THE HIDDEN

Book 3 of The Taken Saga

AVERY BLAKE

NINIE HAMMON

Copyright © 2022 by Sterling & Stone

All rights reserved.

No part of this book may be reproduced in any form or by any electronic or mechanical means, including information storage and retrieval systems, without written permission from the author, except for the use of brief quotations in a book review.

The authors greatly appreciate you taking the time to read our work. Please consider leaving a review wherever you bought the book, or telling your friends about it, to help us spread the word.

Thank you for supporting our work.

THE HIDDEN

Day One

Chapter One

FALLING STAR YELLOWHORSE SAT UP, panting, gasping for breath. She looked around frantically, unable to remember where she was or how she had gotten there. All she knew was that she was terrified of the black orb she had seen behind her eyelids. It was gone now that her eyes were open but the fear was still there. It hammered away in her chest like some Chinese gong. No, not a gong — gongs were slow and deliberate. Her heart was a timpani drum, fast and light, beating so rapidly she couldn't imagine how the beats could be shoving blood through her veins. Squirting though her body that fast, wouldn't a valve blow somewhere, and spew blood out from the pressure? A projectile nosebleed?

She willed herself to calm down, to breathe evenly. To think.

She closed her eyes, then opened them slowly again. It was as dark beyond her eyes as it had been behind the closed lids. Oh, not because she was blind.

Star's blindness was not total. When her drugged mother had pulled out in front of that truck eleven years ago when Star was seven, Star lost images but not light. She could see blobs, shapes, bright colors, and strangely enough, some cartoon figures, probably because they were drawn so simply. Her blind world was not a world without light, just a blurred world without distinguishable images. But it was black now.

The black orb she had seen had been blacker still. A black blotch on the sky. It had come from nowhere. It was simply there. Not there, then there.

Star watched it move slowly across the sky above her, blotting out everything, its gigantic shadow covering the earth. The *whole* earth! It went on and on, gobbled up the sky. Star could not imagine that anything could be that big, to cover up the *whole* sky. But it did.

And because it did, it left no place to run. So Star hadn't tried to run. She had sat down and wrapped her arms around her legs with her forehead resting on her knees and tried to unhook from the gigantic mind that had placed that image in her head. No, not placed it there — that wasn't accurate, but the image had come from that mind, the collective mind, the hive mind, up in the motherships.

She had put a toe into that gigantic mind seven years ago when she and Noah and Paco had been abducted, taken by a shuttle into the belly of a mothership. Once there, they could read each other's thoughts. And they felt around them, well, she did anyway, the swirl of hundreds of *billions* of thoughts, a giant vortex of thoughts spinning around and around like water rushing toward the drain. It was the Astral hive mind and there was nothing else like it in the universe.

Star had tried once, only that *one* time, to tap into that hive mind with her own, to find individual thoughts. It was after she and Noah and Paco had been taken to the haunted house that wasn't real, the one with the holographic horrors. They'd grabbed hands in fear and felt the *snap!* of connectivity, the three of them a mini-hive mind of their own. Noah had been describing Zion Academy to Paco, talking about the monastery with brown-robed monks who tended the huge farm. She had been listening, but then became aware of the background hum of the hive mind. The hum was always there — maybe it was a real sound or maybe just a psychic one, but from the moment Star set foot off the sand of the Taking Place and into the white "plastic" room in the mothership, there was never a moment when the hum was silent. It was as constant as her own heartbeat in her ears.

So she'd ... reached out with her own mind. She just wanted to take a little peek into the monstrous collection of Astral thoughts whirring around her. It had lasted only a few moments, but there was a space of time when she thought she had ... opened a door into it, just a crack. That she had connected her mind to their hive. Then the force of the massive number of thoughts knocked her individual thoughts aside. There were too many of them, traveling too fast, a huge rush, an avalanche, like holding out a water glass to Niagara Falls and hoping to catch just a few drops.

She had instantly retreated, pulled her mind back away from the "peeking crack" and returned to Noah's description of a round man in a brown robe tossing feed to chickens. And after that, she wouldn't allow her mind to go feeling around near the hive.

But the thing was ... she'd always had a niggling feeling that she'd ... left the door open. That when she'd tried to peek into the monster mind through a crack, she'd been knocked back ... and had never closed the opening she'd created.

In the seven years since she and Paco and Noah had been in the mothership, Star had never once felt the presence of the Astral hive mind. Perhaps if she and Noah hadn't been out in the middle of nowhere, perhaps if they'd been in a city with a mothership hanging in the sky above it, maybe then. But out here in rural Kentucky, with no motherships anywhere near, the hive mind was silent to her.

Until today.

Today, the mind had not so much reached out to her as ... the mind was so *full*, with such incredible power, that it had overflowed. Thoughts had ... *spilled out* of the hive mind ... and out through the tiny crack Star had opened all those years ago, and she had been near enough, at least in psychic terms if not distance, to hear them. She hadn't intended to, certainly didn't want to.

Thoughts had spilled out of the hive mind because the entire mind, all the millions of billions of thoughts in the hive mind, had been totally focused on *one incredible image*, one mighty thing. Star caught the thoughts that … *splashed* into her mind through the crack, saw the image all those other minds saw.

Sitting there in the dark, Star tried to sort it out, to figure out what the hive mind had seen that was so incredible she had been able to see it, too. But there was a blank space in there, an empty spot that made it hard to piece the sequence of events together. She had gone to the gymnasium — how long ago? An hour? Five minutes? She didn't know. Holding onto Pumpkin's halter, she had let herself in the side door, hadn't bothered to reach for the light switches, of course. When you were blind, turning the lights on wasn't the first thing you thought of like it was for a sighted person. She just walked into the gym and into darkness.

Along the far wall under the basketball goal lay long sheets of butcher paper and cans of paint. Noah and his cousins Dave and Sam had spent the early morning hours spelunking in Matheson Caverns. Zion Village — the outgrowth of Zion Academy and the huge Gethsemane Monastery — lay between Jessup and the caverns, and once Noah and his father moved there, Noah spent untold hours in the caverns exploring and mapping the tunnels. He had arranged for them to meet Star at nine o'clock to make the gigantic sign they planned to hang in the center of the gym. They already had wires coming down from the ceiling struts. When they were finished, the sign would proclaim Happy Birthday Eagle Feather. Tomorrow,

Eagle Feather Yellowhorse would be seventy-eight years old.

Star knew her grandfather would have a conniption fit when he realized the community of Zion Village was planning a party in his honor. At least an Apache warrior's version of a conniption fit … which was a stone face and a grunt. She hoped that secretly, he'd appreciate the gesture. If it hadn't been for the hunting and tracking skills he had so meticulously taught younger men once they got to Kentucky, their tables would not have been graced with all manner of wild game all these years.

He'd been an anomaly in New Mexico before Astral Day, an old Indian who kept to the ancient ways while the world passed him by. Then the world had turned upside down and wrong side out and he was suddenly as valued as Dr. Mikhail Ziegelman Garczonski, PhD, — Garson — the astrophysics professor who'd been claiming for his entire career that aliens had visited Earth many times in the ancient past.

Value systems had shifted in a heartbeat.

Star had been helping in the kitchen to prepare for the party, had gotten finished half an hour early and came to the gym to wait for Noah, Dave and Sam. She'd sat down on the gym floor beside Pumpkin — and that's where the blank space was. She remembered everything up to that, then nothing until she woke up a few minutes ago from some dream, or from unconsciousness. Or from a vision. She didn't know which. She just knew she had been sitting with her arm around her dog in the middle of the gym and the next thing she knew she was crying out in terror at the black blob, the black hole in the sky she could see behind her eyelids.

She didn't know how long she had been ... what? ... unconscious?

Surely, the others would be here soon and — she stopped, thought for a moment. Was it possible that the same thing had happened to Noah?

She could find out, of course, but that wasn't the way they'd worked things out over the years. When you could read the thoughts of someone else and they could read yours, it was both the most comforting, the most intimate and the most disturbing and intrusive thing it was possible to experience. She and Noah fit together into each other's minds like a hand in a glove. They found that out on the mothership.

And that was glorious. But they still had to get up in the morning and brush their teeth and eat breakfast and lead normal lives. And you couldn't do that when you were constantly being interrupted by someone rumbling around in your head. So they worked it out, the two of them. Speaking to Noah in his mind was just like she would have a conversation with him if he were standing in front of her. She would "talk," to him, an intentional act. She had trained her mind not to just wander in unannounced and he had done the same. Now that reticence was second nature to them. They could, of course. But they respected each other's space and didn't.

Of course, when she did speak to him, he would

see far more than what she actually said so even a casual conversation between them was still very deep and personal.

She felt an overpowering urge to call out to him now in his mind. To tell him to hurry to the gym. To tell him she was scared of the horrible black thing she had seen. She needed his comfort, his support, and the warmth of his presence inside her mind.

But she didn't. She just got slowly to her knees, and then to her feet, and stood there in the darkness with …

What was the sticky stuff all over her hands? She lifted her hands to her face and she could smell it.

Paint!

Her hands were slathered with paint! How had she gotten paint on her hands when it was sitting in unopened cans on the other side of the room? She started to wipe it off on the front of her pants, but then didn't. There was so much of it! It was like she'd stuck her hands down into the buckets … why?

She didn't know. And the not-knowing was becoming as frightening as what she did know — that she had seen some horrible black thing in the Astrals' hive mind.

So she stood, her fingers so sticky she couldn't pet Pumpkin or scratch behind his ears. What was keeping them so long?

As if in answer to her question, she heard a sound in the back of the room, and then heard the *whomp, whomp, whomp* sound of the big banks of lights in the ceiling of the gymnasium being switched on, one after the other.

"Noah!" Star called out to him in his mind. "Something awful just …?"

It wasn't Noah. It was his father. And almost as if she were touching him, she could feel emotions pulsing off him, like when she used to read fortunes when she was a little girl all those years ago in Roswell. What she felt pulsing off Sawyer Matheson was a sudden swirling of confusion and uncertainty, surprise morphing into stunned shock. What had he seen in that gymnasium in the light that she couldn't see in the dark?

Chapter Two

Twenty-three-year-old Paco Sanchez was working out, benching on the free bar. He'd just added two more five-pound plates to the forty-pound free-weight bar and groaned from the exertion of lifting the whole 250 pounds.

He began counting, working in sets of twelve.

... two ... three ...

Grunting from the effort, enjoying the feel of his muscles moving fluidly.

Paco spent at least two hours in this personal gym every day and his biceps, triceps, massive shoulders and broad chest showed with their every ripple all the hard work he had done. In the past seven years, he had become as physically intimidating as he was mentally intimidating. As he grew, matured, filled out as a man, he had become a physical personification of the powerful man he had appeared to be in the minds of his followers, had grown into that role from the teenager who'd stood in an alley barefoot, trying to get his bearings, listening to Santoro talk about his escape plan and grasping for the first time that he could do what nobody else could do. Paco could hear the thoughts of others. He could insert his thoughts into theirs.

It was some time after that before he realized he could also *control* the thoughts of others.

Paco had acquired his telepathic ability as a prisoner on one of the Astral motherships, one of the twenty thousand people who'd been abducted in the early days of the invasion. No, he hadn't acquired it there. He had always known things about people — a stranger's birthday, or what cereal they'd had for breakfast, had always been able to "nudge" others with his own thoughts. What had happened on the mothership was that his simple skill had been magnified tenfold, a hundredfold. He, Star and Noah had been the only "children" on the ship. Oh, he wouldn't have conceded at the time that not quite sixteen was a child. But it had been. He'd been lifted into the ship in a golden beam of light as a child, but he hadn't come down that way.

And while he was there, the three of them had shared a telepathic experience unique among all the humans — they became a mini-hive mind.

Paco shook it off, didn't let his thoughts go to Star and Noah.

... seven, *grunt* ... eight, *grunt* ... nine ...

He had learned long ago to wall off all awareness of them. Maybe someday he could take those memories out and examine them, but not now, not yet, and he was realistic enough to understand he might never again be able to think of those two. That time, those people, seemed to grow darker in him year by year. Sometimes it seemed like the events were twisted into shapes and forms they had not been at the time, that his mind was changing reality into … whatever his mind decided it was. At times, he didn't feel like the master of his own mind at all, saw history, what had been, slide into the open maw of his memories and get changed there. Altered there. Darkened, ever darkened in that place.

It was such a gradual thing he could pretend it wasn't happening, that what had happened between the three of them, the actual reality wasn't somehow morphing into something else, something it hadn't ever been. It seemed, when he thought about it, that every day it grew harder and harder to remember what had happened. What had *really happened*, before his mind began to contort and distort it.

What wasn't hard to remember was the emotion associated with the events. What he felt now was what he had felt then. Violation. Betrayal. *Rage.* They had seen! They had shared with him the most horrible moments of their lives and when he'd refused to reciprocate, when he'd kept private his most closely guarded secret, they had *tricked* him. They had conspired with the Astrals to … what? They'd struck a bargain, they had abandoned him.

The titan's emotionless words rang in his mind.

In exchange for returning them to Earth, they agreed to leave you behind.

Paco had been alone then, truly alone. And the loneliness, the isolation had ... Paco's mind had replayed for him his secret horror — the night he had *killed his best friend*.

Suddenly, Star and Noah were there watching, seeing it all! They had tricked him into revealing what he'd refused to share. It was like ... standing naked in front of the world. And they were *entertained* by his misery. Star and Noah had laughed at him, made fun of him!

They had, hadn't they? Hadn't they?

Yes! They'd enjoyed watching his soul bleed.

And someday ... someday, Paco would collect payment for that injustice. Someday, he would make them pay.

Star.

And Noah.

... eleven ... twelve, *grunt*.

Chapter Three

Eagle Feather knelt down on the damp ground and looked at the paw print that was plainly visible there. It was a bear print, left front foot, showed the foot pad and five toes, with little marks in front of the toes where the claws had dug into the dirt.

He picked up a stick he judged to be about six inches long, stretched it across the print, along an imaginary line atop the foot pad. On the right side, the stick covered the top part of the fifth toe, between the joint and the claw.

Black bear.

Good.

If it had been a grizzly bear, a stick laid on a line atop the foot pad would have passed beneath all five toes. And it would have been bigger, though this track was big enough.

An adult male black bear could weigh upwards of six hundred pounds and he judged that this one was on the higher end of that average.

He stood and looked around into the forest, listening. Unlike mountain lions, bears didn't hide from their prey and then jump out at them at the last minute. If a black bear intended to have you for breakfast, you'd have lots of warning ... not that the warning would do you any good if you weren't prepared.

There had been a pile of spoor about fifty feet back on the rocks, and it was hard and dry. This track was several days old — it hadn't rained in a week. Meaning this bear could be just about anywhere by now. Eagle Feather wasn't looking for bear, though bear meat would be quite a delicacy if he could bag one. He was hunting elk, but would settle for a good-sized white-tailed buck. He'd rather have the elk because Sawyer had specifically requested he look for one — some kind of competition between Sawyer and his brother Taylor. Eagle Feather didn't ask, just said he'd give it his best shot.

He stood still, his eyes flitting from the birds in the trees to the gray squirrels to the red fox that was nestled down behind a log about fifty yards from the creek bed. Game was plentiful here. Thanks to more than half a dozen years without the interference of humans, the ecosystems of the natural woodlands had rebounded remarkably. Game that had been concentrated into the national forests — the Daniel Boone National Forest in Kentucky all the way to the Smoky Mountains in Tennessee — was spreading out, reclaiming the wild as its natural habitat again.

The Hidden

There was a wolf pack operating around here, grey wolf, spreading down from somewhere north. He'd seen the tracks and heard their cry. There was a den in some nearby cave where the kits might be old enough to venture out on their own.

He'd seen mountain lion tracks too, two years ago and never again. He sincerely hoped that meant the big cat had just been passing through. He had had an unpleasant encounter with a puma near Tres Rios, New Mexico when he was a boy and he still had the scars to show for it.

The bear whose track lay at his feet had surely migrated west from the Smokies, where they were plentiful, probably much healthier creatures than the park bears who cut their lifespans in half by dumpster diving and eating human food. The world's most common bear species, the black bears, were way more dexterous than people ever gave them credit for, capable of opening screw-top jars and manipulating door latches — whatever they needed to do to get at whatever food some idiot human left untended. The animals were strong, too, could turn over a 300-pound rock with a single foreleg, run up to thirty miles per hour, had excellent eyesight, a sense of smell like a bloodhound's, were good swimmers and excellent climbers.

Eagle Feather had come by this information not from his lifetime of hunting wild game but from the Great Smoky Mountains National Park bear guidebook he'd found somewhere. That guide had stressed to tourists that bears were, indeed, wild animals, not teddy bears, and that they could be dangerous if provoked.

He'd read the guidelines about what to do if you encountered a bear, that included everything from making yourself appear large by spreading out your coat, chucking rocks at the bear, and backing slowly away. He had smiled at the directive to "fight back aggressively with any available object if attacked and do not play dead."

Whoever came up with the play-dead myth had probably gotten more tourists killed than …

There were no tourists anymore. Not since Astral Day. Not since black Monday, when the population of the world had been reduced from seven billion to three billion — that's what Sawyer had told him.

Four *billion* people — dead. Poof.

And as the years dragged out after Astral Day, Eagle Feather had felt a tightening of the tension string rather than a loosening. He had not bought into the "everything's going to be fine" myth. That was as stupid and dangerous a mindset as playing dead with a black bear. It wouldn't be fine. Eventually, the Astrals would decide mankind couldn't cut it and destroy them all. Eagle Feather hoped he didn't live to see that day, and felt less tied to the world the older he got, as Star was welcomed into the Zion Village community, drawing people to her, with Noah, the "other half of her psyche" by her side. In truth, she didn't need Papa Eagle Feather to look after her anymore, and a part of him yearned to do as his forefathers had done. His

The Hidden

family history claimed Red Fox, his great-great-grandfather on his mother's side, who had simply decided it was time for him to die, had gone up into the mountains and sat with his back against a rock until he did just that.

Might be it was time for Eagle Feather to leave the world, the coward in him whispered, so he wouldn't have to stay around for the end, for the song of the fat lady and the termination of humanity.

His eye caught a movement off to the right, a flag of white, the identifying mark of the white-tailed deer when they took flight, almost begging their adversaries to follow their white flag of surrender until they caught up with them. He turned, but didn't go in the direction of the fleeing deer. He turned up the hill, keeping the brush between him and the trees. He would circle around, be waiting for it when it—

A sound froze him to the spot. A low grumble. He turned slowly, and off to his left was the bear whose paw print he had found on the path. Bears were most active during the early morning and late evening hours. This big fellow was out in the heat of the day for a reason, but Eagle Feather was not eager to find out what it was.

He studied the creature across the breadth of a small meadow, as it studied him. Bear meat? With a rifle, he could have dropped the bear with a single shot. But he had only his bow and arrow and a slightly off shot, and a deflected arrow meant an injured bear, and an injured bear was a dangerous bear.

The bear growled again, grumbled. He swatted the ground with his paw and rumbled.

This animal was demanding more space, and unless Eagle Feather intended to kill it, he should oblige the request. Without turning his back, the old Indian began to back carefully away from the bear. If it followed him, he would change direction. If it continued to follow him, then he would give more thought to the bear-meat solution.

But the bear appeared to be no more eager to make Eagle Feather's acquaintance than Eagle Feather was to meet the bear. It continued to bluster, but clearly it was backing down, just as Eagle Feather was. It backed away, rumbling and swatting the ground.

Truce.

Eagle Feather made a mental note to talk to the monks about the bear when he got back to Zion Village, caution them about trash receptacles, leaving food out where the bear might smell it. And he'd ask the monks about bear meat, too. Did anybody in the whole monastery know how to cook a bear?

In truth, he didn't want to kill the big black beast. His kind in the animal kingdom would rule the earth as soon as the Astrals got rid of his only natural enemy — man.

Eagle Feather had just started across the monks' cornfield when Dave Matheson came running up to him. His Uncle Sawyer needed Eagle Feather in the gym. Star had ... he wanted Eagle Feather to see. The old man felt a fear in his belly then, very different from what he'd felt when the black beast had growled its demand for more space.

Something was wrong with Star. And whether she still needed the old man or not, Star was Eagle Feather's reason for living.

Chapter Four

THE APOLOGY on Sawyer's lips died there as soon as he saw the gym and Star standing with Pumpkin in the center of the floor.

He'd been going to tell her how sorry he was that he'd made the other boys late. Well, lat*er*. He'd caught them on their way to the gym, still covered in dust from a morning spent in Matheson Caverns, and asked for their help moving a chifforobe. Why use a forty-something-year-old back when here were three perfectly good twenty-something-year-old backs available. Noah wasn't quite twenty, of course, but Sawyer was definitely feeling every day of forty-two.

The chifforobe didn't fit where Sara wanted to put it. And so they'd hauled the thing all the way up another flight of stairs to fit it into a bedroom there. Where, gratefully, it fit just fine.

Well, it would once you moved the piano that was taking up all the space on that wall. So he got the boys to help him move the piano all the way down to the basement.

And when the sweet little lady asked the boys if they'd mind helping her move the bookcases as well, Noah had looked at him helplessly, and Sawyer'd said he would go to the gym and apologize in person to Star for making them late.

All those thoughts fell out of his head as soon as he saw Star, and he couldn't quite process what he saw.

She was standing in the middle of the gym floor with paint splattered on the floor all around her. Not just a little paint. Like … lots of it. Like someone had poured out almost all of it. He looked at the back wall where they had lined up the paint cans last night to use today on the sign. Drying paint now oozed down the sides of every one. Sawyer must have gasped out loud because Star asked, "What …?"

Star was covered in splattered paint. It was on her clothes, in her hair, dripping off her hands to the floor. Pumpkin had paint on his paws and his tail. When he wagged his tail, the paint puddle behind him spread out in a fluid swipe like a brush stroke.

And that's what there were. All over the gym floor, taking up the entire gym floor, were *puddles* of paint, smeared around into incomprehensible shapes. The biggest puddle was black, but there were white streaks in it, making it look almost silver in places. But there were puddles of blue, too, different shades of blue.

Sawyer started to go to Star, but that would mean tromping across puddles of paint, getting it all over his shoes. So he stood where he was.

"Star, what happened?"

"I don't know." She started toward him, but he called out for her to stop. "You're tracking paint everywhere. "

"Paint?" She sounded confused. "It's on the floor, too."

"*Too?*"

She held out her hands. "I've got it all over my hands. There's paint spilled on the floor, too?"

"Uh … yes, you could say that."

"Then … you need to get something and clean it up quick. It'll ruin the finish on the floor."

"I believe that ship has already sailed."

"Who spilled the paint?"

"I guess you did, didn't you?"

"No!" Then softer, "I don't think I did. I don't know."

She was about to cry, and he wanted to go to her and put his arm around her and comfort her, but Sawyer still didn't want to track through the paint. At first it was because he didn't want it all over his shoes, but then … He stepped back, trying to make some sense out of the puddles of paint.

"Star, just breathe deep, okay?"

He waited while she took a deep breath.

"Now, tell me what happened. How did all this paint—?"

"I don't know. I didn't even know there was paint spilled until you came in and saw it."

"Tell me what you *do* know. Start at the beginning."

She told him she had been peeling potatoes and got through quicker than she thought.

"... so I just came on in to wait for Noah and—" Then it occurred to her. "Where's Noah and the others?"

"You said ... wait a minute. Back up. You said you were *early*."

"Yes, I got finished about half an hour early so I decided to—"

"The boys aren't here because I commandeered their services moving furniture. I came to get you to apologize that they were so late. They were supposed to meet you here almost an hour ago."

He put it together in his head, as she was doing the same thing.

"So I have been in the gym for almost an hour and a half?"

There was wonder and awe and fear in her voice. And Sawyer started to be afraid with her.

"You didn't know that?"

"I remember coming in here with Pumpkin, sitting down on the floor to wait and the next thing ..." She suddenly remembered. "The next thing I remember was waking up screaming."

"You went to sleep?"

"No, I don't think I was asleep, but ... Oh, I don't know. I wasn't aware. I wasn't *here*."

"Where were you?"

"I was ..." Her words trailed off and he watched recognition dawn, an awful recognition.

"I was in the Astral hive mind."

The Hidden

That was a conversation stopper.

"Star, honey, why don't you just sit down right where you are …"

"But the paint—"

"Don't worry about the paint. Just sit down and try to … calm down, relax."

Conversation was a little awkward from such a distance. The human psyche had set up a distance that was appropriate to stand from another person when you had conversation. Every human knew it, must be stored deep in the DNA. *You stand here and you won't invade my personal space and I'll stand here so I don't invade yours.* The rules and distances changed when people were added or subtracted from the group, But nobody had to ask, *am I too close?* or take out a measuring tape and check the distance to be sure they'd followed the rules.

He and Star were fifty feet apart, way too far for an intimate conversation, particularly alone in an empty gym where every sound echoed and any second you expected to hear the squeak of basketball shoes or the drub-drub-drub sound of a bouncing ball.

It was what it was.

Star did as he'd asked, she sat carefully — he could see her feeling around, trying to find a place to sit that wasn't right in the middle of a puddle of paint. But she couldn't find one. When she finally was seated, she started to drape her arm around Pumpkin, then stopped, held out her hands as if she'd realized she needed to wipe them on something but had nothing.

"Your clothes are already a mess and a little more

paint won't hurt." He was trying to put her at ease. "You'll feel more comfortable wiping them off."

Paint had literally been dripping off her fingertips when he came into the room, as if she had stuck her whole hand into a gallon of paint ... and apparently she had. Why?

"I think Pumpkin wants to snuggle as bad as you do."

The dog was her security blanket and it was clear the dog could tell she needed comforting. When she reluctantly put her arm around him and drew him close, she seemed to relax a little.

"The smell of paint is so strong he's about to choke," she said.

Star could see what her dog smelled, another of the amazing conundrums that when Sawyer thought about it were totally preposterous, but having lived with them for the past seven years, they seemed garden variety normal.

"Start from when you came into the gym. You walked out into the middle of the floor, right?"

"Uh huh."

"Was there paint on the floor then?"

"No, I'd have felt it and Pumpkin would have smelled it."

"So an hour and a half ago, you walked into the gym, the floor was clean, and you went out into the middle and ... what?"

"I just sat down, like I am now, waiting. I knew that since I was early the boys wouldn't be along for a few minutes so I just sat there.

"And nodded off to sleep.

"No, that's not what happened."

She seemed certain of that.

"Then what did happen?"

"I just let my mind wander and …" She paused and he saw realization dawn on her face. "That's when it happened. Maybe even *why* it happened."

"*What* happened, Star?"

"I … there's no way to put words on this. Nothing fits to describe … contact with the hive mind."

Sawyer cringed away from the thought of being anywhere near the hive mind of the alien monsters up in their ships hanging in the sky above a planet they had decimated.

"I dipped into … or I reached into … or I was pulled into … none of those are quite right." She paused, thought. "You know, it was more like, okay, this is going to sound crazy, but it's more like … it *splashed* on me. Like when I was standing down by the barn and Brother Andrew came by with his wagon loaded, hit a puddle and splashed water and mud all over my clean jeans. Like that."

"So something splashed out of the hive mind into yours? What did you see?" He really didn't want to hear the answer.

"It didn't make any sense …"

Noah had told him Star was the only one of the three abducted children who mentioned being aware of the hive mind. They supposed it was because she'd been psychic to begin with. Or it might even have had something to do with Pumpkin's presence. She'd described it as a "constant hum" around her, like a raging river. The thoughts of all the aliens concentrated in one place was a stunning phenomenon.

Star had said she didn't try to connect to that mind because it would be like sticking her finger into a fan and trying to touch only one blade. She feared her finger would get cut off, that whatever thought her mind extended would be sheared off by the force, weight and intensity of the river of thoughts.

"But it wasn't like before … it wasn't a cacophony of thoughts, billions of individual impulses, each thinking something different, shearing like a saw blade. This time, they were thinking the same thing. It wasn't discordant, cacophonous. One thing filled the whole mind until it overflowed with one image."

"And that was?"

"I don't have any idea what it was. It was a black orb the size of, it stretched from horizon to horizon, blocked out the sun, its shadow was so big … it was incomprehensible."

"A planet or a moon?"

"No, it was constructed, it had a surface like the motherships, where you can see indentions and protrusions."

The ships looked smooth and perfectly round from a distance, like a speck of dust looks with the naked eye. But in the magnification of a microscope, the texture, surfaces and angles of a dust mote become clear, and proximity to the motherships revealed their surface structures.

"So this black thing ... what was it? *Where* was it? What was it doing?"

"I don't know, I don't know and I don't know. It wasn't like I could ask questions. I could just see what they were all thinking about, that thing. *They* knew what it was, I guess, it was an image in their heads, but *I* don't ..." Her voice trailed off. When she spoke again he had trouble hearing from that distance because she spoke so slowly.

"I know it was horrible beyond reason, though. Maybe the single most horrible thing in all the universe. Whatever it was, it was death. They were looking at ... *death*."

Chapter Five

Paco dropped the weights and bar on the floor. Slathered in sweat, he turned from the exercise equipment and walked out onto the deck that overlooked the staggeringly beautiful Lake Tahoe. Wasn't interested in the view, though, merely sat down cross-legged on his mat under the flowering tulip tree and willed himself to concentrate.

Paco didn't just train his body every day. He worked just as hard — *harder* — on daily mind training, on expanding it, making it strong enough to withstand the pressure of the thoughts of others.

The smell of the pine needles wafted on the fresh mountain air and the sun would not heat it up to intolerable until later this afternoon. He needed the breeze, the feel of wind on his skin and the smells in his nostrils to help center him.

Sitting perfectly still, he slowly blanked his mind, almost like turning down the dimmer switch on a light, slowly reducing the illumination until there was barely a glow at all. He sat in the dim glow of that light, felt its cool shadows and slowly, *gently* began to reach out with his mind to the minds of others.

He glided swiftly over the minds of the servants, his guards, his militia stationed at the gate, out over the encampment where his army lived and trained for battle. He glided through them because he had long ago reached that far with ease.

It was lifting weights, really, mental weights. First twenty pounds, and you struggled with it, your arms quivering from the strain, sweat popping out on your brow. Still, you added a little more weight every day. He supposed he could have died any one of half a dozen times in the beginning, until he grasped the incredible power of the tool he had harnessed. When the ability to read minds had begun to fade out of his awareness within hours of his return to Earth, he had concentrated to hold onto it, struggled every day, grasped it with his fingernails, and clawed at it until he had a tiny grip and then he worked to tighten that grip. Once he could hold on, he had grabbed power, had gone for broke, had risked his own death and sanity with a gigantic roll of the dice, had spoken into the minds of *hundreds of people* at the same time, turned the whole crowd to his will.

He could still hear the chant. *Kill him! Kill him!* He'd planted the words in their minds, had *controlled* all of them the day he'd fed Spade Jackson into a wood chipper before their horrified eyes.

Paco could dwell on that image, get stuck there almost unable to look away because the image was so pleasurable. Hearing Spade's screams, watching the machine chew off his legs to bare, splintered bones, the way he vomited blood as the machine dug into his bowels. Those images were so delightful and fulfilling that they'd derail his exercise and he hadn't come here today for a walk down Memory Lane, however enjoyable that might be.

He had developed over time a mental strengthening exercise, slowly training his brain to reach into the minds of others — like lifting weights, gradually building up from one person, to half a dozen, to … Now, after all these years, he could speak into the minds of a whole crowd with ease. But speaking into their minds was not enough. He had also taught his mind to do what the Astrals had done to him, Noah and Star in the fake haunted house. He could become in their minds *a thing that wasn't really there.*

That was the mental skill he cherished. He used it seldom because the migraine headache that always followed was debilitating. But he practiced, in small ways, every day. And every day he got better at it.

Over the months that became years, he added space to his routine of mental exercise. And that, too, had served him well as a general. As he was doing this exercise, stretching out to his staff and beyond them to the other men who worked for him, he had uncovered untold number of plots to overthrow his leadership. He had dealt with each one quickly and harshly, mercilessly.

He had chopped off the hands of a man who'd been pilfering food, cut off the genitals of so many men he couldn't even count them anymore for one sexual crime or another. He would *not* countenance any man taking advantage of someone younger or smaller, male or female. Rape was the worst of all possible crimes in Paco's world and homosexual rape in particular was punishable by death, no exceptions, every time, by whatever means Paco determined on the spot would be the most brutal, painful, public and humiliating way to die.

Skimming over the minds of his own, Paco had tiptoed out farther and farther from his Tahoe mansion, where he had moved his troops just before Black Monday's annihilation of Los Angeles. That one had just been a lucky break, but he took credit for it as if he had foretold the future with total accuracy. Every day, he stretched out his mind a little farther, sent his thoughts out through a decimated world, into the remains of small towns, across rural expanses where people driven from the cities had settled, just flitting over people's minds as he went.

His mind presented the process to him as a visual, an image that was both metaphorical and to some extent literal. The image was of a great gray fog spreading out along the ground, moving farther and farther, obscuring everything it came across as it branched out from the source.

He trained his mind every day to stretch out into the wide world.

He wasn't looking for anything or anybody in particular.

Most of the time he believed that lie. Today was

the exception, however. Today he allowed some part small part of his psyche to realize he was searching, poking around, seeking out those who had rejected him, the only two he'd ever cared about ... after Vincent and Tiburon.

Star.

And Noah.

He could direct the progression of his mental reach, the gray fog, but couldn't yet control the outside edges of it with any precision. Once he had cloaked an area and his mind had "conquered" that area, he could reach out to it specifically and be there in a nanosecond, able to pop into the thoughts and dreams of anyone around.

Today he admitted to himself that he had spent two full years stretching out south toward New Mexico. A little farther every day. He was looking for Star and he had found nothing. A couple of months ago, he had turned the creeping fog north, crossed the Mississippi River and began to flow out over Tennessee and—

Bam!

Something hit him, something smacked him with the force of a wrecking ball and he found himself lying on his side beside the mat, trying to get his breath. He felt blood running down his upper lip, draining slowly across his cheek, that lay now on the cool concrete, while he looked at the lopsided world, wondering what hit him.

For a horrified moment, Paco thought he'd been shot, believed that when he found the strength to look down, he would see blood pouring from a hole in his chest.

He lay still, breathing little sips of air.

It took some time to sort it out and he didn't move until he was able to order it in his head.

He knew only two things about what had hit him. No, three.

It had been a psychic blow akin to a spark, hot wire touching hot wire, and though he wouldn't let himself countenance the hope quite yet, he knew of only two psychic forces strong enough to do that.

Two, he knew that the image it planted in his mind was black, a black ball of nothingness. Black stretching out as far as vision went. A horrible blackness that was as certain and cold as death.

Three, he knew the blow had been powered by the black image. The image was the spark that had flared out into the psychic universe, and touched the bare wire of his telepathic mind.

So ... what was the image?

No, he knew three things and *believed* four. He believed the image came from Star. Not Noah, Star. But he believed Noah was there ... wherever *there* was. He believed the two of them were together.

Chapter Six

NOAH STOOD on the edge of the basketball court where Star and Pumpkin sat huddled together in the middle. He and his cousins had shown up at the gym shortly after his father had, and the instant Noah stepped into the interior of the building, he knew what had happened to Star this morning. The images were literally throbbing in her mind, pulsing, and Noah saw and understood it all in a second.

His father had kept him from going to Star, grabbed his arm and signed/spoke his belief that everyone needed to *back off,* not go barreling across the gym floor slathered in wet paint. For practical reasons, of course, but for psychic ones as well. His father wanted the dust to settle in Star's mind so she could help them all understand what was happening.

Because Sawyer Matheson believed that whatever it was — it mattered.

His father had sent Noah's cousin, David Matheson, out to find Papa Eagle Feather. When the old man came into the gym, he said nothing, just stood gawking at his granddaughter sitting in the middle of the gym floor covered in slowly drying paint with puddles of equally drying paint all around.

Eagle Feather didn't ask a single question, just stood looking at Star with that inscrutable Indian-head-nickel face of his. Star had always thought her grandfather looked like the Indian on the nickel but in the beginning, Noah couldn't see it. He realized after a while that it wasn't just a physical resemblance, though, which Star had interpreted with her fingers touching his face. It was his whole demeanor. Oh, the man could be warm and funny and even tender, in a gruff, standoffish, this-makes-me-uncomfortable way. Noah had argued against the whole birthday-party plan, pointing out that Eagle Feather would *not* like the idea.

Then Star'd said, "Okay, he won't like us making a fuss over him. But he's an old man ... whether he likes it or not, he needs to understand just how much he means to us."

That had silenced Noah.

Eagle Feather carried his own silence around with him, wrapped himself in it. He talked when he had something to say, otherwise he kept silent. And that was part of it, part of him looking like the face of that nickel. That Indian was silent and inscrutable, and the more Noah had gotten to know Eagle Feather in the seven years since the man had used his razor-sharp Bowie knife to cut away the noose that Harry Windom had put around Noah's neck, he had come to see the physical resemblance, too. Either the man's face had changed — because the face on the nickel sure hadn't — or Noah came to see how who the man was had fashioned and formed his face so that he had become that image, not just for Star but for everybody. Now that his braids had turned almost pure white, the image seemed so striking that even people meeting him for the first time commented on it.

The look on his face now was even more stern, but Noah had come to know the man — not by poking around in his head, just by daily connection, and he could interpret the look. Eagle Feather was upset, sure. They all were. But he was also scared, frightened by what he saw — maybe in a way the others weren't because he was assigning it some meaning they couldn't yet see.

As soon as Garson showed up, he took up the space for commentary the old Indian had left vacant as soon as he learned Star didn't know who'd smeared the paint around and that she had had a horrible encounter with the Astrals' hive mind.

"You were in here an hour and a half having a conversation with a couple hundred billion Astrals … so is that why you missed seeing who spilled all the paint?"

Maybe Garson was trying to be humorous. Garson could be like that. His jokes were never funny, often unintelligible and just about as often insulting.

Noah had his mouth open to say something about the inappropriateness of the remark when Eagle Feather tapped his arm and pointed to his father.

Sawyer had climbed up into the bleachers of the gym to the very top and was looking down at them.

When he saw them looking his way, he signed and spoke at the same time.

"This paint ... *it wasn't spilled.*"

Chapter Seven

THE NAME of the drug was ayahuasca. Paco had purchased a single dosage of it almost three years ago and understood that now was the time to use it. He'd been saving it, hoarding it, a little like saving a bottle of vintage wine for some special occasion.

This was a special occasion, alright. Getting zapped by a psychic blow that could only have been channeled at him by Star ... maybe Star and Noah, but definitely Star — that was indeed an unexpected turn of events. Certainly, he wanted to explore all that an encounter with the two of them might involve. But that wasn't his primary motivation, wasn't the reason he intended to use the powerful drug ayahuasca. He wanted to know, he *had* to know what that thing was, the horrible cold blackness, the image of death and nothingness.

He had heard about the drug on the mothership more than seven years ago, from a fellow they called the Italian Shoe Man, who'd said the day he and Paco had been sent on an "experiment" together that Meyer Dempsey had taken ayahuasca to communicate with the Astrals.

At the time, he had no idea who Meyer Dempsey might be, had never heard of the film mogul who had been zapped up into the mothership just like he and all the others had been, from all over the planet. But Dempsey had not been returned with the others, didn't return for several years, in fact, and when he did he was the viceroy of Heaven's Vail — the man the Astrals had selected to be their king on the mountain there.

But years later, after Paco had executed Spade in a wood chipper and had established himself as the leader of the S&S Army — who flew the flag of a bleached-white skull with a snake crawling out one eye socket and a spider out the other — he remembered Dempsey. Paco had been struggling to hold onto his ability to enter and influence the minds of others, how to do it without having a stroke, that is. And that's when he remembered the drug, wondered if it might be able to expand his consciousness as it had Meyer Dempsey's.

He'd paid dearly for a single dosage of the drug, holding onto it for just such an occasion as this. His constant mental exercises were straining the physical limitations of his brain. He could feel the blood vessels being engorged with blood, lived through the agonizing headaches that resulted when he pushed too hard, went too far, tried too much.

Now, he had no choice. He had finally found Star

and Noah ... and a power of unimaginable psychic proportions had planted an image in his mind that he would do anything ... *anything* to understand. He would take ayahuasca and reach out ... find out ...

Though he'd made no formal plans, in the back of his mind he had been scheming. He knew that as soon as he found them, really found them, he would go after them. The three of them had been one, until they betrayed him. He wouldn't allow himself to know how much he still ached for that one-ness again, but he would acknowledge his need to make Star and Noah suffer as he had suffered. He would fill up the hole in himself with their presence, and then ... he had formulated no "and then." He might make them his slaves. Or he might kill them.

But he could do neither until he found them. And the drug was going to help him do that.

Without even bothering to shower and change out of his workout clothes, Paco went back inside his Tahoe mansion and called out for his personal servant, Duddits. Duddits had told Paco that his mother had named him after a character in a book — a man who'd had Down syndrome "just like me!"

There weren't a lot of people around who had that birth defect anymore, not after it became possible to see the presence of the extra chromosome in the fetus during pregnancy so the fetus could be aborted.

Paco thought that was sad. Yes, the people were funny-looking, with their flat faces, oversized tongues, and short fingers. But they were also joyful, loving people. Duddits was the son of one of Paco's lieutenants — a man Paco'd had to execute. He'd almost shot Duddits, too, but now was profoundly grateful that he hadn't. Duddits was a little like having a dog that talked. No judgement, perfect obedience and devotion, no questions.

He instructed Duddits to bring him the concoction he kept in a downstairs refrigerator.

"I'm going to take this in a few minutes," he said when the man returned with the vial of liquid. "It's … medicine and I don't know exactly what will happen to me when I do."

Duddits's perfectly smooth brow wrinkled and he looked concerned.

"It won't hurt you, will it? The medicine won't make you sick or nothing, right?"

Paco was touched in spite of himself by Duddits's concern.

"I'll be fine. The reason I'm telling you about it is that I might do or say weird shit and you have to know it's just the drug and it'll wear off soon. So don't open the door and come in if you hear anything strange." Paco paused. "But … if you hear … if it sounds like something is wrong, then …"

Paco stopped. Duddits wouldn't know something was wrong. If he wanted a fallback, he should call for one of the guards stationed at the entrance to his mansion. Yeah, sure, Paco was the meanest dog in the junkyard, so why did he need guards? He remembered plowing into Spade's house that night, took over without firing a shot. *That* wasn't going to happen to Paco.

The Hidden

Duddits was useless as a fallback. Either find somebody with the mental capacity to do the job or forget the whole thing. Paco picked Plan B. He didn't believe anything bad would happen and he'd go with that.

"Never mind," he told Duddits and sent him away. Still in his sweat-damp workout clothes, Paco walked to the couch in front of the fireplace. There was always a blazing fire going there. His air-conditioning adjusted in the summertime so the heat was not troublesome. Paco liked the fire.

He sat down on the cushions, took a deep breath, then drank the nasty-tasting liquid. He'd been told it was bad, but not *this* bad. Like vinegar and wax. It was all he could do to get it down. And to keep it down. But he managed. He leaned back on the cushions then, and waited.

Chapter Eight

WHY WOULD anybody in their right mind think they could keep a secret from Eagle Feather Yellowhorse? Seriously?

Ellie Hampton thought the idea of a surprise birthday party for the man felt a little like a backwards version of the emperor's new clothes. Eagle Feather was pretending he couldn't see all the sneaking around, the surreptitious plans, the clandestine meetings, the hushed conversations. While everybody else in Zion Village knew what was going on. Okay, the analogy didn't fit very well. What did you expect from a dying woman?

Ellie smiled. It almost looked normal. It was surprising how difficult it was to smile when there was no emotion, nothing that physically activated those autonomic nerves that pulled off a real one. It was a challenge to pull all the strings, move all the right muscles, so you looked joyful, at least pleasant, not like you were posing for a toothpaste commercial, or predatory, your teeth sticking out like a vampire. Fake smiling was definitely an art form. Ellie was pretty good at it, if she did say so herself, had had lots of practice, particularly in the past year or so, when the cancer had spread everywhere and the pain level was so intense it was all she could do to breathe, let alone smile.

Do you have a high tolerance for pain?

She remembered the words the doctor in Ft. Knox had asked, and how they had intimidated her, made her cringe away from a procedure she feared was going to hurt a lot.

Hurt a lot … riiiiight. When she'd gone there for help seven years ago she'd had no idea what real pain was. She was an expert now, had earned an advanced degree in agony, courtesy of the lump she had found in her breast on Astral Day.

Though the military doctor had been unable to prevent the pain she now endured, she didn't regret a moment of her horrific trip to the military installation — where Astrals murdered 21,000 people in a single afternoon. Because it was there that chance had hooked her up with the only other survivor of the massacre, a pregnant teenager named Willie Nelson who had given Ellie a precious gift, the child named Diana. And now Diana was what Ellie lived for.

"Do you like it?" Diana asked, her little face a study in anticipation.

Ellie concentrated to keep the moan out of her voice when she responded.

"Oh, I like it a lot. What is it?"

"Don't you know what it is?" the little girl persisted, unconsciously pushing a strawberry-colored curl out of her face as she spoke.

"Yes, it's a picture of a ball." Diana shook her head. "A ... frisbee?" Again, no. "A cookie, a pizza ... a balloon?"

"Yes!" the little girl cried. "Now, Aunt Ellie, you have to figure out why I drew it."

"Why don't you tell me." Ellie had also learned the trick of getting other people to talk so she didn't have to. Talking hurt. Well, everything hurt. Every cell in her body screamed in an agony.

Do you have a high tolerance for pain? the doctor had wanted to know.

Over the course of the past seven years, Ellie had learned that a tolerance for pain was neither high nor low. It just was. It didn't matter how high your tolerance was, eventually pain would outrun it. If you were in pain twenty-four/seven day after day after day, the pain would win, it would overwhelm you. Your tolerance or lack thereof was immaterial, the fiery dragon in your bones would steal your breath so you had to get other people to carry on conversations because if you tried to speak, you'd scream.

"It's a happy birthday balloon for Papa Eagle Feather!"

A smile transformed the little girl's beautiful face into something so lovely it was literally breathtaking.

Willie had told Ellie that Diana's father, who had been kidnapped by the Astrals, had been a strikingly handsome young man ... and Diana was living proof the teenager wasn't exaggerating. Willie's features had been average, but her hair — flaming red tresses! That was her most memorable feature. That and her eyes. Diana had inherited them both.

It was clear that baby Diana had inherited the best features of both her parents, and then somehow blended them into a face that was far greater than the sum of its parts. Ellie knew she was prejudiced, that her love for the child clouded her judgement and made it impossible for her to be truly objective, but she had watched the effect meeting Diana for the first time had on strangers, saw their reactions and knew that she was not exaggerating the child's beauty in her own mind. It was stunning, a little like the perfection of that movie star Elizabeth Taylor when she starred in the classic old movie about a horse called National Velvet. Ellie's father had shown her the movie after it had been reformatted in 3D in the theatre in their penthouse in New York back in the other life. The horse race scene had used holographic images. Ellie'd asked to see it again and again.

Willie had said that Diana's father had been black and she hoped the little girl she carried would inherit his curly hair rather than her straight. And Willie got her wish. But Diana had inherited her mother's hair *color*. The combination was soft, rust-colored curls that hung in a tangled profusion down the child's back.

Beneath her curls, wide forehead and feathered eyebrows were the most astonishing eyes Ellie'd ever seen. Willie's eyes, but even more stunning. They were jade green, a color that almost didn't look real. And the eyes were nestled under eyelashes so long they were like fans on the girl's cheeks. Her red lips were full, almost pouty, and a smile planted twin dimples in her cheeks deep enough to eat custard pudding out of.

The child's complexion had come from her father. Willie had had so many freckles, red ones, that if she'd had one more she'd have had to hold it in her hand. Diana's skin was flawless, a dark cream color. Not the too-white of a redhead, but not the darker shade of a typical mixed-race child. Somewhere in between, an ivory that set off her eyes and curls, to make the total effect one of astonishing beauty.

Ellie would admit that it was at least possible Diana wasn't the single loveliest child who had ever walked the earth. But Ellie doubted that was true.

Diana was speaking again and Ellie tuned back in. That was another skill she'd had to master over the years that the cancer invaded just about every organ in her body. The dissociation skill. Tripping out. Leaving the body full of agony behind and going somewhere else. No, it wasn't somewhere else. It was nowhere else. Nowhere at all. A void that had nothing in it but the echo of the pain the mind was struggling for even a few seconds to escape.

"… going to draw pictures of red ones and blue ones and green ones, like a bouquet of balloons." Diana had never actually seen a for-real balloon. Just one of the thousands of things that ceased to exist after Astral Day.

"How very sweet of you!" Ellie said.

"If you think *that's* sweet, wait until you see what else she drew. It will positively make that place in your jaw under your ears ache."

Ellie caught movement in the doorway and turned her eyes to her daughter Gretchen. Turned her eyes only, not her head. Movement made everything worse, so she remained as still as possible, concentrating on disassociating from the agony caused by her diaphragm muscles' movements to allow her to breathe.

Gretchen signed the words, didn't speak them. She seldom spoke aloud because she hadn't heard speech since the internet ceased to function after Astral Day, rendering her Weiss implant hearing aid useless, and so her speech was flat, nasal and toneless. She was signing now, though, because she knew it was difficult for Diana to read deaf sign language.

Gretchen. Poor Gretchen. Even after seven years, so eaten up with jealousy it defined her. The moment Anna — the registered nurse who provided healthcare for the residents of Zion Village — had placed the newborn infant Diana in Ellie's arms, Gretchen's mind did some kind of twist. That's how Ellie had come to think of it. Like water flowing through a water hose that suddenly gets a kink in it. Gretchen's personality, her … her *soul*, had been a garden hose with life flowing through it and the moment she saw the little baby placed in her mother's arms, she had kinked that hose. And she had never straightened out the kink. Everything froze there. All of Gretchen, her personality, her liveliness, her own growth as a human being, was backed up behind that kink, was never allowed to flow out. And she was left with the constant pressure of all that she should have been battering against the kink of her loathing of the baby Diana. Ellie suspected Gretchen understood that on some fundamental level, and it made her hate Diana all the more because her misery was the child's fault.

Gretchen was eighteen. She had been in Noah's class at Zion Academy, had accompanied her mother to Sawyer's house the day the Astrals kidnapped Noah from the bank of the pond. Over the years, she had learned to mask her loathing of Diana. But doing so had further distorted her personality. In order to be granted the "that's just how she is" excuse when she was snarky, sarcastic, caustic and hateful to Diana, she had to be the same to everyone else in her life. Who Gretchen was had been pulled out of shape and distorted by her reaction to the baby all those years ago. Ellie saw through her act, of course. No, come to think of it, it wasn't even an act anymore. It was who Gretchen was, who she had become — a lovely young woman with her mother's chilled beauty and her father's startling blue eyes, who was as angry and bitter as the old crone stirring a caldron making poison to put into an apple to feed to Sleeping Beauty.

Gretchen had pitched such a supreme tantrum the first time Diana had called Ellie "Mommy" that Ellie had trained the little girl to call her Aunt Ellie. That had been only one of a thousand concessions Ellie had made over the years to try to bridge the rift between her deaf daughter and her adopted daughter. Between herself and Gretchen. Nothing had ever worked.

Diana was blissfully unaware of Gretchen's loathing, which made the child all the more adorable in her loving innocence, and cast Gretchen's wretchedness in even harsher relief.

"Oh, don't tell her, Aunt Gretchen!" the child pleaded. "It's a surprise."

"I'm not your *Aunt* Gretchen. An ant is a bug, and if I'm to be a bug, I want eight legs so I can be a spider."

Ellie closed her eyes. She *couldn't* be responsible anymore for Diana. Because by default, that left Gretchen in charge and at the very least she'd be negligent, and at the worst … Ellie had made arrangements a long time ago with the nurse, Anna, who adored the child, to take Diana when Ellie died. But Ellie couldn't wait that long. It needed to be *now*, because Ellie just flat out couldn't do it anymore. She had to apply all her energy to gritting her teeth together to stifle the scream of agony that was always lurking in her throat, prowling back there like a caged lion.

"She and the other children have drawn a mural on the wall of the cafeteria, Mother," Gretchen said, delighting in spoiling the child's surprise. She had taken to calling her "mother,' instead of Mommy or Mom after Diana came along, surely to emphasize her relationship that trumped Diana's. It was all so tiring it wore Ellie out.

"And they're making a biiiiiig banner for him in the gym," Diana chirped.

Gretchen gave Diana an evil eye. "I bet they didn't spill paint all over the floor in the gym like *you* did in the cafeteria."

Chapter Nine

THE PAINT on the gym floor had not been *spilled*.

That was clear to Eagle Feather the instant he saw it. His eyes widened when he stepped into the building and walked the few steps through the hallway to the gym itself. All the lights had been turned on, bright enough to perform brain surgery, every detail in harsh relief from the glare of the overhead bulbs in the ceiling light fixtures. Though one on the far end was going out. Flickering, emitting a hum that was probably more audible to Eagle Feather than to either Sawyer, Garson or the three young men. His sight and hearing had always been extraordinary, and rather than diminishing with age as they should have, Eagle Feather believed those faculties had grown more acute. His grandfather had once commented about "the special sight of old age," and at the time Eagle Feather had thought he was referring to the wisdom of accumulated years and experiences. And he was talking about that, but he had also been talking about physical eyesight. When you looked into his grandfather's brown eyes, you thought you were looking into wells that revealed the depths of the universe, but you could also see that when he looked back, *he didn't miss a thing*.

Eagle Feather instantly picked up on details that the others had not yet noticed — that the floor was not just some mishmash of color, as if someone had gone out into the middle of the gym floor and poured out whole gallons full of red, black, blue, green and yellow paints and then smeared them all, as a child would smear together the colors of finger paints Oh, the paint had been smeared, but there were clearly lines where blue paint touched green or green touched black, that were intentional, or appeared to be. Certainly more than the random pouring of paint into a puddle. And there were mixed colors, too. The green blotch had not been formed by a gallon of green paint. It had been formed by mixing the blue and the yellow paints, so that it was not flat but textured, more bluish in some places, more yellow in others. And there was an area, a "puddle of brown." He was certain there hadn't been any brown paint.

He'd helped unload the paint cans into the storage building when the truck brought back what had been scavenged from the hardware store in Jessup three or four years ago. Brother Thaddeus wanted to paint the newly erected chapel white, and Eagle Feather had been on the crew sent into town to see what they could scavenge by way of white paint. They'd found dusty cans of paint in the storage room of the old store, the front of which had been gutted in the aftermath of Astral Day when everybody in town suddenly realized they needed one of the four generators that had been for sale. Eagle Feather remembered clearly that there had been only primary colors, red, yellow and blue, and black and white — big drums of it which they'd hauled out to the monastery.

The empty paint cans could be seen at the far end of the gym under the basketball goal and Eagle Feather figured they'd been about to paint some kind of happy birthday banner for the celebration tonight everybody in town thought he didn't know about.

There were drying drips on the sides of each of the paint cans, but it appeared, at least from here, that the lids had been put back on every one. Star couldn't be the culprit in this gigantic display of graffiti. How could she have gotten the paint lids off the cans of paint? That was a pretty delicate maneuver, wedging a screwdriver under the lip of the lid and pounding on the other end of the screwdriver with a hammer until the lid popped free. How had a blind girl pulled that off?

Then Eagle Feather realized he was making excuses, coming up with every reason he could think of why Star hadn't been the person who'd put the paint on the floor. Because to believe she had been was to believe all manner of other things he wasn't prepared yet to believe. But he was sure he would get around to it, he could feel the realization rising up in his consciousness and the harder he pushed it back down, the more determined it became to surface.

It popped right out bright and full into his mind as soon as Sawyer called out from the top of the bleachers that the paint had not been spilled.

Eagle Feather knew then.

Chapter Ten

SAWYER MATHESON LOOKED out at the gym floor from the top of the bleachers and tried very hard not to see what he saw because the implications were staggering. He remembered what his grandmother used to say as she stirred the pot of chili so hot it would burn your mouth and make your eyes water cold out of the refrigerator. She'd put creole spices in it he'd never tasted anywhere else before or since. And whenever she'd fly up to Louisville from Shreveport when he was a boy, he'd stick to her side like a barnacle to a shrimp boat, sitting with her on a high stool in the kitchen talking while she cooked.

"You can't un-know the truth," she'd told him once. "Soon's you know what it is, you're responsible for doing something about it."

He'd hung onto that one. Well, actually, he'd held onto a couple of them, like "Done's done, you can't squirt the milk back up a cow's udder," and "he walks so soft he could sneak dawn past a rooster." But the one that actually provided a usable life lesson could be applied here.

The truth was right there on the gym floor for anybody with eyes to see. And he couldn't unseen it. When he stopped seeing spilled puddles of color and started seeing shapes, the image coalesced in his chest between one heartbeat and the next.

"This paint wasn't spilled," he called out to Garson, after Garson made one of his inane remarks about the mess on the floor.

"What do you mean, 'it wasn't spilled'?"

"Aw, come on, Garson, how many things can 'it wasn't spilled' mean? The paint wasn't poured out in random puddles all over the floor. You can see that from up here. It's not spilled paint. It's …" He hesitated then, not because he didn't know quite how to finish the sentence but because the implications of finishing it were stunning, to admit what it was implied a tacit admission that you grasped the nature of what it meant, and his mind was totally not ready to grapple with that.

"We're waiting," Garson called up.

But Eagle Feather had already walked along the edge of the gym floor to the steps and started climbing up to the stands where Sawyer stood. Somehow the old man had already figured out what it was. And what it meant? *That* was something they'd all have to figure out.

"It's a painting," Sawyer said. "Come up here and see for yourself. From this angle, you can see the shapes clearly. It's not just a painting ... it's a damned intricate painting."

That had been produced by a blind girl, sticking her hands down into buckets of paint.

Eagle Feather got there first, both physically and metaphorically. He merely grunted when he saw it, which on some days amounted to a whole day's worth of verbal communication. But Sawyer was sure this wasn't going to be one of those days.

"Why it's ... oh, my!" said Garson, after he made his limping way up the steps. In another world, he'd have long ago had hip replacement surgery. In this world, he spent the majority of his time in excruciating pain, bone on bone. Somehow it had not managed to dampen the glow of his indomitable spirit, but it had put barbs on his more acerbic remarks ... dipped the tips of some of them in battery acid. The old man adjusted his glasses up and down his nose, the prescription so outdated now he probably saw better without them, and he finally did just take them off altogether.

As soon as Noah saw the image, Star saw the image, and their communication wasn't slowed down by the clumsiness of words.

"It's what I saw in the hive mind," Star cried. "From a different angle, but it's what I saw. The black thing that blotted out the whole sky." She paused, then said in wonder. "Then it *was* me, I *did* do it."

The perspective of the painting wasn't from the ground looking up. It was a side view, like a video shot from the moon, that showed the enormous black ship hanging in the sky above the earth. If the proportions were right in the picture, and there was no reason to believe they weren't, the black ship was as big as ... was bigger than ... it was Texas hanging in the blackness of space above the planet. Not just above the planet ... *above the polar ice cap.*

The detail was stunning. From here, it was possible to see that what had appeared to be streaks of spilled white paint splattered on top of the puddle of black paint actually blended intricately to form gray shadings, was actually the pattern of light and shadow on the surface of an Astral mothership. The huge round spacecrafts looked smooth as marbles from a distance, but closer inspection revealed all manner of protrusions and shapes, crevices, and lines. They almost looked like a view from a helicopter down into New York City — New York City before the Astrals turned it into powder. The protrusions could be cities, vast skyscrapers on the surface of the ship, though Sawyer couldn't wrap his mind around why a race of slow-moving bald white giants, or their counterparts, the insectile reptars with the needle teeth, would live in anything resembling a human city.

But the play of light and dark and shades of gray on the painting, which was drying fast on the gym floor, was detailed enough to see what might have been windows on the buildings — which weren't, because the shapes weren't buildings, but the human mind, his at least, had a bent toward anthropomorphism.

Sawyer had spent the last seven years trying to jam

reality into his own personal belief system, to understand it on human terms, but gave that up on Black Monday. It wasn't possible ever to understand a race of beings capable of murdering four billion people in one day.

The planet was equally detailed, the great blue marble in the sky, with the dark green of land masses, the blue of oceans and the white of the polar ice caps which was where the ship had positioned itself — above the polar ice cap, the roof of the world. Hanging there, a deeper black against the black of outer space.

And the beam of light or power or energy or whatever it was that stretched down from the monstrous black ship to the ice below was so detailed you could almost see the individual pulses, sparkles of color in the brilliance of white.

"What's it ... *doing*?" asked David Matheson, standing forgotten among the young men with Noah who'd believed their day would be spent making a gigantic "Happy Birthday" sign on butcher paper using the paint that had now been subverted into an image that was sinister, rather than joyful.

"Don't be obtuse," Garson snapped. "The ship is melting the polar ice cap."

"But ... *why*?"

"Why to flood the earth, of course."

Chapter Eleven

HALF AN HOUR WENT by after Paco took the drug ayahuasca. Nothing.

An hour. Nothing.

He was beginning to get angry, thinking he had paid for a fake, that what he'd traded an arsenal of guns and ammunition for was worthless. If that was true, Paco would—

Then the flames in the fire turned into birds and took flight. They flew around the room, their wings on fire making the whomp, whomp sound of a low-hanging helicopter, their bodies like hot coals, red and yellow and orange. Their beaks were made of smoke.

The birds began to fly faster and faster, their colors blurring together until there were rings of fire floating in the air around the room. And the fire had an aroma. It smelled like roses. Fire that smelled like roses. Then the rings of fire froze in place, like they'd been projected on the ceiling and walls and someone had stopped the video stream. The rings began to disintegrate, rain down in tiny pieces of red and yellow confetti. The pieces got bigger as the rings broke apart until the hunks of frozen fire clattered down all round him like pieces of shattered glass, but the sound they made when they hit the floor was not brittle broken-glass sound. It was the squishy, moist sound of gobs of mud splatting into a mud puddle.

Paco reached out to pick up one of the broken pieces. It was cold, like ice, then it turned to mist, like dry ice, and his palm was empty.

Then the room vanished. He was standing on nothing. Standing in nowhere. In the black abyss of deep space, cold and lifeless and empty. Slowly a spot appeared out of the blackness, a tiny dot. It grew bigger and bigger until Paco realized it was coming toward him, streaking through space, a round silver Astral spaceship aimed right at him.

Paco tried to suck in a gasp of air to scream, but there was no air, and a scream would make no sound here. He merely watched in horror as the silver ball grew larger and larger. When it was right on him, blotting out everything else, he cringed for the end of life, some little part of his brain wondering if there would be pain when it hit him. Did dying hurt?

And then it struck. Except it didn't. It didn't hit him, it *enveloped* him. He passed through the walls of the ship as easily as water through a strainer. Then he was inside the ship, in the white interior he could remember from before. Only this wasn't like before. Everything was a blur, the walls, the creatures, the titans, everything was smeared like a little kid had smeared paint.

He understood the principle of incredible speed. Unthinkable speed. Grasped on a level his mind was incapable of processing that he was traveling not only through space, but through time, moving forward through it, moving to a time that didn't exist because it hadn't happened yet. Some distant future was here, was now, was gone.

He held out his hand and realized it was smeared, too. Nothing was substantial, everything was …

And then the images began to clear. An eye exam where the optometrist asked, is it clearer here, or here. The fuzzy edges of surfaces resolved into concrete lines. His hand became a hand. The Titans resolved into white giants. He looked around frantically then, to see if there were any reptars, but there were none.

He realized two things quickly. One, the ship that had been streaking through the universe was slowing down now as it approached … what? He didn't know. Earth maybe. And two, he wasn't really here, not in any sense the Astrals could interpret. He could tell by the way they wandered past him without looking that they weren't aware of his presence. But then, he wasn't present. Not really. He was sitting on pillows in his Lake Tahoe home watching a fire crackle in the fireplace.

Except that wasn't real. *This* was real.

Then he heard the hum and instantly recognized it. Star had shuddered when she talked about it. The hive mind. The collective consciousness of all the aliens, all of them thinking with the same brain, but acting independently at the same time, which was impossible but true.

She'd said it hummed in her ears and she went searching for it once with her mind. Just once. Star was psychic, had an unexplainable power long befog the Astrals arrived. When she reached out to the mind, she had been struck down by it. She had described it, a whirling vortex of thought, going impossibly fast inside the mothership, millions of thoughts intricately fit together, all one whole with many parts.

He could hear the hum now, a thrumming sound like a bow string after the arrow is released. He stood, listening to the sound, wondering what would happen if he tried what Star had tried. Would he be …?

He didn't know how and yet he did. It was like reaching into the minds of the people he controlled in California. He sent his consciousness out, seeking, could feel himself getting closer to the vortex, some imagined proximity. He could feel the speed of it, imagined a wind that slicked his hair back on his head.

Like approaching something hot, Paco moved slowly, tentatively, intent on backing up if—

And then the suction happened. One instant he was approaching slowly and cautiously and the next he was pulled forward with a mighty force and he couldn't stop, couldn't help being drawn in. He was sucked through imaginary walls into the hive mind consciousness, like a soft drink up a straw. And there was a thrumming sense in his own mind, as his own thoughts passed through the invisible membrane into—

WHAP!

The force of the psychic blow was staggering. Like his mind had been standing still and had attempted to step onto a train moving a thousand miles an hour. It had sucked him closer and closer by the very nature of its vortex, but as soon as he touched it, he was knocked back with the sensation of a wrecking ball slamming into his head.

Then it was dark. Black everywhere. Was he blind?

No, the darkness had enveloped him. It was more than the absence of light, it was a thing of its own, an entity — *DARK*. It was a single image that took over every one of the billions of thoughts in the hive mind. Paco could see the image. It was a dark *thing* that hung out there in space beyond the motherships, so large the motherships were ... white marbles beside a black bowling ball.

It was quiet then, where Paco was, wherever he was that wasn't a place at all. He hung there in nowhere, his mind a single mind among billions, his thoughts focused with all the others on that *one thing*.

A horrible sense of foreboding came over Paco, a terror that grew in his chest until it exploded out in a shriek of terror that made no sound because he was nowhere sound existed.

He *knew*. He understood without knowing how he could know such a thing that the black orb was death. A death ship that would deliver to mankind the judgement of the Astrals — annihilation.

Humanity would be wiped out, obliterated. All of it. Every human being drawing breath would die.

Then the earth would be clean, and the hive mind could begin again to create a race that would meet the standard it required.

Paco noticed something in the distance hanging in nothingness just as he was … the shadow of a face. Star. She wasn't there with Paco *now*. Not at the same time. Time here was not linear. The Astrals bent and shaped it. But the image of Star was on the other side of the Astrals' bent time. She saw what had been — a millennium ago? Yesterday? Or what would be. The past or the future. But whatever she saw would convey to her the same truth the images he'd seen had conveyed to him.

Judgement had been passed on humanity. Annihilation.

Only two human beings on the planet understood the irrevocable nature of that death sentence. Paco Salazar. And Falling Star Yellowhorse.

The death ship in deep space was coming.

Chapter Twelve

It took a bit longer to get all the paint off Star than expected. Gratefully, it was water-based paint and they just had to hose her down. Noah stepped up beside his father while his cousins Dave and Sam, along with Gretchen Hampton and Jocelyn Conner, squirted water on her. Jocelyn had been working in the surveillance room since the days when they'd spotted Oscar Higgins and the first of the "invading armies" sneaking through the trees.

Star stood in the grass outside the back door of the gymnasium, in the sun, not the shade of the tree. It wasn't full springtime yet, though all the dogwoods on the property were blooming in a profusion of white and pink that sent Sawyer into gales of sneezes.

He'd run out of allergy medication years ago.

"Remind you of anything?" Sawyer asked Noah, and his son nodded. The night they had made the trip to Louisville to rescue Ellie Hampton after she'd driven there alone and got caught in a riot. She'd hidden in a garbage can and insisted Sawyer stop at a car wash on the way back to Jessup to get the goo off her.

"You seen Ellie today?" Noah asked.

Now it was Sawyer's turn to nod. He didn't say more because he didn't have to. Sawyer liked to believe that Ellie had looked a little better this morning. She'd been propped up in bed and Brother Ignatius had brought her a bouquet of tulips from the flower garden behind the hydroponics barns. She'd been in good spirits, asked how things were going with the "surprise" birthday party for Papa Eagle Feather — that Sawyer was certain the man knew about.

But Ellie was in such constant pain it was hard to know how much she really got of what he said to her. He visited her three times every day and understood that seeing her that often, her decline had been so gradual it was harder for him to spot than for Garson, who tried to pop in every day but sometimes went days without remembering the obligation.

For years, they were able to keep Ellie at least comfortable with the drugs they'd gotten from drug dealers willing to barter them for food. The meds were administered by Anastasia Montgomery, a registered nurse who'd worked in surgery and the emergency room in a Nashville hospital before Astral Day. She'd been in on Ellie's treatment from the beginning, had settled the baby Diana under a bilirubin light to combat her jaundice the night Ellie brought the child back from Fort Knox.

The flow of legal/illegal drugs had dried up eventually. Now, there was nothing much more effective than aspirin to give Ellie for her pain.

Sawyer marveled that they still attracted stragglers even after all this time, like the couple from the Florida Keys who had taken literally years to make it back home. Now their community numbered more than five thousand people, as thriving a metropolis as it was possible to have under the circumstances. They'd built housing for the Jessup refugees, the few people who'd survived the Astrals' attack on the town, and for newcomers over the years, individual houses at first, designed by an architect from California named Lars Carlsen who rode a motorcycle and wore a dog muzzle. After that, Noah had designed a remarkable apartment complex that took up almost no space on the ground because it rested on pillars, with one story stacked on top of the next at impossible angles, a domed facility that couldn't possibly stand but did, couldn't possibly house thousands of people, but did, couldn't possibly be heated and cooled using the system Noah designed ... but it was.

In the past seven years, they had built six such complexes, two out by the highway leading to what had been Zion Academy and Gethsemane Monastery and four more, two facing each other on both sides of the road around the academy's outside walls. They'd been named for states: Texas and New Mexico on the highway, California and Idaho on north side of the academy, Vermont and Virginia on the south side.

Noah had designed barns that dried food for storage, using solar panels on the roofs. He'd reimagined the small hydroponics system used by the monks and was working on a system to triple its capacity. Food was the biggie. The farmers here, and the hunters among them, provided what the community needed with no margin for error. It was always a near thing and Sawyer didn't like to think what would happen if there were a drought or any number of other natural disasters. Though they had it far, far better than most people in a post-Astral world, the little community of Zion Village still clung to survival by its fingernails.

Sawyer also marveled at the hidden talents displayed by the remarkable band of survivors who lived in what folks had dubbed Zion Village. Among the most remarkable was the man who had managed over the course of three years to build a remarkable functional septic system for the whole community. The feat itself was extraordinary. The fact that it had been performed by a man who'd spent his life as a mortician was even more so.

Once Star was clean and dry, the elders of the community would get together and discuss ... as if there were anything to talk about — the painting now soundly locked up in the gym. The sign on the locked door was truthful as far as it went, explaining that there was paint on the gym floor that had to be cleaned up. There was no sense alarming the whole community until they had to, and a painting like that was a pretty shocking thing to expect a couple thousand people to take a look at on their way out to the fields to work, something they could chat about over lunch.

The elders had no formal meeting place. They were sorta kinda elected officials that sorta kinda ran the place, though final authority about just about everything was granted to two men, Sawyer Matheson and Brother Sebastian, who had proved to be a competent administrator, and a good friend.

The other elders included Sawyer's brother, Taylor, who'd run the family business, Matheson Caverns, back when there were tourists interested in seeing the second-longest cave system in the world, Brother Sebastian, Garson — Dr. Mikhail Ziegelman Garczonski — and Eagle Feather. From among the Stranded were Nick Wilson, Fred Schwartz and Jessica Maddocks, whose husband had been the first man the monster Bubba Blacksnake had killed years ago as they traveled through Land Between the Lakes. Erika Mason had shown up five years ago, a stock exchange trader who'd managed to survive in New York City for two years after Astral Day in the catacomb-like tunnels beneath the American Museum of Natural History and Science in Manhattan, where her husband was a curator. After he was caught and executed by the Ace Double-Trey gang lord who'd captured the Upper West Side, she had escaped with three little girls and brought them across the wilds of Pennsylvania and West Virginia to find her deaf son, who was at Dr. Weiss's academy. She was one of a small handful of parents who finally managed to make it to Kentucky for their children, and like the others, she'd elected to stay. Anybody who ever showed up at Zion Village decided to stay there. In this New World

Order of fight or die, they had seen the chaos out in the rest of the world and Zion Village was a haven of normalcy. Here, it was almost possible to forget … to *pretend* the Astrals had never come.

Star and Noah were village "elders" too, and even years ago when they were both still children, nobody'd ever uttered a peep of protest about their positions on the "governing board" of the establishment. Nobody needed to be told how special the pair was, many of the residents had come to Zion Village because of the "invisible draw" the two children had, that strange power over people that had moved the prisoners in Bubba's camp all those years ago to protect her, a power that had more than doubled when she and Noah were together.

It was sometimes like having twins, Sawyer mused, *fraternal* twins, definitely. The two so unlike in appearance, Star a lovely, dark-haired young woman of eighteen, clearly Native American. Her Indian features had become more prominent when she lost the chipmunk cheeks of childhood. And Noah, Nordic blond. His hair had not darkened with age as some blondes did, and his eyes were a blue so clear and startling it was sometimes difficult to maintain eye contact with him. The eyes were disconcerting for everyone but Sawyer, and that was because his son almost never made direct eye contact with him, always averted his gaze. At first Sawyer had believed that it was because he was concentrating on reading Sawyers lips, then he slowly realized that there was something behind Noah's eyes he didn't want his father to see, the boogie man that lingered in the strong, handsome young man of almost twenty, a holdover from his haunted childhood — a childhood that'd been haunted even before he and Star had been abducted by the aliens and kept for three months on the mothership.

Part of the reason the elders had no meeting place was the group's determination to keep things as unofficial, and not-governmental as was humanly possible. Zion Village existed on cooperation and collaboration, the whole group's desperate desire to survive the invasion of the Astrals, and all means were eventually employed to that end.

Now, they sat in lawn chairs positioned beside the gym in what would be shade later in the spring, of the not yet blooming — thank goodness for Sawyer's allergies — cherry tree. They'd shown up individually, or by twos, quiet, and sat down. There was no chitchat, and it was clear from the looks on everyone's faces that they were trying as best they could to get their minds around the implications of the painting. They'd all seen it, of course, and basically knew the story of how it'd gotten there, but nobody was quite yet willing to connect the dots.

The silence among them wasn't uncomfortable though. It felt warm and supportive to Sawyer in a way he'd never tried to tack words onto. Old friends — no, more like old soldiers — who'd been through the worst of battle together and survived. Now they were facing an enemy they were no match for.

"I hate elephants, so let's get to it," Garson said,

and it took Sawyer a moment to complete the mental leap about elephants in the middle of the room.

"That painting … confirms what those of us who have studied the aliens, the conclusions we have drawn from the historical record."

Sawyer had first heard this seven years ago when he sought out the comfort of Dr. Garczonski when Noah had been taken up into the beam of light by a shuttle and held for three months in the mothership. He was no less blunt all those years ago than he was now, no less reluctant to … what was it his grandmother used to say, "speak the truth still in the husk."

"The aliens seeded the planet, they are, in effect, our ancestors."

"Nice way to treat your progeny," Fred Schwartz said. He was in his nineties, but still as sharp and with-it as he'd been the day he'd told Eagle Feather they'd hitchhiked across Arkansas and had finally gotten a ride because his wife, Lottie, had "shown a bit of leg." Lottie had died five years ago.

Garson blew by Fred's remark.

"The Astrals have returned at various times over the millennia, and every time the result has been the same. They come, they judge mankind a failure …" He looked at Sawyer as if he thought Sawyer was going to press the point but why bother. They'd talked the topic to death — what criteria did the Astrals use to make a judgment on all of humanity? Nobody had any idea. "After the judgment, they have destroyed mankind, wiped us off the face of the planet and started over, hoping, I suppose, that future generations will get it right, whatever the illusive 'right' is."

He gestured toward the locked door of the gym.

"That's what the painting is. That's how they plan to annihilate us. Melt the polar ice cap and flood the world, that sounds like as good a way as any to destroy all mankind."

"They plan to kill us, they've always planned to kill us," Noah said, *spoke* the words.

Sometimes it was possible to believe that Noah actually wasn't deaf at all. He'd learned speech before he became deaf, but like most deaf people he seldom said anything because he couldn't hear the words himself, couldn't modulate the expression in them, how loud or soft, didn't know if the sounds were right. But with Star — he could hear his own words, through her mind when she heard them. And with that input, over the years he learned how to make his speech sound normal. That input also made him a master lip-reader. When Star spoke aloud to him, he could hear exactly what she was saying as he watched her lips form the words. It was harder for him in a group setting, with speakers switching back and forth, but he still did a masterful job.

"Of course they plan to kill us, Noah," Garson barked. "I have always known that. I just ... had hopes they would wait a couple hundred years to render their verdict and judgement. They didn't even wait a decade."

Astral Day had been seven years ago. Seven long or short years, depending on how you looked at it.

There was silence then. Though what Garson said wasn't news to anybody, hearing it said out loud like that, it knocked the breath out of their bellies.

Eagle Feather finally spoke.

"The painting, that is the gift the gods gave to Star."

That was a conversation starter. Most people had heard the story, but until now it was something like a fairytale.

"Tell us again about the legend," Garson said, though surely he had heard the story a thousand times. He and Eagle Feather had become friends. They felt connected by their shared understanding of the Astrals — Garson's extensive study of the ancient aliens who'd been to Earth in the past, and Eagle Feather's understanding of a new element that'd been added to what came before.

"I don't see what a legend—" Erika Mason began, but Star interrupted.

"It's not just a legend. I wasn't just randomly abducted. Papa Eagle Feather took me to a special place on the mesa called 'the Taking Place' and a shuttle appeared to take me away. Our ancestors must have had contact with the aliens … from before, to come to that place for me. It's not just a story."

Eagle Feather was a man of few words.

"The Great Spirit spoke to my ancestors and said that a girl named after the heavens would go to the gods and would return with a gift that would save her people."

"Her 'people'?" Erika said. "Her 'tribe'?" She

looked from the old Mescalero Apache warrior to the young Mescalero Apache maiden. "There are only two of you left."

Nick tackled that one. "*We* are Star's tribe. Her people. The ones who were drawn to her."

"So ... what's the gift?" Taylor Matheson asked.

"The painting, of course."

Taylor wasn't tracking. "I don't get how the painting 'saves' anybody."

"It's a warning," Eagle Feather said.

"What good is a warning if there's nothing you can do about it and you don't even know when the hammer's coming down? Do we have a month? A year? Half an hour?"

"Actually, we *do* know how long we have," Garson said. Then he turned unexpectedly to Noah with an odd look on his face. "And there *is* something we can do about it. Your special skills, my boy." He glanced at Eagle Feather. "Star's name isn't the only one that was prophetic." He nodded to Sawyer. "I choose to believe it was no accident that you named your son *Noah*."

Chapter Thirteen

"Can we pull this wagon back up to the barn and start loading it again?" said Fred Schwartz, then looked around. "Alright, alright already, so I was never a farmer. But you get my point."

"Indeed," said Garson. "Start over. And—"

"Use little words, professor. I'm a very old man and I'd like to live to hear the end of the sentence."

Garson pulled out a folder full of papers and began shuffling them around. With his penchant for hard copy, Garson had brought all manner of "paperwork" with him from Hillsdale College. When the internet went down ... and stayed down ... there was no way anymore to share images. So the originals were the only thing left and all these years later, those images on paper were even more valuable.

Finally Garson selected a piece of paper and held it up.

"Recognize this?" he asked.

Of course they did. It was a picture of what was

visible through ordinary telescopes on the day before the Astrals arrived, detailed images that showed the surface of the "round balls" were not as smooth as marbles as they'd appeared in earlier, less-detailed images. Instead the surfaces contained structures, complex protrusions and indentions that almost looked like a view from high above a human city, looking down on the buildings below.

"This is a Day Five image," Garson said. "The next day, if you'll recall, we didn't have to look at the Astrals through telescopes, since these little not-marbles were hanging in the sky over cities all over the planet.

Garson selected a second piece of paper.

"This is a Day Four image." He displayed a picture that showed the round marbles in the foreground against a backdrop of deep space.

Then he flipped through the final pieces of paper — Day Three and Day Two images.

"Notice anything peculiar about all those images?"

"Obviously *you* noticed something about them, but I don't see anything other than what we all saw every day, ever larger and more detailed images of the approaching spaceship," Sawyer said.

Then Garson held up a much larger piece of paper, twenty-four inches by twenty-four inches. It was a blown-up photo of the planet Jupiter, the image that would have been visible from any high-powered telescope at any time in the decades pre-Astral Day that you cared to focus on the planet. Jupiter, with deep space all around it. No white dots.

Then he placed another image beside it. It was a blowup of the day the whole world changed. The image billions of people across the globe saw when they opened their Astral Apps on Astral Day and saw the armada of white spots out by Jupiter ... slowing down, as the scientists pointed out, for a landing on Earth.

"How about these images," Garson said. "See anything interesting here?"

The image was so familiar there was nothing *new* to see.

"I see what we've all seen," Sawyer said. "Little white dots, the dots that changed the history of the planet forever." He eyed the professor. "Obviously, *you* see something there that we don't. Care to tell us what it is?"

Garson pointed to an area of space next to the white dots, just space, black nothingness.

"What do you see there?"

Sawyer was losing his patience.

"Stop the science lecture, Garson. We don't have time for this." He pointed to the spot Garson indicated. "I don't see anything there, okay, absolutely nothing."

Garson smiled.

"Exactly!"

Taylor shook his head, holding onto his own impatience with a tenuous grip.

"What?"

"I'm not tracking."

Garson gestured to the previous pre-Astral Day of

the planet Jupiter. The planet, monstrously huge, with deep space showing beyond it and no white dots visible in the foreground.

"Look here, look at the stars you can see out beyond Jupiter, all over the picture." Then Garson directed their attention back to the Astral Day shot. "You *should* be able to see the same things here." He pointed to the area *beside* the white dots of Astral Day. "You *should* be able to see stars there. *But you don't.*"

Suddenly, Sawyer got it.

"You don't see any stars there because there was something blocking the view of them. Something huge. Something black."

"Give the man a Kewpie Doll," Garson cried. "We never noticed at the time. Nobody was interested in anything except the white dots we *could* see, not the stars we couldn't."

"That black ship appeared the same time the other ships did." Sawyer put it together as he spoke. "Of course, it did. The death ship accompanied the motherships. We just never saw it."

Garson held up the Day Two photo, where the dots were larger, still arranged in the neat rows of an armada.

"There are no missing stars here." He pointed to the pictures of the increasingly bigger and bigger white dots. "No missing stars. So that means—"

Sawyer already knew what it meant.

"That means the black ship never got any closer to the earth than their entry point into our solar system.

It didn't accompany the other motherships on their journey here. It stayed where it was."

"They left the black death ship parked out by Jupiter because they didn't need it," Taylor got it, too, "until now."

"And I'd think it's reasonable to conclude" — Garson was back in college professor mode — "that if it took the motherships six days to get here from Jupiter, slowing down for their approach so they could enter our atmosphere without burning up—"

"It will take the black ship six days, too," Sawyer finished for him.

Garson nodded.

The elders looked from one to the other, their eyes wide.

"Six days," Taylor said in wonder. "Just like before."

"Casey Stengel used to say …" Fred began, looked around and realized nobody knew who Casey Stengel was. "An old baseball manager had a phrase for that. He called it deja vu all over again."

"But this time, it's not six days until an unknown fate." Noah spoke for the first time. "We're not wondering … will they enlighten us or will they kill us?"

"Oh no, indeed," Garson said. "This time it's a six-day countdown to the end of the world." He looked at his watch, then back into the faces of the other elders. "Today is Day One. We have a few hours left. May I suggest we cancel Eagle Feather's birthday party and call a town meeting?"

Chapter Fourteen

IT TOOK Paco a long time to come back from the place the drug ayahuasca took him. Not just the place in the heavens, but the place in his own head. He had read somewhere that sometimes people took the drug on long weekends, or spent a week with a shaman somewhere, taking ayahuasca with other people, becoming one with them through the drug. In fact, he remembered reading about a particular man's experience, how the first three nights he drank the foul liquid and watched the people around him respond to it, but felt nothing. He'd been planning to demand his money back until the third night when he took the drink and everything in his world opened up to him. He could see things he could never have seen in real life. But more importantly, he was also able to turn around and look back into himself.

Paco couldn't imagine being able to take the drug more than once. How could you be that ripped apart mentally and psychologically and psychically and spiritually night after night after night? It was unimaginable.

When Paco first came to, came back from the black hole in space where his psyche traveled into the hive mind to see ... *death* ... he was so overwhelmed by the horror of that vision that he could do nothing but vomit. He heaved and heaved and heaved, until he was dry-heaving nothing but stomach bile. His response was because the vision had been horrifying. But that wasn't the only reason. The vision of that end had been only *part of* his ayahuasca experience.

The man who had stood invisible in the alien mothership, saw the death ship hanging in space, preparing to come to Earth to obliterate humanity ... that man had then turned around and Paco found him *facing himself.*

He looked into his own eyes and when he did, he was able to see into the depths of his being in a way that was fracturing, mind-bending, totally life-changing.

The journey through himself went on and on. He thought he was finished, that the drug had finally worn off, so he went into the bathroom ... and watched the flowers on the wallpaper burst out of the paper in a profusion of color, grow incredibly fast until they filled the whole bathroom and he had to back out or be crushed by them.

He had slammed the door shut on them, then watched in horror as leaves and stems began to slide out under the door, growing bigger and bigger, unstoppable.

The Hidden

When he ran from that, he saw other hallucinations too terrible to countenance.

And through it all, he remained the man standing in front of himself, looking inside. He knew the hallucinations were just that, not real. Finally he sat back down on the cushions of the couch and closed his eyes, exhausted. He watched the sun slide down the western sky to the horizon, slip behind the mountains, realized he had been tripping all day.

Now he had to rest, had to let his mind rest.

And so he went to sleep.

Only it wasn't sleep. As soon as he closed his eyes, he was standing in front of his sleeping body, looking at it. The man looking at himself. But this time the man somehow ... entered him. Crawled into his mind. And he had a sense of such utter *violation*, like nothing he had felt since Spade ... But now, he was being violated by his own mind come to look at his mind.

Then he *was* that other man. And what he saw were passageways and tunnels, corridors and hallways, doors, but no windows, going on and on forever.

Paco was looking at his own mind. He was standing outside his own body looking at his brain, seeing it for what it really was — a beat-up prize fighter, eyes blackened, nose broken, lip split, cuts and bruises ... *that* was Paco's mind, courtesy of the beatings he had given it for all these years. He saw dark places in his head where his brain had ... died. Blood had stopped flowing there or a blood vessel had burst from the force of his concentration and destroyed the surrounding tissue. He saw the damage that caused the migraines, the ripping and tearing of tissues and vessels.

Paco stood outside himself and looked in and knew that the damage had affected him in ways he had not been aware of. It had made him paranoid. It had stolen his joy, driven him into depressions he didn't even recognize, impaired his judgement ...

What he had done all these years ... the effort to hold onto his telepathic ability and to control the minds of others ... was slowly driving him insane. Breaking down the tissues of his brain until one day, he would be completely mad.

That's what the man who stood outside himself saw. Watched it while Paco slept.

When Paco awoke, he knew what the other man knew, could remember what the other had seen. It horrified him, paralyzed him with fear ... but the fear faded as the images faded, as the man inside the man slowly evaporated, became mist, smoke rising up from a dying campfire.

Paco still understood that he had learned something profound about himself from the drug. But when he tried to remember what it was, his temples throbbed, so he stopped trying. After all, he hadn't taken the drug to raise his self-awareness. He had taken the drug to see the black ... thing.

In that regard, he had succeeded. He had seen into the hive mind of the Astrals. He had seen the *end of the world.*

Paco walked out onto his balcony overlooking the crystal-clear waters of Lake Tahoe. Sometimes, in the beginning, he'd brought women up here, he would amaze them with the view, dazzle them with his magnificent palace here on the roof of the world, then they'd have sex all night. But gradually, over time, he began to feel the hollowness of it. It seemed that the women became almost interchangeable. They may have looked different — this one a blonde, this a stunning redhead. They might even have sounded different — accents of a Georgia peach or a Scandinavian beauty. But in the end, they were all hollow inside. They were all just dolls. Sex was sex was sex. There were only so many different ways to do it and he realized what he longed for more than the sex or the beauty or the let's-try-a-different-position adventure was someone who would really appreciate the beauty of the world from his balcony. Someone who wasn't there because she was sucking up to him, or because she wanted something from him, or because she was afraid of him. Just somebody who was there because she wanted to be there with him, because she loved watching the sun set behind the mountains, loved looking at its reflection in the lake.

Someone like ... Star and Noah.

Like they had been before they turned on him, and they *had* turned on him, oh yes they had. The acid of those thoughts drained back down into his soul, burned away the awareness the other man had granted him. He was the old Paco, with just a whisper in his head of other things, deeper things about himself that he had known briefly when the drug had enlightened him, but which now were gone. The whispering said he was being paranoid, that they hadn't done anything to justify his feeling of rage at them.

But it was only whispering, and he pushed it out of his head and the man who had looked into the mind of the man who was Paco was gone, banished forever.

What remained was the Paco of old, only more angry than he already was, more filled with something like impotent rage at … at everything and everybody.

And none of it mattered anymore. Nothing mattered anymore, because the world was going to end.

He looked out over the valley as the last rays of the sun danced on the water and tried to picture what it would look like when the black death ship focused its rays on the planet, vaporizing life, turning buildings and people into piles of black dust. They'd already killed billions of people with their death rays, wiped out every major city on the planet. Now, they would do the same thing to the people who were left.

He would die. Humanity would die.

Game over.

But he didn't have to be among the *first* to die.

That thought stopped him. He could run, hide, escape. He had the resources to put off the inevitable. The black orb hung now in deep space, but it would not stay there. It would travel to the earth as the motherships had done, would descend into the earth's atmosphere then … and obliterate mankind.

In the end, Paco would perish with the rest of humanity, but he could survive for a time, a day, a week, a month. He recalled the endless replay of the

The Hidden

annihilation of Moscow. The beam of light, the black dust. It would take time to focus that beam on every man, woman and child on the planet, time to ferret them out wherever they were hiding. Earth might not be a big planet by Astral standards, but there was considerable land mass to cover — annihilation would take a while.

Perhaps it was possible to stay ahead of it, figure where the beams would go next and be ... somewhere else. A game of cat and mouse, with Paco as the mouse. So be it. Paco would wring from existence every second of life.

Paco Salazar would not be the first human being to die. He would be the *last*!

Already moving, he was thinking, planning.

The few cities, smaller ones, would go first. Shooting fish in a washtub. He had to get away from them.

He called out to Duddits. He had a lot of work to do.

Chapter Fifteen

Sawyer looked out over the crowd of people filing into the gymnasium. The stands would hold somewhere between three and four thousand people. There would be folks standing in the aisles tonight. Everybody here was a survivor. They all had stories about what their lives had been once, who they'd been and their struggle through hard times to become, in most cases, someone very different from the person they'd been in Before.

The people in the stands of the gym were much more quiet than usual when the group got together, all of them, for some occasion. Of course, most of those occasions were happy ones, the service before the group Thanksgiving dinner. Christmas. Survival Day.

Yep, they'd designated a day called Survival Day. It was the day the Astrals actually arrived on the planet, though they didn't go boots down then, just set up their stone circles and stone lines all over everywhere.

Most of these people had never seen an Astral,

knew them from descriptions, videos, pictures and jukes back when they worked. People knew what they looked like. The bald white Astrals called titans and the insectile monstrosities with the glittering blue eyes, killing machines called reptars. Sawyer had seen them both and he never wanted to make the acquaintance ever again.

They had left the painting to dry on the floor, so there it was, for all to see. It had looked intricate and detailed wet, when some of the paint was actually in puddles. But dry, it was a masterpiece, an incredibly detailed work of art. And it was an accurate depiction of what Star had seen in the hive mind. It was, as she had said, a portrait of death.

The sun had passed down behind the mountains to the west. The people of Zion Village weren't telepathic by any means, but living as they had together in this tiny bubble of civilization had put them in tune with each other. They knew something was up long before the "doorbell" sounded. That's what Star thought it sounded like — the bell that summoned the residents in times of need. After Brother Sebastian had quashed the idea of a "siren," the bell had been the compromise. They hadn't used it very often … and word spread fast in a small town. There wasn't likely anyone in this crowd who didn't know why they'd been called together.

And that's where Sawyer started when he stepped to the microphone in front of the crowd. They all knew they hadn't been summoned here tonight to celebrate Eagle Feather's birthday.

"Nobody has to tell you what that painting is. I am sure you've all heard about it, how it came to be, what it means and what the elders of the community think we ought to do about it. But to make sure everybody gets the straight story, I want you to hear it firsthand."

With Pumpkin's lead, Star stepped to the microphone and explained in short simple sentences what had happened to her, how she had tapped into the overflow of the hive mind on a mothership and seen this image, because it was the single image all the minds in the hive had been thinking at that time.

Garson was up next and he was the one who felt most at home in front of the crowd. He treated the audience as he would have treated his students back when he was a professor of astrophysics at Hillsdale College. He told them about the study of Ancient Aliens that had gone on both before and after Astral Day, about the work of Dr. Benjamin Bannister in Moab, Utah in particular, delving into the historic record to document what had happened on the previous occasions the Astrals visited the earth.

He was blunt, as usual, but gratefully made no lame attempts at humor. The Astrals had seeded humanity and returned at intervals to pass judgment on their progeny. Humanity always failed.

"They come, they judge, we fail, and they destroy us. Wash, rinse, repeat. That's the history of our dealings with the Astrals and no scientist I know was truly surprised when they showed up again. We had hoped … *I* had hoped that we had generations … but I was wrong. The sentence is about to be pronounced, and"

— he turned and gestured toward the painting that covered the gym floor — "it is a death sentence."

The crowd was hushed after he finished speaking. Eagle Feather was up next and the man of few words was a man of even fewer words stuck in front of a microphone to talk to thousands of people. He described the legend, the Taking Place and how it all referred to Star in three or four succinct sentences, then sat down.

Sawyer took over the microphone again.

"Now we're all singing from the same sheet of music. You know everything we know. We believe that the gift Star brought back to Earth from the Astrals was the ability to peek into the hive mind and see the plans they have for mankind. Eagle Feather believes the 'gift' is that we have been warned. In the past, when the judgment was handed down, the mass destruction fell upon humanity with no time to prepare. We are more fortunate than they."

He motioned for Garson to return to the microphone, and the professor was unexpectedly brief and succinct. He explained that the black spot in the early photos was actually the death ship, and that it made sense to assume it would take the ship the same amount of time it had taken the other ships to arrive — six days.

Sawyer stepped back up to speak.

"We figure the warning gives us time to figure out a way to survive the destruction planned for us." He glanced at Noah, who sat expressionless on one of the benches on the gym floor. Everyone in Zion Village knew he was an engineering prodigy, could build structures unimagined by any other human mind.

"We've only had a couple of hours to brainstorm ... but not surprisingly, we believe our only hope is to build an ark." Sawyer stepped back and gestured to the crowd. "Questions?"

The questions popped up out of the crowd like popcorn in hot grease.

"How long will it take to build an ark?"

"We don't know. Noah is designing plans for it right now, but they're not by any means complete. The actual construction ... part of that depends on how many hands there are working on it."

"If you don't know how long it'll take to build this ark thing, I don't see how this warning does us any good."

"What's the alternative? Do nothing? Sit here and wait for the waves to come surging over the mountains? I don't know about you, but I'd rather die with my boots on."

"Is this ark the only way?"

"I don't have a better idea. Do you?"

"Wait a minute ... are you saying you want *everybody* to work on this thing?"

"What we envision is that our whole, singleminded effort from this moment forward will be to build an ark, as quickly as we can. Stop whatever we're doing, free up every possible hand we can to work on the ark. Use the lumber from existing structures—"

"Whoa, hold on a minute," called out a voice Sawyer recognized. It was Homer Middleton, who didn't technically live in Zion Village. He owned a nearby farm and had managed to hang onto it through the rough spots, raising what he needed for his family, a fiercely independent, irascible old man who always seemed to be looking for something to argue about. And they'd just handed him the mother of all arguments.

"You're saying everybody should just drop what they're doing and come work on this ark thing? We got to raise crops, in case you hadn't noticed. Ain't no way in hell I'm gonna to leave my field to come work on your little floaty-boat."

"Homer's got a point," said Pete Whittier. "If we do this, build this thing … what if you're wrong, this" — he gestured toward the painting on the gym floor — "what if it don't mean what you think it does? You're wrong, and we got us a big boat … and no houses or food."

"Speaking of eating …" said Millicent Kleigelmeyer, who stood amid a group of small children that had all been born at Zion Academy. She'd had two other children born since Astral day, who didn't survive. There was no hospital. And in all the immigrants who'd found their way to the Zion, there hadn't been a single doctor. One dentist and two registered nurses, that was the best they could do. They'd raided all the drugstores that hadn't already been looted of supplies, finding the drugs the druggies weren't looking for. Hard to get high on erythromycin or insulin. What the three diabetics in the village would do when the insulin ran out …

Sawyer thought of Ellie, who wasn't here for this discussion.

"What is it we're going to eat on that ark ..." Millicent wanted to know. "And how long we gonna have to be on it ... and are we gonna, you know, do what Noah did, take animals two by two?"

The discussion went south from there, with some people arguing about whether or not to leave crops to build an ark, other people arguing about what they should take on the ark, while others argued it wouldn't do any good to survive the flood because the earth wouldn't survive.

"If they melt the ice caps, do we got to stay on that ark until they re-freeze? 'Cause the water ain't gonna recede until they do. Reckon how long it takes to re-freeze the North Pole."

"I think I'd rather drown in my own living room than starve to death on some ark waiting for the water to go down."

Garson pointed out then that this wasn't the Astrals' first rodeo. They'd wiped humanity off the face of the earth before ... and then re-seeded a small number of people to start the race all over again.

"If the Astrals can melt the ice caps, I have no doubt they can refreeze them. And there is ample evidence in the geologic record to support that conclusion. They'd have to — at some point — make the planet livable again."

"*At some point* ... and what point is that?"

Before he could answer, Homer Middleton rose to his feet again. "You done told us what you know. Let's just make ourselves a list of what you *don't* know. You don't know if there is really gonna be a flood. You don't know how long we'll have to stay on that boat, how long the earth will be flooded or how the Astrals plan to un-flood it. And you don't know if there'll be a livable world left out there when they do." He spat a disgusting splatter of tobacco juice out onto the steps below him. "Sounds to me like you don't know Jack shit."

And Sawyer thought that was a pretty good summary of their current reality.

Day Two

Chapter Sixteen

THE SUN ROSE on Day Two in Zion Village, peeked up over the mountaintop and shined down through the windows into the office of Noah Matheson, who occupied one of the handful of offices in the main building of what had been the Zion Academy for deaf children. The office was on the top floor, and down the hall gathering dust was Dr. David Weiss's miraculous machine that enabled deaf people all over the world to hear — until the Astrals showed up. Noah had been Dr. Weiss's only failure. No amount of adjusting on Noah's special hearing aids had made it possible for him to hear.

It was in this office that Noah designed the miraculous feats of engineering that boggled the minds of everyone who saw them. Blackboards and whiteboards covered every wall — Garson called them "primitive," Noah called them "intuitive" — that Noah used to sketch out the beginnings of ideas. And there were big parabolic optical image tables where he converted his ideas to 3D designs and made holographic images of plans for builders to use on site.

Noah stood upright and stretched, noticed for the first time that it was morning. He'd been up all night working on the design of the ark. Intricate schematics filled the whiteboards, mathematical equations filled the blackboards. Half-finished holographic images hung in the air over tables all over the room.

None of them was viable.

Not a single one.

Plopping down in his big office chair in frustration, Noah hurled his stylus across the room, followed its progress and cringed as it smacked the robe of an old monk standing in the doorway. Brother Sebastian. The man was about as wide as he was tall. In his brown robe, he looked like a milk chocolate fire hydrant, bald except for a soap ring of brown around the bottom.

The monk leaned over and picked up the stylus off the floor.

"It is proper etiquette when launching flying projectiles to shout, 'incoming round,'" he said.

Noah smiled, or lifted up the corners of his mouth, anyway. The old monk came in, instinctively turned sideways so as not to disturb a holographic image that extended beyond one of the tables, made his way to the chair next to Noah's desk and eased his considerable bulk down into it.

"Why yes, Noah, I'd love to take a seat, but I'm

The Hidden

good. Don't go to any trouble. Coffee and I are going through a very bad breakup right now."

Everybody was going through breakups with coffee. They could raise tea. It wasn't the best in the world and they'd had to wait three years for the plants to mature before they could begin harvesting crops. But it would suffice, and there were enough different varieties that you could find something that suited you. Coffee, not so much. It was either coffee or it wasn't and the supplies of it had dwindled until a cup of it was saved for only the most auspicious occasions.

"Sorry, I'm not very good company right now. Why don't you come back—"

"When you *are* good company? Oh, my dear boy, I would never see half the people I know if I waited to come calling until they were good company. I solve that dilemma by being good company myself, so at least fifty percent of the interaction is companionable."

Noah knew when he was beaten and slumped back in his chair.

"You've been working too hard, son."

"Name me three people who haven't been."

"Touché."

Noah didn't often share his inner feelings with anybody but Star, though somehow that didn't seem to count because she felt so comfortable in his mind that sometimes talking to her felt like talking to himself. But Brother Sebastian was different. He'd been in the mill that day after the Astrals had been sighted, showed Noah how to grind flour, prattling on and on to take Noah's mind off the impending invasion. Noah even remembered what the monk had said to comfort him that day.

"Everybody on Earth was surprised by those spaceships appearing out there by Jupiter, but you know who wasn't surprised — God. He's got this, son. You can relax. He's got this."

In the years since, Noah had sometimes thought about that conversation, and didn't want to broach the subject with Brother Sebastian. But given what the Astrals had done in the past seven years, if God had this, he was sure making a mess of it.

Noah said none of that. Instead, he allowed himself to relax a little and unload.

"It's so complicated, with so many variables. Materials. Where do we get the kind of lumber we'll need to make something that big? Given all the time and resources in the world, we could cut down the forests for lumber. Do you know how long it would take to cut down that many trees, take them to the sawmill, make them into boards … and besides you can't do that. You can't use green wood like that to build with. It has to be dried, cured, or it will bend out of shape and … leak. We'd have to take the lumber from existing structures, tear them down …

"But even if we had the materials, do you know how big that thing would have to be to hold all the people in Zion Village?" The old monk shrugged and Noah didn't bore him with the details. "Let's say it was only as big as your standard naval destroyer. Do you know how long it would take to build something like that, just the hull, not counting anything inside? With no modern equipment — no laser saws, or synthetic seams or ... just your hands and hammers and nails. A destroyer! And—"

The old monk held up his hands.

"It is an impossible task, isn't it, son?"

"No, not impossible, just ..." He let it trail off. Truth still in the husk, yeah, it was an impossible task.

"You nailed it. No pun intended. It's impossible."

The finality of saying it let something loose inside Noah, released some pressure valve and he began to deflate. He couldn't do what had been asked of him — not with existing resources and an absolute *dead*line. No pun intended there, either.

"So what do you do in the face of the impossible? Give up?"

"No! We can't give up. We can't—"

"Then if the solution we have won't work, and we have to keep trying, then wouldn't it be a better use of your time to try to think of some other solution that would work?"

"But there isn't any other—"

"Have you thought about it ... really *thought* about it? Yesterday, when we learned the Astrals plan to flood the earth ... duh, water, a boat — knee-jerk response. That was the first thought of your namesake and it was the right choice for him. If it's not the right choice for us, what haven't we thought about?"

Noah sat very still, his tired mind trying to process what the monk was saying.

"Son, I think it's about time to do more than think outside the box. I think you need to start thinking outside the box the first box came in."

Chapter Seventeen

NOAH ABSOLUTELY, one hundred percent did *not* want to take Josie Wilson on a rowboat ride.

But he had promised!

Josie was Nick Wilson's daughter. Nick and Michelle Wilson had been part of the Stranded Eagle Feather and Star had happened upon in Land Between the Lakes. Josie had been born in Zion Village and was six now. Michelle had died in childbirth. Josie had Down syndrome and was just about the most adorable child Noah had ever met. But still, he didn't want to take the time today of all days, to take a little kid for a rowboat ride on the pond.

Brother Sebastian had shooed him out toward the pond, told him that letting his mind rest for half an hour was a good idea before he tried to focus on the box outside the box outside the box.

Noah never wanted to go for a boat ride, rowboat, speed boat, shoot, he could be on one of those gigantic cruise ships that used to sail the Bahamas before Astral Day. Bottom line: Noah couldn't swim and he was afraid of water.

Only Star knew about what as a child had been his great shame — everybody else could swim and he couldn't. There were so, so many things only Star knew about Noah.

How's the potato peeling going? he asked her in his head as he led the little girl by the hand down to the pond.

Let's just say it isn't very a-peel-ing.

I walked right into that one. Teed it up and handed you the driver.

Have you figured out yet—? Then she stopped, sensed his reluctance to talk about it. *So where are you off to?*

Taking Josie for her long-promised rowboat ride.

You be careful.

I'll wear two life jackets.

Actually, he couldn't find even one. The hooks where adult life jackets were supposed to hang were empty. But little-kid jackets were plentiful and he quickly found one that fit the little girl's slightly rotund figure.

The pond was located in a big field behind the mill and the hydroponics barn, beyond to the meadow strewn with wildflowers that lay across the old road from the stone-walled monastery complex. It had once been seeded every year by the Kentucky State Department of Fish and Wildlife, and it produced fish for the monks. But the seeding had stopped, and the power of the fish to multiply apparently had almost not been sufficient to keep their species alive. If Brother Thaddeus hadn't figured it out and banned fishing for three years, there would have been no fish to catch. Even now, the pond was used mostly for sport, swimming in the summer, and rowboats the teenagers took out and rowed back into the reeds to do what teenagers always did in the reeds.

"We gonna fwim, Unka Noah?" Josie asked. She'd come dressed in her bathing suit, just in case.

"That would be a big NO," he told her. "We're just going for a ride, out and across."

"But it would be fun to fwim, wouldn't it, to go splash down in the water and be a fishy."

"Sorry, but I'm a dry-land kinda guy and we don't have time for that today. Out and across. Okay?"

She looked mildly disappointed for about two seconds, then her bright smile came out.

"Okay, we go wowin', then. Row and row."

He got Josie situated on the seat in the front of the boat and got carefully into the middle seat, where the oars were attached.

"Lookit, swans," Josie cried and leapt to her feet pointing to the two swans swimming majestically across the water.

The boat wobbled and Noah's stomach wobbled with it. "Sit down, Josie. You'll turn the boat over. I see them. They're pretty."

Josie sat back down and Noah lost himself in rowing and thinking. Some structure that was already built — converted into an ark? But what? Most structures were pretty firmly affixed to the ground. He tried to think totally outside all the boxes. Some kind of tower on a mountaintop stretching up above the water. Absurd. Some kind of …

And that's when Josie went overboard. She stood up abruptly and reached down to pick up something floating in the water — a leaf or stick. But she was unstable on her feet and simply toppled head-first into the water.

"Josie!" he cried, and she bobbed up to the surface giggling. "Did you do that on pur—?"

Noah was never sure later exactly what did happen next. He stood, leaned over the side of the boat and extended his hand to the little girl bobbing happily in the life jacket. Then his foot must have slipped. He felt the boat tipping dangerously low toward the water and tried to compensate but his weight was off center now, and his effort merely completed the job of pushing the side of the boat below the waterline and over it went.

Noah had grabbed a breath before his face smacked into the water, but he'd never been able to hold his breath for long and panic instantly welled in his chest.

Noah — what's wrong!

He couldn't order his thoughts enough to answer but Star saw what was happening and understood.

Hold on, I'm coming!

His head cleared the water — he was sputtering and gasping — only long enough for him to see Josie floating nearby, splashing happily.

"Noah go fwimming, too!"

Then his head was under again.

Terror clawed at his throat, his lungs seemed to be exploding.

Noah ... Noah. I'm coming!"

But Star wouldn't get here in time. She was peeling potatoes in the commercial kitchen on the ground floor of the apartment complex called New Mexico out by the highway. With a sickening certainty, Noah understood that no matter how fast Star ran, she couldn't make it all the way to the pond in time. It would be too late.

Noah tried to propel himself upward, but didn't know how. In seconds he would have to breathe. He'd read somewhere it only took thirty seconds to drown. One good lungful of water ... Flailing his arms, trying to make some kind of swimming motion, his hand hit something solid. *The side of the rowboat.* He grabbed it with the strength of pure panic and used it to pull his head out of the water.

He cleared the surface, grabbed a breath ... It was dark. How could it be ...?

He was under the rowboat, could hear Josie's muffled giggles.

Noah! Noah!

I'm okay, I grabbed the boat, I'm okay.

Holding onto the edge of the boat, he could duck back under water and come up on the other side out in the pond.

No way! He was NOT going back under water *for any reason*. There was plenty of air here, thank you very much. He'd wait for help here, safe in the darkness under the boat. In the total silence of his deafness.

Darkness. Silence. Air.

A bright flare of insight, a sudden epiphany lit Noah's whole mind in a brilliant flash of understanding.

At some point after that Star and the rescue party arrived — she'd grabbed people at random as she ran, crying, "We have to help Noah!" She jumped in the water fully clothed. Even though she was blind, Star loved to swim, and she followed Noah's thoughts to where he cowered beneath the upturned boat.

She was talking a mile a minute in his head, but he wasn't attending to what she was saying. Wasn't attending to anything except the excited whirring of his mind. Someone swam out and grabbed the rope tied to the rowboat and towed it back to the dock. Other people flipped the boat over so Noah could climb up the ladder to the dock without having to go under water again. When he finally set foot on firm ground again, he turned, leaned over and planted a smoochy kiss on Josie's wet cheek.

"I had fun today," he said. "We'll do this again!"

Then he took off running.

Noah, what—?

Later!

Noah was a sight, soaking wet, wearing only one shoe — must have lost the other one — as he ran across the meadow to the road, down it to the pathway that led through the rock wall around Zion Academy and across the grounds to the building. He

The Hidden

and his father still lived in a room there, and he stopped briefly to change clothes, before he barreled into the office of "the sheriff" on the ground floor just inside the front doors. He didn't even knock, just barged in on a conversation between his father and Brother Sebastian. A serious one, it appeared. His father was clearly upset, but whatever they were talking about could wait.

"We're not building an ark," he announced. He spoke, didn't sign, stood in front of his father's desk so he could read his lips accurately.

"I gathered that," his father said. "Brother Sebastian was saying he talked to you this morning and—"

"It won't work. But I know what will!"

Noah caught the words 'outside the box' on Brother Sebastian's lips out of the corner of his eye as he concentrated on his father's face.

"We don't have to build a boat. We're not going to ride out the flood *on top* of the water. We're going to survive it *under the water*."

Both men looked blank. He was looking at Brother Sebastian when the monk said, "A … submarine? Well, that's certainly outside the box."

Noah was so buoyed up by hope he actually chuckled.

"No, way easier than that. It's something we don't have to build." He turned back to his father. "We're going to ride out the flood in Matheson Caverns."

Chapter Eighteen

Paco had been up almost all night making arrangements to flee — out into the countryside away from cities the death ship would destroy first. He had finally gone to bed, but slept only fitfully, plagued with bouts of nausea from the drug ayahuasca he had taken. How long would it be before it wore off?

Now he sat at the table in front of the windows that looked out over the lake taking small spoonfuls of tomato bisque soup that Duddits had told the cook to prepare for him to settle his stomach.

He hated to leave Duddits behind, but when he sped eastward later this morning, it would be survival of the fittest. And Duddits wouldn't last long. Inland. No destination. Just *away*. Paco would have to find a place, somewhere to hunker down and make a last stand. He would go down fighting. He'd struggle to the end.

Noah! someone screamed in his head and he dropped the spoonful of soup. The spoon splattered back into the bowl and splashed red liquid all over the front of his shirt.

Star. It was Star. A psychic scream echoed inside Paco's head.

Noah — what's wrong!

Then Paco saw what filled Star's mind — the image of Noah *drowning*.

Hold on, I'm coming!

The words create a video of images and emotions.

TERROR. *She won't get there in time. Noah will drown before she can …*

Noah's heart is thundering in his chest, where the agony to breathe is overcoming his ability to hold his breath.

Paco holds his own breath, feels the fear welling up in him, his lungs screaming for air.

Struggling, trying to make his way up, but he doesn't know how. Flailing his arms—

His hand hits something solid. The edge of the boat. He grabs hold, uses it to pull himself upward until his head breaks the water and he drags in great coughing, sputtering lungfuls of air.

It is dark. He's under the overturned boat.

A bright flare of insight, a sudden epiphany lights Noah's whole mind in a brilliant flash of understanding.

Under.

They will escape …

Under …

. . .

THE IMAGES BEGAN to fade as the intensity of the emotion that amplified them faded.

Total darkness. The silence of deafness.

And then the images were gone.

Paco sat so stunned he had trouble making his diaphragm allow his lungs to fill with air. Star and Noah. *He had heard them.* For the first time in seven years ... the drug. Ayahuasca. It had expanded Paco's mind, strengthened his abilities. And the terror of drowning had amplified Noah's thoughts.

So Paco had heard them.

He sat very still, with his heart hammering.

He had connected somehow to Star and Noah!

Star and Noah!

Yeah, the traitors. The—

But his hatred drained away in the face of the dawning realization in his mind.

Star knew about the end. She'd seen into the hive mind just as Paco had. If Star knew, Noah knew. They both understood that judgement had been rendered and a death sentence handed down to all mankind.

But Noah had figured out a way to escape.

Yes!

The creative insight had come to him with the surge of adrenaline while he was fighting for his life, drowning. He'd figured it out when he was under the boat. *Under* ... Noah meant to hide *under* something, something that would protect him and Star.

Paco threw his head back and laughed out loud. The kid was brilliant beyond all imagining and he had done it.

A dome. A canopy. A shield of some kind.

The prodigy who had built a model Eiffel Tower before his third birthday would build some kind of shield that would withstand the death rays of the mothership. Only Noah Matheson, of all the people on the planet, could come up with a way to trick the Astrals.

"His buildings are like bees — aerodynamically, they can't possibly fly. But they do."

That's what some professor had once said about Noah's creations. Noah would build something that couldn't possibly work. *But it would.*

Paco jumped up and succeeded in upturning the bowl of soup so the whole thing splattered on the table cloth.

"Duddits, get in here. Send for my captains — now!"

Paco was smiling a more genuine and heartfelt smile than he had in … maybe in years.

Not just inland.

No — to a place inland. To Kentucky. What was the name of the little town Noah came from? Jessup. Jessup, Kentucky.

Paco would go there to Star and Noah … and kill them both, take their precious shield *and live.*

Paco Sanchez would *survive*!

He laughed another full belly laugh.

When he stopped for breath, he heard a tiny whisper in his ear, and an image formed. Himself looking at himself, into his mind. At the damage he'd wrought upon his own body and what the damage had made of him.

The ayahuasca had awakened Himself and now the mirror of his soul was here butting into Paco's affairs, trying to tell him what to do.

Fuck that!

Duddits came scrambling into the room, his eyes wide.

"Are you all right?" the man asked, and Paco knew he really cared about the answer. Yes, sir, it was a shame he had to leave Duddits behind, but he didn't qualify for the "lean and mean" force Paco was amassing.

"The five captains — I want them here in five minutes." Paco had blown through hundreds of men in his reign as the leader of S&S, the Spider and the Snake. When you knew a man's thoughts ... you figured out quick that nobody stayed loyal and true for very long. Everybody was expendable.

The current five captains were Radek Nova, Jake Farewell, Hakeem Burchelli, Juan Santiago and Lamont Saunders. Each of them commanded a hundred of Paco's hand-picked soldiers. He'd been planning to replace Farewell and Saunders. They'd started believing their own press clippings, thought they were cocks of the walk. Humility was a virtue, after all. No time for replacements now, though. These five were among the most fortunate men on the whole planet; they would lead his army eastward. They would live.

Live.

Chapter Nineteen

This time, Noah conducted the meeting. It was as jammed with humanity as the one last night, when the Zion Village residents had made it clear they weren't buying the let's-build-an-ark plan he and the elders had tried to sell them. And they'd been right. That plan wouldn't work. But the plan he was presenting now would work. He just had to convince the rest of the community that Plan B was not only a viable option, it was far superior to Plan A.

It didn't take three minutes to outline the plan, because it was simple. There was nothing to build — no issues with a lack of materials or manpower. It could be explained in a few simple sentences — the inhabitants of Zion Village would move into Matheson Caverns and remain there through the flood.

Everybody in the room had heard of Matheson Caverns, the huge cave system south of Zion Village that had been run as a commercial enterprise for tourists for more than sixty years. But the majority of the people had only "heard about" the caverns and really had no idea that the Matheson family owned the second longest cave system in the world, second only to Mammoth Cave National Park, which was the *longest cave system in the world*. Mammoth Cave lay beneath Flint Ridge in Edmonson County, Kentucky, while Matheson Caverns was located within Joppa Ridge, the ridge "next door."

The community's residents had lived in the area long enough that it was unnecessary to describe the basic geography.

They knew that the caverns lay fifteen miles from Zion Village — traveling winding mountain roads. The Twin Forks River provided a much more direct route. The river that flowed past the village wound downstream into the caverns, entering on the west side of Joppa Ridge and traveled four more miles through Level Five of the caverns to exit on the east side.

Noah had asked locals, people from Jessup and the surrounding area, to help him describe/explain the cave system to the others. Herb Wilcox was first up. He was the man who'd owned the warehouse in Jessup that housed all the town's stores for that first winter after Astral Day. The warehouse and all its contents had been reduced to black dust by an Astral shuttle, as had most of the rest of the town. Fewer than half the population had survived. But the few who did, the refugees, moved out to the academy and founded Zion Village.

"I seen the shuttle destroy the warehouse," Herb said. "It was all our supplies, all our stores for the winter. When I look back on it now, I think we shoulda stored them supplies in the caverns. They'd have been safer there." Wilcox had lived in Jessup his whole life, and his two sons worked as guides at the caverns. The two boys, would have been men now, had been on vacation in Florida on Astral Day and Herb never saw either one of them after that.

"Matheson Caverns has got more than two hundred fifty miles of explored tunnels — probably twice that many miles that nobody's ever seen yet," Wilcox said. "The tunnels ain't stretched out straight, like you could drive a train through. Like maybe they could stretch from here to Washington D.C. Them caverns is all twisted up like spaghetti, circling and looping around." He paused. "Think of it like you would a big skyscraper building. Like the Empire State Building — you remember, used to be this big old building in New York City. The Empire State Building was twelve hundred fifty feet tall. Well, Joppa Ridge is even taller than that. It's *fifteen hundred* feet tall. Imagine all the floors in the Empire State Building — one hundred and two of them. Joppa Ridge ain't divided up all uniform like that into floors, but them caverns inside it is on five different levels. That ridge is what you might call a natural-made skyscraper."

He smiled out at the crowd. "I know some of you's thinking — *a cave?* Seriously? But you ain't got no idea how big them caverns are. Roofs hundreds of feet tall, wide enough you could drive five cars abreast through them. They ain't all of them caverns that big, of course, but all of them is big enough you ain't gonna be bent over in some little hole in the ground."

Noah called next on his Uncle Taylor, who had managed the family business as a tourist attraction that entertained more than 1.5 million visitors a year ... until Astral Day.

Noah had made big holographic images to illustrate what Taylor told the crowd.

"Herb told you there are two hundred fifty miles of caverns, but the area we're talking about using here" — he looked at his nephew, Noah, and grinned — "we're calling it 'Noah's Ark.' It's the portion of Matheson Caverns my family ran as a tourist business. The caverns are on five levels, but we'll only be using the top three. All the caverns are stacked one on top of the other beneath a surface land area of about seven miles by eight miles. Each level has a little over four linear miles of caverns, so we'll use between sixteen and twenty miles total. Level One is the cavern that lies in the top four hundred feet of Joppa Ridge, which is fifteen hundred feet above sea level." He stopped and looked at Wilcox. "Three hundred feet taller than the Empire State Building. Level Two is three hundred feet below Level One, Level Three another two hundred feet lower and Level Four is only two hundred feet above the Twin Forks River that flows through Level Five.

"All sixteen of the miles in those levels have flat paved walkways through them. We built railings to keep visitors from falling into the cracks, crevices — like the bottomless pit on Level Four, a gigantic hole fifty feet across and two hundred feet deep — and to help them as they climbed the hills inside the caves, like Mount Rush-More in Level Three that's a hundred and eleven feet above the floor of the rest of the cavern. We installed lighting, bridges … there's a commercial kitchen, grandstands in Carnegie Hall on Level One that seats five hundred people and …" He paused. "Maybe I'm giving you TMI, too much information. Just know Matheson Caverns is big enough to easily house five times the number of people who live in Zion Village. *Ten* times!"

Now, it was Noah's turn.

He knew going in he had two hurdles to overcome.

First, people would not understand that the caverns would not fill up with water when the world was flooded. And second, they would not understand how they could survive there "without air."

He started with Hurdle Number Two.

He picked out a random person from the crowd — selected Paul Balforth, a dentist from Atlanta, who had gotten waylaid by Bubba Blacksnake seven years ago.

"Okay, Paul, tell me this … just your opinion. What if you could seal up the MagnaDome." That was a huge stadium in Chicago three times the size of the SuperDome in New Orleans. Both of them were black dust now. "What if you could stop up every crack, every opening, make it totally airtight. You with me so far?" Paul nodded. "Once it's sealed tight, I want you to place an imaginary canary on the fifty-yard line. Now tell me, how long do you think that canary can survive before it chokes to death?"

"Why would it choke to death?" Paul asked.

"I just told you … we sealed up the whole place, not a single open window or door, not so much as a crack in it anywhere. No air coming from outside."

"Yeah, but it's a *canary*, with all the air in the Magna Dome to breathe."

Noah looked out at the crowd.

"And *that's* why *we* won't choke to death in Matheson Caverns once it's sealed up. We won't have the paltry amount of air you could contain in the Magna Dome. We will have *two hundred fifty miles of open air* — that just's in the explored caves. There are hundreds more miles of caverns we've never seen."

He let that sink in, then went back to Hurdle Number One.

"The other thing all of you are worried about — you're scared that the caverns will fill up with water when the earth floods. And they will. *Some* of the caverns will. But the water will seek its own level and won't go any higher. It can't flood every tunnel and passage and chamber. Picture a boat turned over in the water. You can breathe under that boat." He paused and grimaced. "Trust me, I know you can breathe. There's air trapped under that boat and the water won't flow up into that empty space. The water stays level. The bottom levels of Matheson Caverns will fill with water when the earth floods. But there will still be *miles and miles and miles* of caverns above the flooded ones that are full of air and won't fill with water."

He paused then, looked out over the crowd. Of

course, it felt deathly quiet to Noah ... duh, he was deaf. But it appeared to him that the crowd was silent. He saw no one muttering to his neighbor, no one fidgeting because they were either bored or unconvinced or hostile.

Then the discussion started. But it felt like discussion, not arguments. It felt like the questions came from people who'd turned some kind of corner, who wanted to be convinced.

"What if there's an earthquake and it splits open the cave?" Gino Martinelli asked.

Sawyer had less patience with the process than Noah had.

"I don't know, Gino, you tell me. Or maybe lightning will strike the cave and fry us like we were in a microwave oven."

"Okay, not an earthquake, but what if the cave we're in leaks?" That was Herb Granger, who'd been a pilot for TOA, Trans Oceanic Airlines. Not a single commercial flight ever left the ground again after Astral Day. "That's a reasonable question, don't you think? Even if it's on a higher elevation than the water in the bottom caverns, what if it's got a hole in it we don't know about?"

Garson weighed in on that one.

"Have you ever been to Carlsbad Caverns?" the former professor asked but didn't wait for an answer before he plunged ahead. "It is spectacularly beautiful, with caverns full of stately stalagmites like a city's skyscrapers, fifty-foot stalactites hanging down majestically from the ceiling, flow formations that look like frozen waterfalls. Compare that to boring Matheson Caverns, which is spectacular for its size only, not its beauty."

He stopped, waited to be asked. Herb took the bait.

"And that's significant because …?"

"Because stalactites and stalagmites are formed from *water leaking* into the caves, drip, drip dripping over thousands of years, and the dissolved limestone in the water makes formations like icicles. The limestone in Carlsbad Caverns has been slowly dissolving from water leaking in from above since … since before the Astrals showed up the first time. Matheson Caverns is *not* dissolving. It is capped by insoluble rock, a thirty-foot-thick layer of sandstone tops all of Joppa Ridge — all of Mammoth Ridge, too, where the national park used to be. Sandstone seals all the caverns below it. If there were leaks, you'd know. You could see them — hard to miss a thirty-foot tall stalactite. Matheson Caverns is just a big, dry hole in the ground."

No one else spoke. Then Homer Middleton stood and looked around.

"So we hide in air bubbles in a big hole in the ground for how long …?"

"Forty days and forty nights — ain't you read your Bible lately?" someone else said.

"And then we poke our heads up out of our little hidey-holes and hope the world will be fit to live in and that we didn't almost drown and almost suffocate just to starve to death — that what you're telling us?"

But even Homer seemed more resigned than hostile.

"I'd say that sums up our situation pretty well," Garson said.

Noah spoke then.

"This is it. This is our only hope of survival. Every man, woman and child in Zion Village is welcome in … Noah's Ark. But nobody will be forced to go. If you want to stay here, stay. If you want to come with us … then roll up your sleeves, people, because we have an enormous amount of *work* to do! Today is Day Two. The Astral death ship will be here on Day Six. Between now and then we have to haul into those caverns enough food, water and other supplies to sustain us." His eyes scanned the crowd. "Roughly five thousand people."

He paused.

"Look, I get it. There are hundreds of questions we haven't even thought of. And the answers to most of them are 'I don't know.' All I do know is that we've been given a gift that no one else on the planet has been given." Noah glanced at Star, sitting with Papa Eagle Feather on the bottom row of the bleachers. "We have been *warned*. What we do with that warning … that's on us."

Chapter Twenty

SURVIVING the Astral flood in Matheson Caverns, and planning how to equip and outfit the "Noah's Ark" caverns had begun the moment the crowd walked out of the gymnasium at noon after Noah had outlined the plan.

While Noah, his uncle and cousins went to survey the caverns that afternoon, Garson divided up responsibility among what he called worker bees and thinker bees. Noah and Garson would figure out what to do and how to do it, and Sawyer and his crews would make it happen.

"Heat. Air. Water. And food."

Garson held up a finger with each word.

That was the bottom-line puzzle the thinker bees had to solve.

"Those are the essentials necessary for a human being to survive. But given the nature of our current project, I would add light and waste removal to that list, though they're not technically essential they do make survival more ... palatable."

Heat was not an issue. The cave remained a uniform fifty-four degrees year round.

Air was not an issue, not with the hundreds of square miles of it that would be trapped inside the caverns when the earth flooded.

Water wasn't an issue — they could just pump up water from the flooded passages below. If it was salty as sea water — there was debate about that among the thinker bees — they would run it through an electro-dialysis machine to make it usable for human consumption. If it was fresh rather than salt water, they'd use a simple water filtration system put together with parts from the FreshDrink machines that'd filtered Jessup's water from the tower.

Getting rid of wastes ... Noah would design a method of disbursement that didn't contaminate their drinking water supply.

And light. Three sources — the caterpillar lights already lining hundreds of miles of passages, plus corn-oil lanterns and electricity.

That left food. Food *was* an issue. Oh, they had plenty of it. The frugal monks had built and stocked storehouses of food supplies over the years so the village would never again be facing a winter without provisions, had stashed away a year's supply of the basics of survival for five thousand people. Gratefully, the warehouses for those supplies were on the back of the property by the river. In fact, they'd used the caverns as storehouses for some of it — bags of flour, corn meal, rice, cooked and smoked meat, cheese, wine and salt along with sealed containers of VacuDry vegetables — potatoes, carrots, beets, onions, turnips, beans and peas. There were also barrels of the mix used in the inCarts machines that produced everything from potato chips to roast beef, using a slurry mix of soy-like organic substances. The machines had long since stopped functioning, but the slurry mix was ... edible. Tasted reeeeally bad, but you could live on it.

The issues regarding food were not how to come by it, but how to transport it from the storehouses to the caverns — and how much they would need to transport.

How many people would they have to feed ... and for how long? Zion Village had a population of roughly five thousand people — had almost doubled in size from the rag-tag group of survivors from the Astral attack on Jessup. But right now nobody knew how many of them would choose the ark and who would remain behind.

Those who chose the ark would, of course, present their own logistical problems. They all would have belongings they wanted to take with them. What could they take? And how would those belongings ... people ... supplies ... everything be transported to the caverns and loaded inside?

The Cricket Bottom entrance to the caverns was fifteen miles from Zion Village — US 60 to Tucker Road, and then to Cricket Bottom Road. The route went all the way around Joppa Ridge, snaked down winding roads that meandered through the mountains and foothills in no hurry to take anybody anywhere. Roads that hadn't been re-sealed or repaired, and with potholes that hadn't been filled for seven years! The trip was like negotiating an obstacle course.

Dock Road peeled off Tucker Road and wound around to the west side of the caverns to the dock where the river flowed into the cave, but it was in far worse shape than the highway.

The Village had stored gasoline. The tanker that had arrived with Star and the Stranded had long since been emptied. That was back in the day when they were still figuring things out, weren't as aware of preserving un-renewable resources as they were now. They'd filled it up three times since then, traveled from one gas station to another all over McClintock County looking for one the looters had either missed — not likely — or didn't think to pump dry — very likely. The gasoline tanks were buried under the ground of the gas stations. The tanker trucks that delivered gasoline had the equipment to pump the liquid down into the tanks. Then it was pumped out slowly by the pumps where people filled their cars. What Sawyer knew that the average person did *not* know was that there was always more than one tank, and that sometimes it required some kind of action, flipping a switch or something to shift from the empty to the full tank.

They had found more than half a dozen still-full gasoline tanks and used them to fill the tanker. The work scared the shit out of Sawyer, knowing how volatile gasoline was and that the jerry-rigged contraptions they'd put together to pump the gas back up into the tanker might spit out a spark or two and the whole operation would go up not with a whimper, but with a bang.

There was only a little fuel left in the tanker now and there was no way it would be sufficient to propel vehicles on multiple trips back and forth to Matheson Caverns carrying supplies.

Gratefully, there was a method of transport that didn't require gasoline. The river. The Twin Forks River flowed through the edge of Zion Village. The monks had built a dock on it years ago and even a small bridge — would barely hold the weight of a pickup truck — to access their orchards on the other side of the river. The Twin Forks River flowed from there *right through Matheson Caverns* ... in one side and out the other only a couple of miles east of the village. All they had to do was slap together some barges or rafts and float the supplies down to the caverns. Gratefully, the storehouses for food were right next to the monks' dock, and the four elevators in the caverns were just inside the cave entrance where the river entered.

Of course, that made it sound a whole lot simpler than it would actually be. The logistics of loading and unloading rafts, then hauling the supplies up into the higher caverns that wouldn't flood ... that was staggering.

Sometimes, when Sawyer let himself, he wanted to laugh out loud at the absurdity of it, the ridiculousness of it. How absurd and ridiculous everything in life had become as soon as little white dots were spotted in the sky somewhere out there by Jupiter. Life had been reasonable, and then it wasn't anymore. Everything was turned on its head. People rioted, killed each other over food, scratched and clawed to survive, when a week before the little white dots their biggest concern was the final episode of the remake of *Lost*. They worried about reversing the effects of global warming, and the presidential primaries, and why they wouldn't put a traffic light at the Main Street and Hill Street intersection where auto-drive cars always got confused, and even a little town like Jessup wound up with a traffic jam. People were worried they would lose their jobs with the current rate of Artificial Intelligence robots taking over just about every aspect of human life. And they worried about not having enough put away for retirement, or to pay for their kids' educations, or about their failing marriage, their children's drug use, whether or not their child would decide to get a sex change operation and what that would cost, and how they would afford to pay for their mother's care in assisted living, or about trying to get pregnant, or finding the right doctor to get an abortion. Crime. Racism. Religion ... and all manner of other things that go bump in the night.

And then they woke up one morning and none of that mattered at all. Everything they had worried about, everything they had been striving for, everything they were afraid of, loved, hated ... well, just *everything*. It all stopped mattering. And the only thing that did matter was survival — the phrase Eagle Feather and Nick had brought to Zion from the madman in Land Between the Lakes put the whole situation in a shirt-pocket summary.

In the New World Order there was only one imperative: fight or die.

Chapter Twenty-One

Noah closed his eyes and inhaled deeply. The years had changed nothing. He still thought Matheson Caverns was truly one of the great wonders of the world, and not because it was listed as the longest cave on somebody's book of world records. Even as a boy, he had loved it, knew he would never tire of feeling the cool air settle around him as he walked down into the darkness through the natural entrance. He liked the smell of damp earth. Other smells, too, that when he was a boy he imagined were exotic -- that he could actually smell bat shit.

Matheson Caverns was as wondrous and mysterious now as it had been when he and his father, uncle and cousins used to spend whole weekends in the winter, and almost every evening during the summer, exploring the "undocumented" sections of the cave, carrying on the tradition of Josiah Matheson, who'd bought a seven-by-eight-mile piece of land in

Kentucky right after the Civil War and discovered a cave on the property.

In the almost two centuries since that time, the family mapped 250 miles of cave, but left many more miles yet to be explored. Sawyer, his father and grandfather were certain that somewhere deep in the limestone rock on their fifty-six square miles of property, Matheson Caverns connected with the massive Mammoth Cave National Park — the longest cave system in the world, with more than 450 miles of explored caves.

When the family opened the caverns as a tourist attraction, they built a visitor's center at the natural entrance — the big hole high up on the mountainside of Joppa Ridge that Josiah Matheson had followed bats to hundreds of years before. That entrance opened into the top level of the caverns, Level One, more than a thousand feet above the river flowing through Level Five below. They conducted tours of the top four levels of the caverns, paved the passageways, lit them and built all manner of passages.

In 1964, they built the Cricket Bottom Visitor's Center, an entrance below the natural entrance that opened into Level Four, because that level featured the rock formations many visitors came to see and it was a hike to get down there from the higher levels. That same year, they built the four elevators near the boat dock on the west side of Level Five that rose up through a natural chimney with openings on all the upper levels. Supplies were hauled from the elevator to different places in the cave by mule-drawn carts.

The Hidden

Noah felt a hand on his shoulder and opened his eyes. His Uncle Taylor handed him a lantern and signed, "Go for it, fearless leader." Taylor's sons Samuel and David were behind him. They had been dispatched to the caverns to get the lay of the land — of the cave — viewed as a residence for five thousand people rather than a tourist attraction. They'd come in through the Cricket Bottom entrance and each would take one of the cave levels, traverse it from one end to the other — would climb from Level Four up the stairs to the higher levels, then walk eight miles, four out and four back. Later, they'd report to the council what locations they thought would be best suited for the storage of supplies, and the disbursement of thousands of people.

Noah liked the analogy Herb Wilcox had used to depict Matheson Caverns at today's meeting, where the community as a whole had bought into Noah's vision of using the caverns to escape the Astral flood. Some grudgingly agreed, a handful blew him off entirely, but the majority of the residents of Zion Village began a few hours ago to re-calibrate their thinking — what do we need to survive inside the caverns and how can we get it there in the next four days?

Herb had said Joppa Ridge was the Empire State Building and Matheson Caverns was the interior of the building. That helped residents see what would have taken hours to explain — how the caverns wound around on different levels inside the 1500-foot-tall ridge.

The Twin Forks River ran through the caverns on the bottom level, and those who'd been put in charge of stocking the caverns were already figuring how to float barges full of supplies downstream from the village to the caverns.

So … in Wilcox's analogy, the "basement and first floor" of the Empire State Building — Levels Four and Five of the caverns — would be flooded when the whole world was submerged under the water from the melted polar ice caps, but every floor above the basement would be dry because the water wouldn't flow *up* into the building, couldn't displace the air like that.

Truth was, they didn't have time to do this properly. You could spend months drawing up maps and diagrams of the best locations. It was now three o'clock on the afternoon of Day Two and the earth would be flooded on Day Six. Those organizing the migration might already be hauling supplies.

Noah was assigned Level One, the highest level in the caverns. As he climbed the stairs up … up … and up, his mind was churning. It seemed to him that Level One would be the best of all the levels to "build a community." It had big chambers where lots of people could gather, wide caverns where folks could … pitch a tent, he supposed, and make it a home site. He had to stop to catch his breath at the top of the stairs, then headed out, his mind still churning out all the possibilities when he headed down a gentle decline for about a hundred yards and as he rounded a corner a memory surfaced from years ago.

Astral Day.

He'd been eleven years old and his class of deaf students had been on a tour of the caverns when the little black dots were spotted out by Jupiter. Noah had gotten separated from the group that day because he got his zipper caught in his underwear when he stepped off the trail to take a leak. He had wandered around in the dark for hours and hours, had finally smelled fresh air and spotted sunlight, and came out into a passage beneath the Double Cedars Sinkhole. He remembered how relieved he had been when he saw the sinkhole and looked out at the sunlight above, at the grate that covered the hole so people wouldn't try to enter the cave through it. He'd squeezed between the slats of that grate as a kid but he certainly wouldn't fit through them now.

Of course, the sinkhole was filled in a couple of years after the invasion. The Robertson family, who had grown dope and manufactured hard drugs for years, moved their operation into the abandoned tourist attraction to hide it and because the temperature in the cave was uniform year round. It was the perfect place to put a meth lab.

Nobody was sure what happened after that. There was an explosion and when people came to investigate, they found the Historic Entrance to the caverns collapsed. The explosion had totally blocked the cave, swallowing up the entrance, the sinkhole and a quarter mile of caverns. After that, there was no outside access to the top level of the caverns. You could only get to that level by going through the other caverns, climbing up from lower levels.

As Noah traveled along the passage, other memories from that day surfaced. It wasn't like he'd had the time in the days after Astral Day to ponder it. He'd been at the academy that first week when the director went insane and tried to kill all the students. And after that, he'd been taken up in an Astral shuttle and spent three months in an Astral mothership.

As the memories appeared, he had to blow the dust of time off them to see what they revealed. When he did, he stopped cold in his tracks.

He had gotten to the top level of the caverns, to the Double Cedars Sinkhole *somehow* from the caverns on the tour the students were taking that day and he couldn't imagine how on earth he had accomplished that feat. Other than the elevator shafts on the west side and the staircase on the east, there was *no* connecting tunnel. He'd been feeling his way in the dark, a terrified little boy, going wherever he found space between the rocks, winding upward, higher and higher. Then he remembered the cavern he'd stumbled into that day. The impossible cavern. The one that seemed vast and hollow and had *smooth walls.*

He had found a way out of that cavern, through an opening between rocks just big enough for a little kid to squeeze through, that opened onto a passageway that led to Double Cedars Sinkhole on Level One. He lifted his lantern and looked around. The sealed-up historic entrance and caved-in sinkhole lay at least half a mile away. So where was that passageway that had ended up there? A passage that led to a big cavern *with smooth walls*? Because there was no such thing as a cave with smooth walls.

Chapter Twenty-Two

From his balcony, Paco could see the road and the column of vehicles traveling down it. It was late afternoon, the sun sinking toward the horizon, and he was satisfied with what he'd accomplished since he'd heard Star's voice in his head that morning.

They were on their way.

He watched the caravan, vehicles of all shapes and sizes — trucks, cars, motorhomes, vans, buses, motorcycles. He had emptied out his entire stockpile of gasoline to fill all these gas tanks. The gasoline tanker midway along the snaking line would probably get them all another five hundred miles when the tanks ran dry.

Bottom line was Paco did not have any idea how long it would take him to get from California to Kentucky in a post-Astral America. Seven years of no road maintenance — and hundreds of thousands of cars abandoned wherever they ran out of gas. After he moved his encampment from the little town to Tahoe, he'd had his army clear all the roads for a hundred miles in every direction. But beyond that … it would be what it would be.

It was a journey of more than two thousand miles. Taking a caravan of people and equipment. On uncharted, unexplored roadways. Going through territory controlled by all manner of warlords, who'd snatched land, power and authority just like Paco had done.

Would he have to fight his way through? Maybe. He would be absolutely ruthless. He would kill anybody who opposed him. Anybody who got in his way.

And as they drove along, they would begin to run out of gasoline. At that point, they'd start losing pieces of the caravan. Which was part of Paco's plan. He'd told his men about the impending destruction of the earth, and about Noah's Shield in Kentucky that was their only hope of survival as a "motivational tool."

Doing so ensured that they would pack up and be ready to leave before sundown. He knew when he told them about the end of the world that they'd all demand to take their families with them — of course they would — what were they to do, leave the wife and kiddies, the dog, cat and canary here to drown? But no way in hell did Paco intend to show up in Kentucky with thousands of people — women, kids and goldfish. He'd planned for that eventuality. As the vehicles began to run out of gas, he would consolidate the numbers into fewer and fewer transports. And there would come a point where he would make an impassioned speech to the men that they must leave their families behind and make a run for it.

They'd secure the shield, kill all those who opposed them, steal their gasoline — he assured them he was certain they had two or three tanker loads — and return for those they'd left behind.

They wouldn't like it, but he didn't really give a flying fuck what they liked or didn't like. He could bend them to his will if he had to.

Don't try it ...

The voice spoke into his mind as clearly as if someone were standing beside him.

It was Himself. It was the voice of himself talking to himself.

You saw the burst vessels. How many of those do you think you can rupture before ...

"Shut up!" he shouted the words out loud and cringed at the sound of them.

But the voice was not to be silenced.

VICENTE. *You remember Vicente. He of the spider and you of the snake. You left him to die in a dryer and the person you found later ...*

He put his hands over his ears and shook his head. The boy he had found later ... drooled.

Paco would be careful. He would. He would not employ his mental magic, wouldn't risk any further damage. He would just use simple persuasion, leadership, a dose of fear and common sense should prevail.

Yes, that would be all he needed. Maybe he'd

needed some special theatrics before, in the beginning, to bow the men to his will, but they were sufficiently cowed now. He could get all the mileage he needed out of their fear of him. His plan was to show up in Jessup with a sleek, determined, desperate force of maybe five hundred men, mean and scared. He could take anybody — certainly a little town full of normal folk — with a force like that.

He might even let some of them return to get their families, if indeed there was any gasoline available at the end of the line. If they made it there and back ... well, they'd just be shit out of luck. He and the others would be snug as bugs in rugs, tucked in tight away from harm.

Noah's Shield.

Paco could almost picture what it looked like, designed by the genius of the little deaf boy — who wasn't a little boy anymore. He'd be ... what? Eighteen now. Making a protection shield — it might not be a shield exactly, maybe a special roof on a building or some kind of dome. Something like that — Noah would figure it out. Whatever it was, the people in Kentucky who intended to hunker down under that shield would have prepared to stay awhile, wouldn't they? Until the Astrals thought they'd zapped all humanity and got back in their motherfucking mothership and went back home. He didn't know what kind of supplies those would-be survivors might have managed to gather up and put in their Shield House, but he would cheerfully relieve them of whatever they had.

And he was bringing supplies of his own. He had them packed away separate, sustenance Army meals he'd stolen from Fort Irwin in Barstow and Camp Roberts in Monterey — along with an arsenal of military weapons and ammunition — after the Astrals decimated them. That would be enough to feed a continent of five hundred men for at least three months. Six if they rationed.

He watched the line of vehicles and a smile spread across his lips. He had seen a vintage movie once — the sisters at St. Francis of the Hills School had shown it to the students. *The Ten Commandments*. It had been an alright movie, the acting and plot were fine but the special effects sucked. He did remember one scene, though. Moses was standing up on a rock beside the Red Sea that had parted, and he was watching this huge mass of people, a seemingly never-ending line of them passing by him and out into the dry land on the sea floor.

Paco felt like that now, kinda wished he had a staff to hold up, watching his army, his "people" flee across two thousand miles of dry land to get somewhere that when the water really did fall down and cover the earth, they wouldn't drown. He was Moses, taking his people through danger — there might be danger on the road, who knew? — to the promised land on the other side. The promised land Noah and Star would provide for them once the pillaging horde of Paco's army showed up. Paco would make sure the arrival of his army would make the alien occupation look like a birthday party at nursery school.

When it came time for the final charge, Paco would be out front, taking the lead, rumbling forward on his customized Harley Davidson, a totally unique work of art. It had taken his worker bees several years to find the right parts, the right bike, or the right material to make what he demanded from scratch.

It had what was called a torpedo fairing, a single piece, streamlined shell covering the front half of the bike, resembling the nose of an aircraft.

But Paco's didn't look like the front of an aircraft. It was crafted into the shape of the nose of a shark. Inset in the shell below the point of the nose were razor-sharp teeth, in an opened mouth, so the bike coming toward you looked like a shark attacking with its mouth open. It was a motorized weapon. Anything the front of the bike hit would be shredded on the teeth on both sides of the fairing — before whatever it was fell under the bike's tires and was mashed into roadkill.

Early on, a couple of his Latino flunkies referred to the bike as "tiburon" because that was the Spanish word for "shark." Use of the word in Paco's presence earned the speaker a broken nose and the loss of several teeth.

Paco didn't think of his friend Tiburón when he commissioned the construction of the bike, relentlessly shoved thoughts about him out of his mind whenever they surfaced. But the big dude's words from that first day at the prison where the Scared Straight Program had abandoned him and the other teenagers on Astral

Day often rang in his ears despite his best efforts to ban them.

"I am Tiburon," he had said. "And ain't nothing scares a shark."

When Paco had secured possession of Noah's Shield, he would kill them all. Every man, woman, child and that damned dog of Star's — Pumpkin. He would make Star and Noah watch him butcher them. Then he would ... He didn't have this part planned out totally because it was so much fun to consider the possible scenarios he just couldn't bring himself to select only one.

Killing them both outright was oh so boring and uncreative. Then his mind exploded with fireworks. He couldn't ... could he? A wood chipper ... he couldn't possibly haul a wood chipper that far.

Or could he?

Chapter Twenty-Three

NOAH WAS HOT, tired and disgusted with himself for wasting hours of precious time looking for something that clearly didn't exist. He must have imagined the mysterious smooth-walled cavern. He had, after all, been only eleven years old. He'd been lost and terrified. Feeling around in the dark, desperate.

Not surprising for a little boy like that to imagine things.

But that was the rub. Noah had never been a child given to imaginings. He was very literal, grounded in reality. A niggling part of his mind argued in the boy's defense — he wouldn't have *imagined* a thing like that.

If he thought he saw a smooth-walled cavern, he did. So where was it?

And against his better judgement, Noah started trying to retrace the little boy's route. Explorers in the caves often found little connecting tunnels nobody'd noticed before, and apparently that's what he had done. He'd found a tunnel that connected to Level One and the sinkhole.

So where was that connecting tunnel?

Noah looked.

Looked and looked.

He should have given up a dozen times, but each time he decided to go just a little farther, check out just one more connecting tunnel. The more he thought about it, the more he remembered from the mind of the panicked eleven-year-old, and the more peculiar it seemed. He couldn't make himself let the mystery go.

He climbed up three or four tunnels that petered out, dead-ended. Another one he tried led back to a place he'd been half an hour before.

He kept trying, one tunnel after another, remembered the strange fact that began to haunt him the more he thought about it. He was certain that the tunnel he'd found after he left the smooth-walled cavern had led *down*. Impossible, but down. He had come *up* from one of the lower levels to Level One, then had gone *up* from there. It was nuts, but he distinctly remembered when he had found the tunnel with the sinkhole, he had climbed *down* to it.

Trying to retrace the boy's steps from Level One, Noah climbed *up*. There were no caverns above Level One. Duh — that's why it was called Level *One*. But he kept trying. Time came unhooked. He might have been struggling here in the dark for an hour or a day. He refused to give up. Every blocked passage made him more determined to find one that wasn't. He kept hitting the ceiling, time and time again.

The Hidden

Until he didn't.

He came to a cavern with an odd "stripe" six inches wide all the way up the wall, floor to ceiling. It was only a seam of really dark limestone but its edges were so uniform it looked like somebody'd painted it there with black paint.

If Noah's younger self could have seen it, he could have used it as a touchstone, a way to mark his position, and then he could have … but the terrified little boy didn't see the black stripe in the absolute darkness.

Noah climbed up past the stripe, kept going … and hit the ceiling in that cavern just like all the others. He was so disgusted he might actually have given up at that point, but there was a small opening at the very top he could continue to climb through.

So he followed it. He had no idea how far he'd gone or if it was the direction the little boy had gone, but there was one direction the child hadn't needed a lantern to see — *up*. So Noah climbed up.

Then he hit a dead end and he let fly a stream of expletives. It would take him fifteen minutes to get back down to Level One from here and he'd wasted—

Wait.

He remembered that the entrance to the impossible cavern was a small opening *on the floor*. Noah got down on his hands and knees with the lantern, inspecting the wall at the dead end, looking for any kind of opening.

And there it was, or could be.

A flat rock was leaned up against the cave wall, and behind the rock was an opening. Noah was sure he couldn't even fit behind the rock, let alone squeeze through the opening — if, indeed, it was the one the little boy had used. He sat down, hot, dirty and tired, and tried to reorient. The part of his mind that'd been recording his route knew that if, indeed, there was a cavern beyond this hole it was higher than any of the others. It was *above* Level One.

A *smooth-walled* cavern *above* Level One. Impossible. On both counts. Still …

He turned around in the small space and reached back to where he had set the lantern on the ground. Picking it up, he inserted it behind the rock so he could get a better look at the small hole there in the cave wall.

The flame on the lantern flickered.

Noah got very still.

There was wind sometimes in the caverns, sure … but not *this far* from an entrance. His gut began to tie into a knot.

He scooted the lantern as far back behind the rock as he could, got down on his belly and looked at the opening that led away into darkness. The rock sides of it closed in at the top, widened at the bottom where there was dirt. Crumbled rock, big and small pieces, plain old dirt formed the floor of the space between the leaning rock and the opening on the wall. Noah began to dig, hollowing out a space.

He remembered then — an inopportune time to remember it — what his grandfather'd said once. "Don't dig your way into a passage or you could find yourself having to dig your way back out." Meaning that if the floor of a passage was unstable enough to dig in, the top was probably unstable enough to collapse.

He kept digging, making the bottom of the hole larger and larger. Finally he got about as far as he could go. The hole he'd formed looked impossibly narrow, but he stuck his feet in first, rolled over onto his belly, and scooted himself backwards. Even squeezing his shoulders together they dragged painfully against the sides of the rock, but as he scooted along, he could no longer feel the sides of the passage with his feet and legs. The opening had widened. He kept scooting, his shoulders scraped ... and then he was ... out. The passage was only five or six feet long, and it emptied into a bigger chamber beyond. He reached back out through the opening and grabbed his lantern, pulled it back in.

Then he stood up and looked around.

At the impossible cavern.

The walls of the cavern were smooth, like they'd been sheared off, from the floor all the way up. He held his lantern high and couldn't see the ceiling. At the outside edge of the glow of his lantern, there was a pillar. It was square, with square corners. *Square!*

He had to see it more clearly, but he didn't dare move away out into the darkness beyond the opening where he'd entered ... because he might not be able to find his way back there. So he reached into his pocket and took out the kite cord. Noah always carried it when he was caving; the safest possible way to make sure you didn't get lost in twisting caverns was to leave a string tied to where you came in. But the cavern walls here were smooth. There was nowhere to tie the string.

This was crazy, couldn't be. Cavern walls weren't smooth! Finally, he forced himself to go back through the opening — his shoulders fit a little easier this time around — but only halfway. Reaching out beyond the opening to the spot where he'd had to dig his way in, there was a protrusion on the rock. He tied the string firmly to it, then he slid back through, held the string in his left hand so he could let it out behind him, his lantern in his right hand, and stepped toward the column, the impossibly *square* column.

Perfectly square. Thirty feet by thirty feet. And behind it was another column. It was square, too, the edges as perfect as the crease on a West Point cadet's pants. He tried to see how tall the columns were, but they disappeared into the blackness above him and his paltry lantern didn't cast enough light to see what was up there.

He turned, made his way back to the opening where he'd entered and instead of going forward into the cavern — that might be the size of a football stadium or of a church basement — he began to edge along the wall of it to the right of the opening. Smooth rock, impossibly smooth rock. And what he could see out there in the cavern beyond the walls was one column after another. Square edges. He noted the uniformity and realized the thirty-foot columns were all spaced the same distance apart — about thirty feet. A checkerboard.

The flame on his lantern had not flickered anymore since the opening, but about a hundred feet down the wall, past half a dozen number of the thirty-foot columns, it began to flicker again. By then, Noah didn't need the flicker to tell there was an opening in the cavern wall. He could see the glow of light reflecting off the pillars.

Chapter Twenty-Four

Sawyer paused outside the door to Ellie's room and pasted a smile on his face. He had to have it firmly in place when he walked in because the natural response to seeing her certainly would make nobody smile. Oh, she knew the smile was phony, it was part of the elaborate game they both played.

About a year ago, they'd moved her into a room in the main building of what had once been Zion Academy so she could feel more a part of what was going on around her, so people could pop in to visit her and so it was easy to keep tabs on her needs. They'd filled the room with the expensive furniture that had been the academy's fare, courtesy of a lot of rich parents. They'd brought in rugs, her daughter Gretchen had made lacy curtains and hung them over the window, which faced west, so she could watch the sunset.

Ellie was dying of metastatic breast cancer that had spread all over her body.

Of course, Ellie wouldn't be the first person who had died at Zion Village — of natural causes. With no doctor and few medications, people died. It happened. They had lost three newborns to some kind of illness the registered nurse, Anna, thought was either whooping cough or diphtheria. Nobody'd caught those diseases as infants anymore, thanks to modern inoculations. But the generation growing up in Zion Village wouldn't be inoculated against anything.

Monty Phillips, who'd owned Phillips Foodtown in Jessup, had died of a heart attack. Pearl Oglethorpe had collapsed in the kitchen and the nurse suspected she'd had a stroke. They had started a little cemetery up on the hill overlooking the wheat fields.

Lottie Schwartz was among the first to be buried there. A plot beside hers awaited her husband Fred, who was more than ninety now. The old couple had run out of gas in their motorhome seven years ago and became part of the group Eagle Feather called the Stranded.

Sawyer took a deep breath, then knocked gently on her door.

"It's open" came the weak voice from inside,

He stepped into the room that smelled of fresh flowers, cinnamon sticks and death.

Ellie lay propped up on pillows so it was easier for her to breathe. The cancer had spread to her lungs about six months ago, now she coughed up blood, and there was a horrifying gurgling sound in her chest when she did. She wheezed when she spoke sometimes, too.

The Hidden

She was a skeleton, had no appetite anymore and it was all Gretchen could do to cook any food at all that she'd eat. Her eyes were sunken in dark holes that looked like cigarette burns in her face, desolate pools. All hope had drowned in those lonely depths. Her hands were boney, claw-like, and he was probably imagining it, but it seemed like her smile had changed, like her teeth had somehow grown bigger, more prominent. But that was, he was sure, just her skin receding from them as it shrank and dried out. Her hair was brittle and thin, her scalp showed through in places like a bad paint job.

As he crossed the room to sit by the bed and take her hand, he called to mind the Ellie he had first met, the woman who had rushed up to him after her helicopter illegally landed on the Zion Academy grounds on Astral Day. She'd been lovely, slender, with beautiful chestnut hair in a carefree style that fell back into place as soon as the wind from the chopper blades died away. She was dressed in the most expensive everything. But more than that, she was alive, vibrant. So was the woman who'd bought a car, paid for it with a credit card, and drove to Louisville just days before the Astrals arrived in the sky, determined to find a doctor to diagnose the lump she had found in her breast. She'd walked right into riots, had hidden in a trash can to avoid the mobs, and Sawyer had had to hose her down in a car wash to clean her up. But even as rattled and freaked out as she was then, there was a vibrancy, an alive quality that had been what drew him to her.

So did her compassion and her capacity for love. She'd brought back to Zion Academy a baby girl who'd been born to a teenage survivor of the Astral massacre at Ft. Knox — an incredibly beautiful child named Diana, and Ellie loved her fiercely.

It was all that about her and countless other things that had made him fall in love with her years ago. The life and the vibrancy were gone now in the shell of a woman whose eyebrows were drawn together in a constant grimace of pain. But the spirit, she'd managed to hang onto that.

"How are you feeling today?"

"How do I look like I'm feeling? I feel like shit. I hear that's the natural state of people who are dying."

The spark was still there, in the frail body. Still there.

"That's what I hear, but other than the fact that you're dying, how do you feel?"

"Like shit."

Then the bantering tone and all its energy died away and her voice became wind-driven sand scouring across ancient stone, like the brittle whispery click of scuttling scarabs.

"I … *hurt*. Everywhere."

"I'm sorry." What else was there to say? He knew her simple, "I hurt," was an understatement of grand scope. He was sure she was in agony.

"Is there anything I can get you?"

Meaningless comments. How do you feel? Can I get you anything? Oh, how he wished he had something more to offer her now, during her last days.

"How about you stop squirting out platitudes like a pigeon shitting on a statue."

The spark, it was dim, but it was still there.

"Okay, no platitudes."

"There *is* something you can do for me. I'm ... not going to the caverns."

His mind stumbled, needed a moment to grasp what she was saying.

"Don't make me draw you a picture, Sawyer. I know what Noah's planning and I ... can't. *Won't*. Moving to the ark would be ... an unbearable *agony*! What's the point?" She took his hand in her bony claw. "I'm staying here. I made arrangements with Anna a long time ago for Diana. I'll send her off ... tell her goodbye tomorrow. But I need your ... will you help me with Gretchen? She's going to pitch a royal ... will you help her accept my decision ... *Please!*"

NOAH CREPT SLOWLY FORWARD along the wall. He had no idea why he felt the need to be cautious. But his father, the police officer, had always advised him to *trust your gut*. And right now his gut was sending out alarm signals as loud as a signal on a railroad track.

The light grew brighter. He had gotten to the end of his kite line, but there was enough light that if he put the string down on the floor next to the wall he could find his way back to it.

He went forward another few feet and stopped

with a pillar between him and the source of light. Then he cautiously moved away from the wall to the pillar and peered around it.

His heart froze in his chest. There were machines, not fifty feet from him, robots of some kind, cutting away uniform slabs of the rock. Leaving the walls smooth. If he'd been able to hear, he was sure he'd have heard them as soon as he came into the cavern, maybe even before that. Dust flew around the blades as they sawed through the rock. Beyond the robots was an opening that lead to a passageway and diffused light came from there, meaning there were some twists and turns in the passage before it *opened up outside*.

He reached down and turned off the flame on his lantern and sat it at the end of his string. Then he moved stealthily from one pillar to another, careful to stay out of the spill of ambient light from the entrance. He had to move over three pillars before he had an angle of sight out through the entrance of the cavern into the passageway beyond.

Three titans stood in the entrance to the cavern. Each held a tablet of some kind in his hand and was moving his finger over the top of it, obviously operating the robot machinery that was cutting away the rock slabs. He wondered if the cutting machines were making a lot of noise, but he doubted it. Noise, at least loud noise in an enclosed space like this, would create vibrations he could feel. Other than a low humming sensation, like holding onto the end of a tuning fork, he felt nothing. He moved over one more pillar, trying to see if he could get a line of sight on the opening that led outside, but the passageway turned again behind the titans and he couldn't see out.

Not that it mattered. He didn't have to *see* the opening the Astrals had cut in the side of the mountain to create this ... whatever it was ... to know that it was high up on the *north* face of Tucker Mountain.

He thought of Herb Wilcox's Empire State Building analogy. When water covered the whole surface of the earth, the basement of the submerged Empire State Building would be full of water. But the water could rise no higher into the sealed floors above.

Unless somebody on the top floor left a window open.

In Wilcox's building analogy, all would be well unless some dude in an office on Floor One Hundred left a window open. If that happened, water would flow into the building through that window and down into all the dry floors below, flushing out the air as it went, creating bubbles that would rise to the surface of the water.

In other words, if there were an opening into the caverns high up on the side of the ridge, all was lost. There wasn't one, of course. There never had been ... until now.

Oh shit.

Noah had seen everything he needed to see, backed away from the pillar toward the far wall where his kite string lay ... and ran smack into a robot, one that had a flat platform behind the wheels for stacking the rock slabs. He didn't just bump it, he connected with it, got tangled in its forklift-type arms and crashed to the floor of the cavern with the machine on top of him. It lay there, its motorized treads still moving like it was trying to get traction on the air. He shoved at it, helplessly, but the thing was as heavy as a forklift and he couldn't budge it.

He had to get out of here before one of the titans showed up to see what was going on. Wiggling, squirming and writhing, he tried everything he knew to get out from under the cumbersome piece of … metal? Plastic. Who knew. His heart was a runaway buffalo in his chest, knowing that he only had seconds to extricate himself before one of the Astrals—

A small machine appeared, almost like a model car, on the floor and sped toward where he lay tangled in the machine. The model car stopped about ten feet away, and he saw the face of it. It was a video camera, some kind of device that allowed the titans to see into the cavern from the outside.

He struggled even harder to free himself from the robot, but there was no getting out from under it. The robot was too heavy. His only option was to wiggle toward the back end of the thing, but if he tried to get out of the tangle that way he'd be chewed up by the links of the still-moving treads still trying ineffectively to get traction on the air.

That's when Phoebe showed up. Not just one Phoebe, though. A whole herd of them. They'd come to record 360-degree-angle pictures of him — he'd been there, done that before, a long time ago.

The first Phoebe rolled up to within a couple of feet of the still-struggling robot. The little round ball was slightly bigger than a marble, and no color at all.

Not clear or even translucent, though. The little balls acquired the color of whatever they were near, like a chameleon blending into different colors of leaves. But when the balls got close enough, you could see yourself in them, the image of you they were transmitting to the Astrals.

If a ball was floating above you, the image in it was the top of your head, if one was inches from your face, the image in it was your nose.

It was Star who'd named them the day the little swarm of marbles had shown up as he, Star and Paco sat together alone in the white room, sorting out the food boxes so Paco got enchiladas, Noah got fried chicken and Star got a chili dog.

There were about a dozen of them then, and they were entertaining to watch. They rolled on their own with no method of propulsion they could see. And like everything else that happened in the mothership, they didn't come *from* anywhere. They were just suddenly there, a handful of them on the floor nearby. One of them broke from the others and rolled up to Noah and he could see the toe of his shoe reflected in its surface.

"Phoebe B. Beebe nuked her new canoe canal," Star had said, not out loud. In his and Paco's heads. They almost never spoke anymore. There was no need when they could talk to each other inside their own heads.

"Run that by me again," Paco said.

Star had giggled. "When I used to tell fortunes in the little room at Alien World, I had to sit there between customers. So I made up stuff to entertain myself. Sometimes it was nonsense rhymes, like that: Phoebe B. Beebe nuked her new canoe canal."

From that moment on, the little balls had been Phoebe. And the three of them had become very well acquainted with the Phoebes.

As Noah lay helpless under the still-struggling robot, the Phoebes approached him, then lifted up into the air around him, surrounding him.

"Smile for the cameras," Paco had said that day when the herd of them showed up in one of the nightmare worlds to watch the reaction of their captives — Noah, Star and Paco.

The day Pumpkin had …

Noah actually smiled a little thinking about it, wishing he had Pumpkin by his side now.

Chapter Twenty-Five

They are just "there." It is always jarring. They are sitting in the white room, or in some other place the Astrals have parked them, and then poof, they are somewhere else.

They have gone from the still and quiet of the mothership to this ... war zone between one heartbeat and the next.

Paco looks around in wonder. "Is it real? It's not real, is it?"

They never know. That's the bitch of it. They never ever know for sure. Are they really somewhere, some real place, whether on the planet Earth of some other planet in some other galaxy or in the motherships or ... wherever. Or are they still in their bodies, parked in the white room and everything that seems real isn't, everything that appears to be part of some other world is really only happening in their heads.

"I hope not!" Noah cries out in Paco's head. "It feels real, though, absolutely real.

He, Paco, Star and Pumpkin are on the ground, hunkered down behind a crumbling rock wall. The sounds and sights of war are all around them. There is nothing but ruin for as far as they can see. Buildings blown apart, walls hanging with part of a roof. Rubble. It would look like London, maybe, during the Blitz, except this doesn't look or feel like a modern town. It feels somehow medieval. All the buildings are stone. They're no longer standing, none of them intact, so you can't tell. But it appears that what has been blown up is a city full of stone buildings.

They can hear the sounds of explosions, feel the rumble in the earth when a bomb goes off. But if this isn't the modern world, where did the explosions come from? They weren't blowing shit up back in King Arthur's day.

"I don't think this is real," Star says. "Not one thing. I think we ... our bodies anyway ... are sitting where we were that first day, in that white room. And the Astrals are feeding stuff into our minds to make us think we're somewhere else."

That's when the Phoebes appear. They form out of nowhere, a swarm of angry hornets, making not a sound but he imagines they are buzzing, that they will attack him, cover him like a swarm of bees on a comb and sting him to death.

Then they fly at him, Paco and Star and they realize that the spheres are not insects.

"Smile for the cameras," Paco gasps, his words breathless. Because that's what the Phoebes are — cameras.

They hover above the three of them. Just hang in the air, more like a swarm of gnats than of hornets. Then, they literally surround Noah, like a second skin about twelve inches from him. They take on his form — arms, legs, torso. They're recording everything, not just what he looks like. They are recording ... one has a blinking red dot that is measuring his pulse, another maybe his blood pressure, another his temperature.

The Phoebes desert him and surround Star, taking on her shape as they had taken on his.

The Hidden

That's when Pumpkin leaps into action. The dog snarls and snaps at them, manages to grab one in his teeth and the crushing sound makes it clear there is now one less Phoebe in the world.

Pumpkin goes on a killing spree then, leaping at the little balls, crunching them in his teeth, batting them away with his clawed paws. Clearly, this place is real ... *because in less than a minute, a whole swarm of dead Phoebes lies at Pumpkin's feet.*

Chapter Twenty-Six

THERE WEREN'T AS many Phoebes here today as there'd been that day in the war-zone world. Now, in the impossible smooth-walled cavern, there were only about two dozen Phoebes. They'd didn't outline Noah's body as they had done before. The Astrals must not have brought a full complement of Phoebes with them when they came to cut rock.

Why would they need Phoebes at all, though? Or the little car with its revolving camera eye? Or the robots, even? Titans were huge and incredibly strong. Why didn't they come into the cave and take the cutting machines in their own hands to cut the rock? Unlike their cousin reptars, titans had opposable thumbs. It seemed a convoluted way to accomplish the task — standing outside the cave with tablets, operating the controls on robots to do the cutting.

He had not heard the Phoebes make a sound that day the swarm had come at him, Star and Paco in the war-ravaged city ... somewhere, or maybe nowhere.

And at the time, he'd been able to hear. The Astrals had restored his hearing, so if the Phoebes had buzzed, as it just seemed like they ought to be doing, he'd have heard it. If he couldn't hear them then, he certainly shouldn't expect to hear them now, when he was back on Earth and deaf again. Still, he listened in his deaf silence, irrationally expecting a buzzing sound to waft off the floating, darting, flying Phoebes as they reported every possible discernible detail about him back to the Astrals.

They knew he was here. And it occurred to him to wonder if they even *recognized* him, knew who he was. Did they have … a database of all the people they'd kidnapped? There'd been something like twenty thousand of them. Had his picture, front and side views broadcast beside a ruler to display his height, a post office mugshot — appeared on the tablets of the titans operating the cutting robots? Would they "know" him?

Oh yeah, I remember him, the kid who couldn't hear. The one who hung out with that blind girl and the Hispanic boy who had a chip on his holder the size of Ft. Lauderdale. This is him, that guy, Noah Matheson.

Suddenly, the robot stopped moving, like it'd been unplugged. Noah couldn't be sure, but it felt like all the vibration ceased, as if the motors had been cut on all the machines. With the treads no longer moving, it would be possible to wiggle out through them, through the space between where the tread was attached to the wheels on the bottom. Like on an army tank. If the treads weren't moving, there were empty spaces where you could crawl …

The Hidden

But if the treads started moving again while he was still in them, he would be crushed, pulverized, nothing left of him but a smear like day-old roadkill, flattened by the traffic on a road.

It was his only shot, though. Noah would have to risk dying there to avoid certain death at the hands of a reptar. He'd only seen titans, of course, but he knew their dirty little secret — had seen it while he was on the mothership and that day the shuttle had crashed right outside Jessup. Where there were titans, there were reptars. Where there were "gentle giants" who moved slow and never talked, there were also black insect-like things with carapace scales and needle teeth that chewed up their victims. The yin and the yang. Two sides of the same coin. Piss off a titan and badda boom badda bing, you were facing an angry reptar and an angry reptar could shred you into the consistency of apple butter. If a reptar caught him, it would rip him to shreds, just like he'd watched the reptars rip his father's deputies to shreds the day the shuttle crashed outside Jessup.

Noah had to get out of here now! He squirmed around frantically to free his feet and began worming his way through the mechanical guts of the robot toward the treads. It was a tight fit. He scraped the skin painfully off his elbows and shins as he dragged them through too-tight spaces. The machine lay quiet and still. The treads were within reach now. Beyond the open spaces between them was freedom.

Meanwhile the Phoebes watched, hanging in the air. He remembered the one Pumpkin had snapped at, caught and chewed up with a satisfying crunch, and he so wished he could do the same to these.

He was sweating, his whole body wet, and that helped to ease his passage through the guts of the robot toward the treads which were now hanging still.

He made it through the robot machinery and paused. Then drew in a quick breath and shoved the top portion of his body out into the empty space between the treads. If they began to move, they'd literally cut his torso in half. They didn't. It took only seconds for him to free his butt and legs and stand up on the upside-down base of the robot and he was already leaping out between the treads even as he freed his foot. Diving out between the treads, beyond them, onto the impossibly smooth cave floor. He landed ungracefully in a heap on his right shoulder, grunted and slid a few feet. He was free, and he had to get out of here before …

He was sure he was already too late, that it was a senseless gesture, but he jumped to his feet, leapt toward the stupid little car, drew his foot back and kicked the thing as hard as he could. It bounced off the nearest pillar and came apart. The biggest piece of it slid a couple of feet, upside down, its wiry guts handing out, looking like the autopsy of a robot.

The chunk of miniature car came to rest only a couple of inches away from the two pairs of white feet, belonging to the two titans that had appeared thirty feet away while Noah had been extracting himself from the guts of the robot. They'd seen his image in the eyes of the Phoebes, which were now out of sight, but he was sure not far away.

He stared in horror at the titans. It was the first time he'd been in the presence of one since the day the shuttle crashed and his father's deputies were massacred by reptars. They wore the customary blank look of all titans on their white features, except as he watched, the blank look shifted to a grimace, a matched set of grimaces that didn't seem to have anything to do with his presence. In truth, they looked like they'd both eaten ice cream too fast and had gotten brain freeze.

The titan on the right shook his head violently, then clamped his hands over his ears. The other did a similar head-shake thing, but leapt backward, disoriented and clumsy, would have fallen if there hadn't been the impossibly smooth cave wall to break his fall. Titans, though they were individuals, were so similar it had always been almost impossible for Noah to distinguish one from another. The left one of this set, however, was noticeably larger than the one on the right.

But it was the one on the right that began to transform first.

It shook its head violently from side to side, its hands on its ears, an expression on its normally expressionless face that on a human would have been translated: painful confusion. The titan bent at the waist and Noah watched in horror as its body transformed, its feet and legs becoming the too-many legs of the repulsive insectile-looking reptars. Its arms and hands became clawed appendages, with black armor. Somewhere inside, a blue light began to glow.

The second titan was transforming now, horror legs and black scales appearing as the first titan's upper body covered itself in scales and the bald head with the expressionless — stupid-looking — face turned into a head with a mouth full of razor-sharp teeth, teeth that could rip a man apart, sever arms and legs, chew up a human and spew out body parts. Some body parts. From the one experience he'd had with attacking reptars, it was clear the beasts ate and swallowed some of the bodies they shredded.

Noah instinctively backed away, recoiling in horror, an escape attempt here inside a cave would be futile — nowhere to run, nowhere to hide and the reptars could run a whole lot faster than a man could.

He suddenly felt Star's presence in his mind, felt her instant understanding, felt her terror and even in these last few seconds of his life, he wanted to comfort her, wanted her to know how firmly he believed that she and the others would make it if they went down into the caves.

No words passed from one mind to the other. Sights and feelings and understanding were enough. He felt her gasp and cry out, knew she'd seen the titans become reptars and what that meant—

Still shaking its head, the reptar on the right leapt ...

But not at Noah.

It leapt at the reptar on the left and trapped it up

against the wall it had staggered into directly behind it.

Noah didn't hear the horrifying sucking sound he knew the creatures were making, but he did watch the lights in the reptar's body shift colors, turn from—

The reptar's mouth opened and it closed razor teeth around the extended upper claw of the first reptar and bit it off, flinging the dismembered clawed arm away. The bloody appendage hit the pillar, bounced off it and slid across the floor toward Noah, who was too shocked to breathe, let alone move.

The smaller reptar lunged then, launched its body at the bigger one, sunk its razor teeth into the body of the creature where the too-many legs connected to the torso. It bit down, the lights in its eyes changing rapidly, casting colorful flashes on the walls of the cavern, like watching a crystal refract light into colors. Slicing though the scales like they were the cardboard carton with a pizza inside, it ripped and tore. Bloody guts spewed out of the hole in the creature's side the other's razor teeth had gouged, and gore ran down the sides of its legs.

The reptar's legs buckled on that side, but its own razor teeth were even now sinking into the place where the body of the smaller reptar was attached to its head — the neck except there was no neck, and Noah knew there must be a crunching sound he couldn't hear as the teeth ripped through armor and into vital tissue below.

Run!

The word appeared as a shout inside his head, as

stunning as if someone standing beside him had screamed in his ear.

Star.

Get out of there!

But Noah didn't need the second command. He'd been knocked out of his horrified, transfixed stupor by her first word and was already turning toward the wall he had traced to get here. He took two steps to the spot where he had set the lantern down at the end of the string. He snatched it up with one hand and grabbed the string with the other and bolted back toward where the string terminated in an impossibly small opening near the floor of the cavern.

How had he ever managed to get into the cavern through an opening that size?

Well, he had. Dropping to his belly, he stuck his feet into the opening and began to slither his way backward. In the cavern, the sounds of battle raged. He curled his shoulders and smashed his diaphragm so he could not get his breath. If he'd been claustrophobic …

And then he was out, pulling his lantern after him. He moved on all fours in the dark to a position behind a rock before he relit the lantern. He sat back, gasping, unable to get enough air into his lungs. Then fear grabbed him again, and he turned and raced down an incline that hadn't seemed this steep when he was climbing it. He looked back at the absolute nothingness of the cave.

Somewhere back there two reptars were ripping themselves apart.

Why?

Why had they gone after each other like rabid dogs instead of attacking the threat they'd come to investigate — *Noah?*

Why hadn't they dispatched Noah with a single snap of their razor teeth?

Why had they chewed each other's arms off instead?

Noah.

Star in his head.

Noah, just go. Get away. Garson will figure out why.

He needed no prompting, scrambling down the incline he'd climbed, ricocheting off rocks and boulders and the sides of the cave, leaping down from one big rock to another, fleeing in controlled panic, not the slightest interested in why the reptars had chosen to attack each other instead of him. He didn't care right now. He just knew he was only alive because they had.

Chapter Twenty-Seven

As Sawyer watched Garson's face while Noah described what happened to him in the strange cavern he'd dug his way into that afternoon, it was the first time Sawyer had put it together in his head. Why hadn't he seen it before now? Why had he never noticed that Garson — Dr. Mikhail Ziegelman Garczonski, PhD, professor of astrophysics — probably wanted more than anything else in the world, *to meet an Astral?*

Duh. It made sense. The old man had spent his entire life studying them. He'd suffered the derision of other scientists for his whole career, had been labeled a crackpot, had been a laughingstock in the whole scientific community — until little white dots appeared out by Jupiter and overnight he went from being the butt of the joke to getting the last laugh.

Of course he wanted to actually *see* an alien, and in the seven years since the big silver balls first began to hang over the cities, the old man had watched, gobbled every speck of information he could find, interrogated Eagle Feather about Indian legends, watched videos of the ships and the titans, had seen reptars on jukes — back when jukes still worked — but he had never actually laid eyes on one. The old man wasn't doing a very good job of hiding how delighted he was to hear that there might be half a dozen or more of them almost within rock-throwing distance.

Sawyer and the others didn't share his enthusiasm. Sawyer had seen Astrals up close and personal, had watched reptars rip apart deputies he had worked with for decades, so shredded their bodies that you couldn't even put them back together to have a decent funeral. He had watched a shuttle vaporize most of the town of Jessup — people in their houses indiscriminately fried with the buildings. The monsters had destroyed the whole town's winter food supply in one beam of white light. If Sawyer ever saw another Astral he would …

He was sure Noah felt the same way after three months on an Astral mothership, being studied like a bug on a pin. Sawyer had heard about his experiences, the ones he was willing to share, but he was sure his son had had experiences he didn't tell his father about. Whatever had happened to him and to Star and their friend Paco, whom he had never met, it had changed them profoundly. And he could tell by looking at his son's face that he was way more rattled by what had happened to him on the mountain than he wanted anyone to see.

"Obviously, it's a mine of some kind," Noah said. He spoke and signed, unconsciously doing both at the same time. "It would make sense, the methodical way they were cutting and stacking slabs of rocks."

Star looked at Noah quizzically, and Sawyer explained.

"You've never been inside a coal mine," Sawyer said. "But what Noah described is what one looks like."

He knew that Star could see the images in Noah's mind so he tried to interpret them for her.

"I had to explain to someone once what a coal mine looks like," Sawyer said. "I used this analogy. Let's say you have a thirty-story building and the fifteenth floor of it is solid gold. Now, if you want to remove that gold, how would you do it? Well, you could strip-mine it, rip the top of the building off. But let's say you couldn't do that. Then the only way to get to the gold would be to start removing it from the sides. Problem with that is the top fifteen floors would collapse on top of you as soon as you dug deep enough into the gold. But what if you left thirty-foot by thirty-foot columns of gold every thirty feet to hold up the top fifteen floors, while you dug out the rest of the gold around them?"

He could tell by the look on her face that she got it now.

"I don't get it," said Erika Mason. "A mine? Why would advanced beings like the Astrals cut rock out of a mountain like coal miners? If you could travel across galaxies and bend time, surely you'd come up with a better way than that — melt the side of the mountain and suck it out with a straw or something, but cut out slabs of it with robots?"

Garson peered at her over the top of his glasses. "I suspect that the question is the answer, my dear."

She looked at him as confused as the others.

"They do it that way because … that's the way they do it."

Silence.

"Look … we can't begin to understand how they managed to get here in the first place. Why should we expect to be able to figure out why they cut rocks out of the side of the mountain instead of using some more sophisticated method? I'm sure there's a reason, but what difference does it make? What is significant here that we can't miss, is that Noah first saw this Astral mine *seven years* ago on Astral Day. Before the Astrals arrived. That means that they used this mine, cut slabs out of it for whatever purpose, the *last* time they were here."

Sawyer got up and began to pace back and forth across the room. They were in Dr. Weiss's old office and Sawyer didn't know that he was re-tracing the steps the old man had taken, back and forth. From the window to the fireplace. Turn. Back to the window. Turn … just like the old man did the night before he died.

"So what we know is that the Astrals are mining the rock out of that mountain — for some purpose. I—"

Nick Wilson interrupted him. "Have you seen

those stones lined up like little West Point cadets for miles, leading to circles made out of stone?" Nick was among the elders who'd been gathered up in the middle of the night after Noah got back from the caverns to hear the tale of what happened to him there.

"No, but I've heard about them. People say that when you get near them you can read other people's minds."

"I've seen it," said Jessica Maddocks. "And it's true — that's what the rocks do, they make it possible for you to communicate without talking, see and hear what someone else is thinking."

"So maybe the rock for those stone lines and circles — maybe some of it was mined right here at Matheson Caverns?" Nick asked.

"That would make more sense if they were making stone lines and stone circles now," Sawyer said. "But they're not. They haven't laid down any new ones, as far as I know, for seven years. So what do they want to use that rock for?"

Noah had been sitting quietly reading the lips of the others. He didn't often say much, because it was hard to concentrate on lip reading in a group of people where you had to look from one person to the next to read their lips. In a group situation, Noah spent most of his energy trying to hear and not much trying to talk. But Star was here, listening, and he could hear whatever she heard.

When Noah stood, the others grew quiet.

He didn't often show emotion so when he did the others sat up and took notice.

"Who cares?" The frustration was obvious in his voice. "Who cares how they mine it or what they're using the rock for." He paused. "You're all *missing the point*. The point is that the Astrals are there now, and they have made a hole in the top of the mountain, and when the flood comes, the water will flow in that hole and flood Noah's Ark. Somehow, we have to plug up the hole."

"You said the titans weren't working in the cavern, but were standing outside it … right?" Fred Schwartz asked. When the elders had been summoned, he'd come running — with a severe case of bedhead. With his hair flying every which way he looked so clownish, Sawyer had to concentrate to keep track of what he was saying. "You said they were crowded together in a passageway, right?" Again Noah nodded. "So why were they jammed up in a small place when there was all that space in the cavern in front of them?"

Noah shook his head. "Don't know, don't care. What I *do* care—"

"I think I know why, and more importantly why the reptars went postal and chewed into each other," Garson said and looked at Noah. "And this part really does matter."

"I'm listening," Sawyer said.

"If those stones are what we think they are, the ones the Astrals use for the stone lines and stone circles, then apparently, the Astrals couldn't just use whatever rock happened to be handy to make them —

not if they went to the trouble to dig a hole in the side of a mountain and return to it thousands of years later to get a particular kind of rock."

"But that rock is just plain old limestone," Sawyer said. "The whole cave is limestone. You can find limestone just like it all over the world."

"That's what you and I see, but what matters is what the Astrals see. Apparently limestone, or maybe just the particular limestone in Matheson Caverns, has some property, some component we don't even know about that's necessary in the making of telepathic rocks and circles."

"Okay, I'll bite. So …?"

"So, when people go near those telepathic rocks their thoughts are transmitted to each other, and beamed up to the hive mind in the mothership. But the Astrals' thoughts are *already* in each other's heads and in the hive mind. Maybe being in the presence of rocks that transmit thoughts, when their thoughts are already being transmitted … maybe it causes feedback."

"Okay, here are my crayons," Sawyer said, "draw me a picture."

"Feedback is caused by a 'looped signal.' Think of a public address system. A microphone feeds a signal into a sound system, which then amplifies and outputs the signal from a speaker … which is picked up again by the microphone. A continuous loop."

Finally the lightbulb came on. "And you think that if the Astrals went into the cave with that rock all around them, their presence would trigger whatever it is that makes the rocks telepathic ... and then — feedback!" Sawyer smiled. "I certainly hope so. I hope it makes that awful squawking sound in their heads and drives them crazy."

"Apparently it does something in their heads that's pretty catastrophic," Nick said. "As soon as they got in the cave they tried to eat each other."

Noah grabbed the conversation and dragged it away again.

"I'll grant that we've made a significant discovery here ... that the Astrals go nuts when they're surrounded by limestone ... but right now I don't give a shit! I don't care about anything except that we have to get them out of that mine and close up the hole they dug in the side of the mountain. Or when the flood comes, we are all going to drown."

"Seems pretty simple to me," Nick said and let out a breath. "We get some R8 and blow it up."

Sawyer smiled a little. It was good to be in the presence of a man who knew how to get things done.

Day Three

Chapter Twenty-Eight

ON THE MORNING of Day Three in Zion Village, Sawyer Matheson stood up to stretch his back after spending all night loading supplies to take to the caverns, and he was reminded of the winter when his brother Taylor was ten years old.

The family had been packed up for a family skiing vacation in Vermont … when eight-year-old Sawyer broke his leg in a bike accident. The vacation had to be cancelled. The little boy in a cast was devastated, so his older brother came up with a plan to cheer him up.

"We're going to *pretend* we're in Vermont," Taylor announced the morning the family *didn't* get in the car and leave. And for a solid week after, Taylor staunchly pretended they were in Vermont, dragged the whole family into his fantasy world with him. The boy would stand at the window looking out at summertime in Kentucky and comment on how beautiful the Vermont snow looked. They cranked the air conditioning so everybody had to bundle up in sweaters. They kept a fire burning in the fireplace and roasted hot dogs and marshmallows. It was the best not-vacation the family ever had.

Sawyer hadn't thought about that time in years until Taylor appeared on the loading dock, took him firmly by the arm and announced, "Come with me. We're pretending it's evening. I'm going to grill steaks on the back deck."

Sawyer eyed the sun that had just peeked up over the eastern horizon.

"Steaks? At seven o'clock in the morning?"

"You need a break. And this is the last cookout we'll ever have."

Taylor's family was one of probably a dozen families that Sawyer knew about who actually lived inside Matheson Caverns. He suspected there were dozens of people living there he didn't know about. Taylor's house was on Level Four and it would be under water when the flood came.

The brothers' eyes met and locked.

"Sure," Sawyer said. "Give me half an hour."

"Why ... so you can dig out your winter coat?" Taylor shook his head. "Wimp!"

Say what you will, fifty-four degrees was nippy. His brother and nephews teased Sawyer and Noah, called them sissies, wusses and candy-ass whiners because they always wore jackets or long-sleeved shirts when they went into Matheson Caverns, where the year-round temperature — except right next to the entrances — was a uniform fifty-four degrees.

That was one of the reasons some of the families who lived in the caves had moved there in the first place. After Astral Day, when the whole infrastructure of electricity, propane for gas heating in the winter, fuel oil, and coal deliveries all went to shit, it was very appealing to find a place where you didn't have to worry about blizzards, and didn't have to melt during the dog days of Kentucky summers when the temperature seemed to hang on a nail at ninety-eight degrees the whole month of August.

That wasn't why Sawyer's brother Taylor and his family had moved into a cave a couple of years after Astral Day, though. They'd done it because Taylor's wife, Kelly Jo, had lupus. When medications that helped ease the symptoms of the disease — rashes, joint pain and fever — began to dwindle, the family decided on the one treatment they could effect themselves — a lifestyle change. Exposure to sunlight caused lupus flareups — and Kelly Jo seemed to be particularly susceptible to sunlight as an aggravating factor. Given that she was going to have to live the rest of her life "medication free," and there was no way to know what kind of internal damage the disease was doing to her joints and the lining of her heart and lungs, they decided to join what Taylor called the "Blind Cave Fish Society," and live somewhere the sun would not bother her.

Nobody had to twist Taylor Matheson's arm to get the man to move into a cave. He'd spent his youth as a guide before he took over operation of the whole family business. Even before that he'd spent every spare moment exploring the caves with his father and grandfather. He moved his family into Level Four, a few hundred yards inside the cavern from the Cricket Bottom entrance that had been built to give visitors direct entrance into that level — which the family called "the petting zoo." Level Four featured dozens of weirdly-shaped rock formations that tourists believed looked like carved statues ... of everything from the Statue of Liberty to a fifty-foot-tall carrot. Cricket Bottom was named for the thirty-foot-tall rock formation just inside the entrance that looked like a cricket.

The Twin Forks River flowed through the cavern from west to east on the level below that, Level Five. There was a spiral staircase/ladder at the Cricket Bottom entrance on Level Four that led both down to Level Five and up into all the levels above. Sawyer had never counted the steps in those stairs — didn't want to know how many it took to stretch up fifteen hundred feet from the valley floor, through the Tripoli Cavern on Level Three, the Wiggle Room Cavern on Level Two all the way to the Smiley Face Cavern on the top of Joppa Ridge.

All the levels of the cave were lighted, and had paved passageways — passages no longer traveled by the hundreds of thousands of people who used to visit the cave every year. There were scenic steps leading down into the cavern from the parking lot — better landscaping than you could pay a professional to set out in your front yard. And there was plenty of land area for solar panels to provide electricity inside and for Taylor to plant the family's garden.

Over the years since, Taylor had built a house of sorts in the cavern — didn't need a roof, but there was something comforting about four walls to keep out the vastness of the cave. He'd added on until he had a totally maintenance-free four-bedroom house with a deck out back and a porch on the front. The deck didn't overlook anything scenic, of course — well, except the rock formation that looked like a pig — and you couldn't sit in the porch swing on summer evenings and wave at your neighbors driving by, though it gave a dandy view of the rock formation that looked like a cricket. It was just what Taylor's family needed. As soon as he moved into the cave, he began lighting passageways with caterpillar light. Caterpillar light had been designed for use in coal mines. Essentially, it was clear tubing smaller than a man's thumb that produced a remarkably bright light considering its size by some complex chemical reaction Sawyer could not have understood even if it had been explained to him — a later iteration of the glow sticks the brothers had played with as children.

Caterpillar tubes, once activated, would glow ... well, nobody knew for sure how long, but there were existing tubes that had been lit for almost twenty years and showed no signs of dying. Water didn't faze them. And since they didn't depend on some current running through them you could cut them in two and both halves would keep right on glowing.

The tubes didn't produce bright light, about as much light as a full moon on a cloudless night. But in the coal mines of Eastern Kentucky and West

Virginia, where the shafts were barely four feet tall, that was plenty of light. In the vast halls and caverns of Matheson Caverns, the light was paltry indeed, but it was better than utter darkness and once your eyes adjusted to the dimness, it was remarkable what you could see by the glow of them.

Taylor had stripped miles of the tubes out of nearby coal mines in Eastern Kentucky and West Virginia, and over the course of the past five years — with help from his two sons — he had lit up probably a hundred miles of interconnected passageways in Matheson Caverns.

Taylor was out on the deck, cooking venison steaks on the grill.

"Need any help?"

"If I did, I wouldn't ask you for it," Taylor said. "You suck at grilling."

"Says who?"

"Says anybody who's ever had to eat the charcoal chops you serve—"

"One time, okay. Cut me some slack. I got busy and—"

"Burned them? Oh, no no no. Burned does not do justice to the character of the black things I saw lying on your grill. A lump of coal would have been more tender."

"Eat a lot of coal, do you?"

"Nobody likes a smartass."

"Then you must not have a friend left in the world."

The brothers' banter was as easy and comfortable

as an old house shoe, even if today its presence was a cover for other conversations they did *not* want to have.

Taylor and Sawyer bore a strong family resemblance, in the shape of their faces, their body structure — they were both tall and broad-shouldered — and the way they moved, with the grace of former athletes, which both of them had been back in the day. Still they might not have been picked out of a crowd as brothers. Sawyer's hair was chestnut, his beard red, his eyes gray. Yet Sawyer somehow missed handsome and his older brother had been a heartthrob since junior high school. Taylor's hair was the same color as Noah's — so blond it was almost white and eyes the blue of a robin's egg. Where Sawyer's boney face seemed craggy, Taylor's came off as aristocratic, with high cheekbones and a wide forehead.

Taylor's sons David and Samuel split the difference. Both boys were strong young men in their mid-twenties. The older, David, was as blond as his father, and Samuel had full-bore red hair, like Sawyer's little girl Rosileigh, who had died with her mother in a fire when Noah was eight.

Kelly Jo brought out a bowl of salad and set it on the deck table. She was a pretty woman, had put on a little weight over the years, with hair the color of butter that curled around her face.

"You guys are perpetual tenth-graders," she said.

"Am not," said Taylor.

"Are, too," said Sawyer.

"Not!"

"Too!"

"Put a sock in it."

Sawyer still missed Peanut and Butter. The two German Shepherds used to wander the Taylors' portion of the cave as if on perpetual guard duty. Taylor hadn't trained them to do that, but they came from police dog stock and the instinct to guard and keep safe went all the way to the bone. When someone asked Taylor once how he could stand living somewhere that didn't have a door he could close and lock, he'd said anybody who could make it past Peanut and Butter deserved to steal whatever he owned. The two dogs had died within about a week of each other three years ago.

Taylor took the steaks off the grill, put them on a plate and set them on the table as Kelly came back out on the deck with mashed sweet potatoes, fried okra — she knew that was Sawyer's favorite — and a platter of just-picked corn on the cob.

"I'd have fresh tomatoes ... but the phantom thief struck again a couple of days ago and the tomato plants are bare," Kelly said.

Sawyer rolled his eyes. They all knew who the culprit was for dozens of petty thefts — Gideon Freeman. A shiftless freeloader, thief — and maybe worse, but Sawyer'd never been able to prove it. He'd moved into Level One the first winter after Astral Day and had been stealing the belongings of other cave dwellers, and occasionally from Zion villagers, for years.

Taylor looked up as if he could see into the

caverns above. "Hate to think *his* DNA is going to be in the genetic mix to repopulate the earth."

Sawyer wondered why he'd been surprised by Taylor's morning cookout. It was just the kind of thing Taylor would do … a little thing to lighten Sawyer's load. After all, the world was going to end in three days. The responsibility for saving a remnant of humanity, just plain *people* — like Gideon Freeman — and not those hand-picked for procreation by the Astrals, belonged to his brother, Sawyer Matheson. No pressure.

Chapter Twenty-Nine

STAR SAT on her stool in the kitchen peeling potatoes on the morning of Day Three. Ordinarily, she was a potato-peeling ninja, her hands moving so fast the peelings flew up into the air like leaves before a leaf blower and she enjoyed the soft plop they made on the piece of canvas beneath her stool, positioned there because the majority of her peels didn't land in the trash can in front of her.

But her hands were slow today, the peels dropping slowly into the can, like drips of water off a roof after a rain.

It wasn't that she couldn't concentrate because the clock ticking down to the End of the World dominated her thoughts. The looming Doomsday was making it hard for everybody to stay focused on the tasks at hand — but people understood they couldn't freak out, had to keep on keeping on with their normal responsibilities or the whole village would fall apart before they had a chance to load up the ark.

Star *had* to show up for kitchen duty, do her regular job so there would be food on the table in the cafeteria tonight. But this was her last shift. Tomorrow, she'd be in "Bardstown." Not really in the little community, she'd be working in a "receiving station" for families moving into the ark, set up in the parking lot at the Cricket Bottom Visitor's Center entrance … beneath the Bardstown awning. Back when Matheson Caverns had been a growing concern with hundreds of thousands of tourists, neighboring communities had set aside areas in the parking lot for their tour busses. The shelters were individualized, with every little town trying to outdo the others with their shelter. Now, seven years after Astral Day, the only shelter still standing was the one for Bardstown.

Families seeking sanctuary in the ark could get into it several different ways. Most rode on the rafts down the river, got off at the dock inside the cavern and rode up to the higher levels in one of the elevators. There were some buses running — until the fuel was exhausted — and they were usually jammed, or people could simply drive themselves if they still had transportation. People who showed up at the Cricket Bottom entrance had to be willing — and able — to climb the stairs to the upper levels, and they couldn't take with them more belongings than they could wrestle up the stairs.

A receiving station had been set up under the Bardstown awning in the parking lot and Star would be working there tomorrow, handing out guidebooks that'd been dug from the filing cabinets of the closed-up visitor's center. The books contained maps and all kinds of useful information about the caverns.

That was tomorrow. Today, her task was peeling potatoes, and she was doing a lousy job of it because she was ashamed of herself.

Oh, how she wanted a do-over! She had done what she never allowed herself to do, had trained herself not to do. She remembered the day the women from Roswell had come out to Alien World and begged Uncle Clyde to let Star tell their fortunes. She had taken the hand of each one of them in turn, and the images she got from their minds were so horrifying she couldn't tell them. So she'd made up stories, borrowed a little bit of the truth from the visions and made them pretty and palatable.

Uncle Clyde had explained back when Star had performed Astral Readings as the Amazing Apache Psychic, that customers couldn't ask her questions because she didn't get to choose what she saw. They couldn't ask if they would get a new car or marry the man of their dreams. Star might see the image of a new car and she might see roses and a wedding cake. Sometimes she could reasonably interpret those images to tell a man he'd get his new car and a girl she was going to get married soon. But other times, she got images that didn't make any sense at all, images of random objects — a basketball or a sousaphone. And the wedding cake image — it might really be showing the girl attending the ceremony where the man of her dreams married somebody else.

Star could pick up images from anybody she

touched. But she didn't. *Wouldn't!* She had practiced the self-discipline of never invading — that's the word she used, *invading*, that's how she thought of it — someone's mind without their permission. She touched people every day, bumped up against someone or took a little kid's hand, or hugged somebody. She didn't allow those touches to open a door into their futures, had learned as a small child that that was *not* a good idea.

The restriction was now as much a part of her as breathing, she no longer even had to think about doing it. She'd heard people talk about driving a car on a trip and not remembering a thing they saw on the journey because their minds were focused on something else. This was that. Star focused on other things and genuinely didn't even see the images anymore.

But not today. Today, Star had *purposefully* looked into Mrs. Blinkhorn, looked for images of her future.

Oh, how she wished she hadn't!

Mrs. Blinkhorn was an unpleasant woman. Star had seen her through Noah's eyes, an image, and she looked the part of an old crone. Her mouth turned downward at the corners, even in repose, and from it issued a whiny little voice that sounded like she'd inhaled helium out of a balloon. Her eyes were small and beady, set in a dish face, sunk in so her nose didn't stick out much farther than her chin and forehead. Her most unattractive feature was her hair, or rather the lack of it. The woman was almost bald.

Mrs. Blinkhorn didn't live in Zion Village. She and

The Hidden

her husband had a cabin in the woods near Jessup, but they got food from the monks, and Mrs. Blinkhorn often grudgingly "volunteered" to work in the kitchen. She had complained in the past that they shouldn't allow Pumpkin to accompany Star, that a dog shouldn't be in a place where food was prepared. She was an "expert" on such things because she'd once owned a little cafe, or so she claimed.

Mrs. Ballard, the kitchen manager, had overruled her complaints, pointing out that Pumpkin was Star's eyes, but Mrs. Blinkhorn never missed an opportunity to point out how unsanitary it was to have him around.

Like she had done earlier this morning. As soon as Star closed the kitchen door behind her, Mrs. Blinkhorn said, "I smell dog shit. That dog of yours has been stepping in his own shit. Do you know how unsanitary that is?"

Star said she didn't smell anything, and she even bent down on one knee and lifted each of Pumpkin's paws one at a time and sniffed.

"He's all clean," she'd said and Mrs. Blinkhorn had merely huffed in response.

Maybe that was why Star had done what she'd done. Maybe she'd subconsciously wanted to get back at the woman for her criticism of Pumpkin.

No, it hadn't been that ... it had just sort of happened — after Mrs. Blinkhorn announced to all the kitchen workers that she and her husband, Herbert, weren't going to the ark.

"Me and Herbert talked about it and that cave

business is a crock of shit. Sittin' in the dark waiting for the end of the world. No way!"

The Blinkhorns weren't alone in their determination not to join the travelers on Noah's Ark. The Millers, the Cassidys, Bill Donahue, the Quigleys ... lots of people had announced they were not going, that they were staying right where they were, thank you very much, and then pitched fits about all the supplies that were being loaded into the caverns.

"Why are you listening to this *Indian*?"

Star hated the way she said the word, like there was something wrong with being an Indian. She had not had to deal with racism since they had come north. The people of Jessup didn't care what color you were.

"Her claiming them aliens is gonna flood the earth ... did it ever occur to any of you that she don't know Jack shit?"

That's when it happened. Star wasn't even aware how close Mrs. Blinkhorn was to her, or maybe the woman just moved fast, but the next thing Star knew, Mrs. Blinkhorn had grabbed hold of her shoulder and was squeezing painfully.

"Why don't you spit it out, admit you made it all up."

At that moment, Star burst uninvited into Millicent Blinkhorn's mind.

And she saw ... *nothing*.

It was like being in an empty room.

Did that mean Mrs. Blinkhorn was going to die? It

did, didn't it? There weren't images to read because she didn't have a future.

Star had no right to know that!

It had so rattled Star that while the other kitchen workers leapt to her defense, she shook off the woman's hold on her shoulder and stumbled to the bathroom. Closing the door behind her, she stood with her back against it, trembling.

Pumpkin whined on the other side of the door. He wasn't used to her locking him out of anything. He'd seemed to get more clingy now that he was older. Nine was at the very least middle-aged for a dog, and he seemed to want to stay up close to her now more than ever.

Star stumbled to the sink, turned on the tap and splashed cold water into her face.

There was nothing there. *Noth—*

No, not nothing. Before the nothing there was an instant when Millicent Blinkhorn was terrified … but *not* of the end of the world.

And that fit. Star didn't like it, but it did fit. The woman was afraid of something *worse* than the end of the world. And Star could sense that worse thing coming.

She hadn't told Noah, hadn't let him see it, but it was happening to her again. She was getting some sense of … *danger.* It was like she'd felt the day the townies came to Alien World and shot the place up, killed Uncle Clyde. And like she had felt when they'd been traveling across Land Between the Lakes and she could feel something … *bad* out there in their future.

She hadn't said anything about it to anybody, not even to Papa Eagle Feather, because at first she had just assumed that the bad thing that was coming was the flood and everybody already knew about that.

Now she knew that wasn't it. The bad thing was something else. Something different. Something was coming at them, something really bad. Millicent Blinkhorn had seen it. Star could feel the woman's instant of terror and it made her shudder.

Chapter Thirty

It was a conversation that wouldn't be easy to sign. Shoot, it was a conversation that wouldn't be easy to say out loud with the combined wisdom of Socrates and Solomon, and all the words in the thesaurus. It was a hard thing and he would just need to do the best he could. It was the only thing he could do for Ellie, the last request she'd ever make of him.

He waited until Gretchen left her mother's room to go to the laundry where she worked some afternoons. You couldn't call after a deaf person and have them wait for you to catch up, so he took several large steps and came up beside her as she crossed what had been the lobby of the old administration building. The spot where David Weiss had waited in the dark for the townies' attack on the academy seven years ago.

"Hello Sheriff Matheson," she signed. "How are you?"

"I need to talk to you, Gretchen.

She flinched when he said it and he suspected

she might have an inkling about where the conversation was leading and clearly she didn't want to go there.

She said nothing, though, just went to one of the ornate benches in the big, empty room and sat down.

"What can I do for you?" she asked.

He sat down beside her, wanted to reach out and take her hand, but didn't. Gretchen was a don't-touch-me, don't-hug-me kind of person, at least she had become that after Diana came into her life.

"I want to talk to you about your mother."

"I figured that's what it was." She rushed on before he could formulate a response. "Don't you think she's looking better? I do, but when I said as much to Anna, she looked at me like I'd grown a third eye."

"I'll side with Anna on that one." Gretchen didn't like the response. He felt a little niggle of added apprehension in his belly.

"Well, *I* think she has more color in her cheeks. And I got her to eat three bites of applesauce this morning, so that means her appetite's improving."

A sickening realization began to dawn on Sawyer.

"Gretchen ... do you honestly believe your mother ... is going to get *well*?"

"Of course she's going to get well." She signed the words with crisp assertion. When she saw the startled look on his face, she hurried on. "Oh, I know the odds are against her. I understand that she ... you know, might not make it. But I also know she has a fighting chance and that's all you can ask."

He signed very slowly, making certain she understood the question.

"Do you think she has a 'fighting chance' to survive Stage Five cancer in her bones, lungs and who knows what other organs?"

"Like I said, I know it's a long shot, but—"

"Gretchen, your mother is dying."

She looked like he'd slapped her.

"How can you say a thing like that? I thought you cared about my mother, that—"

"I *do* care about your mother — that's *why* I said it. I care enough about her to be honest with her. And with you. You're not doing your mother any favors with this false hope."

"*False* hope. There's no such thing as false hope. It's just hope. All hope is just hope. It's thinking positively. It's not talking about the ... bad things that could happen, but concentrating on the good things you believe *will* happen."

"Gretchen, when you get to the end, when you know you're dying, you need the help of the people you love — to *help you die* in peace. There are things you want to say to people. I'm sure there are things she wants to say to you, but if you won't let her be honest—"

"She *is* honest with me. I admit she's discouraged right now. I would be too if I were as sick as she is. But I won't let her talk about dying, about the negative. I won't—"

"Gretchen, you have to let her say what she wants to say. You don't have any right to deny her the opportunity to be honest just because it makes you uncomfortable to hear it."

"I'm doing it for her own good."

"What will do her good right now is letting her be real. She's dying—"

Gretchen started to rise, but he put out his hand and took hers and she reluctantly sat back down on the bench.

"You know I'm telling the truth, Gretchen. I understand it hurts to admit it, to face it, but she *is* dying … and she's in terrible pain."

"She'd be in less pain if she had a positive attitude."

"Gretchen, she asked me to talk to you, to help you understand. She intends to die … *here*."

"She's *not* going to die, here or anywhere else—"

"She asked me to tell you — she's *not* going to move to the ark. It would be painful and futile."

There, he'd said it. The words hung in the air between them, floated in the hollow air in the big room.

Gretchen's shock and dismay morphed in a heartbeat into rage.

"How could you say a thing like that! My mother would never—" Then she gasped, so shocked and enraged she was sputtering, half-forming signs, her hands shaking. "You aren't considering *leaving* her … oh, my God, you *wouldn't*—"

"I will not force Ellie to leave. The decision is hers — not mine … and not *yours*. She's not going, Gretchen … she's *staying here*."

The girl leapt to her feet.

"I won't *abandon* my mother, do you hear me? I won't let you leave her here to … *drown!* No, I won't let you *kill* her!"

Then she lost it, burst into tears and ran away. He had suspected something like this might happen, but he'd told himself he could reason with the girl. He'd been wrong. Clearly, Gretchen Hampton was delusional. And if he had learned anything in four decades on this planet it was that most people would give up their lives to keep from giving up their delusions.

Chapter Thirty-One

As Sawyer walked from the academy administration building back to the loading dock, he was mulling over in his mind his conversation with Gretchen, wondering how he was going to tell Ellie that it had gone reeeeally badly. He decided he wouldn't tell her at all, not yet. He'd have another go at Gretchen later. Maybe after she'd slept on it, she'd see reason.

He stepped up onto the dock to find one of his work crews stuck there waiting for the monks to bring down barrels of vegetable oil to load onto a raft, and marveled at the stamina of the old professor. Garson had worked as hard as anybody, stayed up longer than anybody, and still found the energy to lecture any group of people he could hold still long enough to listen to him.

"... power grid is really very simple, when you think about it," Garson was saying, which was horse shit, but Sawyer kept his mouth shut. "Electrical storage of energy is generally not subject to the same thermodynamic constraints as storage systems that involve moving masses of solids against the earth's gravitational field, because of the very low value of the gravitational coupling."

Riiiiiiight.

Sawyer watched the eyes of the trapped audience glaze over. Garson might as well have been speaking Klingon.

"Garson, we don't need to know how the hot dog is made." Garson looked blank — and Sawyer liked to see that look on *his* face for a change so he didn't explain. "All we need to know is — will we have electricity in the cave?"

"I was just explaining how—"

"Yes or no?"

"Of course we will."

"So that means we can run lights and all manner of other electric doodads, right?"

"I shall attribute your hostility to sunstroke." Garson glanced up at the burning yellow orb in the sky. The professor always wore sunglasses and a hat and sometimes even gloves — "melanoma, you know" — keeping his body so white Sawyer thought they might not need electricity in the caves because Garson probably glowed in the dark.

The old man continued to stare upward and his changing expression caused Sawyer to turn and follow his gaze. Visible in the distant sky high above Matheson Caverns was an Astral shuttle.

Apparently, they were back today, working in their mine.

Without a word, Sawyer headed toward the workshop Nick Wilson had set up where he was building a bomb.

Nick was bent over a work table in the monks' woodshop when Sawyer approached.

Nick held up his hand. "Tread lightly, my friend," he said.

"Is that stuff temperamental, like … like nitroglycerin or something?" Sawyer asked.

Nick laughed. "This is so many generations past nitro, dynamite and C4 it's lost the red hair gene." He turned his attention back to what he was working on. "Old habits die hard, though. Military training was both the best and the worst thing I ever did. The best because of the discipline, the loyalty and determination it taught."

Nick smiled again. "The worst because … it's like dog shit on your shoe. You can't ever seem to get rid of it, no matter what you do."

"Default to the level of your training," Sawyer said, and Nick nodded again. Sawyer had known when he first met Nick seven years before that Nick had been a soldier. He had the ex-military vibe. What he hadn't known was what Nick kept private. Not many people knew that Nick had spent his years in the military as a Navy SEAL!

"Yup, and I was taught to be careful with explosives, any kind of explosives, even one as garden variety as this one."

"If it's so garden variety, how do you know it will do the damage we need?"

"Quantity, my friend. Quantity. The monks used a piece of R8 the size of a pinky finger to blow out tree stumps to clear fields for farmland. We will be planting *pounds* of this stuff outside the Astral mine." He grinned. "These explosives will get the job done. I just hope we don't blow off the whole side of the mountain."

He must have seen the alarm on Sawyer's face and backed down. "Just kidding. I was a bit of an expert with this stuff back in the day, and I guarantee I will plant charges around that cave opening that will bring the walls and roof down, seal it up like a stopper in a sink."

Sawyer noted that the substance Nick was working with was brown.

"Don't suppose that color is accidental."

"I'll be drilling holes and planting it deep, but I could just leave pieces of it lying around and the Astrals would think they were rocks. Any word yet from the men stationed in the woods across from the entrance?"

As soon as Noah had reported the presence of the Astral mine to the elders, Sawyer had set up a watch on the site, dispatched a team of men with high-powered binoculars to the woods on the other side of the valley from the rock face on the north side of Tucker Mountain. They reported that the hole in the rock face was as perfectly round as a drainage pipe — probably twenty feet wide. The

The Hidden

Astrals had also cleared out an area in front of it big enough to land one of the large shuttles that carried a full crew — half a dozen at least and maybe more — along with the robots and the cutting equipment they used.

"After about an hour, they saw the Astrals load up their gear and boogie — you know, that thing the shuttles do where they are there and then not there, vanishing because the human eye can't track movement that fast."

"Loaded up their gear, did they?" Nick observed. "Maybe they're finished and won't be coming back."

"Maybe. No way to know. But we can't count on that."

Nick nodded. They had determined that they needed to plant the charge and then wait until the very last minute to detonate it — otherwise the Astrals might come back, find the passage blocked and drill it back out again.

Nick lifted a small gray box that almost looked like a toy. It was about the size of the lunchbox Sawyer had taken to school as a kid, but it was shiny metal, totally unadorned except for a clear, see-through plastic domed lid that was closed over a single red button.

"This is the monks' detonator — intentionally simplistic, for men who wouldn't be able to operate a juke if they had one. But it will work fine. Just unfasten the plastic covering, and punch the red button and … ka-boom."

"What is the range of the signal from this thing?

Will somebody have to be outside, pointing this thing at the opening?"

That, of course would be problematic, since whoever was standing outside would likely drown.

"Six hundred feet, more or less. But it's designed so the signal doesn't travel through the air. It has to be detonated from *inside* the cavern."

"The signal goes through solid rock?"

"That's what this is for." Nick held up a length of heavy wire, with a pointed metal tip about six inches long, that was attached to the detonator. "Stick this into a crack in the wall. The signal through this will go through twenty-inch-thick corrugated steel so a few hundred feet of porous limestone will be just the fuse it needs."

"So we don't have to worry that somebody might be using their garage door opener somewhere near Tucker Mountain while you're planting that stuff." Not that anybody lived anywhere near Tucker Mountain. Or still had a car. Or gasoline to run it. Or batteries for a garage door opener.

"Only one signal will detonate this stuff. There are … just call them blasting caps, though that's not specifically what they are. They're computerized chips I'll imbed into the R8, then program a signal from this detonator to set off the caps. The chips will only respond to the exact signal."

"When do you plan to plant the explosives?"

"As soon as possible." Even Nick unconsciously looked up at the sky, as if he expected to see storm clouds there that would herald the beginning of the storm. "Our plan is to watch the Astrals, and the next time they leave, we'll plant the explosives."

Today was Day Three. People had started pouring into the caverns before sundown on Day Two, when Noah had outlined the plan for the community. There had been a growing stream of them day and night ever since. The plan was to have all the residents and supplies fully loaded by sundown on Day Five, to leave a full day of grace.

On Day Six, the black ship would arrive and do the heinous act the Astrals had summoned it from its parking place near Jupiter to do. It would melt the polar ice caps, but even Garson was unwilling to make a prediction about how long it would be before the water actually flooded the whole earth. They were inland, on high ground. The poles were thousands of miles north and south. The nearest bodies of water that would overflow their banks with the incoming flood were the Great Lakes. Like Michigan was 250 miles north. Both the Atlantic and Pacific were thousands of miles away. How long would it take before the water reached central Kentucky?

And what would it do when it did? Nobody knew that, either. Would it wash over the mountains in a mighty tsunami roaring inland that would obliterate everything in its path? Or would it expend that energy when it broke over the coastlines, and merely come inland as steadily rising water?

Water rising how fast?

All they knew for certain was that they had to be inside Matheson Caverns before the water reached the lowest entrance, which would be the river, and begin to flood the lower caverns as the level rose. It would wash over the beautiful home Taylor and his family had built in Level Four, submerge it and the homes the other cave dwellers had built. No home, at least none that Noah knew about, was in a cavern that was up above the waterline that would establish itself in the cave. People who'd moved in over the years had just come into the cave as far as they thought it was necessary for their purposes — constant temperature and protection from the elements. Nobody that Noah knew about had gone exploring the passageways above.

Those lower caverns would flood. The next level of caverns up, between them and the sandstone cap that protected limestone of the cave from completely dissolving away, were the Noah's Ark caverns where they would wait for the end of the world to … end.

But all the caverns would flood if they failed to plug the hole the Astrals had dug high on the mountainside, right through the cap of insoluble sandstone. Water flowing into that hole would find its way down through all the caverns between it and the water level of the Twin Forks River far below. It would flood them all and drown anybody who'd taken refuge in them.

They had to blow up the Astral entrance or they all would die.

The two men fell silent. Sawyer watched Nick's expert motions as he molded and fashioned the R8 into the shape he wanted.

"You scared?" Sawyer asked. He was instantly

embarrassed for saying it, didn't mean to, it just popped out.

Nick didn't even look up.

"Totally shitless," he said. "I don't think I've had a solid bowel movement since I saw that painting on the gym floor."

Day Four

Chapter Thirty-Two

DAY FOUR in the end-of-the-world countdown came and went without Sawyer Matheson acknowledging its passage. Life had become about getting people and the supplies necessary to ensure their survival into the caverns before sundown on Day Five. Within hours of the rollout of the ark plan, preparation had reached a fever pitch. And the pace never let up. At some point on Day Four, it seemed to take on an insectile frenzy. Even though everyone knew the flood was not going to come from a rainstorm, people couldn't help looking up at the sky in apprehension as they hurried about whatever task it was they had been assigned.

Brother Sebastian had left a handful of monks behind in Zion Village to help with the move while he and the rest set up shop somewhere in Level One and were building a chapel. Garson had moved in already, imprisoned by the rule: *when you get here, you stay.* The overtaxed elevators could not accommodate people coming and going, returning to get more stuff to bring into the caverns. They'd made an exception for Garson, though, allowed him three trips, because he understood as no one else did, that the flood would not only kill millions of people, it would kill all trace of their existence. All the great works of art or science or philosophy would be wiped out. Succeeding generations would not know what it had taken millennia for humanity to learn. Something as simple as how to manufacture a match, or as complex as how to launch a rocket ... it all would be gone.

Nothing would remain except what Garson was able to load on Noah's Ark. No pressure.

Sawyer had watched him agonize. Shakespeare or the Farmer's Almanac? Mozart sheet music or *How to Build a Bridge for Dummies*? He'd selected a handful of textbooks he'd scavenged from the Hillsdale College Library years ago — medical, mathematics (from simple algebra to quantum physics), agriculture and engineering, along with Taylor's copy of *The Boy Scout Handbook*. Sawyer had brought along his own dog-eared copy of *The Worst-Case Scenario Book*.

As Sawyer worked, his exhausted mind pinged from one random thought to another.

There would be gunpowder in the brave new world, which probably was not a good thing at all, but it wasn't an intentional inclusion. The recipe for gunpowder was charcoal, saltpeter and gypsum. Since the all those elements were either available in the caverns already or easily accessible, gunpowder had been manufactured in the cave in the late 1800s. In the early years after Astral Day, several enterprising county residents had operated an ammunition factory there.

Shell casings were the only scarce commodity. They couldn't easily manufacture those, so that was the medium of exchange, ammunition for shell casings. If you wanted a hundred cartridges, bring in a hundred empty shell casings.

Because the caverns had housed gunpowder, several tunnels close to the manufacturing facility had been outfitted to keep the barrels of gunpowder secure. There were warehouse tunnels with metal doors and state-of-the-art — at least for the time period — locking devices, along with at least half a dozen smaller rooms equally secure where Sawyer intended to lock up his arsenal and all the firearms he confiscated from the residents. He and Nick had inspected them, found that the metal doors were equipped with sturdy hasps, and the metal door frames had secure loops for padlocks. Then he'd rounded up a handful of heavy-duty padlocks and loaded them with his things, considering that he might need the capacity to lock things securely away. Those metal doors would be impenetrable.

Nick had almost given him a coronary when he'd reported finding barrels of gunpowder stored back in the dark depths of one of the warehouse caverns — "enough to blow the top off the mountain." Then he'd seen Sawyer's white face and continued, "If it still worked, which I'm sure it doesn't!" He'd said smokeless powder made before WWI was unstable and several ships had been blown up when the powder in their magazines exploded. "There's no sense trying to move it out of there. It's been fine right where it is for a couple hundred years, and if it ain't broke …"

That warehouse was the first of the metal-doored rooms Sawyer fit with a padlock.

In truth, Sawyer really had no idea what *else* somebody might have decided to haul into the ark, had not exercised as tight a control over what went into the cavern as he would have liked, especially as the clocked ticked down on Day Four. Farmers brought chickens, sheep and goats — sometimes managed to talk those operating the elevators into admitting them, sometimes not.

The monks had brought donkeys and carts to use to haul goods around the twenty-four-plus miles of connecting passageways. There were those who wanted to bring family heirlooms, possessions they'd somehow managed to hold onto after Astral Day. It wasn't that there was not sufficient space for all that people wanted to bring. The issue was time and space to load them up.

Sawyer listened to one of the elevator operators engage in a heated discussion with a farmer who wanted to bring his geese with him into the ark and he stepped away from the dock, out into the night air to avoid having to arbitrate the dispute. He looked up at the black velvet sky, dotted with stars. Found the Milky Way. What would the night sky look like after … would it be the same?

He glanced at his watch, the one that would have cost more than his house before Astral Day. Erika

Mason had forced it on him, insisted that "the guy in charge" needed such a time piece and she didn't anymore. So far, the only things he'd found that the sleek, silver band *couldn't* do was make coffee and whistle Dixie. In truth, he couldn't operate more than a handful of its five hundred functions, but he had figured out how to make it measure twenty-four-hour increments of time, so he could keep track of their journey on the ark. He had selected the vintage watch face and while he watched, the second hand swept up to twelve. It was no longer Day Four. It was Day Five. This time tomorrow they'd be snug as bugs in rugs, people and their stuff in the caverns waiting for the death ship to flood the earth — unless something unforeseen came up.

Day Five

Chapter Thirty-Three

Paco's army rumbled into the little town of Jessup, Kentucky, at dawn on Day Five like a swarm of locusts. Paco liked that analogy. Motorcycles and troop carriers emblazoned with the image on Paco's flag — a white skull, with a spider crawling out one eye socket and a snake out the other.

He was pumped, ready. He rode his big Harley past the city limits sign: Jessup, Kentucky, population 5,000, that hung by one chain from the rod attached to a leaning post.

Paco was euphoric. He made it! It had been an amazing trip halfway across the country fueled as it was by terror. He had timed his arrival here to be just after first light. Let the residents of this little burg wake up to a whole new world. Not the Astrals' world. Paco's.

The Astrals intended to wipe humanity off the planet and start over.

Paco had been able to banish that realization from

his mind when they had first set out from Tahoe, the thrill of movement, of taking action, the hope that they could beat the odds, that they could survive when the rest of humanity was reduced to black dust.

But day after day, the fear that fueled that sense of purpose grew. It became a lead ball in Paco's belly that dragged his internal organs down, so heavy he felt them stretch and pull out of shape.

It could be today.

How many times a day did he think that thought? *Today.* The ships could swoop down and begin the annihilation at any moment. He *believed* the Astrals would start with the cities — they would, wouldn't they, where there were concentrations of people?

But the truth was Paco didn't *know* if any of those assumptions was valid.

The Astrals had already reduced to black ash all the major cities in the world, New York, London, Hong Kong, Mexico City, Jakarta — the most populous places on the earth had been vaporized in one day, Black Monday, reducing the population of the earth from seven billion to three billion. Four *billion* humans vaporized. Still, that wasn't every city in the world. The smaller ones, they'd survived, hadn't they? There was no way to know for certain, but he was sure they hadn't sent a mothership to Des Moines. Had they? To Indianapolis? Shreveport? The smaller cities had remained, he genuinely believed that. So the Astrals would go there first, killing those people.

They couldn't go hunting people down out in the

hinterlands until they'd killed them in all the cities. That made sense, didn't it?

So he had time. He wasn't certain when the annihilation would begin, but there was still time even after that for him to make it to safety.

There was, wasn't there?

His belief in his own logic, his interpretation of how things would go was eroded hour by hour, day by day. As they strained forward as fast as they could go, on pieces of deserted interstates, back out to small country roads, bobbing and weaving their way across the country. They didn't stop. Never stopped. Not to eat. Not to sleep. As vehicles ran out of fuel they stopped with the tanker to refuel and then caught up to the rest of the caravan as it traveled on.

They had forged ahead relentlessly, Well, except at the Mississippi River, when they'd run into that rabble they'd had to mow down to cross "their" bridge. He had made short work of those morons. Didn't pause to give them a proper sendoff, just took half an hour to string up the leaders by their heels, pour gasoline on them and set them on fire.

That had cost them only a few hours, not even half a day of travel time.

But they'd made it! They were here. Jessup, Kentucky where …

Paco's heart began to hammer too fast, too much pressure, but what he saw stabbed terror into his chest.

There … was no Jessup.

It was a ghost town.

He rumbled with his armada down the main

street, past empty holes where it looked like Astrals had vaporized buildings, past other buildings not vaporized, just abandoned.

He rolled to a stop in front of a black hole where a sign out front still proclaimed McClintock County Courthouse, and killed the engine on his bike. Made a motion for the others to do the same. He leaned the bike over on its kickstand and lifted his leg over the seat. Then stood, looking around.

The roar of his engine and the others in his ears had left an echo even in the quiet. And it was quiet. None of his people moved or said anything. Some sat astraddle their bikes, others got off and stood beside them. They were looking around, as he was, trying to figure out …

No one was here. The town was abandoned. Not recently, either. This was a place that had not had "population 5,000" in years.

Doors hung ajar on broken hinges on what had once been stores. A lone building stood down the block, windows broken out, a bakery maybe, beside the last of what appeared to be maybe half a dozen empty lots that must once have sported buildings — that had been vaporized.

Paco's mind began to fragment, thoughts flying around in it, out of his reach, where he couldn't grab them, couldn't think them.

Well, looks like you screwed the pooch.

Was Himself … *laughing* at him?

Himself was Paco's constant companion now, but he had morphed through their journey eastward.

Born of the drug ayahuasca, Himself had merely been Paco looking at Paco, seeing into himself, who he really was. But the act of looking into himself didn't wear off with the effects of the drug. Himself became a voice in Paco's head. At first a gentle warning voice, trying to keep him from doing any more damage to his blood vessels, injured through years of projecting his mind, dominating the minds of others and, most draining of all, appearing as someone or some *thing* feared. Pulling deep-seated fear from a person's subconscious, then manifesting in their eyes as the object of that fear, took tremendous concentration and mental clarity. It was a trick right out of the Astrals' playbook, had been used on Paco, Noah and Star when they were in the mothership

Paco had done damage to his brain in those efforts. He knew it at the time, though he wouldn't have admitted it, knew it more acutely as time went by but wasn't forced to face the whole reality of it until Himself confronted him.

Himself said Paco had so harmed his brain that he was going insane, that the impairment was permanent and irreparable, pointed out that who Paco had been when he was abducted by the Astrals seven years ago bore little resemblance to the man who'd sat looking out at Lake Tahoe as he pried his mind open with a psychedelic drug.

Paco tried to shake it off. That was just Himself talking and what the fuck did it matter what that not-person thought or said. He wasn't real. In fact, if anybody was insane, it was Himself, not Paco. Himself was nuts. Paco was sane.

But as Paco raced eastward toward salvation, fear had weighed down every thought, incipient panic crawled on hairy black legs up the back of Paco's throat every waking moment and Himself had become belligerent, abrasive, sarcastic and condescending.

Now, Himself was mocking Paco, making fun of him and the folly of this two-thousand-mile quest to reach a little town in nowhere Kentucky that was abandoned. A ghost town.

Now, what the fuck are you going to do?

Paco had no idea.

He caught movement out the corner of his eye, turned and saw—

"Hey you, stop," he cried, at what appeared to be a figure disappearing into an abandoned store. "Come out here where I can see you."

Had he even seen anybody? Or was it just his imagination? Sounds came from inside the store — it was a department store, and a crash like things falling could be heard through the broken windows.

Paco looked at two of his captains, Radek Nova and Juan Santiago, nodded with his chin toward the sound, and the two men stormed into the building. He heard scuffling sounds and then the two men returned. Nova had an old man by the collar, had dragged him out through the doorless door frame, and threw him roughly into the street at Paco's feet. The man went down on his knees, and stayed there, trembling.

"What's your name?" Paco asked.

The man said nothing.

"You don't know me yet, so I'm going to give you that one. But it's the only freebie. When I ask a question, you answer it. What's your name?"

"Blinkhorn," he said. "Herb Blinkhorn."

Still the man kept his head down.

"Look at me, Herb Blinkhorn," Paco said, and the old man slowly lifted his chin and Paco could see his face. He was a walking skeleton, his skin stretched out across the bones of his skull like the tarp of a tent. His gray hair and clothes were filthy, his beard shaggy and full of … Paco didn't know what.

This guy could have been cast as the town drunk in every black-and-white vintage, "historic" movie the nuns at St. Francis of the Hills Catholic School showed students when Paco was a boy.

"Where is everybody?" Paco gestured to the deserted streets and abandoned buildings.

Blinkhorn didn't seem to understand.

"Where are all the people?" Paco amended the question, with a not-so-hidden threat that the old man had better come up with an answer for this one.

"Gone," Blinkhorn said. "Nobody lives here. Nobody's lived here for … years."

"All the people who left … where did they go?"

"An Astral shuttle attacked and killed most of 'em." Blinkhorn was clearly thrilled that he had actually been asked a question he could answer. "A few survived, half maybe, and they moved to Zion

Village." He straightened and pointed down the road. "It ain't far, just down that way."

"What are you doing here?"

"Me and the missus got us a cabin up in the woods and we come down to see could we find a bucket. Old one's got a hole in it."

"We?"

The old man looked back toward one of the collapsing buildings, and as he did a woman came around the corner of it holding a bucket, clearly unaware of Paco's presence. The woman was ugly as sin, dish-faced and almost completely bald. She froze when she saw Paco and her eyes grew wide in terror.

Paco drew his pistol and blew away her homely face, then turned the barrel on the old man and blew what little was left of his brains out the back of his head.

Chapter Thirty-Four

Six-year-old Josie Wilson, who had gone "fwimming" with Noah in the pond, was the first casualty of Paco's war against Star and Noah. Nick Wilson's little girl had gone out to the road that turned off to the old Zion Academy entrance to pick blackberries from a bush that grew wild beside the road.

She heard the growl and rumble of motorcycles, Harley Davidsons, coming down the road and the sound scared her, so she turned back toward the village and began to run home, down the middle of the road.

Paco was on the lead bike, riding Tiburon — except he didn't call it that, of course, would *never* call it that. Except he did. It was his masterpiece of horror, and riding it made him invincible, totally fearless. Nothing scared a shark.

When Paco spotted the running figure ahead of him in the road, he aimed his bike at it. Not thinking, really, just reacting. He always aimed at dogs or rabbits or anything else in the road. The fact that this was a child didn't matter. It should have mattered, but it didn't. Like other things should have mattered to him, but just didn't anymore. Where those connections had once been in his brain, the wires had been cut, the vessels torn away by the pressure of what Paco forced his mind to do.

And some small part of him noticed now, saw it every time it happened. Ever since he had taken the drug, he had been confronted by Himself, the schoolyard tattletale. The image would flash in front of his eyes, his own image, telling him that the vessels were too stressed, that something was going to blow, that there should be connections here that were gone, that he had destroyed his own humanity.

Himself flashed briefly and was gone. Then time slowed down as it did for him sometimes when he was reading people's minds or appearing to them as the thing they most feared. Everything cranked down into slow motion, as if time itself came unhooked from reality when his mind did those acrobatics — his sanity on a trapeze high up at the top of the tent, flipping and tumbling and gyrating up there ... and there was no net underneath.

He watched each piece of gravel on the road as the front tire hit it and sent it flying out behind, he saw the little girl's back getting closer and closer. She was wearing a red t-shirt and overalls and she was clutching a small straw basket in her left hand and the motion of running was jarring out the contents, blackberries flying in slow motion up into the air, turning over and over. She had long blond hair that streamed out behind her, was barefooted and he could see her footprints on the asphalt as she ran, which he couldn't, of course, but he saw them anyway, they were glowing, bright yellow around the edges, a trail of them, beads on a necklace connected to each other by a filament of yellow light.

The little girl turned to look at him then and he saw.

No! He would never hurt … so pure, an angelic life form. No! She had Down's syndrome.

He tried to swerve, tried to turn the wheel, to miss her, but there was no time and even as he tried he knew he would not make it.

The shark nose struck her in the back and he saw her bend in the middle where it hit her, at the impossible angle of a broken back. She floated there knocked forward by the bike, both of them frozen in time, her basket upside down, dropping blackberries that didn't ever land.

And she looked at him.

Oh dear God in heaven, she looked at him, turned her head and saw him. Saw into him, saw the broken places with clear blue eyes, knew him, knew every thought he'd ever had, everything he'd ever done, saw that all of it was smeared with a black tar of evil, sticky, couldn't be washed off.

Her face became Star's then, as she forgave him.

Elastic time that had been stretched out to the limit snapped back. He saw the teeth on the faring draw blood that flew up in a fine red spray into his face. His tires thumped over a bump. A small one. And someone was screaming, and the roar of his bike and the others ate up the world.

He smiled. The sun beat down with searing heat, making the whole world shimmer as he and his men rumbled under an archway that said Zion something and spread out beyond it. The road led to a loop in front of a big school-looking building, U-shaped with a statue on the island in the middle, and somebody had planted red and yellow flowers around its base.

He cut his speed, rode slowly around the loop and back out to the road.

Sound faded away until all he could hear was the thumping of his own heart. Not the motor of the Harley, not the screaming that came from a long way off. Just his heart. Thump. Thump. Thump. Pumping blood rhythmically around his body.

Except through the broken vessels. Remember those. The ones that don't connect anymore because you burst them. The heart isn't pumping blood into them.

Paco shook it off. The man in town had said everybody'd moved here, that nobody lived in Jessup anymore, which was plain to see. So the shield must be here.

Here *where?* Where was it? Where was the dome?

He'd always pictured it as a dome because that was the kind of thing Noah would build, something rounded and beautiful as well as functional, a "bee that can't possibly fly but does."

But that's just how Paco pictured it. He had no

idea what it really did look like. Maybe it wasn't a dome at all. Maybe it was a bunker. Some other kind of shelter. A shield of some kind, shining in the sun.

Where was whatever-the-hell-it-was that would withstand the Astrals' death rays?

Chapter Thirty-Five

Paco's arrival had created exactly the effect he wanted on the citizenry of Zion Village. In truth, running over the child had been a masterful strategy, if it had been what he intended to do. He made so many statements with that single act, made a lot of explanation, bullying and intimidation unnecessary. Of course, his army was intimidating in its own right, riding into the little "village" as they had on roaring Harley Davidsons and in troop carriers.

The troop carriers with his crest emblazoned on the sides had screeched to a stop, and the men piled out of them and formed a line neat as little West Point cadets. Their uniforms were striking — as black as death. Paco had told the tailor to create a look like Hitler's Gestapo — with Paco's skull, spider and snake insignia on their breasts. They held their rifles at the ready, not pointed at anybody, just ready to be pointed. But the show of force had been rendered unnecessary by killing the child.

A black woman who had some connection to the little girl was screaming, apparently had witnessed the act and raced out to the road to gather the mangled form of the little girl up into her arms. She sat there by the roadside on her knees, rocking the dead child back and forth, her head tilted back, wailing an inconsolable scream into the morning air. She had been joined by several other women, who sat with her, knowing there was nothing any of them could do — the corpse was barely recognizable — to help the child, their eyes huge and focused on the army arrayed in front of them.

The scene had drawn a huge crowd that grew by the second as word spread. People poured into the area, hundreds of them, left their houses and dropped whatever task they'd been performing, and came to stand in a stupefied gathering, staring in slack-jawed wonder at the might displayed before them.

If all the five thousand people who'd lived in Jessup had moved out here, this was a good-sized little burg. Might it be possible they had some kind of … alarm system, like a siren they sounded in an emergency, some way to summon them all, like the bell his aunt in West Virginia told him Amish farmers used to call for help.

Motioning for Radek Nova, he directed the man to "find somebody to show you their … emergency siren, get them to turn it on."

He called another of his five captains to him, told Jake Farewell to "take a hundred men, divide into teams of ten and search this place."

The men ran off to do his bidding. He noticed the woman who'd been wailing beside the body of the dead child, watched her features warp into a mask of rage. She laid the child gently down on the ground, stood and came running at him, screaming, with only a few words intelligible enough to understand.

"What did you ... on purpose ... murderer! Precious little Josie ... *monster*!"

Two of his soldiers stopped her before she could get to Paco, held her by the arms while she screeched at him. He merely stood, looking at her, wondering at the total lack of emotion he felt. It was clear she wasn't the child's mother, just somebody who'd been looking after her. But the woman had loved the child, a child he'd killed, and he couldn't summon even a snippet of sympathy.

The pathways are broken, the vessels blown out.

He casually took the pistol he'd used to shoot the town drunk in Jessup out of the holster at his waist and pointed it at the screaming woman, then spoke to the other women she'd left by the roadside with the body of the little girl.

"One chance, that's it. Get her out of here and shut her up or I will shoot her where she stands."

That was the right thing to do, wasn't it? Show a little restraint. Yeah, that established him as a leader who held the lives of this woman and all of them in his hand. Didn't need any useless brutality.

Bullshit. You need to be utterly ruthless, not compassionate.

He almost regretted not shooting the woman, but

by the time he'd had second thoughts, the other women had dragged her away. One of the women had gone to the body of the dead child, picked her up tenderly and took her with them. He could hear the woman still screaming until a door somewhere shut behind them, cutting off the scream in mid-shriek.

It was only quiet for a few moments before a bell began to ring. A ridiculous sound, like a doorbell. *That's* how they summoned people in an emergency? Paco shook his head. This was going to be even easier than he'd thought it would be.

Showtime.

He was still astraddle Tiburon. No, that wasn't the bike's name, dammit. It wasn't. He kicked down the kickstand, lifted his leg over the seat and strode purposefully out in front of the crowd, which was growing with people summoned by the bell filling in behind. Lots of people ... but nowhere near five thousand of them. They looked like sheep about to be slaughtered. All except the monks. There was a group of them, a dozen, maybe more, in brown robes with ropes tied around their waists near the front of the crowd. They just looked at him, but he could detect no fear on their faces. He felt rage well up inside him. How dare they not be afraid of him. Well, he would start there.

He leaned over and spoke quietly to one of his soldiers, who strode out into the crowd — they parted for him like the Red Sea — and grabbed one of the monks by the front of his robe, dragged him roughly out to where Paco stood, shoved him to the ground so he lay at Paco's feet, looking up at him.

The monk was afraid ... wasn't he? Yes, he was. He had to be afraid.

"What's your name?"

"Brother Luke." The monk made no effort to get up off the ground. That meant he was scared, didn't it?

Then the monk got to his knees and stood up, dusting the dirt off the front of his robe.

"We're going to start with you," Paco said. "And if you tell me what I need to know, if you're helpful as you should be, a monk and all, nobody else will have to get hurt. So tell me, Brother Luke, where is Noah's Shield?"

The monk looked at him questioningly.

"I don't know what you're talking about. *Shield?*"

"Shield, dome, whatever the fuck it is. Where is the thing Noah built to withstand the death rays of the Astrals?"

"Withstand the death rays? Nothing can ... I don't know of anything—"

Paco shot him, lifted the gun, pointed it at the man five feet away and blew the monk's face off. His blood splattered on Paco. Red stains on his black uniform. Bigger stains than the little girl's blood had made.

The crowd shrieked, and that did, at least, get the attention of the other monks. Several of them rushed out of the crowd to kneel beside their fallen brother.

"Let's start all over again, shall we?" His eyes scanned the crowd. He needed someone the others would be sympathetic toward … there was a woman, white-haired, standing to his left. Old, her thinning hair pulled back in a bun, granny glasses on her nose — like a cartoon of a "little old lady." The woman beside her had her arm around the old woman's shoulders, a woman who might have been pretty once — fifty pounds ago. It always amazed Paco how fat made features go away … just go away.

"You there," he said to the old lady and made a beckoning gesture. "Come here." The woman looked around to be certain he was indeed talking to her, then she disengaged from the arm of the woman beside her and walked slowly toward him, probably on legs that felt like they wouldn't hold her up. He had felt that way once, the day he'd been herded into Radcliffe Correctional Facility, a fifteen-year-old kid who had no idea what lay in store for him there.

"What's your name?" he asked.

She said something in a voice so soft he couldn't hear.

He raised the gun and pointed it toward her face.

"I said, what's your name?"

She spoke louder this time, but her voice was quaking and she was hard to understand. He thought she said, Lucy Pruitt.

"Well, Lucy …" He sauntered over to her. She stood with her eyes forward and he walked around her in a circle slowly, then came to stand where he could reach out and put the gun on her forehead. "I need to know something, Lucy, and you're going to tell me."

"I'll tell you whatever … just don't…" She looked

at the fallen monk and for a moment Paco was afraid she was going to faint.

"I will not harm you in any way if you tell me what I want to know. Where is it? The thing Noah designed that deflects the death rays of the Astrals?"

She looked at him like he'd just grown a third eye.

"I don't know what you're … what thing? I don't know of anything Noah—" He took a step back because he didn't want to splatter even more blood on his uniform and pulled the trigger. Lucy Pruitt fell to the ground like a sack of potatoes and now the crowd was seriously freaked out. Women were crying, trying to shush their children, men were grumbling. Fear washed over the people like wind through wheat.

Why wouldn't they tell him? Two people dead and nothing.

"Where is Noah?" he called out to the crowd and several people were more than happy to provide that piece off information.

"… at Matheson Caverns."

"… he and his father—"

"… be there all day."

Paco remembered a cave of some kind. Noah had been there on Astral Day, got lost in it. What the fuck was he doing in a cave now?

"Where's Star?"

Again, the answer came from several sources, all saying the same thing.

"Bardstown."

"She's handing out guidebooks—"

"They're checking people in and she's helping—"

"—won't be back until late this afternoon."

Paco had seen a sign that said "Bardstown, 30 miles" when he had ridden into Jessup.

So these people *could* answer questions. Were eager to answer questions, just not the one he wanted answered.

A wave of blind fury swept over him.

"Where's the motherfucking shield?" he screamed in a voice that didn't even sound like his own. It was too high-pitched and strained.

He shot a monk in the chest.

"Where is it?"

The crowd was in a panic, people on the front turned to run but there was nowhere to run with his men surrounding them. One guard smacked a man in the head with the butt of his rifle. All the guards were pointing their rifles at the people, ready for a command to mow them down.

"Dammit — *where*?" Paco shrieked, and knew he sounded like a little boy throwing a tantrum but he couldn't help it.

He heard a sound then that came from a distance, the sound of an engine racing, like a dirt bike cranking, but it was gone almost as fast as it came. Clearly, somebody'd had the good judgment to run. The rest of these stupid cows would soon wish they'd had the same foresight.

Lifting his pistol, he fired indiscriminately into the crowd, in a blinding rage that turned everything he looked at red. Not aiming — people dropped, others cried out and rushed away from the victims. Paco

The Hidden

pulled the trigger again and again until ... the hammer clicked. He ejected the magazine — not "clip." That was a Hollywood word. Ammo was loaded into magazines — and he reached into his pocket for another one, jammed it home. The act of reloading centered him. This was getting him nowhere. If fear of getting shot wouldn't shake the answers loose, what would?

And then he knew.

He needed to get them all together in a small space, where everybody could see him and he could see them.

"Where is somewhere you can put everybody — I want to talk to all of you at once, where?"

Someone shouted out "the cafeteria," but most peopled called out, "the gym."

He turned to Lamont Saunders, one of his captains. "Herd these cattle into the gym." Paco had to get information and he didn't have time to go through the crowd one person at a time blowing their heads off.

You're not seriously considering ...

Himself was so shocked he couldn't even form the question. For some reason that struck Paco as uproariously funny and he burst out laughing. Some of the crowd looked at him, and so did some of his men. He had seen a couple of them looking at him in an odd way lately. Like maybe they thought there was something wrong with him.

He slipped quietly into Saunders's mind.

... asshole's losing it ...

"Think I'm going nuts, do you, Lamont?" he asked.

The look on Saunders's face was absolutely priceless, so comical that Paco almost laughed out loud again. But he didn't, needed to tone that behavior down. Leadership was a delicate thing even when you had your troops totally under your thumb. Instead, he pointed the pistol at Saunders and fired. His aim was a little off, though, and instead of blowing off the top of his head, the bullet caught him in the face.

The terror that wafted his way from his men coupled with the crowd's collective gasp/groan was impressive.

But he hadn't killed the man, had merely ripped off his nose and jaw, and he dropped to his knees, gushing blood, holding onto what was left of his face with both hands.

Paco raised the pistol … no, his former captain was a better object lesson alive.

"Leave him," he told the other guards, not that one of them had made any attempt whatsoever to go to his aid. "Now, where's this gym?"

Surely, you don't intend to ...? Himself began.

Shut the fuck up!

Chapter Thirty-Six

Sawyer looked up when he heard the whine of the jet ski coming down the river. Whoever was driving it was flying, needed to slow down. The jet ski operated by sucking water up from the bottom and squirting it out the back end. It was temperamental; get into water too shallow and it would suck up mud and debris that would stop up the motor.

He tented his hand to shade his eyes as he watched for the craft to appear and saw it fly around a corner. Derek Roberts was driving it. He was easy to identify, was tall and kept his hair long, in a ponytail. He'd been the little boy Noah had held hands with on Astral Day before he let go so he could take a leak ... and then got lost in the cave. Derek knew better than to treat the machine like that. It was all they had to travel back and forth up the river—

As soon as Derek was close enough for Sawyer to see his face, rebukes died on his lips.

Sawyer, Nick Wilson, Noah and Howard Thomas,

who'd been one of the rangers the day Noah'd gotten separated from the other Zion Academy students, were working with a crew at the dock at the cave entrance where the Twin Forks River flowed into the cavern. The dock and attendant elevators had been pressed back into service when they'd decided to shelter in the caverns to escape the Astral flood. No one had used them in years. When Matheson Caverns was a tourist attraction before Astral Day, one of its features had been to provide a dock where boaters could park their boats and tour the caverns before they traveled down the Twin Forks River through the cave and out the other side. In the summertime, the dock and boat lines were jammed. They'd installed four elevators. One of them carried people up to the other four levels of the cave, the second carried returning visitors back down to the dock. The other two elevators carried freight up into the caverns — food for the cafeteria, equipment and laborers working on the grand Carnegie Hall "auditorium" on Level One.

Now those elevators carried people and supplies into Noah's Ark. Two of them were still reserved for human cargo, transporting residents of Zion Village up to the caverns above. The other two hauled the mammoth amount of supplies that would be necessary to sustain them. There had been a nonstop flow of people and supplies in a frenzy since Noah'd outlined his plan for hiding there on Day Two.

On the other side of Joppa Ridge, where the Twin Forks River exited the caverns, was another entrance that had been set aside for human cargo. There was no elevator on that side, however. People coming to take shelter in the cave through the Cricket Bottom entrance would have to climb the spiral staircase that stretched from the river, through the bottom of Level Four of the caverns that was about two hundred feet above the river and then up to the caverns above. The staircase terminated in Level One nine hundred feet above.

Derek flew into the dock, yanking the handlebars of the ski hard left so it would slide like a slalom skier at the foot of a hill. It was a maneuver that produced a spray of water, which was usually the intent. Derek wasn't trying to drench anybody today, though, had just been going too fast to stop any other way. The water flew up from the ski, splashed the workers standing on the edge of the dock, then Derek killed the engine, leapt off the machine and began to sign frantically.

Derek was not completely deaf, but had only about twenty-five percent of normal hearing. It wasn't only Noah who had worked hard at lip reading — all the deaf "kids" had. It was just that Noah had instant feedback, because he could hear what the person said in Star's mind, and that helped him refine his lip-reading ability and his speech far more than any of the others could.

But Derek was speaking, too, as he signed, and the sputtered words and half-formed signs were hard to follow. Clearly, something horrible had happened at Zion Village.

"... with soldiers ... shot people ... motorcycles

—" Then he spotted Nick Wilson and he went pale. Nick had been one of the stranded who'd come to Zion when it was no longer an academy for deaf children, and over the years living with the deaf, he had learned some sign, but he wasn't in any way proficient. Clearly, Derek was thinking about that because he signed the next part quickly, hoping it would go past Nick.

"He ran over Josie. She's dead," Derek signed.

Sawyer and Noah exchanged a horrified look.

Nick caught the last part.

"Who's dead?" he asked.

Sawyer took hold of Derek's shoulders and spoke right into his face, didn't bother to sign it.

"You have to slow down and tell us what happened. You're not making any sense."

"The village has been ... *attacked*. Some men came, the leader was on a motorcycle." He paused a beat on that before he continued and Sawyer knew that was who had run over Josie. "There were other motorcycles, too, and trucks. Men in uniforms with guns jumped out of the trucks and everybody was taken prisoner and he shot Brother Luke and Lucy Pruitt, killed both of them when they wouldn't tell him what he wanted to know and then I sneaked away and got the ski."

Lucy! An old woman who wouldn't hurt a fly. And Brother Luke.

Sawyer tried to absorb the blows and stay focused ... but *Lucy*?

The young man had said the whole thing in one,

long, breathless sentence, signing it so fast that only an expert could have followed it.

"Uniforms?" Nick asked. "What kind of uniforms? Like soldiers, you mean?"

"Yes, like soldiers. The trucks had this symbol on the sides and all the soldiers had an insignia on their right shoulders. It was a skull, and there was a spider crawling out of one eye socket—"

"—and a snake crawling out the other," Noah finished for him, with no color at all in his face. "Paco."

"Who's Paco?" Howard Thomas wanted to know. Sawyer already knew, and he could tell by the distant look in Noah's eyes that he was talking to Star about it.

Star was on the other side of the cave, at the front entrance where the road ended in a parking lot, with Taylor, his wife and his two sons. She was working with a crew that included Brother Sebastian and some of the other monks, handing out cave fliers to the people who'd come to that entrance to enter the cavern, had set up shop under the "Bardstown" awning in the parking lot.

It was the closest to the cave entrance.

"Paco wouldn't do a thing like that," Noah said, and Sawyer knew he was repeating aloud what Star had just said to him.

"Yes he would, Star. You know he would."

Noah spoke to those who could hear, explaining.

"Paco was with Star and me. When we were abducted and taken up into the mothership, he was there, too. There was some kind of connection between the three of us. Star and I ..." He let that dangle off. Everyone knew about the two of them. "But for a month before Astral Day, she and I were dreaming about that symbol." He gestured to Derek. "We saw a white skull with a spider crawling out one eye socket and a snake out the other. When we got to the mothership, Paco was there, no shirt on, and that was his tattoo, on his chest, the thing we'd been dreaming about. It was more than a tattoo, though. The images were formed by scar tissue, where his chest had been ... cut up. He said he had been dreaming about us, too. And the three of us were the only kids on the ship, at least the only ones we knew about, so we became, you know, a team."

"So why is he—?" Sawyer began.

"I don't know what's going on. Paco was a street kid from Los Angeles. He was a petty criminal, juvenile crimes, and he was in the Scared Straight Program, and he and some other boys got caught and trapped in a prison on Astral Day." Noah took a breath. "Terrible things happened to him there."

"You're still not answering my question," Nick prodded. "Why's he doing this?"

"I don't know, but he and Star and I ... something went wrong. It's too long to tell you now, but ... Paco thought we betrayed him, that it was the two of us against him. That's how it ended. We were never able to straighten it out with him because we were returned to Earth before we had a chance."

The Hidden

Sawyer was still trying to put it together, reeling from the information Nick didn't even have yet.

"Star and I were returned to the spots where we were taken so he probably was, too, which means he's been in California all this time."

Sawyer felt chilled. "Building an army."

"What does he want?" Nick demanded. "Why here, why now?"

"When we were in the mothership, the three of us could talk inside each other's heads like Star and I do now. But after we were returned. Just Star and I. Paco couldn't …"

"It's no coincidence he showed up here right now," Nick said. "Somehow, he knows. He knows the Astrals are going to destroy the earth, and he's here because we have a way out."

Derek burst in then.

"He killed Brother Luke and Lucy when they wouldn't tell him what he wanted to know, asked them, 'Where's Noah's shield?' He wanted to know where was the thing you built that would repel the death rays of the aliens."

"That doesn't make any—" Sawyer began.

"Yes it does," Noah said. "He must just know about the judgement, but apparently doesn't know *how* it's going to happen. If he somehow connected to Star or me, knows we have a way to escape the judgment, that'd be the first thing you'd think, wouldn't it? If you knew the Astrals planned to annihilate humanity, you'd assume they'd do it the way they've been killing off people ever since they got here — with those rays like when they destroyed Moscow and New York."

"So he doesn't know about the flood, doesn't understand about the cave," Nick said. "He thinks you built some kind of shield to protect you from the death rays, and he's here to take it away from you."

"What are we going to do?" Ranger Thomas said.

"We have to get those people out of there. Josie's there with her aunt, and Eagle Feather—"

"Nick …" Sawyer didn't think there had ever been a time in his life that he less wanted to say what he had to say. But Nick had to know.

"What …?" Nick was quick. "What is it? Josie … *what?*"

"Nick, I'm sorry. There is no way to say this but just to say it. Derek said Paco … killed Josie."

Nick took the news like a blow to the belly. All the air whooshed out of him and he staggered back. His face went colorless, and he was shaking his head "no" though he probably wasn't even aware.

"What … how … why *Josie?*"

"Derek saw him kill her." Sawyer wouldn't tell him how unless he demanded to know, but gratefully, he didn't. He was barely upright.

"We have to do something quick," Howard Thomas said. "This guy's crazy, no telling what he'll do to the rest of those people."

Nick was barely tracking, his mind still hammered with the news.

"What *can* we do?" Noah looked to his father. The sheriff. The lawman. And Nick, the Navy SEAL. Two formidable adversaries under other circumstances. But right now …

"We don't have any weapons," Sawyer said. Zion Village counted on the sophisticated surveillance system installed to guard the academy to warn them of danger. They had an armory and Sawyer had trained a contingent of villagers as "deputies." But nobody was thinking about that now. Their survival depended on getting the ark loaded and hiding inside. They'd moved some of the guns to the cave, would eventually move them all, but weapons weren't as high a priority as food. And Sawyer wasn't a hundred percent sure where the weapons had been stored in the ark.

"Taylor has deer rifles at his house," Sawyer said. His brother and nephews were crack shots. His wife, Kelly Jo, might be the best shot of the lot. Deer were most active in the early morning and late afternoon hours, the times she could come outside and count on shade instead of sunlight. But Taylor's house was on the other side of the cave at the front entrance by the road. No way to get to the weapons quickly.

Nick had gotten his breath back, and there was steel in his voice.

"Then we go in unarmed," Nick said. "And find us some weapons once we get there."

Chapter Thirty-Seven

STAR HAD JUST HANDED out a Matheson Caverns brochure to Chad Langhorn and his wife, Millie. They were in their early twenties, no children, and had spent time in the caverns when they were children. They figured they ought to let older people use the elevators on the other side of the mountain to get into the ark. They'd climb the stairs, said they planned to go all the way to the top, through the Tripoli Cavern on Level Three, the Wiggle Room Cavern on Level Two, all the way into Smiley Face on Level One.

Noah suddenly cried out in her head.

The village has been attacked. And I think it's

Then his mind filled with the image of Paco's tattoo, the skull with the spider crawling out of one eye socket and the snake out of the other.

Paco?

That's the insignia on the trucks, the troops. Has to be Paco.

Why would Paco—?

He killed Josie Wilson.

Star gasped.

Ran over her with a motorcycle.

Paco wouldn't do a thing like that.

Maybe the Paco we knew wouldn't, but this is somebody else entirely.

Star considered how much she and Noah had changed in the seven years since their abduction by the aliens. Clearly, the intervening years had changed Paco, too, hardened him, made him into the adult that loomed out there in the edges of his imagination. She'd caught glimpses of that person in Paco's mind, a mean, dangerous man that she watched Paco alternately fight against and then embrace.

The mean man had won.

What are you going—?

We're going there, Dad, Nick, Howard Thomas and I. Try to rescue …

But you said there were hundreds of armed soldiers. How can you—?

We'll find a way.

Then Noah was gone. He was no longer speaking to her, his mind engaged in other activities that she could have watched if she had wanted to but the thought didn't enter her mind, not after seven years of "speaking when spoken to" courtesy developed by two people privy to each other's most private thoughts.

"What's wrong?" asked Sophie Sunderland, speaking in the flat, nasal tones of someone who was at least partially deaf. She was one of Noah's classmates at Zion Academy. Her mother had been a

The Hidden

Vermont senator, but after Astral Day, Sophie never saw her again.

Star couldn't seem to get her breath. The silence inside her head, that had been broken so suddenly when Noah called out to her, now had returned with a pressure like a bomb. Her mouth had gone dry, so dry it seemed, that opening her mouth would require a literal pulling her tongue away from her palate.

"We've been ... Zion Village has been attacked." Star both spoke and signed the words to Sophie. Star was better at signing than any of the people in Zion Village who could hear — because she had learned how inside Noah's head.

She could hear only her heart now, nothing else, not fast, but sledgehammer heavy, pounding and pounding in her chest, slamming blood around her body, into her brain. The doors to a thousand fears flew open in her mind and panic began to well up in—

She remembered that feeling. Listening to the gunfire as she raced through the darkness with Pumpkin, looking for somewhere to hide. And then, in the silence that eventually followed, trying to find Uncle Clyde, growing more and more terrified every second when he didn't answer her calls. And in the featureless room in the mothership, when the reality of it hit home. She had been abducted by aliens — the panic had overwhelmed her then and she had curled up in a ball, sobbing.

And it had been Paco who came into her mind, trying to reassure her. Noah, too, but it was Paco at first. Then she'd seen the tattoo on his chest through Noah's eyes, knew he was the one who had been linked to her, to her and the blond boy, by her dreams.

This was it!

This was the bad thing Star had sensed coming. She had known it was something other than the impending flood, even laughed self-consciously at herself for believing she was afraid of something *else* besides the end of the world. But it was this. She had seen it, sensed it coming, and she refused to let that feeling of panic consume her now. She wasn't a child. This was, as Noah called it, adult-ing.

She stood and took hold of Pumpkin's halter. He was right beside her, knew instantly when the fear hit her. Might even have known it before she did.

"I need to go find Taylor," she told Sophie.

"But what's happening … what? Is everybody alright in Zion? Dear God, what will we …"

Star didn't elaborate. Telling Sophie would only send her off into a panic of her own, given that she was something of a drama queen. Star didn't have time to deal with that.

"I don't know any more than that," she lied. "I have to go—"

"I'll take you."

"No, stay here. Keep handing out the fliers." There was nobody right now waiting for them, but Star heard a car pull up into the parking lot. "Please, please, just keep working. I can find Taylor on my own."

Reluctantly, Sophie agreed.

"And don't … don't tell these people about Zion Village. There's nothing they can do and …"

Star realized she was asking the impossible. Sophie couldn't keep the news to herself.

"Find Taylor," she told Pumpkin, then slipped into his mind and watched the amazing process of sorting through the sensory input from the dog's amazing nose to find Taylor, then cycling so fast she couldn't even follow it, Taylor's scent from yesterday and the day before and the—

He pulled her off to the right, toward a large blob she assumed was a pickup truck.

"Taylor!" she cried, and smelled him, too. Oh, not as Pumpkin did, but the rough, masculine scent of him, sweating, and the slight whiff of cinnamon from the toothpicks he always chewed on.

"What's wrong?"

She told him, trying to keep to just the facts as closely as she could. She could tell that all the people around — Sam, Dave and Kelly Jo — had stopped what they were doing and were gathered around to hear what she had to say.

"You know this guy, Paco?" Taylor asked.

"Is he the guy Noah talks about, the one who was with you when you were abducted?" Dave asked.

"It's Paco, but not the Paco we knew." She leaned close to Taylor and he realized what she was about to say was private, and put his ear close to her face.

"Paco killed Josie!" Even though she'd meant to say it quietly, just to Taylor, there was so much emotion in the words, that they burst out of her throat on a strangled sob and everybody heard.

"Josie!"

"Why?"

"How could anybody—?"

Taylor silenced them all. "This stays right here, do you understand? Until Nick gets back to …"

Then Taylor realized he hadn't heard the remainder of the story. "Where are Nick and Sawyer and Noah?"

So Star told him, told all of them.

"They're going to fight an army? With what? A knife and a tire iron?"

Taylor straightened, told his boys, "Get the rifles out of the house. It'll take us—"

"No! Sawyer wants you to stay here. He says if you come charging in, they'll mow you down."

"I'm not going to sit here on my hands—"

"Noah said to tell you that you're a weapon Paco won't know about. He said they needed to use that weapon as a surprise."

Taylor let out a whoosh of air. "Get the guns, boys. We need to be ready."

The two young men ran down the path into the cave.

"Noah said that Derek told them there were hundreds of men, all of them in uniform, like soldiers, with handguns and rifles."

"Dammit!" Taylor swore, in rage and frustration. He took a couple of breaths, then turned back to Star. "How did this Paco dude know—?"

"Noah doesn't know. He only knows what Derek told them. His dad sent Derek into the cave by the river entrance to warn the people in the ark."

"You'll tell me when ... if—" he began.

"Of course," she said. Then Taylor went off in the direction his sons had gone and Star stood alone on the path with Pumpkin, snuggled right up against her side, knowing she was scared.

And she was scared. So scared she was afraid she might lose her breakfast.

Chapter Thirty-Eight

Paco stood on the gym floor watching the citizens of Zion Village file in. They were a random grab of people, young and old, grownups and children and more than a hundred of the brown-robed monks.

He had sent his men out to scour the property, and bring back anybody they found. Anybody. He figured most everybody had come when they rang that idiot ding-dong bell, that they were gathered around Paco when he'd done his interrogation of the crowd, but he didn't want to miss anybody, didn't want somebody wandering around behind his back.

He saw the women he'd sent away with the mother of the little girl he'd killed, leading her into the gym. She was a mess, barely holding onto hysteria. But she had two other little kids holding onto her, so she'd likely keep it together for their sakes. He hoped so. If she interrupted him, he would kill her.

His men had scared up a number of people who

were working in the barns way up on the back of the property, or in the fields around the farm. People who were busy and hadn't dashed to answer the summons of the bell. A couple of farmer types had on muddy work boots that tracked up the gym floor when they entered. Not that it mattered.

As soon as he flipped on the lights in the cavernous gymnasium, he saw the mess on the floor, dried paint all over it. A big blob of black paint but other colors, too. It might have been some kind of picture, a landscape maybe, but why they would paint the thing on the top of a perfectly good gym floor was beyond him.

He watched the people's faces, let his mind skim out across theirs. Not digging deep, just skimming. He'd learned how to do that when he projected his mind out beyond his home in Tahoe, to skim the minds of the people he passed over, get some sense of what was going on with them, but nothing specific. He sometimes wondered if what he was doing, the information he could gather was similar to what the Astrals intercepted with their stupid rocks and stone circles.

The first time he'd gone anywhere near one of those was when he'd moved his encampment from California, after the near miss on Black Monday, into a safer place in Tahoe. There had been a line of stones set up in the forest. He'd heard about them, but had never seen one. As soon as he got near it, his mind-reading ability soared. Suddenly, he could hear the thoughts of everybody anywhere near him, and it was a cacophony he couldn't turn off. Like being in the room with a hundred people, all talking at the same time. He had quickly retreated from the stones, but the heightened ability lasted for several days. It was maddening.

He had entertained the thought at the time — wouldn't it be great if he could lay his hands on a rock, only one rock, and use it like those things that boosted sound, maybe a cell phone repeater tower. He'd even gone so far as to send his men out to get him one, but they had returned empty-handed. They said the stones were way bigger than they appeared to be, that what you could see on the surface was like an iceberg, with ten percent showing and ninety percent underground. Those rocks weren't going anywhere.

What he got from skimming the minds of these people was fear, fear as big and black as a boogie man in the closet. Fear of him, but fear of impending doom. They must have been told about the Astrals' plan to wipe out humanity — of course they had, and they knew their only hope of survival was Noah's Shield. That's why they wouldn't tell him about it. Oh, he scared them, alright, but the thought of being zapped out of existence apparently scared them more and they wouldn't even think about the shield.

Paco had been systematically narrowing down his army as he traveled the two thousand miles from California to Kentucky. He'd dropped off civilians all along the route as the vehicles carrying them ran out of gas, a few hundred here, a few hundred there. He'd come back for them once he'd secured the shield …

sure he would. He'd roared into Jessup with a five-hundred-man, lean-and-mean army. He left four hundred of them there … he'd come back for them once he'd secured the shield in Zion Village … sure he would.

Riiiiiiight.

Paco knew that whatever their shield thing was, or building or dome or whatever, it couldn't possibly be big enough to accommodate thousands of people under it. And he had no intention of being part of a crowd. Whatever was there, Paco meant for it to shelter him and a few handpicked people. He would go back and fetch some of the civilians he'd left in the ghost town of Jessup — certainly didn't plan to occupy a whole new world without any women at his side, and the ones he'd brought with him from California, and a couple he'd snared along the way, were definitely the pick of any litter. But the rest of the left-behinds … they'd be reduced to black dust. And Paco would only shed tears for them if the black dust happened to blow into his eyes.

The crowd had filed in to fill the gym, directed to the bleachers on one side so Paco could face them all, make eye contact with everyone at the same time.

Paco had posted guards all around the property. Not really because he thought there were people there he hadn't located who would come out with guns and go to battle with him. He had to give his men something to do. They needed to feel like they had a purpose. That was just good leadership. Leaving them standing around, idle … no, that's when doubts surfaced. And a doubt in a group of men would take root and sprout fast if they hauled it out and started talking about it, discussing it. Then they'd betray him.

He held no illusions about the loyalty of his men. They served him because he scared the shit out of them. And because they knew if they didn't, if they doubted or started some kind of mutiny, he would know it before they ever got the plans put together.

In the beginning, he'd had them convinced he was in cahoots with the Astrals, that the aliens were reading their minds and telling Paco what they were thinking. Over the years he disabused them of that notion. He gradually let it be known that the Astrals had taught their trusted ally Paco Salazar how to read minds. They didn't understand how the process worked, probably assumed he was listening in to every thought of every one of his minions all the time. Which was fine with him. Let them think that. But when push came to shove, and it would do that as soon as he found the shield, their loyalty would go poof without even the tiny sparkle of a soap bubble and it would be every man for himself. He would deal with them then the same way he intended to deal with all these people who were planning to hide out under Noah's Shield while the rest of humanity was annihilated. He'd do his own annihilating, narrow the number so that the tiny bit of humanity that would be spared the Astrals' judgement would be small indeed.

His mind flashed to Duddits. Paco should have brought him along. It'd been a mistake to leave him behind in Tahoe. Duddits's devotion was genuine. He should have been among the people Paco had selected to live on an empty planet with him for the rest of his life. As he watched the crowd, he decided he'd make room for a handful of women from the village — he'd seen two teenage girls who looked sweet and a young mother nursing a baby — literally had her tit out and the kid was sucking at it. But the tit was round and full and so was the other one and it excited him. They'd stay big like that, wouldn't they, when he got rid of the baby and she couldn't empty them. They would, he was sure of it.

He'd thought that requiring people to use only one set of bleachers would jam up a crowd there. But there was no crowd. Apparently, there weren't as many residents of Zion Village as he'd thought. Only about a thousand people sat before him when he stepped out into the middle of the floor onto the big blob of black paint and looked the crowd over.

Himself knew then.

You're going to become … what? Do you realize how danger—?

He wasn't about to get into an argument right now with a person who didn't exist. Yes, he understood the risks. When he had pushed that whole crowd of people to demand Spade's death on the great day of wood chipper annihilation, it had left him barely able to function afterward. He couldn't afford that now.

After that, he'd taught himself how to "become" something in a person's mind. Something that terrified them. He'd only done it on a limited scale, but the resulting terror and instant obedience such a display created made it one of the best mental tools in his arsenal. Today, he wasn't going to become a thing, like before. He was going to become flashes of lots of things, images that came and went, like a kaleidoscope of horror. What had been so draining was creating an entity in people's minds and maintaining it, making it real for ... what had it been the last time, half an hour, maybe longer?

He'd never tried what he was about to try. But it was his best option. He had to become to these people something way worse than being reduced to black dust. He had to scare them so badly that death by vaporization would look like a peaceful die-in-your-sleep way to go.

He stood quietly, focusing his attention. He'd plucked images from half a dozen minds and would use stock ones everyone would fear. Every eye in the gym was riveted on him, including the eyes of the four soldiers he'd brought in with him. Two of them stood on either side of him like bodyguards, rifles at the ready. Two others stood on the empty side of the gym, facing the crowd — one on each side of the visiting team's benches. The guards were perhaps more focused than the villagers because they knew what to expect, and hadn't seen "fearless leader" do any transformations in years.

"Let's get something clear right now." Paco said, and what little murmur of voices there had been instantly died, leaving the cavernous room silent. "I can, and if I have to, I will, kill every one of you. You have something I want. Information. And unless you give—"

Suddenly a young woman who was seated on the lowest row of the bleachers in front of him leapt to her feet, and pointed at the other side of the gym and started screaming.

Chapter Thirty-Nine

Sawyer piloted the jet ski upriver, pegging the throttle, but unable to get any real speed. It wasn't far, though. Still, every second counted. He looked back over his shoulder at the raft he was pulling along behind, where Noah, Nick and Howard Thomas had climbed aboard as soon as they'd unloaded the supplies off it. Sawyer had left Derek behind, not because the young man couldn't fight — he was the same age as Noah, though Noah appeared decades older than his biologic years. He needed Derek to go into the caves that were accessed by the river entrance and tell the people there what was going on. The people by the front entrance knew everything Sawyer knew, because Star was there. But those in chambers accessed by the other entrances had no idea the village was under attack.

They needed to know there was danger. Right now, the men and women he'd trained as deputies over the years were scattered all over Zion. Some of them were already in the caverns, others were still in town loading up. If Sawyer could have contacted them, they might have been able to lay hands on some weapons, but it wasn't likely. Paco had roared into town and taken everybody by surprise. The people in the caves would at least have a warning so they could hide in the miles of passages that stretched and spaghetti-ed out under the sandstone cap rock. In the few days they'd had to prepare for the move into the caverns, the people from Zion hadn't had much time to familiarize themselves with the caverns they'd be occupying. That's why they were distributing maps and brochures from the old Matheson Caverns tours — but with warning, they could vanish back into the shadows.

Paco didn't know about the cave — yet. As soon as he figured out there was no such thing as a shield, he would march on Matheson Caverns like Sherman taking Atlanta, and the only hope for the people inside was hiding.

He and the others — Noah, Nick, Howard Thomas — had little more than a vague plan.

There were weapons at various locations in Zion Village. Sawyer had rifles, hand guns and ammunition in cases in his office — which was in the old academy building. There was the academy arsenal, still in the same room off the main hallway that it'd been when Dr. Weiss armed the children to fight off the townies. The door was locked and Brother Sebastian would have a key. Whether or not they'd be able to get to those weapons would depend on how Paco had positioned his troops. Were they trained soldiers? Sawyer didn't know, but he was certain they were more formidable adversaries than the townies who'd tried to take over in the past. It was just that *right now* everything was in a turmoil ... Zion Village had been caught with its pants down.

Nick kept a pistol out of sight under the workbench in the monastery woodshed where he'd crafted the bomb to blow up the Astrals' entrance. The detonator for the charges they'd planted around the entrance of the cave yesterday, was *still in the workshop.* They had to get it to the ark ... how could they do that now?

As soon as Sawyer rounded the bend in the river where you could see the dock on the back side of Zion Village, he cut the engine on the jet ski and let it coast noiselessly into shore. With hand signals, he motioned to Nick and the others that there was a guy in a uniform on the dock. A guard, apparently, though he had been digging into the supplies still stacked there, stuffing his pockets full of something, hadn't even looked up at the sound of the jet ski's engine.

The thee raft riders got off and waded to shore on the village side of the river and Sawyer beached the jet ski on the sandy riverbank. Then they made their way carefully through the woods toward the village. It was worse than Sawyer'd feared. When Derek had said there were troop carriers full of men, he'd thought ten to a dozen per truck. Add those to a handful of motorcycle riders and the force opposing them was about forty or fifty men. But the trucks were the kind that could carry thirty soldiers each. Paco had brought with him an army of more than a hundred men, and he and the others could see them stationed as guards around every building on the property, spaced within sight of each other, so there was no way to grab one and take their weapon.

Paco's army was well equipped. Their uniforms were impressive, with the crest you couldn't make out on their breasts and regulation black army boots. The soldiers he could see all carried sidearms in matching black holsters, as well as rifles, looked like M82s they must have taken from a military installation somewhere.

The four of them crouched behind a bush and signed a silent conversation.

Not a single building we can get into unnoticed.

Where is everybody? Noah signed. The others could hear a kind of crowd sound from the gym, which took up the whole south end of the academy building. There were big doors on the front of the gym and a side door on the side of the gym that faced inside toward the circular driveway. There were neither doors nor windows on the back side of the gym that faced the rock wall.

He's gathered them all in the gym.

Then that's where Paco is, Nick signed awkwardly, then just whispered the rest. "We go after *him*."

It wasn't just revenge talking, though the rage in the man's voice was even audible in a whisper. If they could capture Paco, he'd have to call off all his dogs. The four made their way carefully toward the old academy building, set behind an old rock wall, where David Weiss had dropped Oscar Higgins with one shot. There was corn in the field, tall enough to shield them as they passed behind the sheep pens, chicken coops and the barn with a milking parlor where the monks milked their dairy herd. They made cheese and butter inside the walls of the monastery buildings.

They continued to communicate silently in sign language when they got within sight of the rock wall surrounding the academy. Sawyer motioned for Noah to take the lead, and he led them through the passageway beneath the wall he'd crawled through when he smelled "gasoline" and knew Star was in trouble seven years before.

There are at least half a dozen guards out front, Sawyer signed. Hidden in the bushes beside the wall, they didn't have a direct sightline to the front door itself. All he could see were the soldiers standing outside the gym.

Look. Nick gestured rather than signed and pointed to the low windows near the ground on the back of the gym. The boys' and girls' locker rooms in the gym were in the basement. And they opened onto the rest of the gym.

"We get inside through the locker rooms, then overpower some guards to get their weapons," Nick whispered.

It was a painfully inadequate plan. They hadn't seen any guards they could disarm out guarding the buildings — how could they possibly expect to do so inside the gym itself? Sawyer started to protest, but backed down from the fire in Nick's eyes. If they could get the drop on Paco himself here …

Truth was, Sawyer didn't have a better idea.

Their only hope was finding isolated guards they could pick off with their paltry weapons. Sawyer's knife, a Bowie knife but not near as big or sharp as the one Eagle Feather carried. He'd been using it to cut the tie-downs off the goods floated downstream on the rafts. Nick had nothing but a tire iron they'd been using to break open the wooden boxes the monks had stored cheese in. Noah and Howard Thomas had no weapons at all.

They backed down the wall until they couldn't be seen crossing the side yard to the building by the guards outside the front door of the gym. One by one they Groucho-walked, a running-squat so named for some comedian Sawyer had never heard of, from the concealing bushes to the back wall, flattened against it and edged toward the front until they were beside the ground-level windows.

Sawyer tried to open a window. It was locked. He crawled to the next one, locked, too. It would make far too much noise to break the glass. He inched close to the last window, which was close to the front of the building where a guard was lazily leaned against the wall smoking a cigarette.

Smoking a cigarette. Sawyer hadn't seen a cigarette in … five years? Six? Paco's army was, indeed *well equipped*. But well trained …? Sawyer doubted it. They were playing soldier. They might have practiced at a shooting range, but these men were clearly not a disciplined unit of career soldiers.

For all the good that did Sawyer.

He pushed on the window and it swung easily inward. He turned around backward and lowered himself into the building feet first. He had to let go and drop the final couple of feet to the floor, but he didn't make a sound. Noah was next. It was really hard for Noah to "be quiet." He couldn't hear any sound he might be making, so he could easily try to sneak up on somebody with a clanging keychain on his belt. But he made no noise as he entered. Then Thomas. Nick brought up the rear. As soon as he was inside, Nick reached up and eased the window closed again.

The room still smelled of old sneakers and sweaty gym socks. Even after all these years. There hadn't been a "team" of any kind playing any sport since Astral Day. Life stopped being a game forever then, and the humanity that would have sold its soul to win the Super Bowl or snag gold at the Olympics vanished in a heartbeat, courtesy of white giants and blue-eyed monsters with needle teeth.

There were two locker rooms located in the basement of the building, the home team's and the one for visitors. They sat side-by-side beneath the bleachers on the "Away" team's side of the gym. There was a door between the two, but it was likely to be locked. Each of the locker rooms had a door on the far end that led to short steps up to the level of the gym floor.

Sawyer went to the door that joined the locker rooms. It was unlocked.

He turned and gave a thumbs-up to the others. Then Sawyer went to one of the locker room doors leading up to the gym and Nick went to the other. Each of them eased their door open a crack, looked out, closed the door and met back with the others.

Nick reported in a whisper. "Nobody's in the bleachers on this side. The whole crowd is on the other side of the gym. So the guy" — Sawyer could tell Nick couldn't even stand to say Paco's name — "is facing them with his back to us."

"Three guards that I could see," Sawyer said. "Two are standing back from him, facing the crowd, and the other one is on this side, about fifteen feet down from the door — also facing the crowd."

"*Four* guards," Nick amended. "There's another one standing about twenty feet down from that door, too."

Sawyer and Nick looked at each other.

Two guards on this side, both armed.

"We could wait … who knows why he hauled everybody in here, but if he lets the crowd leave, that's a lot of people to guard and these guys will be focused on them," Nick said.

"Why'd he bring all these people in here?" Thomas asked.

"Paco wants everybody bunched together so he can keep them corralled," Sawyer speculated.

"So he can kill one after another until they tell him

what he wants to know," Nick spoke the words as he thought them.

Much as Sawyer didn't like to admit it, he agreed. If they waited, Paco'd start hurting people. They needed to act before he had a chance.

"The two guards on this side, they're looking the other way, and we have the element of surprise — I say you and I take them both out at the same time," Nick said.

It had to be Sawyer and Nick, of course. However willing Noah and Thomas might have been, he and Nick had been trained for this. They hadn't.

"Two of us trying to take out two guards." Sawyer shook his head. "Timing would have to be perfect — soon as one of us makes a move, we're alerting all of them. I say we take just *one* shot, take out one of the guards on this side." He pointed to the door he'd been looking out. "This guard is closer."

"You slit his throat, grab his weapon," Nick said. "I make my move ten seconds after you do, take out the other guard as he's reacting to your attack on the first guard."

"There are more holes in that plan than a wino's raincoat," Sawyer said. "Either one of us gets spotted before we get to the guard …"

"The other guards behind Paco are going to open fire, unless we drop them instantly," Nick said.

"Lots of moving parts," Sawyer said. "And we have to take Paco alive." He knew Nick wouldn't like that part. "Get him to make his men lay down their arms. We blow him away, it might just turn into a shootout … in which case, we're kinda outgunned."

"Fine. Take him alive. Soon as the others surrender … he's *mine!*" The boiling rage in Nick Wilson's eyes was staggering.

"You guys know what you're doing, and I hate to point out the obvious," Thomas said. "But the people in the stands *are facing this way.* They'll see the doors open. As soon as you start up the steps you'll be in plain sight — they'll see you."

Sawyer shrugged. "No way around that. They'll see us and *recognize* us. All we can do is hope they have sense enough not to give us away."

Nick and Sawyer stood there then, looking at each other. They both knew the harebrained scheme had like zero chance of success. If either of the guards on this side chanced to glance sideways … if anybody in the stands saw them and gawked, and the guards looking at the crowd turned to see what they were looking at …

It was what it was. Just a shot. But it was all they had.

Sawyer nodded at Nick and the other man turned and headed into the other locker room. Sawyer eased his door open a crack. He saw Nick do the same. Then he put all his focus on the man he could see about twenty feet away, watching the goings-on in the middle of the gym, where Paco had begun to speak.

"Let's get something clear right now," Paco said, and his deep baritone voice echoed in the cavernous space. All eyes were focused on him. Good.

Sawyer eased the door open, and creeped out, didn't close it behind him.

"I can, and if I have to, I *will*, kill every one of you." Paco's voice was as cold as a shark in a polar ocean.

Sawyer started up the steps, crouched low, knife out, still partially hidden from the man with the gun.

"You have something I want — information. And unless you give—"

Just one more step and Sawyer would—

"Stop him," cried a woman's voice from the other side of the gym, from among the villagers. "He's trying to kill my mother!"

Chapter Forty

SOMETHING WASN'T RIGHT. Suddenly, an image rose in the minds of the crowd in front of Paco. All of them saw the same thing, men behind—

Then a woman screamed and Paco whipped around and looked where the screaming woman was pointing. A man was standing in the stairwell leading down to an open door, with a knife in his hand. Paco's guard, standing only twenty feet away, raised his rifle—

"Don't shoot," Paco ordered, as his eye caught a second man just outside an open door on the other side of the room, with a tire iron raised. That man leapt at the nearby guard who wasn't as quick as the other had been, brought the metal rod down hard on the rifle the man was raising, knocked it out of his hand and dived for it. The first guard opened fire — not at the leaping man, but at another man a step behind him, caught him in the chest and knocked him back into the stairwell.

"Hold your fire," Paco screeched. The man who'd knocked away the guard's rifle had gotten his hands on it and was rolling over onto his belly, the gun raised toward Paco, ready to fire.

"Tell them to drop their weapons," the man cried, the rifle trained on Paco's chest. "Or you will be dead before you hit the floor."

Paco did nothing, just looked at the man, let the situation settle. The guard who'd shot the man coming up the steps behind him had his rifle trained on the fellow who'd been about to attack him with a knife. The two guards behind Paco had their rifles trained on the lone gunman on the floor, as the guard who'd lost his rifle to the gunman lay stunned a few feet away.

"Don't shoot," Paco said and raised his hands slowly in the air.

"Tell your guards to drop their weapons," the man growled again.

"Listen to me," Paco called out to his men, then spoke quickly. "Johnson, if this man fires, kill him. The rest of you, open fire on the crowd. Empty your weapons into the crowd, shoot to kill, is that understood? Children first."

Paco spoke into the minds of the two guards nearest him, and they both turned their backs to the man on the floor, lifted their rifles and aimed at the crowd.

He looked at the man on the floor, drilled into his mind. He was a remarkably strong man and his mind was closed with staggering rage and hatred.

"Drop your weapon." Then he called out to his men again. "Open fire on the crowd on the count of three and don't stop firing until you run out of ammo. One. Two."

The man on the floor slowly lowered the rifle, and when he did, the guard he'd taken it from grabbed the weapon back and hauled him to his feet.

Paco turned then to the almost forgotten man still holding a knife on the guard who had a rifle pointed at his chest.

"And you, sir ..."

The man dropped the knife. And the woman who had yelled out the warning, began to scream again.

"No, no!" she cried, "you can't *let him go*." Paco noticed what he'd heard before. Her speech had an odd nasal quality, her words flat and almost without inflection. "Shoot him or he'll try again. He'll murder my mother!" She turned her attention to the man then, screamed at him in a toneless voice that nonetheless conveyed a fiery rage. "*I* took her, by myself, last night. I *saved her* so she has time to get well!"

Paco really looked at her for the first time. She was a strikingly pretty girl, early twenties, with long brown hair pulled back in a ponytail that snapped back and forth as she shook her head in rage. He decided on the spot that he'd keep her, along with the other three or four he'd spotted.

"What's your name?" he asked and she totally ignored him, just kept yelling. Ignored ... or didn't hear him. That was it, she was deaf, this place used to be a school for the deaf and he'd seen other people speaking in that sign language. He spoke to the guard nearest him, "I want her. Take her out to the truck."

The guard crossed the gym floor, grabbed the girl and began dragging her out of the room, fighting and screaming.

Paco turned his attention back on the man who'd been hauled to his feet off the floor and to the other—

He suddenly felt like he'd been thumped hard on the head. Not on the head, inside the head. He knew what — no, *who*—

He looked past the man toward the open door behind him where another guard was hauling someone up the steps, a young man with hair so blond it almost looked white. Paco felt hot all over, then cold. He actually began to tremble, inside, deep in his guts but not on the outside where anybody could see it. No, on the outside he was icy calm.

What difference did it make how he looked on the outside? His insides, his mind, were now opened up and he felt a chilling breeze blowing through it.

Noah.

He only spoke the name inside his head, but the young man looked up at him — with those eyes so blue they were almost transparent.

Paco.

Then Paco felt a door close in his face. Noah had … what? Shut his mind? How could he …? But then, Paco had learned a mind trick or two in the years since he'd last seen the boy. Apparently, Noah had, too. He refused to acknowledge that he'd been turned away, behaved as if he wasn't inside Noah's mind because he had other, more important things to think about.

Paco made a gesture and the guards brought the three men to stand in front of him. Paco would not allow his eyes to devour Noah, or let his mind bang uselessly on Noah's until he decided to open up. Instead, he watched for a reaction from Noah to the sight of his old friend Paco.

Paco certainly was not the skinny 16-year-old Latino kid who'd stood with Noah and Star in that white room all those years ago — so scared, holy shit they were so scared. Paco tried to call to mind how he had looked then, but the only image that would form in his mind was the one that greeted him every morning in the mirrors all around his exercise room. He was a hunk, muscled, strong, ripped, stunningly handsome.

Noah just looked at him steadily, showed no emotion whatsoever.

"Want to introduce me to your friends?" Paco said. When Noah continued to look at him, Paco turned mean. "Want me to drag their names out of them — you could watch, it would be entertaining—"

"This is Sawyer and this is Nick," Noah said.

And their minds were not locked up as tight as Noah's was.

"Your father," Paco said, looking at the russet-haired man with the stubble of a red beard who bore almost no resemblance at all to his son. He turned to Nick and felt the rage and hatred again, didn't even have to dig into his mind to find it, you could see it on his face.

The little girl.

Paco felt like he'd been knocked to his knees. In the man's mind was the face of a smiling child, a little girl with Down's syndrome. He wanted to say he was sorry, that he hadn't meant … that he loved the angelic … but he said nothing, just understood and grudgingly respected the man's hatred of him. He had loved that little girl with all his heart and that said something good about him that Paco acknowledged.

My, my but aren't we getting sentimental. Some "leader of men" you turned out to be, pussy!

Himself spoke with such spite and venom it was stunning. Paco reeled, didn't even know how to respond. When had Himself become … the enemy? And he was! He was no longer the voice in Paco's head that warned him about the damage in his brain, that feared for his mental health. That was trying to help him. Himself had turned on him.

Finally figured that out, did you, asshole?

And Himself was no longer just a voice. He was standing there next to Noah. He was Paco. No, he was not-Paco. He was the scrawny little sixteen-year-old kid that Spade had raped for hours and hours, laughing uproariously as he bled on the sheets on Spade's bunk.

Paco's eyes traveled down, he couldn't help it, down until he could see the blood running down the backs of Himself's legs.

No, Paco actually took a step back, away from the

apparition, with the words Himself had spoken to him the night he took the ayahuasca. *You're going insane.*

Dear Jesus-God, he was!

Then Himself burst out laughing. The incongruity, his face was twisted in agony because he could feel, he could *feel* what Spade had done to him. But he was laughing.

You poor, sorry bastard. Himself was laughing so hard there were tears rolling down his cheeks. Tears of pain, because it hurt. It *hurt*! But laughing, still laughing.

Find Noah's shield so you can survive and you can repopulate the new world with your damaged DNA, father a race of crazy motherfuckers who see things that aren't there and hear voices.

Chapter Forty-One

NOAH KEPT his face impassive as the guards hauled him out of the locker room and across the gym floor to Paco. He looked over to where they were also dragging Nick along and saw ... the body of Thomas, lying on the steps, the front of his shirt a black-red and a pool of blood under him. Paco's men had killed him.

Paco ... except he wasn't. Noah was so surprised by the man he saw, all the breath was knocked out of his lungs.

Paco?

Paco had been skinny and trying so hard to be macho. But he sort of gave that up after a while because you couldn't hide much from people who could read your mind. He and Star quickly knew everything about each other. Paco didn't want them to see his deepest secrets, though. He and Star had revealed the worst thing that'd ever happened to them, the events at exactly eight o'clock on the day after Halloween all those years ago, the thing that had hooked the three of them to each other psychically long before there were any white dots out by Jupiter. But Paco had reneged on that agreement, refused to open up and it'd driven a wedge between them. After that it was no longer Star/Noah/Paco. It was Star/Noah … with Paco cut off from them. In the end, they did see, though, saw him smother his friend with a pillow — but that was after the Astrals had tried to trick them all, tried to convince each of them that the others had agreed to leave their friends behind in exchange for being returned to Earth. It was a lie. Noah didn't believe it for a minute. Neither did Star. But Paco … Paco thought he'd been betrayed. Noah remembered the look of shock that morphed into rage on Paco's face when he realized that Star and Noah had seen his darkest secret. They'd wanted to offer comfort and compassion, but the Astrals had not allowed it, had sent each back to Earth, to the spot where they'd been taken. That was seven years ago, and Noah had not seen Paco since.

The man standing in the middle of the gym floor was so very different, in every conceivable way, from the boy on the mothership. Of course, his looks had changed. So had Noah's and Star's, but not so dramatically. He got the sense that Paco had crafted the look he now presented, that he had labored long and hard to become the man he wanted the world to believe he was.

Noah.

Paco spoke Noah's name in his head, a greeting that never left his lips.

And Noah suddenly caught a glimpse of the horrible things Paco had done to become the man standing before him, a whisper of it from his mind — he killed someone with a ... wood chipper!

Paco.

Then Noah had stepped back, unwilling to go any further into Paco's mind, and closed the door on Paco entering his.

That appeared to piss him off. And then he introduced his father as "Sawyer," and Paco instantly knew he was Noah's father. He had not gotten that information from someone's mind! Noah's or his father's or ... which meant ...

Could Paco still read the minds of others? The ability had faded quickly with him and with Star, except with each other. But, apparently, Paco's ability had *not* faded. What else might he be able to do with his mind?

It wasn't an answer to his question — he hadn't asked it of Paco. But as Noah watched, he began to come to a horrible conclusion. Something was wrong ... Paco was ...

Paco was ... not normal anymore.

He stood silent, watching Paco have what was clearly a psychotic episode.

Paco appeared to see someone standing in front of him, talked to that person, called the person "Himself." And he went through a range of emotions that were responses to what was going on in his head and whatever it was, it was horrible.

"You turned on me, Himself. You're ... the *enemy*, now."

Then he giggled, replied in a different voice entirely, "Finally figured that out, did you, asshole?"

Paco ... was *crazy*.

The moment Noah thought it, he felt the truth of it in his soul. Whatever had happened to Paco since the day they'd all stood together in that terrifying white room in the mothership, or whatever Paco had done to himself in the intervening years, had damaged his mind. Paco was psychotic.

And a dangerous, dangerous man, indeed.

As he, Nick and his father watched the mental anomaly play out in front of them, Noah tried to figure out what he should do.

Paco was going to ask him about the shield he thought was going to protect them from the death rays of the Astrals. And he would kill people if Noah didn't tell him the truth.

But he had to confuse and thwart Paco's efforts at every turn because it was clear what his intentions were. As soon as he found "Noah's Shield," and was sure it would protect him from the annihilation that was coming, he would kill everybody and take it over for himself.

Chapter Forty-Two

Paco grabbed hold of himself, not Himself, but himself, the real Paco, grabbed him by the metaphorical lapels and shook him. He had to get a grip, he was losing it and he couldn't do that, not here in front of thousands of people, his men and Noah. Most of all Noah.

He had to get his shit together.

Lots of luck get—

Shut the fuck up, he screamed at Himself, bellowed at him. And Himself disappeared, was gone. Paco began to rearrange himself mentally, put his ducks back in a row, become rational again. How much of his mental turmoil had he shown? He had no idea. He would just have to go on from here.

"So here's the deal, Noah, I know what you know."

"And that is?"

He was speaking aloud, like a normal person, and for a moment Paco wondered if he had somehow gotten his hearing back. But then he saw how concentrated Noah was on his lips and realized he was just doing a masterful job of lip reading. And his voice didn't sound funny and nasal like that woman—

"Who was that woman, the one who screamed?" He turned to Noah's father. "She sure had a burr in her saddle for you. What'd you do, fuck her mother?"

He saw Sawyer wince and for a moment got a picture of a beautiful woman overlaid by the image of a scraggly old hag. This was a rabbit trail and Paco didn't have time for rabbit trails right now.

Back to Noah.

"Let's cut the shit, kid. The Astrals are going to blow us away and you've made something that will protect you against it … and I want it. And, you're going to give it to me, or …"

He turned and looked up into the stands full of people, trying to find somebody he could pick.

Oh, shit!

The smile that spread across Paco's face lit it up like a little boy on Christmas morning.

"Well, attention K-Mart shoppers," he said. Then he strode up the center aisle of steps, up and up, almost to the top row. Then he stopped and looked down at the man sitting there next to a woman with two small children. He smiled.

"Well, hello *Eagle Feather*," he said. "I've been wanting to meet you for years."

The old Indian was wearing a big, flop-eared hat, old, from before Astral Day, and it had probably been an old hat even then. The moccasins on his feet weren't old, though. They looked new, hardly worn at all, and Paco figured the old guy had made them himself, some Indian life skill that hadn't meant shit in years and then suddenly knowing how to make a pair of moccasins made you a very valuable human being indeed. He had a tattered poncho draped over his shoulders, a big one that went down way past his knees and he didn't even look up at Paco, just continued to stare straight ahead, managing to appear he hadn't heard a word. But Paco knew, had been told about the stoic old Indian … who was the beloved grandfather of Star, who was supposed to be home anytime from Bardstown.

He had perhaps found the goose that laid the golden egg. A threat to the old white-haired Indian might just be what was needed to pry loose the information about the shield.

He pointed the pistol at the old man's head. "The knife, or I splatter your brains all over this sweet little boy's shirt."

Paco couldn't see the knife under the poncho, but he knew about it. Star had described it, said her grandfather never went anywhere without it. The Indian reached into his poncho and pulled the knife out of a scabbard, and Paco instinctively backed up from him, just the sight of it in his hand. He cocked the pistol and the Indian turned the knife around and handed it to him, hilt first. Paco took it in his left hand, never lowering the pistol from Eagle Feather. This was a *knife*. He had no scabbard, but it would fit for the time being in his gun holster, and he slid the blade into the holster.

"Down there," Paco ordered, and pointed to the gym floor. "Now."

The old man rose slowly, totally unhurried, and began walking ahead of Paco down the steps. Paco stood, watching, thinking—

It was like metal shavings ... lying peacefully and then suddenly snapped to a magnet, drawn there so fast, fixed there. The image that came into focus as Paco looked down on the gym floor, popped into place that quickly. The paint. The blobs of paint somebody had vandalized the gym with. It wasn't vandalism, or spilled.

It was a picture. Someone had painted a gigantic picture that stretched from one end of the gym to the other, huge, must have taken gallons of paint. But the detail was stunning and the image took his breath away. He stood gaping, taking in the wonder, meaning and terror.

There was the earth, the blue-green marble. And there was the black ship, the monstrous black ship, a ship the size of ... miles and miles across. It hung in the sky above the planet, a black boil on the universe. Above the planet ... the north end.

It hung above the North Pole and the light it shined down on the planet, even rendered in paint on a gym floor, was staggering in its power and intensity. It was two heartbeats and maybe three, before the whole message came through and when it did, Paco thought he needed to sit down or he might throw up.

He did neither, just stared, understanding dawning with a white light of its own in his head.

The old man had reached the bottom of the steps by the time Paco came back to himself and followed. He ignored the Indian, marched right up to Noah. It was clear from the look on his face he knew what Paco had seen.

"What is this shit — this painting? Who did it?" He didn't mean to, but it was instinct. It was his natural way of treating people. He reached out and grabbed the front of Noah's throat and began to squeeze. "Who …?"

Then he realized what he was doing and let go. Stepped back. Took a breath.

"Star painted it," Noah told him. "She saw it in the hive mind, like a vision, not like she looked into the mind but more like things spilled out of it. This, this image. The whole hive mind was thinking about this one image and Star saw it."

It took a moment for Paco to absorb it.

"I saw … the judgement," Paco said. "Ayahuasca showed me …" He let his voice trail off, knowing they didn't understand what he was talking about and not caring. "I knew the Astrals found us guilty, handed down the death penalty. But I didn't know … never *dreamed* …" He gestured out at the paint on the floor all around him.

"*This* is how. This is what they're going to do to kill us all off. They're going to drown us." He was so staggered by the thought that he couldn't form words for a moment. Then it hit him.

"But you know a way, don't you? You were under a boat and you figured out a way." He liked the look of surprise on Noah's face. "You know a way to escape. What is it?"

Noah looked at him carefully. And Paco pulled out his pistol and placed it on the old Indian's forehead. "First him, then your father, then one by one every single motherfucking person in this room until—"

"A cave. Matheson Caverns. We're going there, inside, until the flood waters recede."

"You've fucking lost your mind!" Paco was devastated. He'd come all this way because he believed he would find salvation here, only to discover the kid had some crackpot plan to ... "You're gonna suffocate in some fucking—"

"It will work," Noah said. "This isn't an ordinary cave. Matheson Caverns is the second longest cave system in the world, more than two hundred fifty miles of caverns.

"*Miles!* Are you shitting me!"

"Miles of *explored* caverns and another ... hundreds of miles of unexplored caverns. There's enough air in there to keep thousands of people alive."

"For how long?"

"We don't know all of it. We're taking in supplies—"

"So you're outfitting this ... this cave, got food and what else?"

"Electricity, a water purification system—"

"And it's here, near here. Are you finished, is everything in place?"

"Almost."

Paco's stomach yanked into a knot.

"What if the flood comes before—"

"It won't," Noah said. "We still have … two full days."

"How in the hell do you know that?"

"I can explain it to you …" Noah looked around and for the first time Paco noticed large pictures of the solar system, planets and stars and the white dots, blown up and on easels."

"Give me the CliffsNotes."

Noah pointed to the second of the pictures. The first was a picture of Jupiter, just Jupiter. The second was a picture of what that looked like on Astral Day, with the white dots."

"I can show you how …"

Noah went to step toward the picture and Paco blocked his path.

"Tell me."

"You can see on the pictures … the black ship, it came with the others, appeared the same time they did out by Jupiter."

Paco looked where he pointed and didn't see any black ship, didn't see anything at all but didn't interrupt.

"You can tell from the other pictures that they didn't bring the black ship with them when they first arrived." He pointed to the successive pictures that showed the white dots getting bigger and bigger. "I guess ... they didn't need it then. But they do now, and they've summoned it. That's what Star heard."

"So how do you know—?"

"Dr. Mikhail Ziegelman Garczonski, he's an astrophysicist — he said that it took the motherships six days to travel from Jupiter because they had entered the Earth's time and had to *slow down*. The black ship's in our time, too, so it will take the same six days."

Six days. Just like before. The countdown to the end of the world. That made sense. Paco had seen the black ship out there in deep space. It would take a while ... six days ... yes, that made sense.

"When—?"

"This is *Day Four* since Star painted the picture. We have two more full days, Day Five and Day Six. On Day Six we need to be inside the cave when the flood comes."

Then there was time — the rest of today and one more day — before the day the Astrals arrived. Time to go there, take it over, get all nestled in.

"And with all these people working ..." Noah pointed up into the stands. "This many people can get a lot of supplies stocked in three days."

Paco smiled. Yes, this was going to work after all. These would be his minions. He'd use the labor, and their food and other supplies. The tension eased in his head, the throbbing let off in his temples.

"Where is this cave?"

Noah pointed down the road they had taken into the village.

"It's down that road."

"So tell me how it works, what you're doing," Paco said. Noah hesitated, then looked at his father, who spoke for the first time.

"I'm in charge of getting the caves ready," the man said. "Since we don't have any gasoline, we've been floating the supplies on rafts down the river to the cave. It takes a *whole lot longer that way* — the river winds and bends miles out of the way, but it's all we've got—"

"You could load up trucks, haul shit there, come back for more and get the job done faster, right?"

The man, his name was Sawyer, nodded. "If we had trucks and gasoline, but we don't."

"Well, *we* do now," Paco said. "Those four trucks out there, load up three of them, as much as they can carry."

Noah's father and the man, the little girl's father. He needed to kill them, shoot them right now. They were dangerous men, you could see it in the way they carried themselves.

Well, Paco was a dangerous man, too. And those assholes didn't scare him!

"I should kill you," he said to the little girl's father, and realized with horror that if he'd been close enough, the man would have spit in his face. "Both of you." He hated it that neither of them flinched. "But you, I need," he said, pointing to Sawyer. "And you …" He stood staring, emotions working their way through him. The little girl's face came to mind, the terror on it when she looked back and saw— "You get this one pass."

He wasn't sure why he'd done that and he never liked doing things without an apparent reason. He was just ... saving him, saving them both for object lessons later on, yes, that was it. Object lessons.

He gestured to one of his guards and nodded toward the man standing beside Sawyer. "You watch old Nick here real close." The guard would see to it he was secure.

Speaking to Sawyer, "If your buddy tries anything — sneezes funny or scratches his ass some way I don't like, I'll shoot you first, then him. We clear?" He looked from one to the other of them, waited for assent, a nod, something, and got nothing but stony silence in reply. He let it go.

"So you're in charge of getting things ready, are you — well, don't let me stand in your way. Get out there and oversee the loading of those trucks." He pointed at Noah. "He comes with me, right by my side." He pulled out the impressive knife that belonged to the Indian. "You blink" — he held the point of the blade up beside Noah's face — "and your boy here loses one of them pretty blue eyes. Blink twice and I don't like it, he gets to be both blind and deaf. You hear what I'm saying to you?" This time, Sawyer nodded.

Paco turned toward the crowd.

"These folks, the women and kids, they stay in here, though. You can load supplies using my men."

He couldn't let these people go wandering around, get guns maybe, escape. He'd end up having to kill them all, but he'd get around to that later.

He stood there then, turning the knife over and over in his hand, pretending to be examining it while the guard held a gun on ... what was his name, the girl's father? He didn't know, had lost the name and wouldn't ask because he was sure the man wouldn't tell him, and then he'd have to do something about his defiance.

He shook it off, just stood, letting his mind wander out over the minds of the crowd. Out past the two men, whose minds were pits of hatred and boiling rage. Noah's father, he was as calculating as a snake. He'd try something, as God made little green apples, Noah's father would try something and Paco would have to shoot him. He'd enjoy the look on Noah's face when he did.

The fear and turmoil in the thoughts of those around him was like noisy stage whispers, words said not quite loud enough to be heard, but too loud and abrasive to ignore.

... take our food and leave us ...

... we'll drown, they'll leave us out to ...

... Betty Ann, have to find some way to get her inside the cave even if ...

That was the first Paco realized that not all the people present were destined for the cave.

... happens when there ain't no flood? What ...?

... when nothing happens, what's he going to do then?

So the whole crowd hadn't bought into Star's vision. Paco did, one hundred percent, because he knew, had witnessed what Star could do with the minds of others, how she could collect images of things that might not even have happened yet. If she put the painting on the floor — how? She was blind! — then she got it from the hive mind. It was what they were thinking.

Star.

He didn't turn to Noah, just hovered around the outside edges of his mind. It was locked up like a steel trap. How had he learned to do that? Well, he'd had seven years and look what Paco had taught himself to do in seven years. He wondered if Star could do the same thing, too.

"They said Star's in Bardstown, that right?"

Noah nodded, "Yes, Star is in Bardstown."

"Doing what?"

"What we're all doing — getting ready to move into the cave."

"And she knows all about me, now. The two of you been jabbering in your heads about me since you first laid eyes on me — haven't you?"

"I told her."

"*I told her,*" Paco mimicked and smirked. "Oh, I'll bet you did. Well, tell her I said hello ... and that if she isn't back here before dark, I'm going to make Injun Joe here into a cigar store Indian."

Noah merely nodded. It infuriated Paco that Star was actually hearing Paco say the words to Noah.

He'd break the two of them apart. He'd get inside their minds. Star couldn't keep him out and if he got into her mind, he'd get into Noah's too. And once he was in there ... he was gonna *fuck with them.*

He smiled at the prospect. Yeah, fuck with their

heads. Burst a few of *their* blood vessels. See if maybe he couldn't get one or the other of them to have a stroke. Or maybe a twofer, the two of them sitting there drooling — his mind yanked away from that image like he'd touched a hot stove with his finger.

Somewhere he could hear an echo of chuckling. Somewhere, Himself was laughing.

"She'll be back before dark," Noah said.

Paco grabbed Noah's shirt and shoved him forward then.

"Alrighty then, let's get busy."

Chapter Forty-Three

When Star heard Noah's voice in her head again, she let out a gasp and only then realized she'd been standing with her eyes closed, exercising all the control she could muster not to listen in and listening with all the might of her mind anyway.

Of course she had. She saw what Noah saw, saw the gym, Paco's back — he had grown, must have been three or four inches taller than she remembered, and so much bigger. Even from the back, she could tell he had broad shoulders and a powerful build.

She kept her face as neutral as she could. Taylor was nearby, pacing, waiting for word about Noah and Sawyer. She watched in horror as Noah saw their attack fall apart, saw through the barely open door, that Gretchen had leapt to her feet and shouted something.

She gasped and put her hand over her mouth.

"What?" Taylor demanded.

"Gretchen … she gave them away. Sawyer and the others were sneaking … and she warned Paco."

"She wouldn't …

"She did …"

Then Star watched the soldier burst into the locker room where Noah was, grab him by the arm and drag him out onto the gym floor. Paco turned to face him.

Star was struck with shock at the sight of him. He was … he looked like some comic book superhero. His shoulders were so broad they stretched the fabric of his uniform taut. His face … he'd been good-looking, but now his handsome face was both startling and frightening. His finely chiseled features belonged on some movie set, but his eyes. There was nothing … oh yes there was. There was something in them, alright, some new being. Those were not Paco's eyes. She had never met the man standing in the middle of the gym floor whose eyes bored into Noah's like drill bits.

Star could feel his probing mind, poking, looking for a way into Noah's thoughts. She saw the look of frustration on Paco's face through Noah's eyes, and knew Noah had kept him out. But he had let her in. She knew Noah knew she was there, watching and listening. And she knew he didn't mind.

Star saw the whole thing, watched the drama unfold through Noah's eyes. She told Taylor about what was going on, in snippets. How Paco's soldier had shot Thomas, apparently killed him, had dragged Noah, Sawyer and Nick out into the middle of the gym floor and began to interrogate them. She saw Papa Eagle Feather standing off to the side, like a discarded shoe, looking stoic and uninterested but not missing a thing, not a single detail with his eagle eyes.

"Noah told Paco that this is Day Four," she told Taylor, who had been joined by his wife, his two sons and three other men and women who'd been working with them. "So he thinks there's another whole day left to prepare."

She wasn't sure why Noah had done that, just to throw him off, obviously, but what it accomplished other than misleading Paco for some reason she didn't know. When Paco directed the men out of the gym into the sunlit morning to load up the trucks with supplies rather than the rafts, Noah spoke into her head.

He's bringing supplies and his soldiers to the cave in trucks. I don't know how many soldiers, but I'll direct him to the front entrance, Cricket Bottom. Tell Taylor, Dave, Sam and Kelly Jo … they'll have to be … snipers.

Snipers?

We're no match for his soldiers, too many, too well armed. They'll kill us all and take over, unless we … This is all we've got. Paco won't expect opposition. We have to … mow them down, all of them.

Snipers. Star struggled to get her mind around the word, around the concept.

Tell them to get their deer rifles and go up into the woods and hide. To fire on Dad's signal, when he wipes his forehead with the back of his arm.

Noah, I'm scared—

So am I.

His mind went to other things and she delivered his message to his uncle and cousins.

"Snipers," Taylor repeated the word, grappling with it. Sam and Dave tried not to appear nonplussed but Star could sense both young men were shaken to the core.

"Noah says … it's our only hope."

Taylor didn't have anything like an arsenal, but he was a typical Kentuckian — had collected several different kinds of deer rifles over the years, as had his wife and his sons. As a boy, he'd gone hunting with his father and he'd taken his own sons with him. That expertise, like a lot of other things rural people still knew how to do, had been what kept food on the table for the villagers. All of them were crack shots, but even if they had been lousy shots, their deer rifles had sophisticated scope sights … state of the art a decade ago, kept in mint condition. From a deer blind in the trees, any one of the four of them could drop a buck with a single shot at 250 yards.

This wasn't shooting a deer, though. They weren't soldiers and they were being asked to put the crosshairs of a rifle sight on some man's chest and pull the trigger. Not just one man, but as many as they could kill. Star could hear the gravity of realization in Taylor's voice, and imagined she could see that determined set to his chin that she sometimes saw on Sawyer's through Noah's eyes.

Kelly Jo was the acknowledged best shot in the family. Since deer stayed hidden when the sun was high, came out in the early mornings and late evenings to feed, going hunting was the only time she left the cave and it was her passion. She knew how to work the rise on it and had once dropped an elk in a meadow half a mile away.

She broke the silence.

"The new world order." Her voice was soft but firm. "Fight or die."

There was no further discussion.

Using all Taylor's weapons, they could arm some of the other villagers who'd been working with them. Altogether, they could place ten snipers up in the hills, in the woods looking down on the parking lot where Paco would come with his soldiers. It really would be like shooting ducks in a washtub.

"You need to come with us," Taylor told Star, "up into the woods to hide." Paco thought she was in Bardstown, the mostly-deserted-now little town twenty-five miles from Jessup. "You can help us coordinate our" — he hesitated for just a beat, then she heard the firmness in his voice — "our *attack*."

David and Samuel returned to the parking lot with weapons and boxes of ammunition. Like everyone else with a weapon, Taylor and his sons had kept meticulous track of shell casings since Astral Day, refilled every round they fired. Taylor'd always kept lots of ammunition on hand, so he wouldn't have to go to Louisville to get it, where it was much cheaper than he could buy it locally. He'd had floor-to-ceiling shelves in his basement lined with ammo the day little white dots were spotted in the black of space out by Jupiter. With a foresight that would serve his family well in later years, he'd sent Kelly Jo to Louisville that afternoon — to buy up every shell she could find.

Star figured they were wearing their hunting jackets, which had places to fit shells, and big pockets to carry ammunition. There was little conversation as Taylor distributed guns and ammo among the six other villagers as well as his family. Star could hear the sounds of them loading, pouring shells out of the boxes, of magazines slammed home. With ten snipers in the woods, when they all opened fire at the same time, it would be a bloodbath. And Noah, Sawyer and Nick Wilson would be right there in the middle of them. Papa Eagle Feather, too, if Paco brought him along. David Matheson took Star's arm and walked her beside him up the hillside. Star had "seen" the Kentucky mountains through Noah's eyes, knew the hills surrounding the parking lot of the Cricket Bottom cavern entrance in the valley were steep, with heavy woods. The snipers would be invisible.

"I'll park you right here on the top," David said. He helped her sit down on a small rock next to a larger one. "They might ... return fire, but you're safe behind this boulder. If you need anything, I'll be in an old deer blind about seventy-five yards away and I can hear if you call."

This was a good place for a deer blind. The elevation would give a commanding view of the hills and valleys stretching out beyond for miles in all directions around it.

Star seldom wished she could see. It had been so long that it almost never occurred to her to want to anymore. And besides, she *could* see, out through Noah's eyes when she was with him. It was an odd perspective. Like sitting in a movie theatre where there are images being projected on a big screen in front of you. But you can only sit and watch. You can't change the perspective of the camera, turn it to the right so you can see the rest of a bush there, or look up at the sky. When you saw the world through the eyes of another, you saw what they saw and nothing more.

She could "see" through Pumpkin's nose, too, though even after all these years, it was still difficult to translate those images so they made sense to a human mind.

But today, Star yearned to have vision of her own. She knew they were atop a high hill and she wanted to be able to look out over the land. If she could *see*, maybe she could get rid of the horrible dead feeling in her belly that was lying there like rotting meat. It was the "something's wrong" feeling, only different. The minute Paco showed up in Noah's mind, Star had known *that* was the something wrong she had sensed, just like she'd sensed the men coming to shoot up Alien World and the horrible man who'd kidnapped them in Land Between the Lakes.

She had sensed Paco in Millicent Blinkhorn's future. Star was certain that at some point in Paco's "invasion," he had killed Millicent Blinkhorn.

So that should be over, right? It had happened … so why did Star still sense a bad thing *out there* in the future?

Something else, something different. *More.*

More ... that was it. This was more than just sensing that this ambush might go badly, that she or someone she loved might be hurt. It was somehow bigger than that. What could possibly be bigger than that?

She didn't know. All she did know was there was *something* ... it was like the voice of a thousand flies drowning in unison. Anxiety, like swarms of something winged, flew around and around in her stomach, fluttered in her bones.

Something bad ... something *reeeeeally* bad was about to happen.

Chapter Forty-Four

Sawyer went out of the gym into the sunlight, watched Paco stride out with Noah at his side and thought that the Latino kid Noah and Star had described bore no resemblance whatsoever to this young man with the wild eyes.

Something was very wrong with him. Sawyer could tell Noah saw it too, certainly knew a whole lot more about it than Sawyer did, was considering it in the overall plan the boy was cooking up in his head, and clearly, Noah had a plan is his head.

He'd told Paco that there were two full days left to prepare before the flood, that today was Day Four. But in reality, it was Day Five and the death ship would arrive tomorrow. They had all day today, and had planned to be snug as bugs in a rug in the ark before midnight. And then tomorrow ... sometime tomorrow ... in some form tomorrow, the water would come. Their plan called for everybody to be safe in the ark without even getting their feet wet. He hadn't been counting noses, but he felt sure more than two thirds of the villagers were there already. When the water began to rise, Noah was to climb up near the small opening he'd crawled through into the Astrals' mine, close enough that there would be no doubt the detonator's signal would carry through the solid rock to the explosives they'd planted. He'd set off the explosion that Nick guaranteed would seal up the mine "like a cork in a bottle."

That'd been a great plan, but it was shot to hell now and it was up to him, Noah, Nick, Eagle Feather, Garson … *somebody* to come up with some other plan.

Noah had taken the initiative by telling Paco he had a day longer before the flood than he actually did. Sawyer got it. Noah didn't want Paco to feel pressured, so he wouldn't hurry, would take his time to get his things in order if he thought time wasn't a problem. And in that relaxed rather than hypervigilant state, Noah hoped they'd be able to … something.

Even as Sawyer directed his work crews — under the watchful eyes of Paco's soldiers, mean-looking, rode-hard-and-put-away-wet men — to load the supplies they'd intended to send down the river on rafts, Sawyer did the best he could to keep his eyes on Noah. And as he'd hoped, whenever Paco's back was turned, Noah signed to him and Nick.

When he told him what'd he'd instructed Star to do, Sawyer was impressed that a non-strategist like Noah had thought of it.

His brother, nephews, sister-in law and who knew how many others firing from vantage points high above their targets ... if they played it right, they could drop all the soldiers, or at least enough that the others surrendered. Then they could use those soldiers' weapons to assault Zion Village, free the others and take back their town.

Then Noah signed a very determined "Don't think about it!" and Sawyer suddenly realized that he had to put the assault plan out of his mind, that Paco would find it there if Sawyer thought about it.

Then he watched Paco drop to his knees. Everyone who saw it stopped what they were doing and just stared at him. He turned his face toward the sky, and uttered a cry, wild and Jurassic.

"Vi-cen-te!"

No one moved.

Then just as quickly, he lowered his head, got to his feet in one agile hop, and stood as commanding and purposeful as he had been only moments before. Like it had never happened. He was Paco, back in control. Back in charge.

And Paco could read minds.

Sawyer had never in his life tried *not* to think about something, and he found it impossible. He couldn't blank out his mind ...

But he could think about something else, something so riveting and compelling it would take the place of everything else in his head.

He could remember precious Rosileigh.

Sawyer didn't think of them often. The pain of their loss more than ten years ago still had the power to slice him open and bare his soul to the core. But now he concentrated on those memories, built pictures of his "two favorite girls" into his mind.

IT'S HER SECOND BIRTHDAY, *and no little girl ever looked more adorable than Rosie Posie — that's what Noah calls her. Her red hair is not carrot-colored, as his had been when he was a little boy. When you looked at it closely, hers isn't even a single color. It's a deep wine red, dark and shiny, but it has rust-colored highlights that look golden in bright sunlight. It is thick, too. When Noah was little, his wispy blond hair had barely covered the top of his head when he was two years old, and even now, at seven, it still wisps, a veneer on his head that looks almost white with its lack of color. Just like Taylor's had looked when he was a boy, but it had darkened with age.*

The two children are striking when they sit together, side by side. Their faces bear a striking resemblance to each other, not hard at all to tell they are siblings. The different colors of their hair set them apart, cause the "awwwwww" factor that always pops out on the lips of strangers who see them together.

Valerie has pulled Rosileigh's hair back into two "dog ears." A part down the middle and two ponytails on either side of it instead of one. So the dog ears of russet curls dance around when she moves her head, so long they even bop her in the face when she turns her head quickly.

The child is so excited she cannot sit still. Her birthday dress is a pale yellow, with delicate pink flowers on it. There's a white apron in the front, that has yellow flowers, bigger ones on it, and lace around the collar. Valerie loves to dress the little girl in what she calls "girly" clothes, but in truth the child would rather put on jeans and dig in the dirt with Noah. She'd find her own space.

"Aren't we ready, yet?" Noah pleads, and it might as well be his birthday as his little sister's. He has watched Valerie make the cake, licked all the spoons and the beaters on the mixer, and still has a tiny dollop of pink frosting on the end of his nose.

"Hold your horses, big guy," Sawyer says. "We have to put the candles on the cake so she can blow—"

"REMEMBERING YOUR LITTLE GIRL, ARE YOU?"

The words were so jarring, Sawyer was yanked out of the memory. He had been loading boxes in the back of a truck, stacking them one on top of the other, and he had so filled his mind with memories that he hadn't noticed Paco's approach.

Sawyer just stared at him, and a huge smile lit his face. He was ridiculously good-looking, so handsome it didn't even seem real, but there was nothing pleasant about his features for all their perfection. His eyes ruined the effect. They were black marbles in his face, cold and lifeless. No, not lifeless — when he narrowed them, there was a feral quality to them, almost reptilian, that raised goosebumps on Sawyer's arms.

"I know all about Rosie Posie," Paco said. His attention was unfocused as he moved his eyes ceaselessly over the bee hive of activity going on, alert, on guard for any attempt at violence.

Sawyer didn't even like to hear the child's name come out Paco's mouth.

Then the man turned the full force of his marble eyes on Sawyer, really looked at him.

There was a beast in there. Sawyer saw it! A monstrous beast peeked out the young man's eyes, a horror from some other world, as scary as any reptar. No, more frightening, because it was human. It was a beast, but it was also human.

"Shame what happened to your wife and Rosie-Posie," Paco said, with deliberate offhandedness, like he'd been talking about how they'd missed the bus, or spilled spaghetti sauce on a new blouse. "A real, real shame. You need to have a long talk about it sometime … with Noah."

Chapter Forty-Five

Paco watched and listened, planned and schemed. Wanted to laugh out loud at the profound irony of the story his life was writing. Almost did laugh out loud, but he grabbed hold of it at the last moment and swallowed the sound.

He was having so much fun!

Maybe more fun than he had ever had in his entire life! He was enjoying every moment of the drama playing out before him.

He'd landed on top. Again. He was in charge, the ruler, the man in whose hand rested the fates of every man, woman and child here. He held sway, like a Roman emperor, could put out his hand, turn his thumb down and someone would die.

Oh, how he wanted to laugh out loud.

Instead, he occupied his mind surfing the minds of those around him. He didn't try to go deep into anybody's thoughts. Every time he had done that recently, he had felt a stabbing pain behind his right eye. It was his imagination, of course, not real, a product of Himself's hysteria and made-up images of ruptured blood vessels. But even if the pain was generated by his own mind, it still hurt, so he pulled away before he pushed too hard. Just over the tops of minds, hearing snippets

... son of a bitch gonna leave us ...

... man's batshit crazy, gonna shoot us all ...

... can't swim. Don't want to drown, oh dear Jesus, don't let me ...

... get away and hide in the woods. He'd never ...

... pissed as hell when don't no flood happen and he's ...

He let them swirl through his own consciousness, listening to whispers.

The old Indian was having a rough go of it. Loading up supplies into the back of one of the trucks, he kept having to stop to get his breath, got slower and slower.

Shit, he didn't want the motherfucker to have a heart attack. He wanted that som-bitch alive and kicking when Star rolled in from Bardstown.

"Sit down, asshole, before you fall down," he called to the old man, who set the last box in the truck bed and almost staggered over to a nearby wall. He sat down next to a pile of discarded blankets at the edge of the building and leaned carefully back against the wall, careful to rest in the shade of the overhanging roof, that dappled the area in shadows. Then he drew his knees up and wrapped his arms around them, pulled his poncho over himself and disappeared under his hat. He looked like a painting Paco'd seen somewhere. It had had a poem under it and the words bobbed to the surface of his mind.

Each day he sits and stares into the distance that is great.
And things are in his eyes words tremble to relate.
A chambray shirt and flop-eared hat,
And wire-tied shoes worn thin and flat.

Where had *that* come from?

He felt a chill. It was happening to him more and more lately. Memories from out of nowhere would suddenly bob up into his mind as if the scene had just happened, in fact sometimes he thought the scene *had* just happened.

Hey kid, you new here. Want to come with me?

Paco's body went limp and he dropped to his knees, a psychic blow so staggering the world pulsed in and out of focus around him. He tilted his head back and cried out a single word, a cry of such incredible pain and longing it ripped over his vocal cords and exploded out his mouth in a raspy, harsh voice.

"Vi-cen-te!"

His friend. His only friend. And Paco had—

It was gone. Where he had felt anguish to his core, an agony of loss — there was nothing at all. He found he was on his knees for some reason, and quickly hopped back up to his feet. Everyone was still for a frozen moment, or it seemed to him they were staring at him, and then like a paused video clicked back on, everyone continued whatever it was they were doing.

Noah appeared not to have even noticed Paco had been on his knees in the dirt.

On his knees in the dirt — that was ridiculous.

His eyes slid over the people nearby.

Sawyer, Noah's father.

He was thinking about a little pixie-faced girl, her red hair in twin ponytails, wearing a yellow dress with pink flowers and a lacy collar. Rosileigh.

Ahhhh. Noah's little sister who burned to death, a crispy-critter.

Paco wanted to laugh at the thought but he didn't right then because if he did the others will look at him again like they did before when he was on his knees in the dirt. Why had he been on his knees in the dirt? He didn't remember, so it must not have really happened at all.

He allowed his eyes to slide out over the workers again. While three men haul out barrels of monk's cheese and began to set them up one at a time in the back of a truck, Winslow and Haycraft stood nearby, guarding them, with their legs spread, rifles in the crocks of their arms, looking mean and menacing.

Mean and menacing ... riiiiiight. Haycraft was so claustrophobic it was all he could do to sit inside a vehicle. He must be shitting bullets right now at the prospect of having to go down into a cave. And Winslow — menacing to little girls, alright. He had a thing for little girls.

The man named Nick was standing with Hawthorne not three feet away with a rifle leveled at his chest.

The little girl had looked at him, turned her head and looked at him and he saw that she had Down's syndrome, was an angel but it was too late for Paco to swerve and he had—

There were no Down's syndrome people anymore because it was easy for a doctor to do a test on a pregnant woman to see if the fetus had the extra chromosome that caused it. If the fetus did, the mother aborted. But this man and his wife ... they had *known*, and had kept the child. Had had a baby in the first horrible days after Astral Day who was handicapped, and—

Paco turned away. He'd save the mother of that little girl and her other children if there were any. He'd find them in the cave, wouldn't kill them or turn them out to drown with everybody else. He'd let the woman live ... she might produce more Down syndrome children to seed the new world and that would be a good thing. He would actually like to save the father, too, but he was too dangerous. No, once they got to the cave, he would execute him and Noah's father and Papa Eagle Feather.

He swung around to look at the old man, sitting up against the wall of the building in the shadows. His brand new moccasins stuck out from under the front of the poncho he huddled under, his flop-eared hat covering his head and face.

Paco thought about the poem, and wondered where he'd heard it and why he remembered it. Maybe it was because ...

He'd been turning away but now he stopped, continued to look at the old man in the shadow. Something was different. Wrong. Something was—

There had been a pile of blankets beside him and now the blankets were gone. Had somebody decided to load them into a truck? He hadn't noticed anybody loading blankets into the truck.

A pit began to form deep in Paco's belly, an empty black place like a drain hole where foul water was spinning around and around rushing to the pipe …

Something was—

He took four long strides and came to stand in front of the Indian.

"Wake up, old man," he snarled, and kicked the Indian hard in the shin.

But his boot tip buried itself in a soft poncho instead of striking the bone in the old man's …

Then Paco saw it, and kicked furiously at the poncho, knocking it and the hat off the pile of blankets where two moccasins stuck out on the front.

Papa Eagle Feather was gone.

Paco saw red. Literally. Suddenly the whole world was red, like there was blood dripping off everything. Like he was seeing the world through the walls of a broken blood vessel.

Nooooo! he screamed and began kicking the blankets, screeching obscenities.

He turned, pulled his pistol, and shot a man who had stopped loading the big boxes and was just looking at him, stupefied.

Paco just shot him, watched the blood squirt out of his chest into the air, a spray of red droplets. Then it was like Paco was looking through a window glass out on a world where it was raining blood. All the people were standing there as the rain poured down, drenching them in blood. The window glass was cool,

The Hidden

the rain hit the window glass, spattered it the way rain splatters on the windows when there's a slight breeze. But there was no wind in this blood storm. The blood fell straight down, hard, a torrential rainstorm. The buildings were slathered in blood. He could hear it pounding on the rooftops. But he was on the inside, on the other side of the glass from the blood. He looked down at his hands and arms. He was clean. There was glass between him and—

He was inside a bubble, a glass bubble like the one Mama Rosa had had sitting on the mantle in her home in California, which was black powder right now, had been black powder since Black Monday ... Mama Rosa's black power blowing around with all the rest of it.

She'd had a globe on the mantle that showed a city. He thought it was Chicago but he never went there and after the Astrals came there wasn't a Chicago anymore just like there wasn't a New York, or Boston, or Houston, or Atlanta or ...

But that glass globe had shown the skyscrapers of this big city sitting beside a lake, the blue painted on the bottom of the globe. And when you turned the globe upside down, then righted it again, the snow fell on the scene. Fell on top of the lake water and covered it, fell on the buildings, falling hard and covering them.

Paco was in a globe and outside the globe it was raining blood. He was horrified, saw the drips of blood squiggling down the glass in front of him, bloody worms, like the ones Vicente had shown him how to impale with a fish hook so they could not catch fish in the river that didn't have any motherfucking fish in it.

The blood was Paco's rage. He knew that, understood it, saw that he was protected from his own rage, sealed away so his own anger couldn't harm him, while everyone else was covered, slathered …

It was gone. The blood was gone. The man was lying on the ground and a couple of the men who had been helping him load boxes were kneeling beside him, turned him over, then one of them looked up at Paco with loathing and Paco raised the gun to kill him, too.

But didn't.

"We're done loading," Paco called out.

They had enough shit, or if they didn't, he'd send for more of it tomorrow. Right now, he just wanted to get to this cave, this hole in the ground where Noah had figured to hide his people from the flood and where Paco now would take over, and put his men, the ones he selected.

"Get in the trucks. Get them in." He indicated Nick Wilson and Sawyer Matheson. "All of you, get in the trucks."

He snatched Noah by the arm before he could take a single step.

"You ride with me."

Then he got into a truck with Haycraft driving and Noah in the middle. The back was loaded with his men, and the deaf girl who had called out. He wondered if she'd be safe back there and smiled. Surely not.

A second truck at the end of the line would transport another twenty men and the other four trucks, partially loaded with … he didn't know what was in them … would be in between. Sawyer had been in charge of seeing that the ark was outfitted so whatever this shit was they'd been hauling there was obviously necessary. He could see the food, the bags of flour, packaged dried meat, and barrels of cheese. They left behind as much as they loaded, but there was still time. They'd come back for it.

He wouldn't let himself think about the old Indian who had disappeared, probably should have told the soldiers he was leaving behind to search for the old man but in truth he didn't give a shit where he had gone. He meant to move himself and his men into the cave, kill whoever he had to kill. And not come out. The old man could drown with everybody else in the world.

Chapter Forty-Six

Eagle Feather had often talked to Nick Wilson about it. Nick had been a Navy SEAL and Eagle Feather enjoyed listening to him describe his training, what he had to do to become a SEAL. It was very similar to what was required of young Indian men as part of their initiation into manhood ... at least, it once had been.

"Endurance was the thing," Nick told him one night when they were seated around the campfire they often lit behind the cafeteria in the fall. There were no marshmallows anymore for kids to roast, but universal delight in poking sticks into a fire was not an activity the Astrals could take away from mankind. "You had to be able to take it, whatever it was, and not let it affect what you had come to do."

Eagle Feather could relate.

"For instance, you had to be totally immune to heat or cold. It didn't matter how cold it got, you didn't let it be relevant. In the end, we found out that the ones who made it ... most washed out ... but the ones who didn't had that place in their heads where they could go and what was happening to them physically, how hot or cold or tired they were, was of no consequence."

Eagle Feather recalled the ritual when he was a boy. It wasn't as it had been in days of old, back when being an Apache warrior meant just that, a warrior. Someone who had to fight to survive. Part of knowing how to fight to survive was turning off senses. He had been in initiated in the wintertime, and his grandfather had taken him and the other boy up into the mountains around Ruidoso. It was snowing, he remembered, the big hunks that fell out of a sky of gray stone, the kind that would leave a foot or two feet or more on the ground before the storm was done.

He had had to go out into the storm in nothing but moccasins, a leather shirt and pants. No buffalo robe to keep out the cold. He remembered fearing that he would have to grit his teeth to keep them from chattering, remembered setting his jaw, fiercely determined not to show any sign of weakness.

But it hadn't been that way at all. He had just not felt the cold. Not registered it. He had no memory of "going to some special place" or anything like that. And that's not quite what Nick said either. He didn't say the men who succeeded went to some "special place." He said there was a special place in their heads that was where their consciousness took them that was beyond their control. It was a product of their will, of being steadfast and strong and then one day you realized it just didn't matter what the hardship was, you could endure it.

He'd once had to swim in a swollen river. A rowboat he and two others were in turned over and like idiots, the other two — not Indians — had gone after their floating coolers to make sure they still had their beer. And they'd let the paddles float down the swollen river.

So Eagle Feather had tied the rope on the front of the boat around his shoulders and began to swim, pulling the boat along with him. He swam like that for three hours, was so exhausted that when he finally found a place to tie up, his legs wouldn't support him. And he had been aware of none of it.

Another thing that SEAL training taught men that Indians understood from generations was that "the human eye is drawn to movement."

"You'd be amazed where you can hide, like right out in plain sight …" Nick had said. "But if you don't move, the enemy's eyes will skip right over you and they won't register the sight."

When Nick said, "not moving," he had meant not moving *anything*. It was a state of slowed breathing and heart rate where your chest showed no sign you were alive. And if you had to move, you got there a millimeter at a time. It could take three hours to make a foot of progress.

That's what Eagle Feather depended on now. That the human eye was drawn to movement. That as long as he kept absolutely still, the idiots in their black uniforms and their skull insignias would not see him.

His "old man" ruse had worked to get off the loading detail so he could sit down next to the blankets. Then he had stuffed the blankets up under his poncho. Reaching slowly over and grasping the corner of one, pulling it slowly out of the pile and up under the poncho with him. One after another until he had enough to make his own shape. Then he had eased gently out behind the form he'd made. That part had been right out in the open, and he hadn't relied on the eye being drawn to movement so much as waiting until everybody was concentrating on something else, and moving quickly. He made it from his stuffed scarecrow Indian to the side of the building in a single, quick-as-lightening movement. Then he vanished into the nearby bushes.

Eagle Feather was not "escaping." He was making for the woodshop in a stone building behind the monastery where Nick had built the detonator. Paco's soldiers were everywhere, but Eagle Feather knew the property. He slipped unseen into empty buildings, passed down hallways and up stairs as silent as a ghost, out windows, through bushes and trees, moving from one puddle of shadow to another, just a deeper shade of dark than the shadows around him.

Nick and his men had just gotten the explosives in place last night. They'd waited until the last minute to plant them, for fear the Astrals would become aware of them in some way the humans didn't even understand. Nick had drilled down into the rock of the entrance, that had been cut into the sandstone as smooth as cutting marble for a statue. He'd planted the R8 deep, in the walls, and then set smaller charges outside buried in the rocks on the sides of the entrance. Eagle Feather knew Nick planned to move the detonator down to the cave today.

But then Paco had shown up.

When Eagle Feather slipped unseen into the workshop building, he found the detonator sitting on the counter where Nick had assembled it, a small gray box that looked like a child's toy. Attached to the box was a three-foot-long wire with a metal tip that reminded Eagle Feather of the meat thermometer his wife had used on Christmas turkeys. The box was totally unadorned except for a clear, see-through plastic domed lid that was closed over a single red button. Shove the meat thermometer into a crack in the cave wall, slide the cover back on its hinge and punch the button, and the charges would go off.

Eagle Feather had never actually had a conversation with Nick about the device, but had been present, doing his cigar store Indian imitation, when Nick and Sawyer had discussed it. He put the detonator into a pillowcase he'd snatched off a bed in one of the monks' bedrooms, and closed it at the top with zip ties he'd gotten from the kitchen. He left as silently as he had come, dodged carefully to the back of the monastery building and slipped inside. He went to the second floor on the back side of the building where a huge oak tree stretched up taller than the roof. Climbing out a window into the tree, eased himself down the back side of the trunk. He didn't know where Paco might have stationed guards, but surely there were none behind the academy's administration building, which was encircled by a huge rock wall that Dr. Weiss had topped with broken glass after Astral Day as a deterrent to the first group of townies who'd tried to take over the academy.

Eagle Feather eased himself along behind the bushes next to the wall. Then he saw him. One of Paco's guards was standing with his back to the wall, smoking a cigarette, with his rifle leaned against the wall. There was no other cover; Eagle Feather couldn't get past him.

Unless he climbed up onto the wall, and crept along it until he was above the soldier and could jump him. But he would have to negotiate the top of the wall without getting sliced open.

He backtracked until he reached a small dogwood tree, climbed it and inched out on a limb that extended over the wall. Soundlessly, he moved from the limb to the top of the wall. He would have to make it sixty feet in absolute silence to a position above the guard. He couldn't stand, so he had to place his hands carefully, crawling, finding a place where there were no broken shards of razor-sharp glass. And he had to move fast. Anyone who chanced to come around the side of the administration building wouldn't miss the old Indian crawling along the top of the wall toward the soldier.

He moved carefully, but still felt a stab of pain on the edge of his palm. Looking down, he saw blood flowing out, staining the concrete where the glass was embedded. He went on, leaving wet red handprints behind him.

Before he made it to a spot where he could jump the guard, he had cut both hands, one slightly, one that was bleeding profusely, and his lower leg. But he was finally in position. The guard had finished his cigarette, and when he dropped it on the ground and stomped it out with his foot, Eagle Feather fell on him from above. He slit the man's throat with the knife he'd pulled from a kitchen drawer along with the zip ties. The man's eyes were huge, his lips working in soundless horror, with blood pulsing out his neck in heartbeat bursts.

Eagle Feather turned the soon-to-be dead man's body over and split the back of his uniform jacket and the shirt beneath it, putting the point of the blade at the neck and drawing it downward to the bottom of the jacket. With the coat, shirt and undershirt beneath it now in two pieces, Eagle Feather pulled them off the man's body and stuffed them into the sack with the detonator. He pulled the man's handgun out of his holster and slipped it into the belt of his jeans in the back, slipped the strap of the rifle over his shoulder and climbed back up the side of the wall to the top. But he just crossed it this time, carefully avoiding the sharp edges, and dropped to the ground on the other side. Then he vanished into the trees like a ghost, from one shadow to another until he reached the fence of the corral where the horses where kept. Naki Kiiya was there. Chelee had died two years ago. The horse lifted its head and neighed in greeting, and Eagle

Feather froze, but then relaxed when he realized the uniformed idiots who could hear it wouldn't know the difference between a greeting neigh and the feed-me-now neigh that greeted Eagle Feather in the evenings when he came with the bag of oats for the old horse. And couldn't tell either of them from the oh-shit-there's-a-rattlesnake neigh.

Eagle Feather paused then and cut the pieces of fabric he'd taken from the dead soldier into strips to make bandages for his hands and leg. He pulled the bandages tight to staunch the blood flow. Any horse could spook at the smell of blood, and the best Eagle Feather could do was keep it from running down his leg.

He slid though the slats of the fence, making his way through the other horses silently. The animals knew and trusted him and moved willingly out of his way. He took hold of Naki Kiiya's mane, guided him to the gate in the fence on the other side of the corral, lifted the catch, opened the gate wide enough to lead the horse through it, then closed it behind him.

Eagle Feather didn't mount the horse until they were safely in the woods, then he threw his leg over the animal's back, didn't groan at the pain that shot through it as the motion pulled the cut open and sent fresh red out to stain the bandage. Then he urged the horse forward with his knees.

Eagle Feather was certainly what the kids would call "old school," but in truth, he hadn't ridden a horse bareback in decades. It was as uncomfortable as shit, holding onto the animal with his knees, and using them to help guide him at the same time, as he pulled slightly on the animal's mane with his right hand, the one with only a small cut. The left had been opened up all the way to the bone and the bandage holding it together was already soaked again. The wound needed stitches, as did the wound on his leg.

Once he got to the trail in the woods, he didn't have to do much guiding. He and the horse had taken this trail many times. It led through the woods roughly in the direction of Matheson Caverns, then veered off and out over the mountain to a spot where Eagle Feather tethered the animal by the side of a creek where the glass was tall and green, while he slipped into the trees to bag a squirrel, a brace of rabbits from the meadow or a deer if he could locate one grazing and then track it through the trees.

Naki Kiiya thought that was where Eagle Feather was going and was surprised when the Indian pulled right on his mane at a bend in the trail and took out through the woods. The mountains around here were dotted with caves. Eagle Feather had stumbled upon one of them a couple of years ago, and that's where he was going. Its position on the mountainside would indicate that it opened into Level Four of the caverns — which, along would Level Five would flood when the waters came. It was the closest entrance and beyond that … he hadn't planned beyond that.

No telling how long Paco would take to load the rest of the trucks, or how long to drive down the winding road from the village to the Cricket Bottom cave entrance. He didn't know what the madman would do once he got there, either, but given that Noah was certainly talking things over with Star, who was with Sawyer's brother and his family at the entrance, Eagle Feather suspected there would be some kind of surprise waiting for Paco when he got there.

But Eagle Feather had learned as a young boy at the feet of his father and grandfather not to concern himself with things he couldn't control. Whatever happened there would happen and he wouldn't be able to affect the outcome one way or the other. What he could do, however, was make sure there was a detonator waiting for Nick or Sawyer or Noah to use when the time came to plug up the entrance to the Astrals' mine, high up on the north face of Tucker Mountain. Otherwise, everything they were doing would be futile once the water from the flood poured into the mine, far above the elevation of all the natural entrances

Then the water would flood the ark.

Chapter Forty-Seven

DAVID MATHESON WAS up in the tallest tree on the crest of the hill that butted up against Tucker Mountain. On the other side of the mountain, high up under the ridge of sandstone, was the entrance to the Astrals' mine. David looked out all around, and could see for miles from this vantage point. But what he had been placed here to see was the parking lot in front of the Cricket Bottom entrance. Soon trucks would come rolling into the lot. Six of them, that's what Noah had told Star. Two of them, the ones in the front and in the back, contained soldiers and the trucks in the middle contained supplies that his Uncle Sawyer had been preparing to send on rafts down the river.

David had gone over the plan several times with his father, mother, brother and the other villagers they'd armed. It wasn't much of a plan. They would have the parking lot covered from 360 degrees. There was no cover anywhere in the lot, nothing at all there but the poles where community awnings once provided shade for tour buses. Only one awning, Bardstown, still stood. When they opened fire, they would mow down whoever was in the lot below.

David Matheson was about to kill somebody.

He had managed to shove that out of his mind when he was getting ready, listening to the instructions, making sure he had plenty of ammunition. But now, sitting here in the silence, the prospect came roaring down on him and he began to tremble.

He was going to *shoot* somebody. A person. He'd spent his life hunting, started out as a little boy with a rifle that was taller than he was, shooting birds and rabbits and squirrels. He'd graduated to deer and elk, and in recent years had added in "livestock," once-domesticated cattle, sheep, goats and pigs that now ran wild.

Today, he was going to shoot a man. He was going to … commit murder. Wasn't it murder when you plotted it out to kill somebody and then did it, didn't give them a chance?

No, this wasn't murder. This was war. The new world order — fight or die.

This was a war and David sure as shit wasn't going to let the monster who had killed Nick Wilson's precious little Josie win. Yeah, he could shoot that guy, and all the guys like him, lined up on his side.

David glanced at the northern horizon, the line of hills connecting to the sky …

There was something there. Something dark. Almost like smoke, like the distant hills were on fire. He watched for only a few seconds, and as he did the darkness shifted upward, grew. Maybe it was smoke. What could possibly be burning?

Then he heard the roar of the trucks coming down the road and the smoke was forgotten.

His stomach flutters eased away. He felt a steely calm settle over him. Not the calm of trying to be still, not move when you were in a deer blind so you wouldn't scare up the buck you were hunting. This was the calm of resolve and resolution. Yes, he was about to kill someone, a whole lot of someones. He was doing it to protect his family and everyone who mattered to him. Glancing down, he could only see the top of Star's head. He was protecting Star, who … was special, somehow.

He watched the trucks pull one at a time into the parking lot. The lead truck drove all the way across the lot to the steps of the main entrance of the cave and stopped. The other trucks went along behind it, an elephant with his trunk hanging onto the tail of the next. But then the truck in the back broke ranks and pulled up beside the front one.

The trucks were probably what would be called troop carriers. They were military, green with fabric stretched over a canopy in the back. When the tailgate let down, men poured out of the backs of two of the trucks. They were all dressed in black uniforms, with some form of insignia on their breasts. They all had sidearms and rifles. He didn't count, but there were twenty or more in each truck. Forty, maybe as many as fifty men.

The door opened on the first truck and a man got

out that David knew instantly was Paco. He wasn't in a black uniform. His was a deep red, a strange color of red, and the insignia wasn't just on a badge on his chest. It covered the whole back of his uniform shirt.

A white skull with a big, hairy black spider crawling out one empty eye socket and a snake slithering out the other. Star had told him that she and Noah had dreamed of that insignia, the skull and the spider and snake, for a month before Astral Day. And she said that when they were beamed up into the mothership, Paco had been dressed in a pair of sweatpants and nothing else. His feet were bare, his chest bare, too, and the insignia was a giant tattoo that took up most of his chest and belly.

Noah had told him that the tattoo was odd. It wasn't just lines and colors that an artist had drawn. It was raised skin. Scars. The shapes had been *cut into Paco's flesh* — the shape of the skull, the head and body of the snake, the black legs of the spider. They all were scars. The tattoo merely added color to the forms already there. Paco had literally cut the tattoo into his chest and belly, and David couldn't imagine how he had forced himself to do that. But apparently there was more to the story, because Noah didn't want to go into the rest of it.

David raised his rifle and sighted in on the man with the ugly shapes on the back of his shirt, but it was a dicey shot. He was standing too close to Noah, Sawyer and Nick Wilson. The others, the soldiers, were out in the open. He could sight in on any of them, just standing there. Sitting ducks.

He concentrated on the rifle in his hands, looking out through the sight. He found a shape, a man in a black uniform who didn't look any different from the next guy, just that this one had blond hair. When his uncle gave the signal, David and all the other snipers would open fire at once.

Placed in trees in a circle around the lot, the snipers had clear shots at everybody in that parking lot. Every soldier was in the line of fire of one or the other of them.

He let out a breath, then pulled another slowly into his lungs and held it.

Down in the parking lot below, his Uncle Sawyer lifted his arm and appeared to wipe the sweat off his brow. Then he, Noah and Nick collapsed, like their legs had been turned to bags of water, they folded up and fell to the ground, dropping out of the line of fire.

David squeezed the trigger and the blond man in a black uniform staggered a step and then fell forward. David was already sighted in on another soldier before the first one hit the asphalt.

Chapter Forty-Eight

PACO'S HEART began to hammer as soon as he caught sight of the cave entrance. He had never imagined anything like this. Noah had said "a cave" and he had pictured "a cave." Even when Noah said the cave had 450 miles of passages, Paco never connected to the magnitude until now.

There was a hole in the side of the mountain in front of them. Concrete steps had been fashioned to lead at a gentle angle down into the hole, so the grade wouldn't be too steep. The hole in the mountain must have been a hundred feet tall and at least as wide. You could have driven a truck in through it. No, bigger than that. You could have driven a tank in though there. He couldn't think of a vehicle so large that it wouldn't be dwarfed by the size of the hole.

Haycraft pulled the truck to a stop at the edge of the parking lot where a sidewalk stretched out to the top of the stairs, that had metal railings around it.

That cave was so big even claustrophobic Haycraft wouldn't get his ass puckered about it.

The second he stepped out of the truck, Paco felt something like a breeze, a cool breeze, wafting up out of the hole in the ground. He was so astounded, so thrilled and surprised that he could do nothing but stand there, gaping.

No wonder there had been so many supplies! The caverns that a hole like this would lead to ... would be enormous. No wonder they'd planned for thousands of people to hole up here ... get it, *hole up* here ... he almost giggled, but didn't. No wonder Noah had thought of this place and the air that'd be trapped here. This wasn't a small cave where you'd huddle in the dark, claustrophobia making you slowly lose your mind. This was ... this was a huge coliseum, a place where you could ...

He was aware that Sawyer had come up to stand beside him and Noah, felt a movement of his arm, like it was hot and he—

Noah collapsed away from beside him — he was standing there and then he wasn't. Sawyer was gone, too, and it took Paco half a beat to realize they had just collapsed.

The gunfire was deafening. It was from everywhere around him. The roar of it tore into his ears, and he could actually hear ... he could hear bullets zapping into the truck, the door, the fender, the road, all around.

His men were falling like dominoes. Nothing could have prepared him for ... there were four or five men instantly dead, and he didn't see any of them even go for weapons. The shots were coming from all around and there was nowhere—

Paco was only alive right now because he was in close proximity to Sawyer and Noah. His men fell around him with cries of pain, grunts, thuds, screams. All around. Paco crouched to the ground between Noah and Sawyer.

Sawyer didn't stay where he'd fallen, though. He rolled away toward the nearest fallen soldier and Paco realized he was pulling the man's pistol from his scabbard. His rifle had fallen several feet away.

It happened in slow motion then, or seemed to. Paco watched Sawyer roll the dead man over onto his back and reach for the weapon. It was in a holster that had a strap across the top that snapped, so you had to unsnap it to draw the weapon.

Paco felt Noah moving beside him, and he just reached out blindly, grabbed his arm, and dragged him in front, squatting down behind him. Paco had a pistol in his hand. He'd been holding the gun on Noah in the truck, and now he brought it up and placed the barrel on the side of Noah's temple. He watched Sawyer turning as he was lifting his weapon, wondered which of them would be the fastest, which of them would get their weapon into place first.

If it was Sawyer, he would pull the trigger and Paco would die. If it was Paco, Sawyer would hold up, hesitate. He would understand the threat and back off. Paco won the race. He watched the rage and calculation on Sawyer's face drain away and knew he had him.

The sounds of slaughter around them was a cacophony of dying men shouting, screaming. One of his soldiers made a break for it and ran down the sidewalk to the steps and a shot in the back hurled him forward down the steps. Another soldier crouched down beside the truck only a few feet away from Paco, hiding from the gunfire coming from the north side of the truck. But the truck provided no protection from the weapons on this side of the truck, and the man suddenly jerked, his gun flying away, blood squirting out the hole in his back.

Several men sprinted for the hillside and the trees. He watched two get cut down in their tracks, didn't see whether the others made it to cover or not.

Three of his soldiers tried to climb back up into the truck for cover, but the bullets ripped into them. Another man did make it into the back of one of the trucks with supplies. Maybe he still had his sidearm, but he had dropped his rifle as he climbed.

The carnage was so deafening, so sudden and shocking that it was stupefying how quickly it was over. One second there were bullets flying everywhere, thunking into metal or the rubber of the tires, the asphalt, but mostly into bodies …

Thunk! Scream. Thunk, scream. Men leapt every which way, their weapons flying out of their hands. They fell on top of each other, in silent piles.

Thunk. Scream.

Thunk.

The Hidden

Thunk.

The roar of a rifle in the hills.

Quiet.

Not silence. There were cries from injured men, but not many. And those died away after random thunk-thunk sounds. The people in the woods finished off the soldiers who had survived, shot anybody who moved, as quickly and efficiently as they had mowed the men down.

He'd brought fifty-five of his best soldiers. They all were gone now, in less than thirty seconds — dead, he assumed, didn't think anybody had survived the lethal barrage of gunfire. Then he found himself crouched up against the truck, the door open, his hand an iron grip on Noah's upper arm, the barrel of his pistol pointed at the boy's temple. The hammer cocked.

Staring at Sawyer, not five feet away, with a pistol leveled at Paco, the look of determination on his face morphed into something else as Paco watched. The man knew he'd been beaten. It wasn't like Paco had to threaten to pull the trigger unless Sawyer dropped the gun. He didn't have to. Sawyer simply lowered the weapon and placed it quietly on the asphalt.

Then it really was quiet, the only sound the rasping of his breath as it tore in and out of his throat in gasps.

His men were dead. All of them. Maybe not the guy who had jumped into the back of the truck with the supplies but Paco doubted he'd made it. The back of the truck was riddled with gunfire, the cloth canopy dancing from the impacts. No, he was gone, too.

Paco was all alone.

Holding the ace of spades that won the hand.

He had Noah.

Game over.

He glanced up into the woods, knowing the snipers were so well hidden he'd never spot—

Something had come up, was there in the sky above the trees. What in the world—?

Chapter Forty-Nine

DAVID PULLED the trigger and there was no sound of a shot. Just the firing pin landing on an empty chamber. He looked down to discover that there were three empty ammunition magazines in his lap. He'd already slapped three of them into the rifle — after he fired the twenty rounds that were already loaded. He'd used up four magazines with twenty rounds each. Eighty shots, and he hadn't been aware of reloading a single time.

He ejected the empty magazine, shoved home another full one, but could see no targets. The parking lot was full of bodies. Dead bodies everywhere. He had shot some of those men, had killed them, but right now David had no memory of any of it.

He heard a sound, a strange whump-whump sound. Star leapt to her feet, stood up from behind the boulder and screamed,

"They're coming. All of them, from everywhere."

A cloud passed overhead, blotting the sun with its

shadow. He looked up at the cloud and it wasn't a cloud. It was birds. A flock of birds.

Not a flock. A blanket of birds. A solid mass of wings and feathers too thick to see through, blotting out all light.

Not starlings, their acrobatic movements synchronized, twisting and turning and coiling back on themselves in perfect unison. It wasn't any kind of bird, not any *one* kind. The cloud was every possible species of bird — small ones, sparrows and wrens, cardinals and robins but bigger, too, owls and hawks, ducks and geese, *long-necked cranes*, falcons ... shit, even an *eagle*.

Thousands ... hundreds of thousands of birds — the blanket of them filled the whole sky, was a solid canopy as far as he could see.

What ... why ...?

Not swooping and diving — flying straight, due south. All of them in the same direction. He looked back toward the horizon he had seen darkened, where the smoke — but it hadn't been smoke, it'd been the birds. He couldn't breathe then because there was no air in the world. The birds were fleeing, desperately trying to get away from—

Chapter Fifty

STAR COULD SMELL the magnolia bush near the boulder David had set her behind. She could smell the warm grass and feel the breeze on her face. She tried to concentrate on those things, to calm her hammering heart, but it didn't do any good and she finally gave up.

Something was wrong with Pumpkin. He was snuggled up against her as if he were terrified of something, but he wasn't whining or trembling. He kept sniffing the air, then emitting low growls or whines.

She knew he could sense her fear and tension and the fear and tension of everyone around. That had to be it. The dog could smell fear wafting up off David, his father, mother, brother and the other snipers in the woods. And most certainly off Star.

We're coming, Noah said in her head.

"They're coming," she told David. "Noah says

they just rounded the corner by the red-and-black barn, a couple of minutes out."

She wanted to keep talking to Noah in his head, but his mind was concentrating on keeping Paco out and she didn't want to distract him.

Besides, there was Pumpkin ...

She allowed herself to slip into the mind of her dog, allowed herself to feel the sensations, see the images generated by the dog's incredible sense of smell. Those images were always jumbled and mostly impossible to interpret.

They weren't, after all, meant for a human mind. Another dog would have understood perfectly, but Star only got flashes of images, and layers ... always layers and layers. Pumpkin was smelling what was here right now ... here was a squirrel around very close, maybe up in the tree on the lowest branch near her, but there had been a different squirrel, more than one other squirrel in this vicinity recently, and the scents of them were layered on top of the *now* scent.

Star heard the sound of the truck engines and she put both arms around Pumpkin and pulled him tight against her. Not to comfort him. But to let him comfort her. She heard the trucks pull into the parking lot below. Heard the engines die. Heard a truck door open, several doors open and close, and a whacking sound like a tailgate or—

Then the world exploded in a roar of gunfire and she held her hands over her ears and squeezed her eyes shut. She was terrified, the sound of gunfire so horrifying she couldn't seem to breathe. Pumpkin tensed, heard the sounds ... but he didn't seem to be interested in the gunfire. It was a roaring cacophony and she was sure he could smell the blood, hear the screams, smell the fear, there were dozens of men down there, and they were being shot and—

Pumpkin pulled out of her arms ... and *left*.

"Pumpkin!" she called out, oblivious to the sound she was making that could give away her position to anyone who might want to shoot up into the woods from the parking lot. But she hadn't heard any return fire, not a single shot. She had heard the rifles on all sides of the parking lot let go, but nobody down there was firing—

Pumpkin came back to her, snuggled up to her, whining pitifully.

What was wrong?

The dog was paying no attention to the sounds of gunfire. They were far back in his consciousness, like the canvas on which a much more important picture was being painted. What he was attending to was a sudden plethora of images, his whole sensory system was suddenly overloaded with images.

He had his back to the parking lot, was standing beside her, wouldn't sit down. His tail was down, not between his legs, a sign he was frightened, but down. He didn't understand, was confused about something.

He let out a yap. A single bark.

Star knew Peanut and Butter were around here somewhere, the German Shepherds that patrolled the big cave where the Mathesons lived. Was Pumpkin communicating with them? Pumpkin began to whine, put his tail between his legs and made sounds she'd never heard him make before.

Slipping into the dog's mind, Star was slapped down by images. Like you'd pick up a picture book and thumb through the pages, let the pages slide off your thumb so fast it was more like shuffling cards than looking at a book, no single page visible.

Pumpkin's images were smells, what his fantastic olfactory system was sniffing right now on the wind, and the images were horrifying in their complexity and their total absurdity.

He was smelling squirrels, rabbits, snakes, deer, a skunk, a badger and a beaver. A black bear — the bear was very near! — and *birds*! The images of them were so smeared together in Pumpkin's brain that it was nothing more than a freight train of feathers and wings — and a fox, more squirrels. Mice — hundreds of them! Snakes.

Pumpkin smelled snakes. Snakes plural. Not just one snake, more than one, more than one *kind*, why would there suddenly be snakes …

Lizards, crawly things on the ground with too many legs, bugs and locusts and ants, moths and beetles and spiders—

It was all in there together, in Pumpkin's mind, swirling around and around like food in a blender. The dog was totally freaked out, whining, growling, starting to bark but only yipping instead. He moved nervously, beside her, behind her, cuddled up close to her … trembling.

Pumpkin was trembling like he was freezing!

It made no sense.

Star was aware of the gunfight, her attention was on that, the sounds of rifles firing. Men were dying! She could hear their screams of pain and the gunfire was a single sound all its own, a combination of all the shots fired by all the snipers at one time, fusing into a single horrendous roar.

But when she let herself touch Pumpkin's brain, the freaky menagerie of animal smells was so overwhelming it was like she'd been slapped. Why would …?

Then she saw the darkness in the sky. Star was blind, but she could distinguish between light and dark. Something huge was overhead, a big cloud — no, it was too solid to be a cloud, too dark and thick. An Astral mothership, then?

Noah.

Paco had grabbed Noah, and shoved the barrel of a gun up against his temple.

That's when the first of the snakes slithered across Star's foot and she began to scream.

Chapter Fifty-One

Paco was looking up the hill toward the source of the gunfire when he saw them come over the crest.

Birds!

Thousands of birds. *Hundreds of thousands.*

Their cries were as cacophonous as the gunfire that had only just died away. The thumping of their pumping wings made a *whump-whump* sound that became so loud it roared like the thunder of a waterfall.

Every kind of bird … little, big, sparrows and ducks and …

What the fuck!

They were all flying in the same direction.

A voice — *Star.* It was Star. She was up there on the hillside, not in that little town. How had they been able to lie to Paco and he didn't know?

It was Star up there, her voice high and shrill. "They're coming. All of them, from *everywhere*."

Sawyer was still only feet away, just staring at Paco,

menace in his every cell, but as long as Paco had his precious son—

"Snakes!" Noah cried, his eyes wide. "They're everywhere, all over the ground. Snakes and lizards and they're — so thick you can't even walk."

"Snakes? Where?" Sawyer asked, confused.

"On the mountaintop. They came up the other side."

Everyone looked at the mountain. Above it was the insane blanket of birds and—

Star screamed again, and Paco saw a young man suddenly drop to the ground off a tree limb. He reached out toward a boulder and grabbed—

Star.

Paco was unprepared for the impact of seeing her for the first time since a white room in an Astral mothership. All he could do was stare, couldn't breathe, wasn't looking anymore at Noah, whose arm he held in a death grip as he jammed the pistol into Noah's temple.

Star!

The young man began dragging Star behind him down the hillside.

What in the—?

Paco could see that the ground on the hillside was ... *wrong*, something was ... It was like the ground was moving, was alive, wiggling and writhing with movement.

Star was screaming as the young man dragged her behind him.

Paco could have shot her. A shot from this distance

with a pistol would be iffy at best. Or he could have shot the young man, who had a rifle in the hand that wasn't clutching Star's hand. At least waste the damn dog that never left Star's side. Neither of them seemed to care that they were running out in the open toward armed men ... dead men. But Paco was armed!

The young man was shouting something but Paco missed it.

Sawyer caught it, though. Paco could tell by the look of sudden horror on his face and all the color drained away.

"What?" Paco demanded.

"The flood." Sawyer spoke the word barely loud enough to hear, so much airiness in the sound it was hard to understand. "David said the flood ... he could see it from the trees up there. Coming this way."

Paco stood with the others in total shock. Staring. His mind refusing to process the information. The flood. It wasn't supposed to happen for ... it was too early ... They'd said it wasn't coming for ... They had *tricked* him!

No, they hadn't lied to him. One look at Sawyer's face and it was clear he was as surprised as Paco.

The snakes had made it to the parking lot by then and came slithering out across it, up and over the bodies of dead and dying men lying in puddles of blood.

Snakes, *everywhere*. A solid surface of writing reptiles ... flowing toward them along with a black, boiling mass of other things, too — bugs, creatures, moles or mice and spiders, holy God, the spiders. All flowing in an endless sea across the asphalt toward them.

And there was a thundering sound now, coming from that direction, a rumble.

"They're running from the flood," Sawyer said.

"Tell those motherfuckers in the trees to hold their fire or I will kill the kid and you." Paco pressed the gun tight against Noah's temple.

"Don't shoot," Sawyer called out.

But it was clear the ambush was falling apart anyway, snipers climbing down out of trees, out of hiding in brush, running with the stampede of wildlife down the hillside toward the cavern.

"Don't you get it, asshole," Sawyer growled. "The flood's coming. Run right now or—"

The rumble got instantly louder as the first of the animals crested the top of the hillside. It was a stampede of every creature in the forest, rushing forward in blind panic, side by side, united in terror.

Like running from a fire.

Paco had seen one of the infamous California fires, way too up-close-and-personal. The fire ate up the forest in huge gulping hunks and it was all Paco could do to get to his vehicle and run from the flames.

There'd been terrified animals then, too, deer with such fear in their eyes they were totally blinded by it and ran into trees. Bears, shit, there had been half a dozen black bears, and every other—

That — that tangled multitude of wildlife was what came surging down the hillside toward them now.

Paco stood, dragged Noah closer.

"Get me into that ark. Right now or I will blow your pathetic brains out, splatter gray goo all over your father's shirt."

Sawyer said nothing, just watched from his position on the ground.

"Haycraft, Winslow, Hawthorne … anybody," Paco called out, knew no one would answer but miraculously two men crawled out from under a truck where they had taken cover when the snipers opened fire. Hawthorne and Winslow, who dragged the deaf girl out from under the truck. Her clothing was torn, her lip bloody. Winslow crouched behind her, using her as a shield.

Paco turned toward Sawyer.

"So long, motherfucker," he said and moved the pistol from Noah's temple to shoot Sawyer in the chest with it.

That's when the deaf girl broke free, wrenched out of Winslow's grasp and raced as quick as a baby rabbit toward the steps leading down into the cavern. Noah was just as quick, slammed his body into Paco, knocking him off balance and causing the shot meant for his father to go wide and ricochet off the truck fender.

Sawyer instantly rolled under a truck. There was no time now to chase him. No time for anything except get into that motherfucking ark.

Star and the young man had made it to the edge of the parking lot and were racing across it. Paco could wait for her. He could take her captive, force her to—

"Now or never," Noah said next to his ear, as if he knew what Paco had been thinking and maybe he did. Then the kid lurched toward the sidewalk leading to the steps into the cave that the deaf girl had just raced down. He tried to drag Paco with him, but Paco yanked him back a step, staring a hole in Star, whose boyfriend had dropped her hand and was raising the rifle to point it at Paco.

No time.

Paco turned and used Noah as a shield. "Run!" he cried, and clutched the boy tight as he took off toward the cave. They barely made it two steps before gunfire erupted from the mouth of the cave. The shooters in the dark there were careful not to hit the deaf girl or Noah — and Paco — but they dropped Winslow and Hawthorne in a hail of bullets.

Paco was trapped between the boy with a rifle accompanying Star and the shooters in the cave. He froze, lifted the pistol to Noah's temple. He'd take the boy with him if they—

"Over there, down that hillside is the river." Noah pointed off to the left across the bottom of the parking lot. "It flows through the cave. We can get in that way."

"And drown when the river floods?"

"There's an elevator from the river to the top level."

"Bullshit!"

"How the hell do you think we got supplies enough for five thousand people up there?" He pointed to the top of the ridge. "Joppa Ridge is fifteen hundred feet tall."

Five thousand people?

Dammit, there was too fucking much Paco didn't know about all this, about the cave — how could it be that big, *miles* long?

"If there's no elevator, you're dead," he snarled.

"No elevator and we'd all be dead."

Paco shoved Noah toward that side of the parking lot and kept his gun in his back as they ran.

Chapter Fifty-Two

BOTH EAGLE FEATHER and Naki Kiiya were old.

Though his hearing and vision had seemed actually to improve with age, the rest of Eagle Feather's body hadn't been so accommodating to the years. He was seventy-eight, and had really begun to feel his age about three years ago when stiffness had settled into his bones like starch into a shirt. Where once he had been nimble and quick, now he was neither. But he was still mobile, strong and healthy — *without* enhancing drugs. That was something in the era of age regression gene therapy that could give old men back their vigor and old women their beauty, and medications that had all but eliminated all the major illnesses. Had before Astral Day, anyway. Now the world was devolving back into pre-magic-cure life — which meant poor Ellie was dying of a disease that would have been totally curable if she'd been able to find treatment instead of closed labs and absentee doctors, and no way to travel from point A to point B for medical care even if there'd been any.

He thought about those things as he and the old horse struggled up the mountainside, making for the entrance into Matheson Caverns called "The Drain," about three hundred feet above the Twin Forks River. Must have gotten its name because it was a round hole in the base of Joppa Ridge, and in front of it was a meadow roughly the shape of a bathtub, with tall hills on three sides. It was the largest of at least half a dozen, maybe more, natural caves that poked through the rock into Level Four of the caverns, and it was the closest cavern entrance overland from Zion Village.

The Level Four cavern was the longest of the five caverns, by virtue of its tangled-up twists and turns. It was probably four and a half winding miles from the Cricket Bottom Visitor's Center on the west to the dock on the east side where the river flowed into the cavern and four big elevators were now being used to take people and supplies up into the upper levels. The Drain was roughly halfway. Once inside, Eagle Feather would still have to make it at least two more miles through the cavern to the elevators.

In addition to the one in which the main four elevators had been located, there were half a dozen other chimneys, natural "elevator shafts" between Level Four and Level Three. You could climb up through them from one level to the next, and the Mathesons had also built crude freight elevators in each one to transport ... Eagle Feather didn't know

The Hidden

what. There was bound to be one of those chimneys close to The Drain, but Eagle Feather had to find *somebody, anybody* to hand the detonator off to and there might not be anybody in that part of Level Three to take it from him.

Making their way through thick woods, the route became steeper. Eagle Feather had to backtrack around windfalls and gullies, and sudden overhangs that blocked their way, trusting in his once-unerring sense of direction as his only compass.

The old Indian often imagined the mountains naked — devoid of the lush green vegetation — and he did so now. In truth, the mountains here were mesas just like the ones in Sedona — red buttes that rose up off the flat desert like blocks left on the floor by giant children. But these buttes were covered with vegetation, trees and bushes and brush, and the rainfall here over millennia had carved them in ways nature had not shaped the desert monoliths.

Picturing them naked helped Eagle Feather visualize the location of the cave. As exertion and strain stacked up, Eagle Feather felt his energy sapped by the gash across the palm of his hand and the cut on his leg. He hadn't lost a tremendous amount of blood in the beginning. He'd stopped the bleeding with pressure bandages quickly. But bouncing around bareback on Naki Kiiya, using the animal's mane for reins, had opened both the wounds and they were bleeding again, had soaked the bandages and he had nothing with which to repair them.

The old paint horse was trying, too, rising to the occasion, sensing Eagle Feather's urgency. He was not surprised. He and the animal had been friends since the day Eagle Feather had purchased him from Running Buck Thompson, using for barter a fancy set of pots and pans made from some kind of steel alloy that cooked food in minutes using almost no heat at all. His daughter-in-law had given him the cookware for his birthday, or maybe Father's Day, and he'd never even opened the box.

He'd brought Naki Kiiya, whose name meant "two spot" in Apache, and Chelee, whose name meant simply "horse," with him and Star to Kentucky, had buried Chelee when he found him dead in his stall one morning two years ago.

Both the old Indian and the old horse were struggling now more than they'd struggled in years. Eagle Feather's strength was draining away with his blood, and the spotted horse was foaming at the mouth, even had little flecks of blood in the foam, which meant he was working too hard and that his lungs had begun to bleed inside.

Naki Kiiya would die if Eagle Feather didn't stop soon and let the animal rest. That was if the old Indian didn't pass out from blood loss himself first. But he pushed himself and the horse, sliding in and out of consciousness from the strain and the heat, watching the trees bend and blur like they were special effects in some movie.

They got to a small rise where there was a break in the thick forest and Eagle Feather could see the top of the hillside ahead — the "rim" of the bathtub meadow and Joppa Ridge beyond it. They had to turn then, as the trail tracked along beside the top of the hillside to a spot where the grade wasn't as steep. That's when Naki Kiiya suddenly began to act up.

The animal didn't want to move sideways — it wanted to move forward! It wanted to go *up*, and it had nothing to do with exertion or the difficulty of the trail. Eagle Feather understood every nuance of the horse's body language — the animal wasn't exhausted, he was *scared*. Something was frightening him. He looked around, seemed confused, refused Eagle Feather's urging with his knees to move across the hillside instead of up it. Something was very wrong somewhere beyond what Eagle Feather could see, but he couldn't fathom what it might be.

His force of will was stronger than the animal's reluctance, and slowly they began to move sideways below the hilltop, the last incline that would take them to the open meadow in front of the rock face where The Drain led into the cool seclusion of the cave.

Naki Kiiya balked again, neighed, then without warning *stood up on his hind legs*. Eagle Feather would never have dreamed the old horse had it in him. It was so sudden and unexpected that Eagle Feather slid backwards off his rump and tumbled to the ground. Then Naki Kiiya turned and bolted, scrambling up the incline and then vanishing into the trees higher up the hillside, leaving Eagle Feather sitting in disbelief on the dead leaves of the forest floor.

What on earth could have spooked the animal like that?

The old Indian got slowly to his feet. He wasn't sure he could make it the rest of the way under his own steam.

He shook his head, vigorously. Negative thinking! Crazy thoughts. He would do what he had to do because he had to. There was no going back or giving up. If his strength failed him and he couldn't walk, then he would crawl.

He kept going. Not running exactly, more like staggering, something like lurching from tree to tree, leaning forward up the incline, grabbing hold of bushes and vines to pull him upward. He was winded, gasping, seeing stars before his eyes. Then the world darkened, and at first he thought he had actually lost his sight. The darkness had come too quickly to be a cloud across the sun.

He looked up then and saw ... *birds*.

What in the—?

He could do nothing but stand and stare, gawk at the mass of birds suddenly overhead so thick it was a dark umbrella above the woods, blocking out the sun. Never in all his years had he seen anything like it. Every kind of bird, large and small, predator and prey, owls and robins and ravens and eagles, swans and ducks and ...

They had all taken flight, formed a solid mass of ... *fleeing birds*.

He felt fear, nameless apprehension grip his guts and squeeze. They were fleeing ... *what?*

His heart, already hammering a hole in the side of his chest from exertion, found a whole new reason to pound as the explanation began to seep into Eagle Feather's mind, much like the image on the gym floor had coalesced out of formless puddles of color into the image of the black death ship and the ray of white power. He hadn't wanted to see it, had refused at first to believe it was what it was.

Eagle Feather knew what *this* was, too, didn't have to see to know. The knowing froze his breath, sucked the air out of the world. It couldn't be *now*, not yet. They still had another whole day!

The feathered creatures that blotted out the sky were not in denial like the old Indian. They knew. Time had run out.

It was now. Ask the birds.

Then Eagle Feather's fatigue was gone. The pain from his bleeding palm and leg receded into the background of his consciousness and vanished there in the uproar of other thoughts.

He was running.

He was too tired, too old and too weak to run but he was running all the same. Racing past the last outcrop of protruding rock, up the last steep incline to the edge of the high meadow. Ahead was the cliff face where a round, black hole at the base of the ridge looked out of the caverns toward the sun.

He could see other cave entrances in the ridge face from here as well, none as big as The Drain, rips in the rock wall that didn't even have names. The rock face curved around toward him, so that the closest of those rips was not down at the bottom of the meadow at all. It lay where the top of the hillside joined the ridge, a jagged crack about twenty feet wide at the bottom, then angled up, getting smaller and smaller until the sides met and closed thirty feet off the ground.

He was too winded yet to move, stood gasping for breath. Suddenly, the woods below and behind him came to life with movement. He turned to look and …

What …?

There was nowhere in his mind that could interpret what he was seeing. It was such an impossible sight that it was, in a way, like being struck blind.

The animals weren't blind, though.

They were running out ahead of what was chasing them. And as he watched in slack-jawed amazement, the first of them reached him and the ground came to life with small things, snakes and moles and mice, creatures with six legs and eight legs, rabbits, foxes, raccoons, squirrels and … deer, with white tails at attention, raced out of the trees toward him, past him, almost knocked him down.

Everything alive on the floor of the woods was racing out ahead of the flood that was surging across the mountains and valleys. It couldn't be. But it was. Now he understood what had so terrified his horse.

The flood that was supposed to happen on Day Six day was happening *right now*.

They had no more time to plan, prepare or get the detonator in position. And all their preparation would be futile unless Eagle Feather could get into the caverns and use the detonator he'd intended to hand off to somebody else. He would have to *use it himself*. He would have to get close enough to the entrance to the Astral mine high up on the mountainside and set off the explosion that would block it. If the mine entrance remained open, all the caverns below it would flood. Everyone in them would drown.

Chapter Fifty-Three

THE WATER WAS FLOWING MORE than six inches deep across the parking lot before Paco and Noah got to the woods and Noah chanced a look back to see that the flow of it over the hillside was rising.

"Go on, dammit, and if you're lying to me …"

"I'm not lying," Noah talked to Paco out loud and concentrated on keeping Paco out of his head.

They crashed through the trees at the end of the parking lot and down the slope, which was slick with fallen leaves and a steep grade with water flowing over it now in a cascade. The two were about halfway down when Noah lost his footing and landed on his butt, then slid on it down the hillside much faster than Paco could keep up with him remaining upright. He felt bushes and stems whacking him in the face but didn't try to grab anything to slow his descent. As soon as he hit the ground at the bottom of the hillside, he heard a shout, not in his ears, but in his head, a strangled *"wait!"* It was clear it had taken enormous effort for Paco to shove the word into Noah's closed mind.

Noah looked back up the hill at Paco, who was miraculously still on his feet, pointing the pistol at him. As soon as Noah turned and Paco could see that he was looking, that he could read Paco's lips, he spoke words out loud.

"Try to ditch me and I'll shoot you in the back."

Noah had no doubt he would do exactly that.

Paco made it to the bottom of the slimy hillside still on his feet. The water flowing down it had now reached a foot deep and was getting deeper by the second. The cave mouth with the river flowing out of it yawned in front of them and Noah led the way.

He blocked his mind as strictly as he could, didn't allow the image of the staircase just inside the opening to appear in his mind. He would run past it quickly, and all he could do was hope that Paco didn't notice it. The staircase was the only way up to the next level, where his father and the others had sought refuge through the Cricket Bottom cave entrance. He would *not* take Paco there! The elevator was a ruse and Paco would soon figure that out. Oh, there really was an elevator, all right, four of them, next to the dock at the other entrance to the cavern … four miles away! There was no possible way to get to it before the cavern flooded.

Noah ran full out, dashing out of the heat and the bright sunshine into the dim light and cool air of the cave, where the water had risen above the channel worn through the solid rock of the cave bottom by the

The Hidden

Twin Forks River. The staircase was back in the shadows against the front wall, in the corner of the cavern. It certainly wasn't hidden, but you could easily miss it if you didn't know it was there. The string of lights on the ceiling didn't give enough light to illuminate it ... and with Paco's eyes not yet adjusted to the darkness.

Noah could only hope, and keep running. Paco followed, looking neither right nor left. The cavern turned to the left about sixty yards from the entrance and Noah made it there with Paco on his heels. Beyond the turn, the stairs were blocked from view.

It wouldn't take Paco long to figure out there was no elevator. Noah had to figure out a way to—

Face Planter.

Yes!

The cave floor wasn't completely level anywhere, but about fifty feet beyond the bend, the floor dropped like a shelf, like you were stepping off a stair tread. The drop was only about eight inches, but it was almost impossible to see in the gloom, particularly with eyes unadjusted to the darkness. Noah knew it was there and sometimes he still stumbled over the spot — and *face-planted* on the rocky floor.

Noah had to be far enough ahead that he could leap over the spot. Paco wouldn't see it coming if Noah could distract him, even for an instant.

Ten feet away from Face Planter, Noah put a bright image of the stairs in his mind, as clearly as he could visualize. And just as he'd hoped. Paco turned back to see what he'd missed. He hit Face Planter with his head turned, and miraculously kept his footing — he was like a cat. But he was off balance and that's all Noah needed. Spinning around, Noah shoved Paco and he helplessly tumbled into the water.

Noah dived away from the riverbank, hit the rocks and rolled away into the shadows behind the big gray not-statue rock formation that visitors swore was a rhinoceros complete with horn. Could Paco come up to the surface of the river and shoot him? Would the gun even fire, full of water like that?

Paco surfaced downstream. Without the gun. He'd dropped it. In just the few minutes they'd been in the cave, the water flowing down the hillside had grown from a stream six inches deep to a raging flood that almost reached Noah's knees. Flowing into the cave like that, going against the current trying to flow out, the water became tumultuous and Paco was caught in the frothing rapids. He was a good swimmer, at least he'd told Noah once that he was, laughing at Noah for his own inability to swim, and his horrible fear of water. But the current carried Paco backwards nonetheless, and he scrambled toward the nearest shore, on the other side of the river. He made it, got a foothold, was washed away farther downstream, then got a grip and held on and crawled up onto the bank. He got to his feet, looking back at Noah on the other side of the river. He was unarmed, but the hatred in his gaze was almost like a knife, striking a blow in Noah's mind.

The water had risen far out of the riverbank now, a boiling tumult of river water flowing one way — crashing against the water flowing down the hillside and into the cave. Even a champion swimmer wouldn't have been able to fight that current. If Paco went back into the water, he'd never make it across to the other side.

The cave would be full in minutes, and the only way out was the stairs on Noah's side of the river. Paco was trapped. And even if Noah'd been inclined to help him, there was nothing he could do.

And so they looked at each other across the bubbling, frothing river. Noah blocked his mind, didn't want to hear, but he was tired and the words burst through even though he tried to keep them out.

"... not over, motherfucker! I'll get you, kill you and the little bitch ..."

There was more, but apparently it had taken a huge effort on Paco's part to break through Noah's wall with even that much.

Noah said nothing, just turned and began to slog against the current back around the bend in the cavern toward the stairs. His last image was Paco flipping him the bird.

Chapter Fifty-Four

As soon as Paco turned his back and started dragging Noah toward the trees, Sawyer scrambled out from under the truck. The water was several inches deep in the parking lot already and rising fast. His gun was ... where? Then Paco, holding Noah at gunpoint, disappeared down the hillside.

Suddenly, Nick crawled out from under a truck. He'd obviously been hiding there, waiting for a clear shot at Paco. Grabbing one of the pistols dropped by Paco's men, he tossed it to Sawyer. "I think a couple of them made it to the woods — I'll cover you, go!"

Sawyer hesitated. He'd been trained to make instant decisions and he'd been pretty good at it. Once. But he hadn't had to be the man in charge, the dude with the gun and the badge, in a long time and his mind stumbled for a beat before a plan registered. Even before he was finished forming it in his head, he took off running — *not* toward the hillside, toward the cave entrance. Right out in the open, with the rattling fire of Nick's barrage fired into the trees, keeping anybody with a clear shot at him pinned down.

There was so sense following Noah and Paco down the hillside. But they'd be coming up the stairs from the river to Level Four and he'd be waiting to greet them when they did.

He was halfway to the cave entrance when a bullet ricocheted against a rock and he dropped to his knees, sheltering behind the two-foot concrete footer the metal railing was sunk into.

One of Paco's men had made it to the far hillside and had gone up it, found a tree to hide behind. Sawyer began to inch his way down the steps, with gunfire right over his head. He made it another three or four feet down the steps, where the metal railing was installed directly into the rock without even the small footer.

He saw Nick dash from his position behind the first truck to another spot behind the one next to it, watched bullets splash into the water around him that was now more than a foot deep in the parking lot.

"Idiot," Nick called out to the man on the hillside. "You're gonna drown in ten minutes if you don't come down from there and get to safety in the cave. Put your weapon down and I won't shoot."

"Fuck you!" More bullets accompanied the epitaph.

Nick dashed from one truck to another, and then to a position behind a car in the lot that was parked in front of a rock outcrop jutting out from the hillside.

The outcrop carved its way all the way to the top of the hill.

That was it, though. No other cover for fifty or sixty feet where a big green metal dumpster sat by itself in the lot. Sawyer couldn't even provide cover fire for Nick to make a dash for the dumpster, not with nothing but a pistol.

The water rose higher, flowing down the steps now, threatening to wash Sawyer away.

Suddenly, Nick stood and began to race toward the dumpster, zigzagging in the knee-deep water, his body low. Sawyer recalled the words of his sergeant when he was in basic training a lifetime ago: "It is seriously difficult to deliver a fatal shot to a moving target at more than twenty feet."

Nick made it to the dumpster. He turned to Sawyer and used hand motions — not deaf sign language, military signals — to tell Sawyer he planned to go behind the rocks, up the hillside and circle around behind the man on the hill. As soon as Nick was no longer a target, the shooter turned his attention back to Sawyer and laid down a blistering barrage of bullets that pinged off the concrete and rock all around Sawyer, pinning him to the spot.

Then the shots stopped.

The man was out of ammo. It would only take him seconds to eject the cartridge and jam in a fresh one, but Sawyer could use those seconds. Of course, if Sawyer was wrong and the man was just waiting for him to show himself ...

Leaping to his feet, Sawyer bailed down the steps,

then dived for the bottom, which was now submerged in rising water. He rolled through the water and splashed into the cave.

Whoever had been inside the cave firing out at Paco's men was gone now, had made for high ground, up the stairs into Tripoli on the next level. The stairs that led down from Level Four to Level Five, the level of the river, were in the right corner of the cavern. The top portion of stairs was a spiral, cut right through the rock, and it had a decorative rock wall surrounding it.

Noah and Paco were nowhere in sight, apparently hadn't made it all the way up the stairs yet. He opened the wrought-iron gate to the top of the steps and closed it behind him. The wall and gate would keep the water from flowing down the stairs for a little while. It would slow the water down even when it washed out the gate so it wouldn't be water gushing down the steps like water flowing down a drain.

He peered carefully down the stairs, the pistol out in front of him in a two-hand grip.

The stairs were empty. Where were Noah and Paco? They should have been on the steps. Had Paco merely forced Noah to run blindly into the cave *past* the staircase to safety? That was crazy. The river would flood soon and fill the whole Level Five.

He plunged down the stairs, took the steps two at a time, leaning on the railing around and around, the first hundred feet of spiral. Then he stopped before the steps came out of the rock ceiling of Level Five. At that point, he'd be out in the open.

The Hidden

He moved slowly down the steps and was astonished to see the river flowing backwards *into* the cave instead of out. Paco and Noah were nowhere to be seen.

He raced down the final steps and plunged into water that was already up to his waist and rising. The current was so strong it was all he could do not to be carried away by it.

And then he spotted Noah, coming around the bend in the cavern, and his relief was momentarily overwhelming. The boy was alone, struggling against the rising current. Sawyer dropped his gun and hurried forward toward him.

Noah saw him, called out, "Paco's gone."

He grabbed Noah's hand and turned, the two of them fighting the current together, struggling against the mighty force of the water to get back to the staircase in the front of the cave. It was incredible how quickly the water had risen. By the time they made it to the stairs, the water was chest high, and Sawyer knew that any second the water pouring into the chamber through the Cricket Bottom entrance would crest the staircase wall and come gushing down on them. They struggled out of the water and raced up the steps, only made it half a dozen steps before the deluge from above slammed into them.

Sawyer held on to the railing and forced his way upward, with Noah behind, climbing steps up into a waterfall. When he finally popped up out of the hole of the stairwell, he could see water flowing over the retaining wall a foot deep. The steps leading up into

Tripoli on Level Four were on the *other side* of the cavern sixty feet away.

The water was chest high and rising. The current was so swift Sawyer feared to let go of the railing of the spiral staircase, afraid they'd be swept away. He could read the terror in Noah's eyes. The boy couldn't swim, had always been terrified of water. The strength of that current …

Taylor suddenly appeared on the stairs on the other side of the cavern that led up to Tripoli.

"Catch!" he cried. He was holding a red fire extinguisher to which he had tied a length of something. Sawyer held out his hands and Taylor heaved, but the throw was short and the fire extinguisher splashed into the water and was instantly carried downstream.

Samuel suddenly appeared on the steps behind his father, as Taylor frantically pulled in the length of cord.

"Let me, I'm stronger!" Samuel said and Sawyer saw Taylor hesitate, then hand the fire extinguisher he'd just fished out of the water to his son.

Samuel reared back, like he was throwing a pass, though he'd never played football anywhere except in the powder-puff games they had on weekends. He heaved the red metal container high into the air above the flowing water and it came down only inches behind Sawyer's reach.

"Grab my belt and hold onto the railing," he told Noah.

Noah grabbed his father's belt and Sawyer edged

out into the raging torrent, only a couple of steps, but it extended his reach ...

Samuel heaved the red football again and this time Sawyer caught it, momentarily juggled it, then grasped it firmly to him.

"Hold tight," he said to Noah, but didn't turn his head so the boy didn't hear him. But he'd hold tight.

Then Sawyer edged out farther into the water, fighting the current as hard as he could. One step, two. Suddenly, Noah was swept off his feet and carried Sawyer with him. Sawyer held onto the fire extinguisher and Noah held onto Sawyer's belt as the two of them were swept away from the far wall of the cavern out into the middle.

Taylor, Samuel and David all had a grip on the extension cord tied to the fire extinguisher and began hauling Sawyer and Noah to their side of the cavern. The current threatened to rip his grip off the fire extinguisher but Sawyer clutched it to his chest, knowing that Noah's grip on his belt meant water was gushing up into his face.

Twenty feet. Fifteen. Ten.

David was at the end of the line and Taylor called out, "Can you tie it off?"

He nodded. Taylor and Samuel secured their footing while David let go his own grip and tied the cord securely to the metal support on the stairs. He'd have been an Eagle Scout if those things had survived in the new world, but the whole family had become a "Boy Scout Troop," the boys earning badges. Taylor's doing ... like pretending they were on a skiing vacation in the mountains. Samuel and Noah were close to Eagle Scout status, but David was the only one who'd made it so far. And the boy knew how to tie knots!

"Secure!" he said.

Taylor eased off his grip and held onto the rope as he moved down it, extending his hand toward Sawyer.

Farther.

Inching farther.

Then he had a handful of Sawyer's shirt and was hauling him and Noah toward the steps. The other boys, trusting the cord and the knot, let go and struggled down to grab their uncle, cousin and father and the five of them staggered through water, sputtering and splashing until they came out onto a few dry steps at the top of the stairs not yet submerged by the rising water.

Sawyer saw Star and understood that she'd been inside Noah's head the whole time, encouraging and supporting him. The smile on her face would have melted frost off a windowpane.

Then it was group hug time. The whole family holding on, shaking, happy and in shock.

"Paco?" David asked.

"Gone," Noah replied. 'Washed away."

"Where's Nick?"

Sawyer had been too focused on Noah to think about Nick.

"He's …" That's when it hit him. "… *out there*." Out there, where water was flooding the earth. Nick had provided covering fire for Sawyer to make a break for the cave … but Nick hadn't made it inside. And now, all the entrances to the cave were submerged. "He's *gone*, too."

"And the detonator? Where's—?"

Taylor read the answer on Sawyer's face. So did the others.

"It's still in Zion Village," Sawyer said, finding that the terror in his chest froze his diaphragm, and his ragged breathing stopped abruptly.

The plan was to set off the blast sometime tonight, before *tomorrow's flood*. Nick had rigged a detonator that'd belonged to the monks, adjusted its signal to travel through solid surfaces instead of through the air, so it could only be detonated from inside the cave. Once the probe on the detonator was attached to the cave wall, pushing the toy-like red button beneath the plastic domed lid of the detonator would send a charge to the receiving unit with blasting caps to set off the charge. The detonating signal would travel out in every direction, like electricity through a piece of metal. How far? Nick had been vague about that. Said it depended upon the type of rock, and umpteen other variables, but that had not been a concern when they were designing the detonator because Sawyer intended to be standing on Level One of the caverns — a safe distance from where Noah had found the massive mine — when he pushed the button.

"You mean, we can't blow up the …?" Taylor didn't finish.

Terror as real as a gust of wind passed through them all.

"Unless somebody got it and brought it …?" David launched the words out into the air.

And how likely was that? When Sawyer and the others had been forced at gunpoint to get into trucks and drive with Paco and his men to the Cricket Bottom cavern entrance, the few people left in Zion Village were held captive there by the "soldiers" Paco'd left to guard them. There was nobody …

No, there was somebody.

There was Eagle Feather.

Chapter Fifty-Five

From where Eagle Feather stood at the edge of the high meadow, he could turn and look back north and nothing blocked his view. He could see the valleys and hills in that direction all the way to the horizon. But they weren't right, nothing was right — stretching out to the north was water, *rising water.* It flowed along the valleys, surging into them and filling them, leaving little islands of hills behind, little pieces of land higher than the level of the water.

The animals in the woods had fled from the water flooding their worlds, drowning the rabbits, flushing out the deer, flowing over bushes and then trees so the flock of fleeing birds grew bigger and bigger. Joining the birds from farther north, fleeing the water that had already submerged their trees, were birds from the trees only a few miles away, leaping up into the air to join the terrified flock, moving in the same direction, all of them racing toward … nothing except maybe a brief respite before the water caught up to them.

He couldn't seem to move, just stood there as animals from lower on the mountainside began to run past him and down into the meadow. When he saw the black beast lumbering in his direction, he couldn't make his mind define what it … It was a black bear, of course, surely the one whose gigantic paw print he had spotted in the mud the day before the latest and final edition of the-world-is-coming-to-an-end began with Star's painting of the images that'd splashed out of the Astral hive mind.

The bear paid him no mind, and it wasn't the only predator. Among the other animals he saw coming toward him and bursting out of the woods all around the meadow were bobcats, several of them, racing along beside coyotes and what … *holy shit!* Yes, it was cougar. He hadn't seen a mountain lion since …

Then his body finally came unhooked from the ground where his shock and surprise had nailed him to the spot. The land where Eagle Feather stood was high ground, at least temporarily, but it was on the edge of the "bathtub" meadow that stretched out in front of The Drain. Once the water crested those hills, the animals fleeing from it would be trapped, with nowhere to go. And they'd be funneled by the rising water into The Drain at the base of the meadow, where they'd drown in the flooded caverns.

He had to get in another way, at a higher elevation.

Eagle Feather turned to the crack in the mountainside at the edge of the hilltop where he stood and raced toward the black opening in the rock as fast as ever he'd run as a young man. His heart pumping furiously, probably *squirting* blood out his broken-open wounds. That cave would get him into the main cavern on Level Four — Cambridge Avenue — then all that mattered was *up*! He'd use one of the chimney freight elevators to take him up to Level Three, then another to Level Two. He had to get as high as he could in the caverns and then *set off the detonator.*

He didn't pause or lose a step when he burst into the sudden darkness of the cave. It wasn't completely dark. Sunlight shone in through the crack behind him, and in the caverns ahead, he knew he'd find Taylor Matheson's Glow Worm lights strung on the roofs. But they gave precious little light and Eagle Feather had no idea where he was going — just through the cave to the Level Four tunnel, then find a chimney shaft with a freight elevator. With at least half a dozen chimneys, all with elevators in them, Eagle Feather figured to be less than half a mile from the nearest one. If he weren't ... his strength would give out before he made it. And he had to make it.

Eagle Feather heard the low rumble of growling and realized what he had done.

Time slowed down then, but it was already too late.

They had smelled prey, smelled the blood pouring from his hand and the gash on his leg. He knew there were wolves in these mountains, that they had returned with the other wildlife when the influence of man on mother nature was ... downsized after the Astrals killed billions of people. The annihilation might not have been good news for the species homo sapiens, but it was great news for all the other species that had been displaced by the aggressive sprawling world of humans.

He'd only seen the wolves at a distance, though, had watched them take down an injured deer in a meadow two years ago and marveled at the effectiveness of their pack — as disciplined as any army military assault team.

It had not occurred to Eagle Feather to wonder then where the wolves had made their den. It occurred to him now, though. Too late.

A wolf pack had made its den in this cave. And he had just stumbled into it unannounced, uninvited and unwelcome.

A wild thought, born of exhaustion, age, and probably loss of blood, rode the bolt of terror into his brain. The sign over the pizza place in Roswell: *Food right to your door. We deliver.*

Chapter Fifty-Six

NICK WILSON OPENED his eyes and the world spun around him, swirling strips of green and blue and white. He closed his eyes but the world beneath him seemed to be spinning so he opened them again. He blinked. The green solidified, became the leaves of overhanging branches. The blue sky, the white clouds.

And memory instantly returned.

But he remained still, closed his eyes again. He now knew he'd been shot, had obviously barely missed a fatal head wound. But he didn't know where the shooter was. The shooter obviously thought Nick was dead and Nick didn't want to disabuse him of that notion. So he listened, heard no sound, looked out through a forest of eyelashes, saw nothing but the leaves. He moved his eyes without moving his head, searching whatever his field of vision would allow him to see.

He remembered now.

He had climbed up the hillside, sheltered by the rock outcrop, almost to the top. Even with the shooter, below him, he still didn't have a clear shot at the man. So he had slipped soundlessly down the hillside. He could only see a small portion of the man in his sights. Another step or two and he'd have a shot—

The scrabble of slate rocks beneath his feet were hidden by the carpet of leaves on top and he didn't know they were there until he stepped on them, and they slid out from under him. He was only off balance for a second or two, saw the man turning, the barrel of the rifle coming up toward him. He pulled the trigger on his own weapon and—

That's where the memory stopped. The man must have heard the rocks, turned and fired. He was either a damn good shot or got lucky to drop a man above him with a headshot.

Safe money was on lucky. The guys in Paco's army were in uniform, but that didn't make them soldiers any more than being in a garage made you a car. Nick had served years ago as a Navy SEAL and it had been obvious to him within seconds of encountering the force of men in black uniforms that they'd had only the most minimal training. Nick had had half a dozen opportunities to overpower the moron Paco'd set as his guard, would have, too, were it not for what Noah had signed to his father behind Paco's back. Told him *Paco could read minds.* If Nick overpowered his guard, Paco would *know* … and he had a gun to Noah's head. So Nick banished all thoughts of the coming ambush from his mind, knowing he'd have a chance to make his move then.

If Paco's men had been trained, Nick would be dead now because the idiot below him would have aimed at the biggest target. You never went for a headshot. But then, maybe he'd aimed lower and was a lousy shot. Either way, he had dropped Nick in his tracks and the fact that Nick was still alive was testimony to the fact that the man thought he was dead.

So where was the man? How much time had elapsed since he'd been shot?

Nick moved his head now, searching. Then carefully rolled onto his side and sat up.

Holy shit.

Either he had been out for a really long time or the water of the flood was rising incredibly fast. He got to his feet, stayed low, searching—

The shooter lay below him on the hillside. Nick's off-balance-shot had found its target.

Nick was no longer in danger of being shot. Just drowning.

The water now filled the whole valley below him.

The cave entrance was completely submerged, and his only shot at survival was getting into that cave.

Dropping his weapon, he shrugged out of his shirt as he raced through the trees until he was — as best he could determine — on the hillside directly above the cave entrance. The water was now lapping up the side of the hill twenty feet below where he stood. Which meant the cave entrance was more than a hundred feet below him.

SEAL training had been a lifetime ago. In desperation, he called to mind every memory of that training.

He'd only get one shot at this.

The water was dirty, full of silt and debris, so he'd be diving totally blind. He would have to go down maybe as deep as two hundred feet to the entrance, through it and back up to the roof of the chamber, to the opening in it where the stairs led up into Tripoli in Level Three which wouldn't be flooded. Once he got about a hundred feet down, the water flowing into the cave, into the miles of empty caverns on Levels Four and Five, would suck him through the entrance. And it would carry him away into the caverns. He would have to keep himself from being sucked farther into the cave. The stairs into the Level Three were right beside the entrance. How could he keep himself from being sucked past them and swept away into the depths of the cave? If the bottom two levels of the cave had been full, there would be no current. But there was more than 250 miles of winding tunnels like spaghetti beneath the Matheson property. Sawyer'd said there were probably twice that distance in unexplored caverns. And if, as Sawyer suspected, somewhere down there this cave system connected to the longest cave in the world, Mammoth Cave, that'd be another *650 miles.* Nick would be long dead before the lowest levels of all those caves filled up and the water settled. He couldn't wait for the current to ebb. He'd have to fight it, hold onto *something* to keep from being swept away.

Hold onto what? Bare rock? He'd never get a grip.

The Hidden

A rope tied to … he didn't have a rope. A vine, then. No time to find and secure one and where would he possibly find one long enough?

The power cable!

Years ago, there had been a visitor's center at the now-sealed natural entrance to the cave on Joppa Ridge. Then the Mathesons built a visitor's center in Cricket Bottom, six hundred feet below the one on the ridge, because many of the most popular sights, the ones most visitors wanted to see, were only found in the bottom two caverns — really weird rock formations that looked like carved statues. People swore they could see everything from a walrus to Jesus on a cross in the shapes of the rocks. Cricket Bottom got its name from the thirty-foot-tall "cricket" just inside the entrance.

Sawyer had shown Nick where they had strung cable from the big visitor's center on the ridge down the rock face of the hillside. The Cricket Bottom Visitor's Center had burned to the ground on Astral Day after a tour bus's terrified driver slammed into the building. But the inch-thick power cable was still there, stretching from the top of the ridge down the face of the hill. It divided then, with one section going to the ruins of the visitor's center and the other into the cave entrance in Cricket Bottom, across the roof of Level Four and up into the stairway opening into Level Three, where the electricity from it was used to power the cave lighting — that with some tinkering was still functional, turned on for the first time in seven years when residents of Zion Village moved into the cave a few days ago.

He had to find that cable. Fast. The water level was now only a few feet below him.

Chapter Fifty-Seven

NICK SCRAMBLED AROUND, frantically looking for a cable on the ground. Black, it would be covered with leaves and rocks and overgrown—

There it was. Snaking across the rocky surface of an overhang and tunneling back under the overgrowth beyond. He raced to it, digging it out as he followed it to the waterline, which was obligingly rising up to meet him.

Now that he'd found it, he had to switch gears. The next challenge would be a whole lot harder than finding a piece of rubber tubing on the ground. Deep diving — and this would be *deep*, maybe two hundred feet — required training. He'd been trained, but his training was a decade old and he was sure it didn't count anymore. Much of deep dive training was mental exercise, though, denying your body's signals to breathe as the carbon dioxide level built up in your blood, controlling the autonomic effort of your diaphragm to expand and take in air. *Willing yourself not to panic!*

The confidence to do all that came with hours of anaerobic training, which literally meant "without air," working hard while denying your muscles the oxygen they needed.

But SEAL training had taught him that humans shared special diving adaptations with marine mammals, which helped the body to adapt to surviving without oxygen. The most dramatic was the "mammalian diving reflex."

The training officer had demonstrated it by measuring his standing heart rate, then he bent over and immersed his face in cold water. A reflexive slowing of his heart rate was immediate. The spleen releases extra blood cells and blood vessels in the skin and large muscles constrict, reserving blood for vital organs, squeezing the last dregs of oxygen out of your blood in order to subsist on much lower levels than any human being normally does.

His body would take care of that part. The difficulty would be convincing his mind — *his will* — to trust that it would.

Getting started on a deep dive was hard because the body is naturally buoyant and for the first thirty to sixty feet, the pressure of the water is pushing you back up. But at about sixty feet, your body begins to sink like a stone.

Free divers, who dived down hundreds of feet for sport, called that the most beautiful part of the dive, when they stopped moving altogether and sank steadily downward.

He remembered deep dives, the euphoric feeling produced by changing blood chemistry caused by the increased pressure, that allowed gases to dissolve more easily and exert their effects more profoundly. The increased effect of nitrogen created a sensation of well-being. Coupled with the euphoria of oxygen starvation, the combination masked the life-and-death struggle going on inside your body. Some divers responded emotionally to the euphoria … stopped swimming and floated blissfully, until they gave in to the instinctual need to draw in a deep, cleansing breath — *and drowned.*

At the water's edge, Nick stripped to his skivvies, sat and kicked off his shoes. He paused, trying to center himself. He needed to enter the water with as low a heart rate as possible. And he needed to hyperventilate before he sucked in the final breath to hold.

He had decided to hyperventilate even though it was a dangerous technique because he needed every edge.

Hyperventilation would lower the level of CO_2 in his bloodstream and thus reduce the power of the gasp reflex. He could go longer before feeling the need to breathe. It was a trick, of course, and dangerous because it allowed divers to stay under longer — longer than the oxygen level in their blood would allow … and they passed out.

Nick had calculated that he was willing to take that chance.

Without training to prepare him for the effects of oxygen deprivation, Nick knew how hard it was going to be to ignore the ever-increasing desperation to breathe.

He heard the sound at the same instant he saw the bullet ping off a rock a few feet away!

How had anybody survived … he didn't even try to locate the shooter in the trees — the son of a bitch. He just sucked in a breath and jumped into the water.

Without hyperventilating, his survival would depend less on circumstance and more on the strength of his will alone.

He grabbed hold of the cable he couldn't see in the muddy water and began using it to pull himself down through the rising water to the depths below.

Chapter Fifty-Eight

NICK KNEW it would be hard to ignore the need to breathe, to ignore the panic of dark, cold water and no air, to continue to go deeper and deeper when every fiber of his being was screaming that he go up, not down.

He knew it'd be hard, but *holy shit!*

He dragged himself down into the frothing darkness, turned and went feet first, hand over hand on the cable, fighting for a handhold in places where it fit so tightly to the rock he couldn't get his fingers under it. He tried to recall the early days of deep dive training, how it had felt then, and tried to mentally walk himself through the days of training afterward where it got progressively easier and easier to wall off the urgent commands of his body.

He tried, but still the need to breathe clawed at his throat, sent a horrifying ache into his chest.

How much farther? Surely he'd come …

Why hadn't he counted the number of handholds?

If he had, he'd know how far. Well, he hadn't, so he started now.

One.

Two.

Three.

Each pull on the cable lowered him about three or four feet. He was still fighting his body's natural buoyancy, so he couldn't have descended more than sixty feet, which meant he had at least another 140 to go.

No way.

This was madness.

He should just let go, shoot to the surface, breathe air as long as he could after the landmasses sank and there was nothing but water as far as he could see in every direction.

Float there … until he couldn't float any longer. How long could he do that before he couldn't keep treading water?

Fifteen.

Sixteen.

Grunt!

Seventeen.

Would he last a day on the surface? Maybe if he found something floating he could grab hold of, he would last longer.

Three days. Four.

It took the human body several days to die of thirst, but maybe he could drink this water.

Twenty-eight.

Twenty-nine.

Thirty.

Thirty times three was ninety feet. Added in the distance before he started counting. Halfway. More than halfway.

He wouldn't make it. If he were only halfway down now, he'd never make it.

He went back to calculating the alternative. If he could drink the water, then he could survive ... how long? With no food, how long?

The pain in his chest was increasing. But he could also feel the water begin to pull him downward. He was getting closer to the cave opening.

His mind was growing foggy.

The urge to drag in a breath was becoming overwhelming.

Thirty-nine.

Forty.

Now, the sucking action struck with a fury. One moment he was propelling himself downward. The next he was holding onto the cable for dear life to keep from being swept away.

Shit!

The strength of the current was unimaginable. Now, his body was being sucked through a gigantic straw, feet-first toward the cave, a hole in the side of the mountain where water was pouring in. It took all his strength to hold on.

Changing his decision to Plan B, death by dehydration and starvation was no longer an option. The force of the current was so strong now he would never be able to fight his way back up the side of the mountain to the surface. He felt the muscles in his arms bulge from the effort it took to continue holding onto the cable.

He felt panic again begin to rise up in his chest. If the current sucked him away from the cable, he would drown in the depths of the cave, in the cold dark. Alone.

Josie!

He tried to picture her face, framed in a lace of pale blonde hair.

The pain of grief would have stolen his breath if he'd been breathing. His precious baby girl, his angel. Murdered! The man who'd murdered her, who'd run her down in the road … maybe he had made it into the cavern. Maybe Paco was there, alive.

The rage and hatred that swelled into a bright white flare in his mind momentarily replaced the aching agony, the crazy rat inside his chest trying to chew and claw its way out.

If Paco were still alive … Nick had to survive. He had to live long enough to kill the monster with his bare hands.

The added adrenaline rush of pure hate empowered him briefly. But it was cold and dark and the reality was that he was moments away from drowning.

How far down? He'd gotten distracted with thoughts of Paco, had stopped counting.

He felt his arms beginning to cramp. His fingers ached, he was losing his grip.

The pressure of the water flowing through now was unbearable. He knew he'd not be able to continue to hold on, and he began trying to decide if he'd rather just die now, suck in water into his lungs, ease the raging agony, or be washed …

He continued hand over hand, one after the other, and he felt the cable suddenly make a right angle turn. His feet shot out away from the wall, not sucked *down* anymore, but at a right angle. He'd reached the mouth of the cave. Two more hand-over-hands and he was inside and the cable slanted down the wall to the floor of the cave, where it would be strung along the crack where the wall met the floor until it got all the way across the cave and started to snake its way back up the wall toward the top.

Toward air! Nick clung with his fingers, his arms, clung by gritting his teeth. Clung with his mind.

Hand-over-hand-over-hand.

The floor. Another turn in the cable, left along the wall. He grabbed the cable and pulled himself along.

One more handhold.

One more.

As soon as he left the cave entrance, the water pressure lessened. It was merely turbulent, buffeting him this way and that, his body still perpendicular to the floor and the ceiling, pulled as the water wrestled him for control.

The image of Josie's face burst into his consciousness again, from the deep cavern in his mind and heart where he'd banished it. He couldn't think about her, couldn't think about her death or he would be so overwhelmed with grief he couldn't function. But the image of her now didn't debilitate him. It strengthened him, warmed him. Paco. He would kill that man, strangle the life out of him, squeeze his throat until his bulging eyes—

The cable turned again, going up the wall toward the cave ceiling.

Toward Paco and revenge.

Nick held on.

One hand over the other.

Again.

Again.

As he began going *up*, he felt contractions in his diaphragm and throat, knew they were not signs of real distress, but felt panic welling in his chest in spite of himself.

Picturing throttling Paco wasn't working. His mind was consumed with the need to breathe and he knew he would not be able to fight it for more than another handful of seconds.

Hand over hand along the wire. Holding tight. His fingers and the muscles in his upper arms cramping.

The cable took another ninety-degree turn and started up the wall. Toward the hole in the ceiling of this cavern and the floor of the one above where the stairs connected them.

Mind foggy.

Dizzy.

Let go and swim to the *surface*!

He released the grip of one hand but the cramped fingers of the other didn't respond, held him there long enough to realize if he let go he'd be sucked into the depths of the cavern.

Hold on!

He grabbed the cable again.

Climb.

Swim.

No, climb!

Hand over hand.

Two, maybe three seconds left.

So close.

He felt his diaphragm muscles break free of his grip. Shoved himself upward with all the strength in his right arm as he clamped his jaw shut and let go of the cable to hold his nose.

His diaphragm tried to suck in air. Couldn't. Jaw clamped, nose pinched.

One more second.

His head burst the surface as his grip on his nose let go, and his mouth flew open, gasping air — precious air — along with water.

Coughing. Choking.

Sounds — voices.

"Nick!"

"Grab him, get him up—"

Hands clutched his arms and began to haul him upward.

Training spoke in his memory. *Wait before taking that first breath, then exhale it immediately and take another breath, holding it before slowly exhaling ...*

Fuck that!

He sucked in great gasps of air, coughed, choked, cried.

He had made it.

By holy Christ, he had survived!

Chapter Fifty-Nine

николаевское's sudden appearance was so abrupt, so unexpected, that it was enough to draw everyone's attention away from the possibility that everything they had done was for nothing, that the detonator was sitting in the workshop in Zion Village, and when the water level got high enough to start pouring into the Astral mine, they all would drown.

For a moment, Sawyer thought there was some kind of sea monster emerging from the depths. Then everyone was talking at once, lifting Nick out of the water, pounding him on the back to get the water out, which probably wasn't the best way to do it but it was the natural instinct.

"How did you manage—?" Taylor asked.

"A Navy *SEAL*, hell yeah!" Sawyer said. "Good thing you didn't join the Air Force."

Gasping and sputtering and still choking on the water he'd swallowed, Nick said, "... held onto the electrical cable ..."

"You shinnied down that cable?" Samuel was incredulous.

"… going to be sick …"

"Pal, you can puke all over the place," Sawyer said.

"Not that kind of sick." He was still coughing and choking, but they clearly heard his next words. "The bends. I came up too fast."

That sobered the group.

"The bends are …? I think I know …" Star began.

"It's when you come up out of deep water too fast. Bubbles form in your bloodstream," Sawyer said.

"What do the bubbles do to you?"

Sawyer paused before answering.

"Well … just about anything."

"Not a problem … not fatal… I'll be sick is all. I'm good."

Sawyer knew that dying from nitrogen narcosis was virtually unheard of, that modern decompression chambers … But they didn't have a decompression chamber. Since the bubbles could form in or migrate into any part of the body, the range of symptoms was pretty much endless — joint pain, rashes, temporary paralysis, dizziness, headaches …

"I figured my odds of surviving the bends were better than the odds of surviving the Astral flood."

The Astral flood — that had come earlier than they'd thought it would, caught them unprepared. There were people in Zion Village who didn't make it before … Sawyer hadn't had a chance to consider those people. And Ellie did *not* number among them.

She wasn't there ... where she'd chosen to die. Gretchen had screamed at him in the gym that she'd taken her mother to the caverns last night. How horrible that must have been for Ellie, the *pain*! But her self-absorbed daughter didn't care what her mother wanted.

Sawyer looked at the group of people huddled around the stairs they'd just raced up from Level Four, watching the water rise in the stairwell hole. There were maybe thirty people, the armed men who'd shot Paco's soldiers before they could get down the steps into the cavern, some women who'd been—

There she was. Gretchen Hampton stood off by herself with her arms crossed across her chest. Her clothing was ripped, her face bruised. Maybe she had been assaulted by Paco's men on the drive here from Zion Village. Sawyer tried to summon sympathy for her, but couldn't find it anywhere in him. She'd betrayed him and the others to Paco, ruined what was a real chance to stop him. And hauled her dying mother ... Then he realized he wasn't sorry about that. He should have been, but the reality was that Sawyer was *glad* Ellie was alive, which made him just as self-centered as Gretchen.

Nick got to his feet with the help of Taylor's two sons, looked at Sawyer and demanded.

"*Paco!* What happened to the motherfucker?"

"He's gone," Noah said. "I pushed him into the river and he washed away."

"You sure?"

"Unless he pops up here like you did ... no, nobody could have survived those rapids."

Sawyer knew what Nick's next question would be, too.

"Is the—?"

"We don't know about the detonator."

No one spoke into the silence that followed, then Star asked, "If the charge didn't blow and close the hole ... I know the water will come in ... but what ... how will it ...?"

She tried to swallow her emotion but couldn't.

Noah answered. He spoke aloud so they all could hear, rather than just into Star's mind.

"It'll flood Level One. And then it will seek its level, leaking into Level Two. Down the stairs into Wiggle Room and down the elevator shaft at the other end into North Main. If the elevator is at the top, it will slow the flooding, serve as something like a cork, but water will still flow in."

"After that, how long to flood Level Two?" Star was on one knee beside Pumpkin with her arm around him, holding the wet dog close. Sawyer wondered fleetingly how they'd gotten the dog to climb the stairs, but this was Pumpkin after all.

"And then Level Three?" Sam asked.

"Hard to say. Remember, the water is spreading out into hundreds of miles of caves and that will take a while."

"How long is 'a while'?" Sam was trying not to sound afraid, but fear made his voice tight. "A day? More than a day — two or three? A week?"

Noah merely shrugged. He didn't have any idea.

They all were quiet, thinking their own thoughts.

"Any chance somebody brought it?" Nick asked.

"Can't think who," Sawyer said.

"Papa Eagle Feather," Star said and the longing in her voice broke Sawyer's heart. "Noah said he got away. He wouldn't have just run off. He knows how important ... he's *somewhere*."

"I guess he could have gone to the workshop, gotten the detonator. It's possible. But if he did, he'd better stick that thermometer thing up a cavern's ass quick." Sawyer lifted his eyes to the roof of the cavern, as if he could see through the layers of rock to the top of the mountain, and the water lapping around it. "It might ... already be too late."

Chapter Sixty

EYESHINE, all around him.

Twin orbs reflecting the light from the Glow Worm lights on the ceiling of the cavern. Half a dozen of them, at least. The pack leader, some females and young males.

A wolf pack.

The growling that preceded their attack rumbled in their throats. They surrounded him on three sides and when the pack leader gave the signal, they would all fall on him at once, ripping his flesh from his bones with their fangs, tearing out his throat with their powerful jaws.

Eagle Feather understood that he was moments from death. Time slowed down then, perhaps because that was just the way of it, before you died. The Great Spirit granted you time to consider before he called you to his bosom. Or perhaps it was just that Eagle Feather was teetering on the edge of unconsciousness from blood loss and exhaustion. He considered that it was fitting for him to die like this, ripped apart by prey animals. As an Indian warrior, he had lived his life as a predator, killing what he needed for food, living off the land. And the rule of nature was harsh. He had lived off his own prey, now he would provide food to sustain a pack of wolves.

Except he wouldn't sustain them, of course. They had only minutes to live themselves, just like every other creature on the planet. The flood the white giants had unleashed would take them and drown them here with him.

And more important, all the people in the upper chambers would die now because he had failed, had not set off the explosion that would seal the Astral mine entrance. The flood water would pour in when it reached that height and they all would die.

He shook his head. That should not be. *Could not be.* The Great Spirit would not allow it.

There'd been a time when Eagle Feather Yellowhorse put the Great Spirit right up there with Santa Claus and the Easter Bunny. Now, he knew different. He didn't like it, of course, not even a little bit, but he did have to accept it — the Great Spirit had orchestrated events that had unfolded in the past seven years, had "ordained" it to be. That was reality, and it pinched at his psyche like a new pair of boots pinched his toes. Until they were broken in. It took a considerable amount of time before the reality of the Great Spirit's meddling in the affairs of humans was "broken in" enough so he didn't flinch every time he thought about it.

He'd always said he believed the old Apache "oral history." Raised by his grandfather, he'd said he believed the story about the white giants from the sky and the Falling Star, the Apache to whom the Great Spirit would give a gift to save humanity. The white giants had been real. The taking — Star's abduction by the Astrals had been real. They'd brought her back, too — just as the prophesy foretold, and he had no doubt that the Great Spirit had orchestrated that. She had brought something back from her time on the mothership, too — a connection to the Astrals' hive mind, and she *saw* when that awful image consumed the whole Astral consciousness.

She'd fulfilled all the prophecies, she'd gone to the heavens and returned with the gift — the warning — that would save her people, a tiny remnant of humanity, normal humanity, not some select group hand-picked by the Astrals to repopulate the earth. But how had a blind girl painted the image in intricate detail on the gym floor? *That* was the Great Spirit.

Only her people had *not* been saved. They would be wiped from the face of the earth. She and the others would die here because Eagle Feather had proved to be inadequate to fulfill the task he'd been given. He was a warrior and he had failed his people. He was dishonoring his family and his ancestors.

"The wolves owe your family a debt," said a voice that was vaguely familiar. "You must collect payment."

He turned and a man was seated beside him. An old Indian, so wrinkled his features were all but lost in the folds and creases. His face was marked by a scar that cut from his hairline, across a scarred and empty eye socket and down his cheek. It glowed silver in the Glow Worm light that was like moonlight. But the lone remaining eye that looked out the cavern in his face below his cratered brow was bright and alert. He was dressed in native garb. Only it didn't look like "native garb," made by the reservation Indians using the old ways, the traditional methods of tanning hides. Those hides were not sewn with needles made from bone, though, pulling strands of rawhide and horse hair through the tough skins, but with metal needles and thread made to look like rawhide strips. Some garments were even put together with sewing machines and sold to the tourists from the booths set up to peddle roadside pottery and Indian headdresses using duck and chicken feathers.

This man's garments were real. Authentic. Worn and stained by years of exposure to the elements.

He wasn't real, of course. He was a product of Eagle Feather's fancy, brought to life by blood-deprived synapses in his brain, conjured from his consciousness at this extreme, the moment of his death.

But Eagle Feather knew who he was. All right, who he *wasn't*, because he didn't exist at all. The apparition was Wolf Brother, his grandfather's grandfather's grandfather who had lived before the pollution of the white man had stained the lands the Great Spirit had given to his people.

The wolves continued to growl as they edged closer.

The Hidden

The old man seated beside him paid them no mind. But then, he wasn't real, and the animals would not moments from now leap on him and rip him apart. He was nothing but air, so he could afford to be calm about it.

"Do you not know the story?"

Maybe he did. His mind was so muddled right now it was hard for him to pull anything from it. He did remember that his grandfather had told him a story once, just as he'd told him about the prophesy that Star would be taken up into the sky and returned with a gift to save her people. That "story" had been true. Was it possible the story about Wolf Brother was true, too? What was it ... something about finding an injured wolf ...

"He was the biggest wolf that ever stalked the mountains, the leader of a pack that was so strong and stealthy they could bring down an adult elk. I watched from the trees in awe. Surely, I thought, these were not mere wolves but spirit animals walking the earth on an errand from the Great Spirit."

The man's voice was deep and gravelly, scratchy, and the overall effect was hypnotic. Eagle Feather fell into the telling of the tale as if he were a boy listening to his grandfather as the potbellied stove in the corner superheated the drafty little house and the smell of the horse shit on the old man's boots mingled with the aroma wafting off the rabbit stew bubbling on the stove.

"A flash flood had swept down a dry creek bed. The great white wolf leader had been in its path, was washed away and I found him downstream, pinned down by a log. I was just a boy, looking down from the rocks to the creek bed below. His pack surrounded him. I could see where they had dug into the dirt and rocks trying to free him. He could reach the little stream of water to lap it up so he did not die of thirst, and the wolves brought him food. They would stay with him until he died.

"I returned the next day. And the next, stood on the rocks above and looked down as he grew weaker and weaker. I told no one, knew that if I did, the other warriors would come and kill him for his skin, and kill the other wolves, too, pick them off from the rocks above where they kept vigil.

"On the third day, I made my way down the rocky overhang until I was on a rock directly above him. I looked deep into his eyes and knew that I could let him lie there and die. So I climbed down off the rock, jumped into the creek bed and crossed it toward the huge log. The wolves could have attacked and killed me in an instant, but they didn't. They let me approach the great white, allowed me to take the tomahawk from my scabbard and chop at the huge log. I worked all day. Returned the next day and the next. On the fourth day, a full week after the flood, I finally broke through and the log fell away, lifting off the huge wolf. He staggered to his feet and approached me, his ears laid back, as if he were going to attack. Then he knocked me down and raked my face with his claws."

The old man pointed to the scar on his face. "Left

me with only one eye. But he didn't kill me. He turned and hobbled away and the other wolves went with him. When I was old enough, I went up into the mountains with the shaman, smoked the peyote and had a vision. The great white came to me in the vision, said he had marked my face to let all wolves know that he was my brother, that he owed me a life debt.

"I died an old man in my sleep with the debt unpaid. But you are my kin. And now it is time for the wolves to repay the debt owed to my family."

Eagle Feather looked at the old man, tried to look through him because he was, after all, only an apparition, no more solid than the smoke from a campfire. He looked solid, though, as if Eagle Feather could reach out and touch him. He didn't.

"Stand up, Eagle Feather, grandson of the shaman Silver Moon. Stand tall as a man and demand your life be spared."

That sounded like a line from a cheesy black-and-white Western where the Indians were always heartless savages and the white men who committed genocide against his people were the conquering heroes. As soon as Eagle Feather moved, the wolves would pounce.

But wouldn't that be better, provoke them so they'd make short work of him? When survival was not an option, a quick death came in a close second.

Instead of commanding the wolves to honor their ancient debt, he whispered softly, "I'm sorry, Star. I'm so sorry I failed you."

Then he got to his feet. Didn't move slowly, just got to his knees and stood immediately. Not tall, swaying.

The wolves around him continued to growl. But that was all. They didn't lunge and rip out his throat.

That's when Eagle Feather got it.

Duh.

The wolves weren't any more real than the old man. They were *all* products of his exhaustion and blood loss, conjured up by the mind of a man who was about to die alright, but not from a wolf attack. He would bleed out soon, pass out sooner. He had almost no time at all.

"Tell the wolves you claim payment of the debt owed by the great white wolf in the days when the earth was young," the old man said. Of course he did. He sounded like the soundtrack of a bad B Western because that's where Eagle Feather's mind had glommed onto the dialogue.

"Tell them yourself, Grampa," he said. "I'm busy right now."

Then he stumbled down the tunnel, the wolf pack parting to allow him to pass, growling menacingly, their teeth bared — vicious, murderous apparitions that they were. There was a bend in the tunnel just ahead. If he didn't get to the elevator soon …

He heard them then, sounds from the mouth of the cave where he'd entered. Not apparitions conjured up by the dying synapses of his mind — real wildlife, running in panic into the cave, the oncoming flood literally lapping at their heels.

The Hidden

He staggered forward.

Just as he felt his step faltering, he saw it, lit by a brighter light on the right side of the cavern. A huge hole opened up in the cavern ceiling and an apparatus with an old-fashioned steel cage sat on a platform there.

He staggered up onto the platform, got into the cage and punched a button and it began to rise slowly into the air, up through the dark recesses of the column.

He heard sounds in the cavern where he'd been running — raccoons, squirrels, foxes and snakes that streamed into the cool of the cave after Eagle Feather.

The cage came to a stop on Level Three in the main cavern called Cambridge Avenue and he opened the door, staggered out and collapsed on the cavern floor. Only the main elevator went all the way to the top of the ridge, stopping at all five levels of the cavern, and that elevator was ... how far away down this shaft? A shaft that would not flood as would the one below him. He heard a noise behind him, and spotted a raccoon, that had either climbed the column walls or shinnied up the cables that held the elevator. It quickly vanished into the shadows of the cavern.

There were probably cracks and crevices everywhere between the levels, spaces big enough for all manner of wildlife to transverse.

As he sat gasping, trying to catch his breath, Eagle Feather could hear them below him, the movement and animal sounds. When the water came, all those animals in that shaft would die. Except those that climbed up out of it through some opening or another. He saw a pile of supplies, stacked against a cavern wall. It'd been transported here by barge in the past couple of days, and there was much more provision still sitting on the dock in Zion Village. They should have had time to finish off the job.

Except they didn't.

The end of the world was right now. Happening.

He lifted the knapsack made from a pillow case he'd tied to his belt, opened it up and felt around inside. It was there. He withdrew the ridiculous-looking apparatus, like a child's toy, that would seal up the Astral mine entrance. The device appeared to be in working order, but how would Eagle Feather know?

He stared at it, wondering if the detonating signal from it would reach through the hundreds of feet of solid rock between him and the charge that'd been set inside the mine entrance. Was he high enough here in Level Three, which was about halfway up the 1500-foot ridge? As he recalled the conversation he'd overheard about its range, Nick had said the detonator had a vertical range of right at six hundred feet, and an almost limitless horizontal range because ... Eagle Feather didn't remember why. Didn't care. Had he come up high enough?

Well, it would have to be high enough because he would never make it ... what? Two miles? Maybe more than that to the elevators in the chimney that rose up above the dock where the Twin Forks River flowed into the cave. He staggered to the far wall, looked for a crack in its smooth surface, somewhere—

Found one.

He pushed the probe as far as he could into the crack, then stepped back and looked at it there. That was it? Unhooking the catch on the clear plastic hood, he lifted it and — feeling like a fool — he slowly punched the red button, pushed it down all the way, like the plunger on a toy detonator box.

Nothing.

But would he hear anything if the charge had detonated? Through six hundred feet of rock? Probably not. He sank to his knees, his strength now totally spent. He'd done all he could. Either it had blown up or it hadn't. This cavern, and all the caverns above it, would flood. Or they wouldn't. He'd find out eventually.

No, actually, he wouldn't. He would die of blood loss before he had a chance to drown.

He wished the old man and the wolves would come down the cavern to where he lay — when did he lie down? — and keep him company while he died.

The real animals that had been funneled into The Drain had gotten this far in the cavern below. He could hear them skittering around, panicked. Then he heard it, distinctly.

The growl of a black bear.

A black bear … riiiiiiight.

Eagle Feather closed his eyes and the world went dark.

THE END

The Series Continues...

The end of the world is here. Who will be saved?

Continue the adventure of Star, Noah, and Paco as they struggle to survive the great flood.

Pick Up Your Copy of The Saved Today!

A Note from the Author

Thank you for reading *The Hidden*.

If you enjoyed this book, you please consider writing a review on your favorite bookselling site so other readers might enjoy it too. Just a couple of sentences would mean a lot to me.

Thank you!
Ninie Hammon

About the Authors

Avery Blake doesn't want you to know where she lives, or what she does. She travels the world, moving from place to place quickly to ensure she can't be tracked. It's safer that way.

When she's not looking over her shoulder, you can find her in the corner of a cafe, facing the exit, typing as fast as she can.

Ninie Hammon (rhymes with shiny, not skinny) grew up in Muleshoe, Texas, got a BA in English and theatre from Texas Tech University and snagged a job as a newspaper reporter. She didn't know a thing about journalism, but her editor said if she could write he could teach her the rest of it and if she couldn't write the rest of it didn't matter. She hung in there for a 25-year career as a journalist. As soon as she figured out that making up the facts was a whole lot more fun than reporting them, she turned to fiction and never looked back.

Ninie now writes suspense--every flavor except pistachio: psychological suspense, inspirational suspense, suspense thrillers, paranormal suspense, suspense mysteries.

In every book she keeps this promise to her Loyal Reader: "I will tell you a story in a distinctive voice you'll always recognize, about people as ordinary as you are--people who have been slammed by something they didn't sign on for, and now they must fight for their lives. Then smack in the middle of their everyday worlds, those people encounter the unexplainable--and it's always the game-changer."

Also By Avery Blake

The Invasion Series

Longshot

Invasion

Contact

Colonization

Annihilation

Judgment

Extinction

Resurrection

Save The City Series

Save The City

Save The Girl

Save The World

Stonefall Series

Alienation

Stonefall

Snowfall

Downfall

The Taken Saga

The Taken

The Changed

The Hidden

The Saved

The Next Evolution

Transition

Convergence

Evolution

Stand-Alone Novels

Analog Heart

Family Royale

Ruthless Positivity

Vicarious Joe

Also By Ninie Hammon

Cornbread Mafia

Fire In The Hole

Blown' Up A Storm

Ridin' For A Fall

So Shall The Tree Grow

Nowhere, USA

The Jabberwock

Mad Dog

Trapped

The Hanging Judge

The Witch of Gideon

Blown Away

Nowhere People

Through The Canvas Series

Black Water

Red Web

Gold Promise

Blue Tears

The Taken Saga

The Taken

The Changed

The Hidden

The Saved

The Unexplainable Collection

Five Days in May

Black Sunshine

The Based on True Stories Collection

Home Grown

Sudan

When Butterflies Cry

The Knowing Series

The Knowing

The Deceiving

The Reckoning

The Fault

Stand-alone Psychological Thrillers

The Memory Closet

The Last Safe Place

www.ingramcontent.com/pod-product-compliance
Lightning Source LLC
LaVergne TN
LVHW031535060526
838200LV00056B/4500